Jesse's Return

Karen Norrod

ISBN: 0615814085
ISBN 13: 9780615814087

Library of Congress Control Number: 2013908966
CreateSpace Independent Publishing Platform
North Charleston, South Carolina

Prologue

"Have you lost your fucking mind? No! You can't even consider this an option. I'm not letting you do it! Think of your family, damn it! It will kill your mom and dad!" I scowl at her as she screams at me. I know she's hurt and doesn't understand. "And what about me? Are you going to stand there and turn your back on me? That is not what a best friend does!" Oh, she's pissed, like I knew she'd be. I knew she wouldn't take this well. I've come to terms with it and will not change my mind. "I'm sorry but this is my choice, my decision." She shakes her head vehemently at me, tears streaming down her cheeks. All I can do is stand and stare at her while she pleads her case once more. "Please, don't. It's not fair. It's not right! Everyone has problems. I have problems but you don't see me running away from them. Please, stay. We will help you! I know he's a fucking asshole but you are a smart educated woman. Think about this! Please. This is not right!" April sobs and wipes her tears off her face with her shirt. "Please, stay and we can work this out together! Please." Big crocodile tears fall from her puffy eyes.

My chest is tight and I am short of breath. I feel weak and exhausted. Does she think I haven't thought this through? I am angry at her for acting this way. Particularly now when I really need her support. Frustrated and growing angrier by the second, I shout back at her. "Damn it April, you are not listening to me! I haven't slept for a fucking week! I have thought it through! That's all I've done is think about it! I have not made this decision lightly and I would appreciate some goddamn support!" She angrily wags her finger in my face. "No! I cannot let you do this. It's absurd. No, it's beyond absurd. Why the hell would you even consider something like this?" April sighs and paces around the apartment. "I will never give you my approval. No way. Not for this Jessie. I mean, once you do it, it's final. The end. You know that. So why? What is it? Whatever it is, tell me. I will help you through it, but please don't do this!"

Tears cloud my vision and trail down my face. I take some slow, deep breathes and try to get my poker face back on. I knew this would be difficult. Damn it. I told myself I wouldn't cry. I pull some tissue out of the box and hand to her. I pull more tissue out and use them myself. This is getting us nowhere. "I know you don't understand my reasons, but I have them. Good reasons for needing to do this. I am the only one who can make this decision and I am going to do it. You cannot change my mind, so please, be my best friend and spend time with me and my family until I go. Please." She gazes at me with an incredulous look, swiftly grabs her purse off the couch and runs out of the front door, slamming it behind her. Yeah, she's pissed. Maybe I can make her understand the next time I talk to her. All I can do is hope. I know it's the right decision for me and I am resolved to go through with it. She can't talk me out of it, no matter how hard she tries. I know my family will be okay. I have already discussed the details a lot with my mom and dad, but will do so even more before the big day arrives. I yawn. I am exhausted. I plop down on my couch and stare down at the big pineapple on my living room rug. I am cried out. I lean to my right onto big fluffy pillows and close my eyes. I will rest, and later, if she is not back, I will try to call her to see if she wants to talk. I grab the navy and beige plush velour throw off the back of the couch, cover myself, and drift off to sleep worrying about my best friend. Hoping she will be able to see things my way. I only have a few more weeks. I have to make her see things my way.

The dinner party was great. All my friends and family showed up to support me and say goodbye. April is still angry at me. But she showed, and I am so glad she did. However, now that I am back at mom and dads, I am getting a little anxious about tomorrow. I somehow managed to hold it together at the party. I sigh and take off my black dress and hang it up in the closet. I climb into my pajamas and wonder how I will get through the morning. Will I, in fact, be strong enough to turn around and walk away from my mom and dad? I have to. No. I want to. I want this. I have thought a lot about this and I will do it because I want to. That is what I will keep telling myself. Thanks to the asshole my choices seem limited now. I feel boxed in. Trapped. I know I feel this is my way out. In a way, I guess it is cheating. I will worry about it all later. Now, I am going to hang out with my parents like tomorrow is just another day. I want to spend this time with them. I want to reassure them. And, of course, go over the details one last time.

1

Damn it. It's dark and I am cold. I feel groggy. I want to wake up and I will my eyes to open. They betray me and do not respond. I only hear mind numbing silence. Unable to wake I slip back into the darkness. Drip. Drip. Drip. A cold darkness surrounds me. I am groggy. I want to wake up but I am sluggish. I try to force myself awake, but cannot manage this monumental task and I quickly submit to the darkness. Drip. Drip. Drip. I sense something is wrong but I don't know what. The bone chilling cold surrounds me. *What the hell?* Drip. Drip. Drip. I drift in and out of sleep for what seems like days. Are the images I conjure up dreams or are they real? There was the party. Yes. I'm sure I was at a party. I have flashes of eloquent evening wear. I can't recall specifics about the party. Drip. Drip. Drip. I feel so strange. I'm shattered. I desperately want to wake up but my body doesn't. I want to jump up and finish what I was doing. What was I doing? I struggle to remember? What the hell is going on? Why am I so cold? Drip. Drip. Drip. *Come on, Jesse, wake up.* Hmm. Not working. My eyes are not attached to my brain. Try harder. A random thought of a birthday party crosses my mind. It was one of my favorite happy times. How old was I? A shiver runs through my whole body and the thought is lost. Drip. Drip. Drip. I slowly feel myself slipping into unconsciousness. I go unwillingly into the darkness. Drip. Drip. Drip.

Once again, I am aware of the freezing and dark conditions. I think I might feel a little warmer than before but I can't be sure. I am still cold and so exhausted. Suddenly a fleeting glimpse of a tall, handsome man enters my thoughts. For a brief moment in my mind's eye I see his muscles flex when he picks up a large weighted bag. The man has light brown hair and hazel eyes. Who is he? Drip. Drip. Drip. Do I know him? I think I do but can't remember how. I feel warmer now. I feel stiff all over. I suddenly want to rub the sleep out of my eyes. The urge grows with each passing drip. Drip. Drip. Drip. *What the hell is that?* The rhythmic drip is really annoying. Mental note to get a plumber to check things out. I feel a rush of warmth spread throughout my body. Oh I feel strange. Inside my head I scream at myself to wake up! I know I must be dreaming. I want some hot tea and a warm bath. I struggle to ignore the darkness that threatens me.

Drip. Drip. Drip. I scold myself for sleeping this late. I tell myself to get out of bed. I think I have to do something. There's something I'm late for. I am much warmer now and much more aware. My toes tingle and I realize that I've been flexing and releasing them over and over again. I feel pins and needles move from my toes to my legs in a painful sweep. Why am I so stiff? Drip. Drip. Drip. I know that if I stretch a little the stiffness will go away. I slowly try to move my legs. I shake them both. In my head I think I am shaking them but physically I am not sure they are actually moving. I try to raise them but they feel like lead weights. I lie still for some time. I think I fall back asleep and wake again but I am not sure. I have no sense of time and it's cold and dark. I muster all the strength I can and once more I try to raise them. This time they actually lift up into the air. The feeling of pins and needles quickly moves into my thighs. *Come on, Jesse, just wake up.* I feel like I'm awake but my body wants to sleep. This is like that time I took extra strength cold medicine and couldn't get up the next day. I just wanted to sleep for hours. I was so groggy. Like I am now. Did I take any pills last night? Drip. Drip. Drip. *What is that?* I force my legs to move a little more. After what seems like hours I am finally able to move the rest of my legs and shake my arms to wake them up. This feels weird. Really weird. *What the hell is happening to me?*

Drip. Drip. Drip. I slowly try to open my eyes but I can't see any-thing. There's something on my eyes. Reaching up slowly to my eyes I touch a gauze covering. I slowly remove it from my left eye first and then my right. Drip. Drip. Drip. *Come on Jesse. Get your ass up now! You know you're late - as usual. Move it.* Trying to open my eyes is too hard. Maybe I'll just lay here and sleep a while longer. *No! Get moving.* No ice cream for you for a whole month if you don't! Why am I thinking about ice cream at a time like this? I am cold enough already. My eyes feel like they are crusted over with sleep. I struggle to barely open my eyes into a small slit of a line. Bright light fills my eyeballs and they hurt. It's so bright I can hardly stand it. There is a huge strain on my eyes and I feel them trying to adjust to the intense brightness. Finally, as my eyes are adjusting I can see something. It's a bubble around me. No, maybe not a bubble, but something. Now I am officially freaked out! *What the hell is going on here? What is this? Am I locked in this …thing?* Struggling, I reach up and touch what feels like plastic but looks like glass. Drip. Drip. Drip. There's a big light directly above me. My eyeballs are seared with pain again from the bright light. *Could somebody turn off that fucking light!* I am warmer. I am awake and aware now. Drip. Drip. Drip. How long have I been sleeping here?

I feel adrenaline surge in my veins as panic starts to overwhelm me. *What the fuck is going on here?* This doesn't look like my house at all. Where the hell am I? Slowly I turn my head and look around. I can see different types of equipment. I think it's mostly computers and lab equipment. My mind immediately thinks of a sci-fi movie and I am the star. I seriously cannot be here. This cannot be really happening. Drip. Drip. Drip. *Damn it! What is that dripping noise?* I don't know what this place is but I know I have to get out of here. Panic grips me. What if I can't get out of this thing? This bubble or whatever it is. Adrenaline rushes throughout my body. My mind is racing as it feverishly works faster trying to comprehend my present situation. What if I'm stuck here? What if my air runs out and I can't breathe? What if the aliens return to find me awake and they do experiments on me? *Stop it, there are no aliens! Jesse, get a grip. This is not a sci-fi movie!* My blood runs cold because I know that I am not dreaming and this is real. I am really here, in this sterile place. In my head I scream at myself. *Get the fuck out of here… now!*

Looking side to side there's no handle or knob. I notice a slight seam to this bubble. There's got to be something to push or turn. I run my hand up the sides and around the circular top, up over my head. Drip. Drip. Drip. If only there was enough room for me to sit up and turn around. Wait, here's something. It feels like a button. I run my fingertips over an elongated circular shape protruding out from the rest of the bubble. What if I push it and an alarm sounds? Again, I rebuke myself, *Stop it, Jesse; get a grip!* I know I am late and need to hurry. *Come on!*

With my limited strength I slowly push the button. What am I late for? I know there's something I'm supposed to do. What was it? I absolutely hate it when I do this. Sometimes I can go for hours trying to remember things and then the next day or next week it will suddenly pop into my head when I am thinking of something totally different. I drive myself nuts over it sometimes. Once I forgot what my best friend's mother's real name was and it bothered me for a week. We normally call her by her nickname Dot, because of her infatuation with polka dots. You can be in any room in her house and you can spot something polka dotted. She somehow makes it look chic and elegant. I finally had to call my friend and ask her. She thought I had just been under too much stress at the time and that I needed to rest. I remember that condescending tone in her voice while telling me "Just get some rest, you're fine. Don't worry about it." It was like she said, "Oh, you're not going crazy. It's completely normal for a young person like you to forget things like that. It's not the start of anything serious." Yeah, right... April's mom practically raised me. You'd think I'd remember her name.

A low mechanical groan from the bubble shocks me back to the task at hand. I have got to get out of here. The earth seems to shake as the seam to the bubble begins to open. This is weird. I know I watch too much sci-fi but this is ridiculous! I am really here and this is really happening. I pinch myself to see if I am awake. Damn. That hurt. I'm definitely awake. I'll have a bruise tomorrow. The dripping noise is louder now that the bubble door is open. A surge of cool dry air hits my face and makes me realize that I am actually damp. Maybe sweat, I'm not sure. My hair is wet and stringy across my face. *What the hell is this place?* A sharp pain surges in my elbows and lower arms. I look down to see that I am up on my elbows. I must have been in this position for a while, trying to process my whole situation. Now that the top of this bubble is open I sit up and my head starts to spin. For a brief moment I see spots and think I am going to pass out. I feel so weak, so lethargic. I sit and look around for what seems to be hours. I finally gather my strength to try to stand up.

Drip. Drip. Drip. Using the sides of the bubble as railings I pull up to get my lower half underneath me. Next I push up to my feet. I have to take my time because standing is extremely difficult. My muscles ache and I'm stiff all over. It feels like I have been sitting cross-legged on the floor too long and it's hard to get back up. I have noodle legs that are quite wobbly and unsteady. I always kid around and say I'm getting old. When in fact, I know I just need to get back in shape. I know I need to exercise a little bit more and loose that ten pounds I've been hanging on to for the last year. I make a promise to myself to do that once I feel better. This place is overwhelming. I see additional things I couldn't see before. The lab is enormous. There are individual work stations with other bubbles like mine. They all have the computer equipment and hospital equipment to monitor a person inside. The other bubbles are all empty.

Near my work station I see a tray with surgical equipment partly covered by a green towel. There's one of those machines that shocks a person's heart. Over in the right corner of my work station there is an oxygen tank with a mask hanging from the tubing. Locking back to my bubble I am slowly realizing it's not a bubble at all. This is some kind of chamber I was locked in. Fear surges through my body. A bead of water, sweat I think, drips down my forehead. There are tubes running in and out of this chamber which I now see could be attached to my body. Thankfully they weren't! I don't see any marks on my legs and arms.

My legs almost give way underneath me as I first notice that I'm naked and then how my legs and arms look. They are very different somehow. They seem...*skinnier*. They are way too thin and pale. *What have they done to me?* I am nauseous at the sight of me. *I've really got to get out of here!* My chamber I am now standing in is only about two and a half feet off the floor. I awkwardly climb over the side of the chamber, clinging to it for dear life. There is no step so I gently lower myself down onto the cold floor. This place is frigid and unfriendly. Like a hospital. If this was a hospital wouldn't there be doctors and nurses all over the place? Wouldn't someone rush to my aid? Or tell me to lie down? Or tell me to take some medicine? Or at least get me some clothes? Where is everyone? I see an intravenous bag used up and hanging on the IV pole in my work station.

Drip. Drip. Drip. The more I try to comprehend where I am the more I panic. *Where the hell is that noise coming from?* I look around my chamber and see the floor is wet. The floor has two layers to it. I think they planned it this way. I now see that the dripping noise is a liquid dripping off of the outside of the chamber and onto the floor. The liquid is passing through the top layer of flooring and draining down into the sub-floor underneath where it is being caught in small tubes and drained away to some undisclosed destination. *I have got to get the hell out of here now!* I am scared and short of breath. There is a wall lined with cabinets. I am weak and stumble over to them, stubbing my toe on the layered floor. It feels like my toe is being ripped off. *Fuck!* The pain is intense and I see white spots. I have that pins and needles tingling sensation in my whole body and I somehow know that if I were to hit my arm on something that the pain would be unbearable. I am still cold and my nipples hurt from being hard. What I wouldn't give to take a nice long bubble bath. That would be heaven. A cup of hot tea afterwards would be nice. *Hurry up and get out of here!*

I find some hospital scrubs in one of the cabinets and quickly put them on. Another cabinet has blankets and I take one and wrap it around my shoulders. Not the good kind of soft velour blanket that I like. Instead, it is the thin, cheap hospital blanket. It is the standard sterile white, of course. My feet are freezing. What can I do about my feet? Searching further I find a pair of wool socks and some hospital paper shoes. Holding them in my hand I try to hurry but I only manage to slowly proceed to the door. When I get to a dry floor I'll put them on. Man, I hope this door is not locked. That would be my luck. Then what would I do? Hang out here and play with this computer stuff? I don't think these are the kind of computers you can play Asteroid's or Frogger on. I'm positive they wouldn't have Pac Man. I start to laugh at the thought but I ache all over and it hurts too much to laugh. That would be wild, hanging out, playing games and then the aliens come back and can't believe what they are seeing! I frown and scold myself. *Stop it; there are no aliens! No more scary movies for you* I tell myself. Only love stories from here on out. Wouldn't I just love for a gorgeous man to sweep me up in his arms and make me warm. At least just to hold me to get my breast warm. My nipples are still too cold and are tingling slightly. They hurt. I try to slow my breathing down. *Come on Jesse.* My inner voice is screaming *get out of here while you can; before someone shows up and stops you!*

To my surprise the door opens without a hitch. I look out into a long corridor with white walls and a white tile floor. Spotless. It doesn't surprise me. Hospitals are always spotless. One time April's mom had minor surgery on her knee and I had to sit with her for two days in the hospital. The food was terrible and that smell. There was always that smell after they cleaned. It was a bleach smell. I do not smell *that* smell now. There are no doorways on the immediate right or left. Further down I can see a light on at what looks like a nurse's station. Maybe there is someone there that can help me. I want to just get out of here. How am I going to take a cab home? I don't have my purse. I don't have any money on me. Oh, this is a bad situation. *"I'm sorry Mr. Cab Driver. No, I'm not crazy and I always dress this way. I have lost my money. Could you give me a ride home anyway?"* Okay, that sounds more than a little nuts. Maybe I'll just walk home. *If I can find my way out of here!*

I walk down the corridor and the door closes behind me without making a sound. I am still holding the socks and paper shoes. I hurry and put them on. I am anxious for my feet to get warm. The paper shoes make a slight shuffling sound when I walk in them. It is barely audible and anyone else probably wouldn't hear it. At least I hope not. I do not want to draw attention to myself. Walking further down the corridor I notice that there doesn't seem to be anyone at the nurse's station. Fear has kept me from calling out for help up to this point. I don't know if any sound would come out of my mouth anyway. I'm panic stricken. This whole experience will take its toll on me. This I know. I need to get home and get into my own clothes. I need to sit on my own couch and try to figure this out. This place gives me the creeps. I'm not sure that I want anyone's help. I'm not sure that I want to know what is going on here or what they have done to me. I just want out.

As I walk up to the nurse's station I see it's empty. I go around the counter to see if I can find out any information that will help me sort this all out or at least what floor I'm on and how to get out of here. There are only a few call buttons on the panel to the left. I assume that one is for the room I was in. There must be another room at the other end of the hall. Straining my eyes I look in that direction but the lights are not on at that end of the hallway and I can't make out a door. I think I see one but can't be sure. Should I go down there? *Forget it Jesse. Come on, no time for that. Just get the hell out of here. Now! Find a way out. Now!*

I choose to ignore my inner voice that is screaming for me to exit this place. There are papers sitting in a messed up pile on the left along with some medical charts. Looking through the charts I see that they are all empty. Hmm. The papers are blank information sheets that nurses write blood pressure, heart rate and temperature on. To the right side is a newspaper. I glance right over it to see a medical chart just beyond it on the counter. There is no name on the front of the chart from what I can tell. I take a few steps to the right and pick up the chart. This one is definitely not empty. It's full of papers. In fact, it's so thick that it's busting out of its jacket and it won't shut evenly anymore.

A sick feeling overtakes me. Nauseous, a thousand thoughts go through my mind. It must be my chart. I open the front cover and see my name, address, birth date with all my routine personal information that I give when I go to the doctor. There are psychological test results. I think

I vaguely remember taking some type of psychological exam. They said it was also to test my thinking and something about the way my brain worked. *What in the hell am I doing here?* I'm a little freaked out but keep reading. My chart is filled with medical graphs with lines going up and down in a steady pattern. *What am I looking for?* Toward the middle of my chart I see it. My breath hitches in my throat and I am even more confused. The word that halfway explains what could have possibly happened here. It is so farfetched that I just can't believe it. *Cryogenics.* There has to be some mistake.

I am staring at a cryogenics report. It includes a lot of medical jargon I have never heard before and then has some numbers vertically in a row. There are a lot of these reports. In fact, they make up the majority of my chart. Cryogenics. Isn't that where they freeze dead people? I think I remember news reports about scientists trying to figure out how people could grow their own organs in a lab and freeze them in case they get sick when they get old. That way it would be the same tissue and there would be no chance of a body rejecting its own tissue. I don't think they have the technology to do that. I frown and inwardly my heart sinks. What the hell do I know? Didn't I just wake up in some weird bubble sphere? A shiver runs down my spine and I tell myself to get a grip for the umpteenth time.

A wave of fear, panic, weakness overwhelms me again and my noodle legs feel like they will give out any second. I try to sit down in the chair behind me. I almost fall out of the chair. It has wheels and starts to roll out from underneath me as I sit. But I am able to get a firm grasp on the chair and sit uncomfortably as I try to process this information. My mind cannot take it all in. This is bizarre. I am not dead. I wasn't harvesting my own organs, was I? How do I remember that whole harvesting organs controversy and not the way out? What am I doing here? I'll have to try to answer those questions later. Right now I'm getting out of here. Taking my chart in my hands I stand up and I see the newspaper. The date on the top is June 2021, but I don't process it. Instead I grab the paper too, thinking I'll look at it later, at home. Looking around I see an elevator to the left of the nurse's station. Something's not right. If this were a hospital there would be people everywhere. Nurses dumping used bedpans, sick people calling out in pain. There should be buzzers ringing at the nurse's station. There should be phones ringing and monitors beeping. There would also be other patient rooms down this corridor. My fear and panic level is rising fast and I take some slow deep breathes tc try to calm myself. I've got to get out of here.

Reaching the elevator I wait for what seems to be an eternity and then the doors open. I unwrap myself from the blanket and drop it on the floor in front of the elevator. I step into the elevator with my chart and the newspaper and the doors close. There is no basement to this building. I push the number one and wait to go to the first floor. I can see I was on the eighth floor. What is this place? The elevator bell rings and the doors open. I look out into a lobby filled with bustling people all in a hurry to be somewhere else. Some have white coats on over their hospital uniforms. Some are dressed in regular clothes. I step out of the elevator before the doors close. No one seems to notice me at all. I see a receptionist looking down at her stack of paperwork and she answers the ringing phone. To my left is a long hallway with doors opening and closing on either side. Another hallway intersects with this one about halfway down. People are walking down this long hallway. Some turn to the left while others go to the right. That doesn't look like the way out. To my right I see bright light. Past the waiting room I see a door opening and closing as people come in and go out. Past the door I see freedom.

2

I walk toward the door and continue to take slow deep breathes and try to steady myself. As I pass people in the waiting area I hear a mother tell her child that he can't have candy until after his treatment. There is an older man sitting across from them reading. He looks at me and then looks back down at his magazine. I think he looks familiar but I can't remember where I know him from. If he knew me he sure did not act like it. A pregnant woman is sitting against the other wall in a row of chairs all to herself. She looks like she could go into labor any second. The rest of the waiting room was empty. None of them have any idea what is going on here. Don't they know they'd better get out of here? I realize that they don't. They are here at a regular hospital as far as they are concerned. They are here to get their treatment or wait on a spouse. They don't have any idea where I just came from. I am not sticking around to tell them either. Past the waiting room now I reach the doorway. As I step forward to walk through the door I glance back over my shoulder to take a final look. No one notices me and no one is following me. As I turn to look toward the parking lot I bump into someone and drop my chart and the newspaper.

The man stares at me as I reach down to pick up my history. I notice he has big feet. He is wearing dark shoes, dark pants and a light blue dress shirt. He has on a white lab coat over his blue shirt. Standing back up I see he is looking at me with a dumbfounded look on his face. I wish he would move out of my way so I can get out of here. He's blocking the doorway. He has a slender waist with broad shoulders. He is familiar to me. Do I know him? Why is he just staring at me? He speaks to me with a shocked tone, "Jesse, Oh, You're, ugh… awake! Are you okay? Well, of course you are if you've made it this far. That must be your chart you're holding. Don't worry about a thing. I have helped take really good care of you." He stares at me a moment longer and then blurts out, "You're even more beautiful than I expected, even as pale as you are." As he speaks I can see what I think may be excitement beaming in his eyes. He was clearly not expecting to see me and certainly not expecting to literally 'run' into me. He looks shocked and yet happy. He reaches down and takes the chart and newspaper from me. I am shocked that he knows me so I let him. He slowly puts his arm around me and does an about face with me in tow and marches me out of the facility. I don't think I know this man. Should I be going with him? He apparently knows me; but how? He's getting me out of here so I'm not going to argue. Maybe he will take me home. I just want to go home.

Once outside, my senses are overloaded with information all at once. I hear various muffled conversations of people walking around us, hear the noise of traffic in the distance, and I feel the warm sun on my face. I see trees and hear birds singing. It feels so good to be outside. I love the outdoors. My hair, now drying, has started to blow across my face. I feel the sun burning into the delicate, cool skin on my arms and cheeks. I glance at my arm and see that some of my color is slowly coming back even though I am still very pale. I cannot move. I feel like my feet are glued to the concrete underneath them. Just standing here enjoying the warmth and the birds is enough for me at this moment. The man reaches over and gently moves the hair from my face. He tucks it behind my ears and just looks at me. He then looks around and it seems to me that he is a little nervous. He puts his arm around me to guide me and says, "We really need to go. Don't be afraid. I'll explain everything once we get there. Just trust me and don't be scared of me. I promise I'll take care of you...you can trust me." There was a husky tone in his voice, especially when he said that last part. There is a gentle kindness to his nature. The pleading look in his eyes makes me believe he is telling the truth. Or maybe it is just the white lab coat. Regardless, I let him lead me away from the facility. We walk down the sidewalk toward the farthest parking lot, past the end of the building. As we walk I think how good it feels to walk. My legs are still stiff and weak but the kinks are slowly starting to get worked out. The warmer I get the better I feel. No one seems to notice that I am dressed in scrubs. I can't believe no one stopped to question me or even look twice at us while we walked to the parking lot.

We are standing at a car now. I do not recognize the year of the car or the type of car and I don't care. I just want to leave this place. Get back home. Get back to a normal life. What was my normal life? I can't really remember much of anything right now. I'll worry about remembering later. Right now I am really exhausted. My escape was too much. I lean over onto the car and take a few deep breathes. The man sees I am weak and opens the door for me. He helps me into the car and, careful not to touch any part of my body as he does it, puts on my seat belt. I let him do it. I am limp and out of breath. Before he gets into the driver's side he takes the lab coat off and throws it in the back seat. He then gets into the car, puts on his own seat belt and starts the engine. It starts up right away. The car looks to be well taken care of. It looks new. I guess that it is maybe a year old or less. He puts on the air conditioner and begins to drive out of the parking lot. He does not turn on the radio. I shiver and hug myself to get warm. He notices and quickly turns the air conditioner off.

I lean my head back and close my eyes and I begin to think about the events of the day. This has truly been one of the strangest days of my life. It almost seems that the dripping noise woke me up. Would I have woke up anyway? I don't know. I do know I'm tired and confused. Question after question runs through my head and I have no answers. At least right now I don't. I do intend to find out though. As soon as I feel up to it I'm going to get answers to all of my questions with or without the help of this man sitting next to me. I have a lot of questions about him too. Is he a doctor? How long has he been…taking care of me? What's his name? Why didn't he rush me back up to the lab and run test and take notes? Why didn't he alert other doctors that I was awake? He doesn't treat me like a circus freak. He seems nice. But can I trust him? I open my eyes, briefly look at him and take a deep breath. I am exhausted to the point that I can't summon the energy required for speech. I put my head back on the headrest and close my eyes. I think I nod off for a few minutes. Moments later, fearful that I am back in that sterile place, my eyes fly open and look at my surroundings. My heart is racing and my breathing is fast.

He has a calm exterior and looks to be deep in thought. The buildings and trees fly by as he drives a little over the speed limit. It seems like I've seen some of this before but I can't remember anything specific. He turns left at a red light and drives a few more blocks. Then turns right and drives for what seems an hour before turning left again. I can't really tell where we are at other than we are entering a neighborhood. The road is a two lane road that is initially straight. Then the road begins to wind back and forth while going up an incline. We must be on a hill or a mountain. There are a lot of trees here, large ones. They must be hundreds of years old. After reaching the top of the hill he quickly turns to the right.

There is not a visible road here. How does he know where to turn? As he keeps driving it turns into a gravel road. Approximately a mile down it turns into a paved road. Very well hidden and it looks like he wants it that way. After another five minutes of driving straight through a forest we reach huge stone pillars that hold a large iron gate. He pushes a button and the gate opens. Once through he pushes the button and closes the gate. There are more trees directly in front of us. He drives on for another five minutes and then I see the house. The house is not a house but instead, a small mansion. He drives up to the circular tiled driveway. I think it is some type of Italian tile. It's absolutely beautiful. How can he stand to drive on it?

He brings the car to a stop and for a moment the world stands still as he looks me over from head to toe. I must be a sight to see. I'll bet he thinks I look ridiculous. I stare at him bewildered. Jake cannot believe his luck, running into her like that at the hospital. It's not her fault she bolted like that. He knows she is probably freaking out right now. He understands she doesn't remember things right now. But oh god, she's more beautiful than he imagined. He knows she is weak and pale, and finds himself wondering what she will look like with a little color in those beautiful cheeks and lips. He imagines how soft and silky her hair will feel. He shakes his head a little and tries to regain control of his wayward thoughts. He says, "I know you're confused. Let's go in and get some soup. I'm getting a little hungry myself. Then I'll run a bath for you and we can talk later. I have some clothes you can put on. I think they'll fit you." What? Am I hearing him correctly? It strikes me a little odd that he is being so nice to me and seems to know just what I want. How can he know what I want? How can he know me? Too tired to argue with him I just nod my head yes. He walks around to my side of the car and helps me out. Seeing that I am still weak and unstable he helps me across the beautiful tile and up the long, wide stairs. I think I could manage them but I hold onto his arm. Better to be safe than sorry. Even in my exhausted state I can't help but notice his muscular arms and his quiet, steady strength as he helps me to the door. How does he know me? Who is he? Why is he helping me?

Suddenly the door opens and an older woman rushes out to help us in. "Mr. Bradley, I didn't expect you so soon. And you have brought a guest. My, oh my! How can I help? What can I get you, sir?" Clearly, she was a good employee. I imagine that she probably keeps the whole house in order herself and makes sure the other employees do their jobs well. Her face looks young but the gray hair around her temples tells a different story. I'll bet she's worked for him a long time. He laughs a little and says, "Fran. You sweet woman! What would I ever do without you? Please get some soup ready for Jesse. Do you have beef broth with just a touch of salt and some French bread on the side? Also, Jesse needs some water. No ice please. I'll have the same if it's not too much trouble." Fran returns a smile and dutifully says "No trouble at all, sir. I'll have it ready in ten minutes." With that she scurries off to the kitchen. We step inside a huge front entrance. A large chandelier hangs directly above marble flooring. The lighting is soft and warm and the room is very inviting.

Everything in the house seems to be ornate and beautiful. My tired eyes open wide as I begin to take it all in. Just inside the entrance stand two marble pillars on either side. The pillars nearest the door are taller than the other two. On the right side they both hold planters with perfect arrangements of white and purple flowers. To my left only the shorter pillar holds a planter with matching flowers. The taller pillar is empty. I wonder if there are always flowers at the entrance or if Fran got them ready for a special visitor. There is no way she could have known I'd show up on her doorstep. Is there? I am making too much of the flowers. I look at this stranger next to me, still holding my arm to steady me. My brief impression is that he is taller than me and has dark blonde hair and hazel eyes. He is incredibly handsome. I notice of course, but it doesn't really register with the rest of my body because of my current situation. My world has turned upside down and I feel like my feet are lifting up and I am about to be flung off the planet at any second.

My racing thoughts almost make me dizzy. I am weak but I summon the strength to speak. "Mr." My voice is gruff and I clear my throat and start again. "Mr. Bradley? Is that what she said? I wondered what your name is. It's not fair you know my name and I don't know yours." He flashes a boyish grin at me. "Jesse, we will talk soon." His grin is disarming. Wow. He doesn't know me. I don't know him. So how, then, do I feel safe with him? Somehow, I trust him I can't explain it. I try to make sense of it all and my thoughts are reeling. I try to take some deep breathes and get a grip on both my thoughts and emotions. "Jesse, I promise to tell you everything, but it's quite a lot of information to take in at once. It's probably best if we talk in increments to give you time to digest the information a little at a time, because it is so much." I think quickly to myself that he doesn't know how I am. He doesn't know I like to approach things head on and cut to the chase.

He leads me to a sitting room with a fireplace off to the right. It is beautiful, classic and very traditional. Indeed a very cozy room with two huge mahogany colored leather recliners situated in front of the fireplace. It looks like they are leather. I really hope so because I hate the way that vinyl sticks to the back of my legs. *What am I thinking?* I have completely lost it! I should be and I am grateful that he's brought me here and that I am away from that awful place. *Come on Jesse. Don't be materialistic.* There is a small table in between the two chairs. In the back of the room hidden in the shadows I see a leather couch. It looks to be the same mahogany color as the two chairs. Back behind the couch is a wall of books. He turns to me and takes another long look. I know he is doing some sort of mental assessment but it is unnerving. Why does he keep looking at me like that? It's like he's seen a ghost or something. Let's hope this one is not a psycho like my last date turned out to be. I tell myself this isn't a date. Activities like that will have to be postponed until I am feeling better.

He starts to say something but just at that moment a man walks in the room. "Mr. Bradley, is there anything I can help you with, sir? I hear we have a guest." The man is maybe twenty-five years older than the illustrious Mr. Bradley. "Oh, hi Sherman. It's good to see you" Mr. Bradley says as he extends his arm to shake Sherman's hand. To do so he had to let go of my arm but I am holding my own and am stable at the moment. "I'd like to have a fire started please. Plenty of wood and kindling as well. We may end up talking half the night. Don't worry, I'll attend to it." Sherman looks at him with a raised eyebrow. Mr. Bradley states again with his boyish grin, "I promise I'll take care of it." Sherman starts laughing and shakes his head, "As you wish, sir." Then he turns to set about his duties. As he leaves the room I can't help but notice he is dressed in jeans and a button down short sleeve shirt. He acts so formal but yet dresses so casual. Fran on the other hand is dressed completely in uniform.

Mr. Bradley looks around the room and then at me. He sighs deeply and runs his hands through his thick blonde hair. "After we get you taken care of, a little more comfortable, we can sit here and talk all night if you'd like. I know you have a lot of questions. Just please be patient with me. I'm not quite sure where to start with you. I am honored to have you as my guest. I don't usually have many guests here." The way he interacted with Sherman, his strong quiet voice, his words...it's all reassuring to me. Why? How can I feel comfortable with him? He is a stranger to me. There is something about him, something I can't put my finger on. Something about his whole demeanor makes me feel safe and eases my nerves, which leaves me battling my fatigue. I want to ask him why he is being so nice to me and a thousand other questions. My opportunity slips away from me when Fran comes in to announce our soup is ready.

He swiftly thanks her and holds out his arm to me, "Shall we?" I take hold of his muscular arm and allow him to lead me to the formal dining room. I see that it is indeed formal. An enormous table sits in the middle of the room with twelve armchairs neatly tucked underneath. Fresh flowers are placed strategically in crystal vases. These are not the same kind of flowers that are near the front door. I am stunned. I am not accustomed to such lavish décor. "What a beautiful room Mr. Bradley". He nods and gestures for me to sit but I do not, "Glad you like it. It'll do in a pinch" he says grinning and stares at me again. Oh god, that grin warms me head to toe. He doesn't hold my gaze as long because I look directly into his eyes. Instead, he turns his head. Hmm. I think Mr. Bradley is shy.

"Well Mr. Bradley, I do seem to have gotten myself in a pinch now haven't I?" We both laugh. I see that Fran was thoughtful and put Mr. Bradley at the end of the table and I am supposed to sit to his right side. He pulls out my chair and I sit. He sits. We look at each other again. He sighs because he knows I have too many questions. Looking down I see that my soup looks great. It's just broth but the aroma hits me all at once and my stomach growls. The French bread is soft and warm. Now how did she make homemade French bread in ten minutes? She's got some secrets I'll have to convince her to share. As far as my cooking skills go bread is not my forte. Yep, there is definitely room for improvement in my bread making.

"It seems like I haven't cooked in ages" I say flatly. I feel like I should say something else but I am not sure what. So, I decide to thank him for his hospitality instead. "Please let me thank you ahead of time. This is wonderful. You, helping me make a run for it, this dinner, later talking. I really do appreciate it. I don't mean to intrude and as soon as I am feeling up to it I will leave. I just need some answers. I have so many questions. I think it's strange that I don't really remember much. Some things about myself and my life I know but it's... fragmented." Jake realizes he is staring at her lips as she talks. He would love to kiss those lips today. Forcing himself to look anywhere else, he looks down at his bowl and breaks a piece of bread off. "There's really no need to thank me. I just want to help you get back to normal, that's all. And I know you will need a friend in the near future so I'll let you know right now I'm here to help you. And I mean it, with anything." Jesse takes note of the look in his eyes. It is almost pleading. I can't believe this guy. Is he serious? He seems genuine. I think he is flirting with me. I can't wait to tell April about him. She'll be so jealous. "I will be grateful for anything you can divulge. I will be grateful for any help at all."

He nods at me and we eat our meal in silence. We are both thinking about the other. I hate that I can't tell specifically what he is thinking. He is deep in thought and his lips are a tight line. Again, I see his handsome features but they don't really register in my numb over stimulated brain. I don't pay attention to just how handsome he is. I wonder about him and about this house. I wonder about his position at the facility. I wonder if he'll truly be a friend or just one of those people that come and go. I eat half of my soup and am already full. I finish a little more than half of my bread and just can't take another bite. "Make sure you at least drink all of your water. I'm sure you're a little dehydrated. In fact, I'll have Fran bring a pitcher of water and one of juice into the sitting room before she goes. Is there anything in particular you'd prefer?" he asks. It's funny because I can't remember what I like. I think I like juice. Looking at him I have no idea how to answer that. I just say "No, that's fine. Anything will be fine. Where is Fran going?" He takes a drink of water and wipes his face with the napkin before responding. "All of the staff go home in the evenings. Actually they only work four days a week unless I ask them to come in on an off day. Tuesday through Friday. It's a pretty good schedule for them. You know, allows them to work another job if they want to. Get their errands done, etc. Sherman was off today. Had something personal he had to take care of. When he heard I had a guest he just had to swing by and meet you. I think he approved of you."

"Well, I hope so. That's a great schedule. I wish I could have found a job like that. I don't really remember where I work. I know that I work five and six days a week though. I know April keeps telling me not to work so much. She insists I slow down and take it easy. She says I do deserve it occasionally." A strange look sweeps across his face and then disappears. He looks away briefly and then focuses his gaze back on me. I fold my napkin neatly and place it next to my bowl. He makes me nervous. I look around the room at the pictures on the wall. I try to look anywhere but at him. A large framed painting of a woman hangs directly above the buffet. She is stepping down the last of eight stairs holding the bottom of her dress in her left hand so she doesn't trip. A mansion looms in the background. The woman is leaning over to smell some flowers in a tall planter. There is another planter on the opposite side. A dog prances gleefully at her feet. She looks extraordinarily happy.

"I really love the colors in that painting. She looks very happy. Even the dog looks happy" I say with a slightly jealous tone I did not mean to impart. As soon as the words fly out of my mouth I suddenly become very sad thinking about my situation. Will I ever be that happy again? What is going on with me and will there ever be a time I'll be able to escape it? As if he knew my thoughts he says, "I'm sure you will be happy again too. I'm sure it will be soon. Not to worry. I'm taking care of you tonight. Let's go upstairs and I'll start your bath. You can relax a little. Maybe get your thoughts together." He stands up and holds out his arm for me. I accept his arm partly because I know it's what he wants, and partly because I am still weak and unsteady. I let him guide me. We turn to the right and go up a winding staircase. I see pictures of prominent looking people hanging in the hallway. I do not ask who they are and he doesn't offer up any information. Once upstairs we turn right. He leads me halfway down a wide hallway and enters a room on the left. It is another beautiful room. Antique furniture fills the room. It all looks brand new. I think back to what he said about not having many guest here. I doubt if he has had any guest here.

The four poster bed is centered in the room and has an eloquent sheer lace draped across the canopy at the top. It spills over onto the four post and flows to the floor. A step stool is built into the side of the bed. The room has a fireplace which is already indulging a roaring fire. Round marble top tables with impressive claw feet are on both sides of the bed. The table on the opposite side of the bed has fresh flowers in baroque crystal vase. A queen Ann chair sits next to a desk with a reading lamp. Books line the back wall of this room as well. A set of French doors are opened and part of a lovely balcony shows. I see window boxes full of colorful flowers. Mr. Bradley lets go of my arm and heads to the back of the room. His posture is straight and confident and he moves with grace.

He enters the bathroom, flips the switch and I hear the water start to flow. He starts back in my general direction but unexpectedly turns to an armoire instead. He pulls out a pair of women's flannel lounge pants and a short sleeved flannel shirt to match. "These should do nicely for you". Pointing at the top drawer he says "You will find the rest of what you need in here. I'll come and check on you in a few minutes. The bedroom door locks but please leave it open so I can check on you. I promise to be a perfect gentleman". He grins shyly before he leaves. Standing in the middle of the room, alone and weary, I think that he is one of the good guys. There is just something about him that calms me. Thinking about the events of the day makes my head spin. I am so confused. I don't even know what to ask him first. It is clear I do need to get my thoughts together.

3

The water running in the bathroom gets my attention. I pick up the flannel set and head to the bathroom. The tub is only half full. It's an oversized tub with jets. There is a built in step and the sides of the tub are very wide. It looks divine. I feel like it's been a year since I've taken a hot bath. Even though I have had hot soup I still feel the bone chilling cold of that awful place. I shiver. I leave the water running and go to the armoire. I am amazed to find matching black lace panties and a bra that I think will fit. There are various matching sets in different colors and style. Did he put them here for me? How does he know my size? Oh god, I hope these are not his girlfriend's or worse, his wife's lingerie. It's been an exhausting day and I can't worry about the bra and panties. I go back to the bathroom and I turn the water off. Peeling off the scrubs I am shocked to see how thin I've become. I toss the socks and paper shoes into the trash. Next I toss the scrubs. As I throw them away I realize that the people at the hospital thought I worked there. That must be why nobody stopped me. I left the bedroom door wide open. The bathroom door I closed halfway. The tub is situated to the back left corner of the bathroom and there is a half wall that separates it from the rest of the bathroom. Elaborate flower arrangements sit on the half wall and extends over it. There is a separate shower and the toilet is around a corner on the right. Nice layout. I like it.

I feel the water and it feels great. I carefully step into the tub. The warmth of the water is divine. I quickly immerse myself up to my neck. Ah. Yes. I might stay in here for hours. He did say take as long as I want. After a few minutes I scrub myself with soap from head to toe. A bottle of shampoo is sitting on the tub. It is a brand I don't recognize. I use too much and have to rinse my hair twice to get it all out. It feels so good to be clean. To have the creepiness of that facility washed away. After soaking a while I hear Mr. Bradley call out from the bedroom "Are you all right?" I shout back that I am and he says he was just checking to see if I need anything. He asked me to meet him in the sitting room when I am finished. Question after question starts running through my head. My eyes are heavy and I am drowsy. I sigh. What am I doing enjoying a long hot bath when the man downstairs has answers to my questions? *Come on Jesse, get down there. And don't be slow about it either.*

I carefully get out of the bathtub and dry off. I dress fast and dry my hair almost all the way. After brushing my teeth I see a pair of black slippers sitting on the floor outside the bathroom. He must have put them here for me when he came to check on me. They may be a half size too big but they fit well enough for me. I slip into them and make my way downstairs. The house is quiet. The main lights are off. Lamps are turned on near the foyer and formal dining room. The light is off in the sitting room but the dancing light from the fire spills out of the doorway. As I enter the sitting room I see Mr. Bradley sitting in the left chair in front of the fire. Crossing the room to the other chair I see he has also changed into a pair of jeans and white T-shirt. When he sees me he smiles. "Well, I see you look a little more relaxed. How do you feel?" I sit down in my chair and take a deep breath. I shrug my shoulders, "I am ok. It feels great to be clean and the bath did warm me up." I look at his face and can see that he is tired. I really didn't pay much attention to his features earlier other than the fact I know he has dark blonde hair and hazel eyes. With the lights out and the fire roaring I can barely make out his blonde hair. His eyes are mysterious in the light of the fire. He has a slender long face with a square jaw. He's handsome in the glow of the fire and I find myself sitting up straighter and adjusting my shirt nervously.

I think that me being here is a big deal for him. I ask him, "How about you? Are you tired? You have had a pretty eventful day too." He nods his head, "I am tired but it doesn't matter. I am looking forward to talking to you". He reaches for a crystal pitcher on the table between us and pours some orange juice into a Champaign flute. He holds the juice out to me and our fingers touch briefly as I take it from him. My cheeks flush and I feel anxious. He looks at me as I sip on the juice but neither one of us say a word. Finally, the dam breaks and the questions fly out of my mouth before I can stop them. "What's going on with me? Why was I in that…lab? Or was it a hospital? Why was I so cold? Was cryogenics involved? How long have you been taking care of me? And who are you? What's your first name? Are you a doctor? When can I go home? I want to see my family". He holds up a hand, "Whoa, wait a minute. We have to take this one question at a time. It's a lot of information. So, step by step. Okay?" Looking at him I just say "Okay" as I anxiously await some answers.

He has an honest demeanor and again, I mentally note how odd it is that I feel safe and so comfortable with him. "We were taking care of you in the lab. I was assigned to your team. A year after I was assigned the budget was cut and some staff members took better paying jobs at other facilities. I felt that I had an obligation to you so I stayed. I was fascinated by your case. That was four and a half years ago and I've been taking care of you since then." What? He's been caring for me for five and a half years and I know nothing about him? I awkwardly stare at him and I will him to continue. He does when I don't say anything. "Yes, it was a cryogenics project." My breath catches in my chest and my throat tightens. I feel tears start to well up in my eyes but I blink them away. I refuse to cry, damn it. I stare dumfounded at him and he continues, "I have a cryogenics specialist, a cryogenicist whom I consult about you. He basically makes sure I get the mechanics right. I have an incredible nurse who comes by every evening to see if I need anything for you. She has been a huge help. Usually stays with you at night. My first name is Jake. I'm a doctor. I pretty much quit practicing regular medicine when I had the chance to work with you. It was a full time job taking care of you so I really had no time to deal with sinus infections and flu". To me he doesn't look like a doctor. His broad shoulders and square jaw makes me think of the military. I think he looks more like a soldier. So, I was frozen. I am shocked and it seems it is what I suspected. How can this be? He interrupts my thoughts, "I want you to stay here with me for a while. I'd like to get to know you, and help you while you are trying to regain your memory. I want to make sure you're fine from a medical aspect as well. So, no, you can't go home yet."

I try to take in all he divulged. I just can't seem to process it all. "So, you're telling me that I was frozen? How can that be? I mean, do we even have that kind of technology? I remember that there were some people frozen that had serious illnesses. Like brain tumors, cancer, aids. I guess they allowed themselves to be frozen in hopes that when they would be brought back that there would be a cure for their particular disease. And most of them were older people, right? I am young and healthy. This is all a little bizarre. So, don't take it personally but you're freaking me out! So, wow, I was frozen?"

He has his poker face on. I search his face for answers but can't tell what he is thinking. He looks off into the fire and doesn't look at me when he starts to speak next. "Yes, Jesse. That's what I'm telling you. I am sorry. I know it's a bit of a shock. I'm sorry you don't remember. I'm sorry this is so confusing for you. I'm sorry for the difficult days to come. I want to help you get through this. I want to make it all go away for you, but I can't. I want to make you feel whole again. I want to help you be happy again." He is still starring into the fire and I don't understand. Why does he want to help me? Why does he feel obligated to help me? He still doesn't look at me. "Please don't be angry with me Jesse. I had the chance to terminate the whole project but I just couldn't do that to you. After reading about you and working with you for five years I just couldn't. You see, Jesse, I've grown quite attached to you. I've told you my most intimate deep dark secretes. I use to talk to you in the evenings. I did not have anyone to talk to and I was going through a lot of stuff, you know, with my family. I would sit for hours and pour out my heart to you. I guess in a way I hoped that this day would come. That I'd have the chance to meet you while I was still a young man."

I can't believe I'm hearing him say this stuff. I mean, this is nuts. Okay, let's say he's telling me the truth. It could be possible, I guess. Although I never thought anything like this would happen to little old me. *Come on Jesse. Pump him for information. Get the details. This is only your life we're talking about!* He looks rattled. I have the sudden urge to reassure him. "Hey, Jake, it's okay. Don't look so scared. I'm the one who is freaked out, remember? Now, please, tell me. I want to know what you mean by 'terminate the whole project'. I want to know how I was thawed out like a Thanksgiving turkey. You mentioned five years. How long was I frozen?" I blanch, and I am not sure I want to know the answers. Jeez. I brace myself. Fear has me. Oh shit! How long? Have I outlived my friends and family? I feel sick, nauseous. Oh God no!

Oh no, oh no! Please let there be someone left. Even though I don't remember everyone now I know I will. Oh, please God, please let there be someone who remembers me, who loves me. Panicked, I jump up and pace in front of the fire. Oh whoa, I am short of breath. I try to push back my tears but I can't. I stand still and double over to take some deep breathes. Jake sees my reaction and he does not look surprised. He knows exactly what I am thinking. "Now, Jesse. Don't panic. Let's just have you sit back down. You're still weak. You're not yourself yet." He helps me back to my chair. He doesn't leave my side. Instead he kneels in front of my chair and grasps my hands tightly.

"Jesse, I know you're wondering about your family and friends. Let me go through it very fast first, and then you can ask more questions. You were frozen for thirty-one years." I gasp loudly. I suck in air trying to get control of my panic and fear. Oh fuck! No way! I half shout at him, "You've got to be kidding me. Thirty-one years! What about my parents? Are they alive? What about my friends? Ugh, that would make April sixty-one years old! Oh God! I can't see her. She'll hate me that I still look the same and she's aged. She will not want to have anything to do with me! We were best friends but I know she'll resent me now!" Tears flow down my checks. No! I don't want to cry but I can't stop myself. This can NOT be happening. I'll wake up. This has got to be a bad dream! Jake gets a tissue off the table and gently wipes my tears. "Oh, Jess, don't worry. I'm here with you. April is not sixty-one years old. I'm sorry Jess. She was killed in a car accident in 1995. She died immediately, she didn't suffer. I'm sorry, I'm so sorry."

What? Gone? I can't believe my lifelong friend is gone. I can't stop the tears. I cry hard. I sob uncontrollably. He remains kneeling in front of me. Jake takes me in his arms to comfort me. I throw my arms around his neck and I bury my face in his neck and shoulder. "Oh Jake, I can't believe it! My best friend! I love her so much! She is such a good person, my best friend!" I ask the question that burns into my brain. "What about my parents?" Jake shakes his head no. I sob uncontrollably for what seems like an hour. Jake lets me cry on his shoulder. He makes no effort to move. I can tell he is genuinely sorry for me. He is so sincere. I pull away from him and see that his beautiful face is tear streaked as well. He wipes my face and eyes gently with a fresh tissue. "I know that April must have been special to be your best friend" he murmurs softly. "I am sorry about your family too. I know this is a lot for you to bear. But I think it is better you hear it now and get it over with. There's so much to talk about." I nod my head for him to continue.

4

He wipes away more of my tears and also his own. "I know you prob-ably don't remember any of what I'm about to tell you. But just hear me out. The federal government approved a cryonics project and an A-list of scientist were put together to work on the project. The subjects were to have no lingering ties. No family alive that would have a difficult time with it. They didn't want interference. The government certainly didn't want family members going public or to congress demanding the subjects be regenerated or "thawed out" as you stated. I think there was more to it than I'm aware of. I do know the powers that be wanted to keep the project close to home. They chose our state because it was close. They could easily check up on the project."

"We had the best facilities here. They could look at all of them and see which one suited their needs the best. The hospital you were at was the chosen one. It was a classified project and at first they only froze the sick and the elderly. Once they believed that the process was perfected they wanted to test it out on a young healthy person. Secretly, they froze a nine-teen year old girl for a year. She was regenerated and had no side effects. Two years later she married her high school sweetheart and they had a baby the next year. Needless to say the scientists were ecstatic that they had done it. After news stories and rumors flew around for about five years, the government acknowledged that the field of cryonics was flourishing. They told the public the nice part of it. They left out the mistakes and the people who were killed due to human error. Then came the contest. They decided to have a contest on the local radio station to pick another subject. This time they wanted someone in the prime of their life. Male or female they didn't care."

Jake is saying all of this but I'm not remembering any of it. He's right. This is too much at one time. My head is spinning. I am scared. It will take a long time to really absorb all of this. Can this really be happen-ing? He eyes me warily and ask, "Are you all right?" I nod, "Please go on, I'm okay." I know I need to hear it and can pick it apart later. "So, is that it? Was I in this contest?" It astonishes me that I don't remember any of this. How is it that I don't remember any of it? Jake turns and reaches for the poker and mixes up the fire. It doesn't really need mixing. I think he just wants the distraction. "Well, not exactly. They advertised for the contest for months. They did get some calls but they did not want to accept any of those people. It looked like the whole thing would be called off. That's where you stepped in and volunteered to do it. I am not sure what initially prompted you to want to do it, but as the testing continued they decided that you would work perfectly. They completed all the pre-requisites and gave you a few weeks to get your personal affairs in order. A car was sent for you. You had to be in their care for a few days to prep you physically. Once it was all complete they began the process. The records state that you walked of your own accord into the lab and climbed into your cryo-cooler. Also, that you made a few jokes about when they wake you up they'd better have a steak dinner and a sports car waiting for you. Once they started the process you simply fell asleep. The actual cryogenics process took place once you were unconscious."

He took a long look at me. I have a strange look on my face. After what he just told me, well, who wouldn't? Jake turns to me and wraps his large hands around mine, which are shaking at the moment. He pulls me up out of my chair and guides me to a sitting position on the floor in front of the chairs. The fire is warm on my tear streaked face and I can see that the Oriental rug suited this room perfect. "Jesse, are you okay? Do you want to take a moment or do you want me to continue?" I do not respond but in my head I am saying "yes, continue...tell me". "Jesse, you're pale. I think I have shocked you enough for tonight. This is just too much for you. Why don't we just call it a night and I'll let you rest?"

I can't believe he thinks he's getting out of it that easily! No way, he's stuck here and he's going to tell me answers to all of my questions! That's how it has got to be. After voicing my opinion he smiles and shakes his head. He can see how strongly I feel about it so he does not try to argue with me. I'll admit it's all a little freaky, but I can't stop now. I have to know what's going on. I'm so tense and anxious. I need to try to relax. "You got anything stronger than orange juice? Or better yet, do you have anything I can put in my orange juice?" At first he doesn't understand what I am asking, then that boyish grin crossed his face. "I know exactly what you need. Be right back." He gets up and gracefully steps out of the room.

He seems like such a nice guy. I am stunned at the fact he didn't leave me. Not when I was frozen, and not now. He stayed with me, he cried with me. I exhale in a long, drawn out sigh. It's hard for me to understand that he wants to help me with the mess I've made of my life. I'll have to really find a way to thank him later. He has been so caring and kind to me and I realize that he doesn't have to be. I hear a few muffled noises on the other side of the dining room. A moment later he reappears with a bottle of rum and a cheese ball and crackers. The cheese ball is on a marble top silver platter with its own small cheese knife with a marble handle.

"In case you want a snack. As for me, I always have the munchies." He sits back down on the floor across from me. I didn't notice when he came in but he has a large napkin draped over his arm. He spreads the napkin out and then places the cheese ball platter on top of it. He opens the crackers and places them next to the platter. He reaches over with his long arms and takes the crystal pitcher with the orange juice off the table. He could not reach my glass and asked me to hand it to him. When he took the glass from me his fingers touched mine. We both pause for a brief moment. I feel shy and look down at my too thin thighs. When I finally do look up at him, somehow I know I could love this man. Not just the new kind of love you have for someone in the start of a relationship. I'm thinking more along the lines of an eternal earth shattering love that can never be broken. The "I never want to be without you" kind of love. The "best friends" love. I snap out of it and see that he is filling my Champaign flute with orange juice. *What the hell is wrong with me?* In my situation, that kind of thinking is dangerous. I have to get back on my feet...put my life back together somehow.

"Now, Jesse, as your physician I will tell you that your body has been through a lot and it will take some time for you to fully recover from your ordeal. I don't want you getting fall on your face drunk, so I am only going to give you a little bit of rum. I do understand this is rough, and this will certainly take the edge off." He only pours a few teaspoons of rum into my juice. He swishes it around a little and then hands it back to me. The first sip was delicious. It warms my throat all the way down. I smile and look up only to see he is halfway smiling back at me. The look on his face is that of longing. I recognize that look. I may be newly thawed but I'm not an idiot. I am sure my expression has changed because all of a sudden he gets an embarrassed look on his face. Is he flirting with me? I'm probably just being stupid. I mean...How could he want me? I'm a complete mess! Physically I look like a train wreck. I am worse than a train wreck emotionally, all sobs and tears and snot. I do the only thing I know to do which is thank him for the drink, "Thanks, this is good. Please continue, don't stop at nothing. Tell me all of it. And by the way, thank you for...Ugh...taking care of me. It's very nice of you."

He flashes me the poker face look and then responded "Awe, shucks ma'am, t'aint nothin'. Always glad to help a lady in distress." We both start laughing hysterically. I can actually picture him with a cowboy hat and a horse. It feels good to laugh. Like a weight has been lifted off my shoulders. I can't remember the last time I laughed. "Oh, is that what I am to you, a lady in distress?" I murmur and take another sip of my drink. His smile vanishes quickly and just like that the poker face is back. "I am just joking around. You're much more to me than that. Not just because I spent the last five years taking care of you either. On some level I feel a strong connection with you that I just can't explain. It's like I've known you my whole life. I feel like you're my best friend even though this is the first day we've ever spoke to one another."

All I could say is "Wow." He must think I am a complete idiot because of the way I stare at him. I watch him cheese a cracker and choke it down. He fixes a drink of his own and gulps it down. I do not miss the fact that he puts a lot more than just a few teaspoonful's of rum in his glass. "Okay, enough, let me continue before I lose my nerve. If you're sure you want me to, that is." Loose his nerve? Holy shit! Is he nervous too? Do I make him nervous? He cheeses another cracker and holds it out to me. I take it from him and slowly nibble at it. The cheese is sharp and delicious on my tongue. I drink the rest of my drink as he eyes me. Once I finish I voice my opinion about how I must find out the whole truth and try to figure out how to put my life back together and go forward.

I glance over his broad shoulders and notice that the sun has gone down. There is the faint glow of the sunset still noticeable through the sheer curtains of the French doors. I find comfort in the cracking and popping of the fire. The house is completely quiet until he speaks again. "Where was I? Oh yeah, the actual process began once you were unconscious. I can't say for the first twenty-six years what took place because I was not actually there. I only know what is recorded in your files. I have read extensively the history of your procedure and know about it that way.

I can say that you did have the very best physicians. Brilliant minds ahead of their time. You have had the best care physically and medically. Some of the older doctors have passed on. When I first became involved with the project, uh, with you I mean, as I said before, you had an A-list team working for you. I only had a short year to work with them before it all fell apart. Some of the other older doctors retired and moved away. Some of the younger doctors took jobs elsewhere. I was the only one that could or would stay with you. There was talk of terminating the whole project. That's when I put my foot down. That's when I made the decision to complete this project no matter what it took. No matter how long it took."

5

As he spoke about me in that 'project sense' it seemed weird. I do get the feeling he is sincere when he says 'no matter what'. He is very passionate about taking the project on by himself and not allowing it to be terminated. Not allowing me to be terminated. That's what I need to find out. I spoke up, "Whoa, wait a minute. What exactly do you mean when you say they wanted to terminate the whole project? Does that mean what it sounds like it means?" He looks lost. He looks down for a moment, sighs, and fixes himself another drink. After taking a few sips he looks up at me with tears in his eyes. Oh my god, he is going to cry! "Jesse, I'm sorry to say it does mean what it sounds like. They were simply just going to turn you off. There's a whole process that has to be done to bring you back, regenerate you, to unthaw a person so to speak. They didn't have the manpower or the money. They just wanted to forget the whole project. They had the research they needed, and you had cost them more in time and money than they ever dreamed. I had only worked with you a year at that point and resolved I'd do it on my own. And that's exactly what I did." I just can't get past this. Starring down at the cheese ball I listen to what he said but what it boils down to is he saved my life. They were going to let me die. If it had not been for Jake I'd be dead now. Wow.

How do you ever repay someone for saving your life? I sat dumfounded at it all. I am certainly grateful to him. I motion for him to continue. "Jess, are you sure? It's an awful lot to take in." Jess? Did he just call me Jess? I look up at him and he wipes tears off my cheek that I didn't even realize were there. He put the cheese ball and crackers on the table. He topped off his drink and made me another, added more nip to his than to mine and put the orange juice and rum back on the table. We both took another drink. He held out his free hand and nodded his head. I am frozen all over again. "Come here, sit next to me, I want to be close to you while I finish telling you the rest." For a second I am a stone statue and can't move. I think events of the evening are getting the better of me. I think my brain is numb. Is that even possible? My body aches all over. My mind races. Is this all really happening? It's just been a strange day.

I finally do as asked and scoot over until my thigh touches his. He wraps his arm over my shoulders and squeezes my arm. We both lean against the chair. We sit quietly for a minute, getting acclimated to each other's close proximity. He is warm. His touch burns all the way down to my soul. My skin is sensitive to his gentle touch. I feel so safe with him. I don't think I have ever felt so safe with a man in my whole life. Then again, I can't be sure seeing as how I don't remember my life! He asked if I am ready and I nod yes. I manage to say "Please, continue" out loud, my voice small. Inside I am devastated.

"Jess, please know that I'd never do anything to hurt you. This is a lot...weird... I know. Just let me get the truth out and then you can ask me questions later. I come from a prominent family. My father and mother were both doctors, specialist. I always knew I'd follow in their footsteps. I've lived a full life but never had time for...um ... relationships. Don't get me wrong, I've sewed a wild oat or two along the way. Nothing serious though. My father and mother were together for over forty years. They were married thirty-five of those years. They were so happy together. That's what I want out of life. I want to have someone to share my life with, forever." Oh, wow. How has this handsome man not been involved in a serious relationship? It is amazing to me that some lucky woman hasn't snagged him yet. It's unbelievable, really. I know I must have my stupid girl face on. I motion for him to continue. "My father died suddenly. They told me it was a heart attack but I've got my own suspicions about his death. My mother just couldn't take it when he died. She lasted two years. I believe that deep in my heart she died of depression and loneliness. Physically they tell me she had cancer. I am not sure if I believe that either. She would have told us if she had known. I know she would have."

Why is Jake telling me all this? What does it have to do with me? And why is he bearing his soul to pretty much a complete stranger? I think he feels like he can trust me. He said he feels like I am his best friend. "Oh, Jake, I am so sorry to hear about your parents. How long ago has this been?" He shifts his weight and squeezes me closer to him. He doesn't say anything. When I look up at him I see tears on his face. Returning the favor, I gently wipe away his tears and he composes himself. "My mom has been gone for two years now, my dad four. The house I grew up in was just too big with too many memories there. With just me in the house it seemed odd. Plus I did want a new place of my own. I had to handle both of their estates and was surprised to find out just how wealthy we really were. I mean, don't get me wrong I knew we were well off. I just never gave it much thought. I was young and stupid. I never dreamed what my parents had done as far as investments both here and abroad. You name it they had it, stocks, bonds, oil, wheat, cotton. They owned a tremendous amount of shares of different research labs around the world."

I am glad Jake feels that he can share things with me. I know he's going to have to put up with a lot of my problems in the near future. The least I can do is listen and help him when he needs it. Thinking of just how curious his life seemed I lost my attentiveness to what he was saying and he noticed. "I am sorry, I am rambling now. Let me get back on track...this actually does have something to do with you. Jesse, the whole point is that your project was partly funded by my family. Things had been going on for a long time. Things I didn't know about and things my parents shielded me from because they didn't want to worry me while I was in school. I'm not even sure my mother knew all that was going on around her. I was not even supposed to be involved in the project at first. My dad ended up telling me about it one day while we were boating. Said he needed someone on the inside. Someone he could trust. With me having just completed my internship and my first few years of actually working, he thought it would be a good change of pace for me and I'd be able to get some good experience out of it too. Or at least that was the front he put up with the other doctors. They only let me participate because of my father's fortune. That, I do know. They were careful at what they said around me. I used my eyes and ears though, and, partly because of my training, I knew when something was up. Like I said it had only been about a year when I alerted my father to the possibility that your project secret was actually out."

I wasn't quite sure what he meant. "Wait a minute. Do you mean I was a secret? What about the contest? I thought it was widespread knowledge? You know, on the radio. This is turning out to be quite the drama!" My leg started falling asleep. Of all times! I am now comfortable sitting this close to him and I don't want to move, besides that, he is warm. I like sitting next to him. I like talking like this. I feel like it's been forever since I've really talked to anyone. No choice left, I have to move. I scrunch my legs underneath me and get on my feet. Jake watches my every move. "I'm sorry Jake. My foot is falling asleep. Pins and needles." I hop on my other foot back over to my chair but do not sit down. Instead I stand using the chair to keep my balance. I must look ridiculous because he laughs at me and shakes his head. Jake stands up as well. He stretches his legs and while doing so says, "No, you were not widespread knowledge." He straightens up and picks up the cheese ball and crackers. "Carry the glasses for me, will you?"

I do as asked and I hobble behind him toward the dining room. We walk through it and end up in the colossal kitchen. It's tastefully decorated. There is large crown molding all over this house and it sprawls around the top of the kitchen, above the cabinets. "The woodwork, the cabinets, are beautiful", I say in a small, weary voice. He has already put away the crackers and is now putting the cheese ball back in the refrigerator. There is a keypad of some sort on the front of the refrigerator. To the side of it is some kind of display screen. "Thanks. I hand-picked the craftsman myself. I knew just what I wanted and I wasn't going to take a chance on just anyone doing the work." He pointed to my foot and asked if it felt better. I said it does. "Jess, I think that after the contest applicants did not work out that the public was told that it was scrapped. I mean, you were not on the radio or anything in regards to the contest. I think that very few people knew that you were going to do this." He looked at me and I motioned for him to go on.

"Fast-forward twenty-six years and that's when I joined your team.

The next year, well, that's when my dad died and the whole project team fell apart. I was grieving and trying to console my mother and take care of her. I still went to work every day knowing that's what my dad would have wanted me to do. It is a good thing I did too. I overheard a couple of the other doctors talking about lack of funding and how anonymous threats were coming down from above....from someone in the government. Someone powerful. They felt they had to make a decision. They thought if they went their separate ways they would be safe as long as they quit the project. I heard them talking about what to do about me since I'd most likely be the one who would not quit. Before they could scheme or make any plans for me, I walked in on them. I let them know I heard every word they said. I told them I recorded the conversation. I had not of course, but they didn't know one way or the other. I told them that they could go their separate ways if they wanted to but I would not let you just die like that.

They warned me of the danger and the threats but I told them I'd cross those bridges when I got to them. They tried to weasel me out. You know, convince me to just let you go. That was around the time I was handling the estate stuff for my dad."

The only thought that keeps running through my mind is if it were not for this man, I'd be dead. I didn't stand a chance with the others working on my 'project'. Oh, thank God for Jake! We are still standing in the kitchen. I am not ready to sit. I am fidgety and nervous. Anxiety runs through me and there is a palpable tension in the air. I feel it, and, judging by the way he is looking at me, Jake feels it too. It feels good to walk and move around. I stretch big and tall with my hands up over my head and he eyes me from head to toe in a very sensual gaze. I can tell he's thinking something dark because an intense look flashes in his eyes. He's not going to tell me what it is. Instead, swiftly changing the subject, he looks at me and asks, "How about a short walk?" I say, in my small, weary voice, "Yes, that would be nice." Jake turns to walk ahead of me and then unexpectedly turns back around. He closes the distance between us and when we are face to face he puts his arms around my waist. It shocks me but I make no effort to stop him. I know the look, of wanting and longing that is now consuming every fiber of his being. Jake leans in towards me, our lips almost touching. "Jess, I'm sorry for being so forward and I don't mean to scare you. It's just that, well, that... that I think I'm falling in love with you." *Holy shit! Did he just say that?* I take a deep breath and let it out slow, trying to calm myself down. Right now, I only know one thing with every fiber of my being. His close proximity is burning me up. I want him to kiss me. I need him to kiss me. He pauses, looking for permission to proceed. I tilt my chin up and our lips touch. He kisses me gently at first but then changes it to a deeper, more passionate kiss. I wrap my arms around him and pull him closer to me. His mouth is on mine, his tongue is forcing my lips further apart and is reaching and probing into every part of my mouth, searching, yearning for something more. I am full of sensation everywhere and I feel it especially low in my belly. He runs his hands up and down my back stopping short of grabbing my backside. I moan into his mouth and kiss him back hard and fast and do not want it to end. He pulls away, our foreheads touching, we are both breathing heavy. Wow! Nice. This man can kiss! He panics and takes a few steps back giving me space. "Wow, look...um, I'm really sorry, I hope I didn't scare you." I can still feel his hungry lips on mine. What am I supposed to say to that? I smile shyly at him, "No, you didn't. It was….nice…really nice." We have an awkward moment where we both stare at the other and we both want to be back in the other's arms. "Wow, I haven't been kissed like that in decades" I say smiling. I don't know what else to do or say so I add, "Hey, let's take that walk."

Smiling, he takes my hand and turns to walk out of the kitchen. We walk to the other side of the kitchen and through the doorway. There is a small hallway that goes straight. Halfway down at a fork in the hallway one part turns to the left. I'll probably get lost in this house it is so big. We head straight and ignore the intersecting hallway on the left. At the end of the hallway he opens another door. A soft fluorescent light spills out onto the floor. As I pass through the doorway I can't believe my eyes. Well this is not what I was expecting. The room is warm but not uncomfortable. We are in some kind of greenhouse I think. I see plant after plant lined up in a row. "Wow! Look at all of these plants. This is so great." I am sure I look ridiculous with a face splitting grin I can't wipe off my face. He smiles and says, "Yeah, I like a lot of landscaping and the gardener had this great idea. Actually, I liked the idea as much, if not more, than he did. I had this built when the house was built. That way we always have the plants we want for the outside landscaping. We can move things in here if we need to due to inclement weather. It just works out great. I always have the option to add something if I get the urge. It's kind of a neat hobby."

With his hand still in mine, he leads me further down the path. I think to myself but said it out loud, "I can't believe it, look at all of those roses! I love roses." He immediately frees his hand from mine, pulls a pocket knife from his right jean pocket and cuts me a fresh bouquet of roses. "Here, baby, these are for you…for your room." Wow. I am speechless. I graciously accept them. The sweet aroma of the flowers drifts up to my nose and I bend down to get a better smell. I look up and see Jake smiling a shy, boyish breathtaking smile. "Thanks, they're wonderful. You did not have to." He motions for me to walk so I do. Finally, we reach the back of the greenhouse. There is a row of benches. He motions for me to sit and I do. He picks up where he left off. "As I said, I was handling the estate for my father. I was quickly left alone to care for you. Of course, I had the Cryonics specialist I could always call and also an incredible nurse came in every evening to see if I needed anything for you.

She usually stayed with you at night. I became even more fascinated by the whole process and began reading more research info to pass the time. I did get some threats that I will not go into now. Someone in government did not want this to become public knowledge. I hired my own security. Once I realized I could do it, I bought the hospital. They can't tell me what to do on my own property. I made additional upgrades regarding security. Oh, no! I'm making it sound bad. Please don't be scared. I think it's under control."

He thinks? And I can't wrap my mind around what he has just told me. He bought the whole hospital just so he could keep me safe and alive! This just keeps getting better. I have to clarify, "Did you just say you bought the whole hospital?" His lips twist up into a shy smile. "Well, yeah, what was I supposed to do? I couldn't let you be 'turned off' now could I?" If he only knew how much he was turning me on right now! I can't believe he's done so much for me. This incredible stranger has given me so much and all before I even knew he existed. What have I done to deserve him? I asked, "Is that it? So, is that when you decided to defrost me like a turkey?" He laughs at my ridiculously simplified version.

I am looking down at my flowers, playing and moving them around by size so that they form the perfect bouquet. When he doesn't speak I glance up at him. He has his poker face back on. Dr. Bradley is back. "No, there was a problem with either the cryopump or pulse tubes. I checked the cryostats and they were working as far as I could tell. I never actually tried to 'defrost' you as you say. I wasn't really sure that I knew how to do it correctly and I was waiting for the specialist to come by to tell me what needed to be done or fixed. He didn't show and it was after midnight. I decided to come home to sleep and shower. I overslept. I had a few things to attend to here and a business meeting right after lunch. When it was over I immediately rushed to the hospital, and, well, I ran into you!"

Whoa, wait a minute. He was not 'trying' to defrost me! I am standing here now because there was 'a problem'. My head is spinning, my thoughts racing, and I am nauseous. I suck in as much air as I can and then sigh big. I can't comprehend this. "You've got to be kidding me?" I ask. He shakes his head, "No. I had a message on my disk this morning from the specialist that he did show up last night after I left and did what he needed to do. He instructed the night nurse and she stayed with you until she had to leave this morning. So actually, you were really only alone for a short while. Without the support of those two I wouldn't have been able to take care of you. I made sure they were the best, for you."

This is all so bizarre. I know it may be a stupid question but I ask him what a disk is. "Do you mean a computer diskette?" He says it's a new kind of messaging system. The information gets recorded on a little disk that you remove from one phone or device and put into your travel phone or other device. It can also work in your computer with a thing called Tech-M. He said it evolved from a thing called e-mail. It seems like I've heard of the e-mail thing before. It all sounds so complicated but to him it seems easy.

6

Jake is quiet. I know he is giving me time to try to comprehend all of this. I think of all he has told me. He just sits and looks at me, poker face on. I sense that he has taken a great risk to take care of me. I get it. All of this information is overwhelming. Hard to comprehend. Is this really happening to me? I realize I am feeling quite warm. My cheeks flush. I shake my head, "Jake, you were right. Earlier. When you said it is an awful lot of information to hear at once. I want you to know that I really appreciate you helping me." I am holding the roses in my right hand, so with my left, I reach over and touch his hand gently. "Thank you for taking the time to take care of me, for saving me, for the past five years and for today." I feel the tears forming in the back of my eyes. Damn it, I don't want to cry! "I feel a little better knowing about all that's happened. When I do get my memory back I know I'll still be grateful for all of your help."

"Jesse, you don't have to thank me. I was doing what I wanted to do. Really. Now how about let's go put your roses in a vase from the kitchen. You can take them to your room later. I'm getting a little warm in here. I'll show you the rest of the house tomorrow. We can talk more tonight if you feel like it. I just don't want to overwhelm you. You tell me and we'll go at your pace, okay?" I definitely want to talk more. I do, however, want to go back into the house. "Jake, you're not off the hook that easily. I want to hear more, but I am a little warm myself. So, lead on, to the kitchen." We passed back through the hallway and into the kitchen. Jake went to a large pantry and opened cabinet after cabinet until he found what he wanted. He pulls out a beautiful crystal vase. It has a frosted look with soft pink roses on the sides.

He looks at me and then looks down at the vase. "This is a special vase" he murmurs. "I bought this vase for my mother when she got sick. She loved it. I made sure to keep fresh roses with baby's breath in it for her the whole time she was sick. I instructed the gardener and housekeepers to change out the flowers in her room every other day. Sometimes I'd walk by and see her staring at the vase. She had so much weighing on her mind but most of all I think she was worried about me. About me being alone once she was gone." He is lost in thought staring down at the vase. It was all so sad. Looking at him now I can see the lost little boy alone and scared, the little boy that his mom wanted to protect. Clearly they had a strong bond. I picture her lying there wondering what would become of him. If he'd be safe. If he'd be alone his whole life. I wonder myself if he has any other family here. He hasn't mentioned anyone.

"Jake, do you have any other family here? You have only mentioned your mother and father. Do you have a brother or sister? An aunt or uncle? Anyone?" I was almost afraid of his answer. He walks over to me and gently takes the roses out of my hands and places them in the vase. Next he goes to the sink and fills them with water. In a cabinet above the sink he finds a small packet and opened it and pours it into the water. Once it has dissolved he sits the vase on the counter near me. "That will keep them fresh for a while" he said. He looks at me as if trying to figure out what to say. "No, unfortunately, I don't have any siblings and not really any other family here. My father and mother was both the only child in their immediate families and both their parents are long gone. My father had family in Europe when he was a young child growing up. His parents moved to the United States when he was just seven years old. They kept in contact with the family for a while. I think he did know some of his cousins and spoke with them occasionally. I, however, don't really remember them. That is one of my goals. I will eventually look them up. I'd like to see if they have any pictures of my father when he was young. I'd like to have some sort of legacy to hand down to my own children someday. If I have children, that is."

It is all so dramatic. It seems like everything has been difficult for him. Even his history sounds rough around the edges. "Oh, Jake. I'm sure you will have a very nice family someday. You're still so young. What about your mom's family?" He takes my hand and leads me through the dining room, across the foyer and into the sitting room. The fire is still going strong. Instead of sitting in the chairs near the fire he stops at the couch in the back of the room. It is darker back here and I can't see his features as well. He motions for me to sit so I do. I sit in the middle of the couch and tuck my legs up underneath me. Jake sits to my left. He turns his body toward me and begins to speak. "My mom grew up in New York.

Her family was not a *warm* family I guess you could say. Prominent, but not very loving to her. They supported her financially but she never really had a close relationship with them. She went to medical school. Partly to get away from her family. She loved living away at school and learning new things. She worked hard and got a really good job working in a pediatric unit at a burn center. I can only imagine the horrible injuries she had to treat."

"She worked there for six years and actually helped to modernize the treatments for burn victims. It was there that her interest in genetics began to grow. As she grew stronger and more independent of her family, she decided to pursue her interest in genetics. She took a job working for the government in a genetics lab. It was there that she met my father. He too had conquered many obstacles to be in his job. He had been there for approximately five years. He was instantly attracted to her and although she'd never admit it, I think she was to him as well. He showed her the ropes and they became fast friends. They dated for five years and then they married. She continued to work until I arrived. My mom had the strongest duty to her family. She quit work and stayed home to raise me. Once I became a teenager and off to a private school she went back to work. Only this time, it was in one of the labs to help my father. She did a lot of research and administrative things too. She really kept my father organized and on track. When my mother's parents passed away she never kept in touch with anyone else. I guess she never liked them much anyway."

Jake swept his large hands over his whole face. He rubbed his eyes for a minute and then his chin. After looking at me for a second he said, "So, that's it. It's just me. I never feel alone though. Fran and Sherman have been like family to me, along with a few others. They worked for my parents for years. They insisted on coming with me to this house. I have other employees to keep my parent's house. I'll take you there sometime. It is a beautiful place. On a lake and all. I use it as my vacation spot." He looks at me and takes my hand in his. "I am so sorry for everything that you are now facing. Are you tired? Do you want to call it a night?" I shake my head no. He smiles warmly at me.

It was hard to believe that this wonderful man did not have anyone to share his life with. No family, immediate or otherwise. No girlfriend. He hasn't mentioned anyone…and, he did say he thought he was 'falling in love with me'. I am glad he has such devoted employees to help him. I know I have my own problems but when I get my full memory back I'll be able to piece my life back together one day at a time. Jake has his life and has nobody to share it with. It's all so sad. I put my hands over his and said, "I'm sorry too. It sounds like you've been through a lot the past five years. All of that and still you took care of me. That just proves how strong of a man you are. I know eventually I'll get my full memory back and when I do, I won't forget what you've done for me. I would like to think that this is the start of a long friendship for us and I'll be here for you if you ever need me. I owe my life to you Jake. Thank you." I lean into him to hug him. He puts his arms around me and hugs me back. "Thanks Jess. I know our paths are forever entwined and that this is just the start of our friendship too. You have enough to deal with. It's nice to know I can lean on you if I need to though. I've been alone for so long. Way too long."

Jake squeezes me closer to him. I can feel his heart pounding in his chest. My legs are falling asleep again. I stretch them out. My feet do not touch the floor. There are so many other questions I should be asking him. My brain is so overloaded with all this information. It's numb. I am worn out. Exhausted. Sitting here next to Jake like this makes me feel like I could sit here forever. It is nice to feel content and happy. Was I happy before? Maybe something happened and I wasn't happy. Maybe that's why I volunteered for the 'project.' A huge yawn escapes me. Before I realize what is happening I put my head on his shoulder and drift off to sleep. What seems like moments later Jake stands and scoops me up in his arms. I stir a little and ask him what time it is. He says it is almost midnight.

I can't believe it's so late already. No wonder I am tired. "Put me down, I'll walk" I say in a small, weary voice. "No way baby, I want to take you up" he says in a soft husky voice. Even with my eyes closed I know he is smiling because I hear it in his voice. I wrap my arms around the back of his neck and relax on his shoulder. He carries me up to the guest room and puts me on the opposite side of the bed. The fire is still going, but needs attending. I sleepily open my eyes to see him walk to the fireplace where he mixes it up and puts on a few more logs. Jake goes to the other side of the bed and removes the extra pillows and turns the linens down. He puts his hand down on the bed, "Scoot over here" he says. I do as I'm told and scoot over and he tucks me in. He sits on the side of the bed. "Jess, I know it's been a long day and I know you still have so many questions. We have all the time in the world to get to know each other and for you to find out who you are. I do need to go into work for a few minutes in the morning. I need to tie up some loose ends. I won't be long and then we can do anything you want."

I know the loose ends he is talking about has something to do with me. I yawn again. He continues, "Just make yourself at home in the morning. I'll have coffee made if you'd like some. I'll probably be back before you wake up but if not, you'll find what you need in the pantry or fridge." He starts to stand up but I reached for his hand. It has been an exhausting day and I am still scared and anxious. "Don't go", I say. "Please stay with me until I fall asleep." He agrees and gets up and turns off the light. In the glow of the fire I watch him walk across to the empty side of the bed. He lies down next to me and holds my hand as I drift off to sleep. I sleep peacefully for a long while. Nightmares eventually creep in and interrupt my calm slumber. I dream of a man with dark hair and dark eyes, dressed in khaki pants and a black, long sleeve shirt. We are in a park having a picnic. We look so happy.

We start fighting about something but I can't hear what we are saying. Before I know it we are screaming at each other and people in the park stop what they are doing and stare at us. He slaps my face and gets up to walk away. I am so mad I throw things at him. I feel like my world has ended. Whoever this man is, whatever he means to me, I am devastated to think he is walking away from me. I am angry. The park suddenly changes to a living room. My parents are there. Dad is sitting in his favorite chair reading a newspaper and mom is handing me a packed suitcase. She is telling me to have a nice time on my trip. April busts through the front door full of excitement. She grabs my bag and rushes me outside. We start to get into her car but before we can it turns into some huge ugly furry creature with red eyes and long sharp nails. It kind of looks like a werewolf or something but it is ten times as big as we are. It starts to chase us and we run.

I wake up in a cold sweat out of breath. I feel like I have really been running from that thing. I am still mad at that man. Who is he? Do I really know him from before the 'project'? I lay there for a minute trying to catch my breath. I look over and realize that Jake is fast asleep. His hair has fallen almost completely into his eyes. He looks so peaceful. I do not want to wake him and since I cannot go back to sleep, I find a quilt in the armoire and cover him up. I look over to the bedside table and see the roses Jake cut for me. He must have gone back downstairs after I fell asleep and brought them up for me. He really is such a nice guy. I slip into my slippers and head downstairs. I find the bathroom downstairs and wipe my face with a warm washcloth. I feel the first pangs of hunger in my stomach. Wow, it hit me all at once. I am getting really hungry.

I find the kitchen and search for a clock but I don't see one. Finally I spot a small digital clock on the stove. It is five-thirty in the morning. I hear a gurgle in the corner. It is the coffee pot starting to brew. I look at it a little closer to see that it has been set on a timer. I retrieve a cup and saucer in the cabinet. I check the fridge to find half and half. I hate to drink black coffee. *Thank you, Jake for the half and half.* I pull out the eggs, sausage, butter and jelly and sit them on the counter. I fix my cup of coffee and go to the sitting room. The fire is still burning but needs another log. Jake has one sitting off to the side and I put it on the fire. I sit in the wing back chair near the fire. Before long the fire is crackling and burning bright. I drink all my coffee and then just sit there thinking. I do not know exactly what to do.

Last night I learned a lot of what I needed to know. Where to go from here? I am not quite sure. I know there are more questions I need to ask. I think of Jake and *that kiss* and can't help but smile. Wow, he can kiss. He is very handsome. I laugh at myself because I wasn't too tired to notice that! I just don't know what he expects from me. How long does he think I will stay here? I have so many other things to worry about right now. Should I allow myself to get involved with him? Probably not. I sit sulking for a while and then a joyous feeling of being alive overtakes me. I am so happy just to be here. While thinking about how lucky I have been I am re-energized. I want to do something fun today. I feel so alive. More than yesterday. More like myself today. It helps that I have slept some. I decide to think positive about my whole ridiculous situation. I might as well because I can't change it. I go to the kitchen to get another cup of coffee. While I am standing at the coffee pot two arms wrap around my waist. Jake hugs me tight and kisses my neck. "Good morning baby. I was hoping you were not a dream" he says. I smile and turn around to hug him back. "Ugh, let's not talk about dreams" I say. "Coffee?" He shakes his head yes and I fix him a cup. He says no to half and half. I hand him black coffee. "Why" he asked. I told him about my dream. We go to the sitting room. He takes his chair and I take mine. "Jess, I'm sorry. I never intended to stay in your room all night."

Jake blushes a little and looks shy. "I was just so tired that I guess I fell asleep. I went down to get your roses. Then, I sat there for a long time watching you. You are so beautiful. I promise I won't do that again. I don't want you to feel uncomfortable.. . in any way." He runs a hand through his bed head. I can't help but notice he is gorgeous in the mornings. "Oh, don't worry about it. No big deal. Besides, I asked you to stay until I fell asleep. Remember?" He shrugged his shoulders a little. "Yeah, I know. But I still feel like I acted irresponsibly. Jess, I want you to know that you will probably get your memory back in bits and pieces like that. You could get it back in an instant too. But I think it's more likely that you'll remember a little at a time. This dream might be the start."

Jake finishes his coffee. My stomach growls. How embarrassing! "Come on, let's go back to the kitchen and I'll whip up a delicious omelet before I duck out on you." He flips on the lights as we walk. It is easy to see that he loves to cook. He is right at home in the kitchen and before I know it he hands me a plate with an omelet and hash browns. There is a large bay window in the kitchen and a table that seats eight. The table is the same wood that the cabinets are made out of. It looks like it was custom made as well. Jake urges me to eat and I try. I can only eat half of the food and am full. He finishes his food and takes both of our plates to the sink.

"I am going to shower. Please make yourself at home. There are books in the sitting room and also in your room. Roam around if you wish. I haven't shown you the rec room yet. It's in the back of the house, downstairs. Don't be alarmed if you see security around. There's a squad at the front gate. There's also a separate detachment of eight men that work the grounds and house. There is nobody in the house except us. So you have your privacy. If you need help please get me or them. They are here to help you. We can talk more when I get back. Any questions?" I shake my head no and watch him leave the room.

7

I don't know what to do first. Stuffed and just happy to be alive, I walk back to the sitting room. Looking at the books on the bookshelves I am impressed. He has a little bit of everything. This is quite a collection. I was never an avid reader but it was always due to a lack of time. Now I guess I'll have time to read a few books. Right now I feel like being lazy. Maybe even go back to sleep. No way, I am not going to go back to sleep and miss out on one minute of this day. I'll sleep really good tonight. Maybe if I'm really tired I won't have any dreams. Do I dare roam around the house? I could find the rec room. I walk out of the sitting room and pass the bathroom. At the end of the hall I turn to the left. There is a winding staircase that goes downstairs. I followed the stairs and end up in what can only be the rec room.

It is a huge room built like a log cabin. Beautiful hardwood floors and large crystal chandeliers create a stately effect. The walls are logs but they are very smooth. The room is broken down into different areas. There is a bar halfway down on the right side. Hanging on the wall above the bar are antique mining lanterns, a horseshoe and some old photos. To my immediate left is a game area. There is a large pool table, an air hockey table and a few bowling lanes with the actual row of seats where you sit and keep score. In addition, there are five different arcade games. I recognize Galaxy Quest and Frogger. The others I have never heard of. To the side of those are a couple of pinball machines. There is a row of leather chairs opposite a large leather couch. A coffee table and end table were thrown into the mix. They are either dark cherry wood or maybe walnut. They looked to be expensive hand carved wood. The claw feet are lovely.

In the back left section of the room stands an upright piano. Sheet music is sitting out. A guitar is leaning up against the brick of the large fireplace that's centered in the back of the room. The brick of the fireplace nearly covers the whole back wall. There are wing back leather chairs near the fireplace. A leather couch is centered opposite the other side from the leather chairs. A large handmade wooden trunk stands in front of the leather couch. The trunk is made out of that same dark wood and has Viking carvings on the top and sides. To the right of the fireplace there is a stunning armoire. It's large and ornate and is made from that same dark wood. The elaborate carvings are stunning. The same Viking theme. In the very middle and center of the room is an oriental rug. The largest one I've ever seen. Throw pillows are arranged at each corner of the rug. There are pillows of every shape, texture and color. There's a long bookshelf that extends approximately eight feet. The bookshelf backs up against the large leather couch. It is the same dark wood. Low to the ground it had three shelves. It's completely full of books. On top of the bookshelf are miniature replicas of baseball and football stadiums.

If I had a room like this I'd spend a lot of time here. Does Jake? I wonder. I can imagine him playing games or reading. I envision him having guest over and serving drinks at the bar. I imagine him sitting in the wing back chair near the fire during a time of quiet reflection. Walking through the room now, touching various items, I really get a sense of a lonely man. He has all of these things to occupy his time. I get the funny feeling he's never offered a drink to a guest in this room before. No parties to speak of. Just Jake. It made me a little sad to think of him alone here. Just living his life, going about the day to day business of living. Missing his family. I walk over to the Oriental rug. At first I sit on it. There must be a huge cushion underneath it because it's really soft. I sprawl out on it. I lean over and grab a pillow, knocking down the neatly arranged stack. OOPS! I'll have to fix those.

I just lie there thinking about all that's happened to me. Thinking about Jake and all he's done for me. I am still in my pajamas. It would feel great to get dressed today. To actually dress, look and feel like a woman. It seems like it's been so long since I've dressed nice. I look down at my nails. They are long and need some serious attention. I really need a nail file. I don't know how long I have been nosing around in the rec room. Doesn't seem like that long, but I'd best get upstairs and see about getting dressed. I try to arrange the pillows like they were before. They finally stay stacked up but are not how they were. This will have to do. I make my way back upstairs to the main floor. Past the bathroom the sitting room is to my right. I slowly make my way up the second set of stairs. My legs trudge along, almost unwillingly. I have aches and pains all over but I just pushed them to the back of my mind. I could use some exercise. I am sure that the more active I am the better I will feel.

At the top of the stairs I turn right and my room is to the left. Past my room near the very end of the hallway there are a few more doors to the left. Bedrooms I assume. Since I am exploring I decide to go see what they are exactly. I pass my room and head to the next door on the left. It stands partially open so I walk in. This must be the master bedroom. It's an absolutely huge room. This bedroom is also filled with antique furniture but a different style than the guest room. There is the largest sleigh bed I've ever seen centered against the wall on my right. The sleigh bed has a solid canopy that drapes over the top. There is a black pair of men's dress pants and a beige dress shirt at the foot of the bed. This room is navy and gold. I mentally note the luxurious feel of the room. There is an armoire, a long tall dresser that has twelve drawers and marble top round tables on both sides of the bed. This room also has French doors that open out to a balcony. There is no bookshelf in this room. The ceiling of this room is some type of large gold tiles with their own individual molding. Incredible. The whole back wall of this bedroom is a large fireplace. Brick surrounds the fireplace on the outer edges but the inside trim is a marble tile. A single armchair sits near the fireplace. In the back right section of the room there is a door partly open. A light is on but I don't hear anything. I feel like I am in an ancient castle in Europe somewhere. As I stand thinking of how luxurious and beautiful the room is the door in the back right section of the room opens. I am a statue, frozen and shocked when Jake walks into the bedroom. He is in a pair of navy boxers and has a towel thrown over his left shoulder. Wow! His boxers are hanging low on his hips in that sexy way that shows off very nice abdominal muscles. I feel frozen in place but my traitorous body automatically responds to the sight of an almost naked Jake. There are drops of water on his tan, firm chest. I can't take my eyes off of them. I have the sudden urge to lick them from his incredible chest. His hair is wet and messed up, as if he just ran the towel through it. Embarrassed at the direction of my thoughts and my body's sensual reaction to him, I quickly turn away from him. I feel myself blush. Damn it, he is sexy as hell! I tell myself when I turn around to try to focus on his eyes. "Oh, Jake, I'm so sorry. I um…didn't realize you were in here. Ugh, that this was your room. I was just being nosy and looking around." I am sure my face is beet red and stumbling over my words doesn't help.

Shit! I don't know what else to say. I start to walk away. "Wait, Jess. It's okay. I'm sure you've seen a guy in boxers before. Besides, I'm not embarrassed. What have you been up to?" I told him I walked around the house and found the rec room. "Face me baby, its fine. I can't stand talking to your back. We're both adults here" he says. I turn to see him drying his hair with the towel. He has that shy grin on his face. I notice that both his boxers and the towel were etched with gold initials. He is firm all over. His arms are long and muscular. His chest is not overly hairy. In fact, it's pretty damn perfect. His abdomen is ripped, divided into delectable muscular sections. Mmmm. He's really sexy. Damn.

Ah, yes, both adults here. That's what I'm afraid of. Looking at him now makes me want to do adult things with him! I am shocked to realize I am thinking about him on top of me. I force myself to look at his face. I wonder what my face looks like. Can he tell how he affects me? Now, he has a face splitting smile. Shit! He can tell. "So, what did you think of the rec room?" he asked. The only thought that is going through my mind is how extremely sexy he is in those boxers. Focus Jesse, "Uh, I thought it was great. Really great. I can't believe all the stuff you have in there. The game area is fun. The furniture is beautiful. Nice bar. I tried the rug and pillows. I was surprised that it was so soft and comfy. The rustic look is awesome for that room. The chandeliers bring just the right amount of elegance." I watch as he slides into his pants and zips up. He goes to the large dresser and pulls out a pair of black socks. He sits in the arm chair and puts them on. I am sad to see his feet covered because his naked feet are sexy. *What the hell is wrong with me? I need to get a grip!*

Jake slaps both of his hands on his knees. "That's exactly what I thought about the chandeliers. I wanted to have that rustic look but still keep it first class. Not over the top. Good, glad you like it." He stands, leaving the towel on the chair, goes to the dresser and pulls out a white undershirt. I noticed his muscular back before he turns to face me again. Our eyes lock and he slips the undershirt on and tugs it down covering those incredible abs. He goes to the bed and picks up the dress shirt. He pauses, staring at my lips with a burning in his eyes. I blush because of the look and I think he might be thinking about our kiss last night. I swear, I think he wants me. Or is it just my wishful thinking? Jake sighs and breaks the tension in the air by moving to put his shirt on. He asks if I'd like to ride horses later. Do I feel up to it? Or would I rather sit and talk more? The thought of being out in the open air, on a horse, in nature sounds great to me. It is very different from that cold lab environment that I never want to be in again. Enthusiastically I nod, "Oh yes, please, that would be so much fun. I would love to." He smiles warmly at me. "Well, then, it's settled. I should be back by eleven-thirty or so. Be dressed and ready and we'll go on a horseback picnic. If you want to go ahead and pack a lunch, you'll find what you need in the kitchen. The picnic basket is in the pantry where I found your vase. Now I need your advice on a tie."

Jake opens the dressing room door and I can't believe my eyes. The door is like any other closet door. Just a regular size door and yet, very misleading. Inside is a very large dressing room. Shoes of every style and color are lined up neatly on shoe racks on both sides of the entry. Also on both sides, hung neatly on tie racks, are hundreds of ties. Pants are hanging on the left side after the ties. Black dress pants hang on the top rack, blue ones hang on the bottom. The next top row has brown and khaki colored pants and underneath them are corduroy pants of different colors and jeans. The right side of the closet is filled with dress shirts, both long and short sleeved. White and blue shirts hang on the top. The bottom row is filled with beige and light green shirts. The next top row consists of yellow and pink dress shirts. Underneath that row are purple and brown dress shirts. Past the shirts on both sides hang suit jackets to match the pants. There are built in drawers on the left and additional shelving on the right. The back of the dressing room has a large oval mirror and an arm chair that matches the one near the fireplace.

My face must have shown my surprised because he laughs and says, "That's the same reaction I had the first time I saw this dressing room. I think it's twice the size of my old closet. I didn't want to get lost, that's why I asked for your help with a tie." He laughs again. He really has a great smile and nice teeth. He took good care of himself and it showed. "Sorry" I said, "It's just that, Jake, I think this is the largest closet I've ever seen!" My mind shifts to the task at hand. Find a tie to match his beige shirt. That shouldn't be a problem. "I'll take the right side and you take the left" I say playfully. He gives me a quick salute and says "aye aye captain." He begins thumbing through the ties on his side. Smiling I search my section of ties. I find several I think will look nice. He also finds a few. Jake holds them up to his shirt one at a time. I step back to get a good look at him. Not the first one, it's too dark. Not the second tie, it's too whimsical. Now this third tie matches his eyes. I did not notice yesterday because I was just overwhelmed. I now see he has blue eyes with maybe a touch of green in them. They complement his dark blonde hair. I could get lost in those eyes. Wow!

He holds up the fourth tie. It doesn't match as well, too much red and not enough blue. "No, let me see the last one again." He holds up the third tie again. "That's the one" I say, confident of my decision. "It matches your eyes perfectly." He nods his head and thanks me. I watch him go to the back of the closet and put on his tie. He ties it great, it is just a little crooked. I go to him and straighten his tie. When I am finished he grabs my hands and holds them tight. "Thanks again for your help." He kisses my hands. "Jess, I am really looking forward to spending time with you this afternoon. It's been so long since I have had anyone to talk to. I really enjoyed last night. You are beautiful when you sleep." With that he quickly drops my hands and took a step away from me. "You should find anything you need in your room. You may not have noticed it yesterday but there is a dressing room similar to this one in your room. I don't really know what you like so there's a little bit of everything in there. Some of the sizes might be a bit off but that's easy enough to fix. So, it's a date then. See you around noon."

He goes to the front of the closet, bending down to pick up a pair of shoes as he walks out. I'll bet he's done that a thousand times. Excited about the possibilities of the day and full of questions I step out into the bedroom and close the dressing room door. Just as I am about to walk out into the hallway I glance over and see his towel on the back of the chair. Boys will be boys. I could hang it up for him. I go pick up the towel and head for the bathroom. My every intention is to just hang it up quickly and leave. I stop dead in my tracks when I see the master bath. It is ridiculously huge and absolutely beautiful. It is also gold and navy. I have never seen navy marble flooring before.

The first area is a large marble top buffet. I look closely and realize this is no regular buffet. It is really like an entertainment center. There is a small thing that resembles a computer on the left. That can't really be a computer can it? I am sure I remember them being a lot bigger. There is what I think is a phone next to it. Front and center on the marble top was a valet where Jake had left a watch and a pair of cuff links. Hanging above the buffet is a large portrait of who I assume are his parents. Then again, maybe his grandparents for all I know. Opposite the buffet is a pair of armchairs that match the one near the fireplace in the bedroom.

Past the buffet and armchairs is a doorway that goes into a second area of the bathroom. I walk through the doorway and feel like an intruder. Well, I guess I am intruding but now I just have to see the rest of it. Besides, I haven't seen a towel rack yet. Instead of the normal bathroom things you would expect to see there was a large navy blue Jacuzzi. Golden swirls race through the navy blue. Surely that's not real gold! Only the bottom two feet of the Jacuzzi was encased in dark wood. At least ten people could fit in it. I feel the water. Hot, but not too hot. I'll bet it feels great to be in there. This is one type of relaxation I have always liked. Above and behind the Jacuzzi the wall was layered in a unique fashion. The level closest to the Jacuzzi held three long grapevine planters. The greenery drapes down the tile wall almost to the top of the Jacuzzi. The next layer consists of four long ten wick navy candles. They too had gold swirls. I don't think I have ever seen a ten wick candle before. In fact, I'm positive I never have.

On the next layer of the wall there are a couple of oil lanterns on both ends. The middle was full of different sizes and shapes of navy and gold swirl candles. More flowers line the top layer right up to the center. There was an empty spot in the center. I wonder what is supposed to go there. Opposite the Jacuzzi stands a row of cabinets. Above the cabinets is a screen of some kind. Next to the cabinets is an armoire. It looks a lot like the one in the rec room except the wood is a lighter color. I pass through another doorway. Finally, here is the bathroom. The whole left corner of the room is a shower. There must be at least fifteen shower heads strategically aimed. Hhmm. No shower door. Navy tile walls and floor made this room really neat. Some of the tile had gold stars, planets and moons in them. The left side of the shower is a large wide bench big enough for Jake to lie down on. I could see droplets of water still lingering from his shower. I think again about the drops of water running down his firm perfect chest earlier. I let my mind wander to a naked Jake. What if they were a couple? Oh the things they could do in this shower! *Stop it! Get your mind out of the gutter! Damn it! What the hell is wrong with me?* To the right there is a half wall like the one in my bathroom. The other side of the half wall is an extra-long and extra-wide garden tub. At each end of the tub there is a built in head rest. Nice. Opposite the tub is a row of three sinks. A lone razor sits on the sink to the far right. Further back there's a door ajar. I can see the toilet and small vanity through the crack in the door. I could get lost in this bathroom it is so big. Man, what a way to live. I may not be able to remember my past but I am sure I didn't live like this.

I spot a towel warmer on the wall next to the tub. I hang his towel there, careful to make sure the monogram part shows. I quickly exit through the bedroom and go out into the hallway. What a nice diversion that was. However, I need to dress. Therefore, back to the task at hand. I would really like to look nice today. What to wear for horseback riding and a picnic? I think about it all the way down the hallway and back to my room. I have a good three hours before he returns. Surely I can do something with myself by then. While I really feel like looking nice today, what I really want and need is to find out more information about me, about him, about the project. I would like to go back to my own apartment. If not to stay then to pick up a few things. That might not be today but I'll mention it and maybe another day we can go. If it still exist. Who am I kidding? I'm sure my stuff is long gone by now. I don't even know if the building is still standing. I'll ask anyway. Couldn't hurt to try could it?

8

Jake mentioned a dressing room in my bedroom. I did not understand what he meant when he said there was a little of everything in my dressing room. I have a lot of things to ask him. We have so much to talk about. I guess jeans and a nice tank top or maybe just a short sleeved shirt would do. I definitely need to get some sun today. I walk over to the closet door. Jake was right, I had not noticed it yesterday. That doesn't surprise me though. I was not myself yesterday. I was pretty weak. Today I feel much stronger though. I am still not feeling quite back to normal, but compared to yesterday I feel like I'm ready to take on the world. Well, maybe I'm not that strong yet, but I will be soon. I open the closet door. After seeing Jake's dressing room I am not surprised to see the size of this one. Mine is not quite as wide or as long as the one in his room. It has a similar layout though. I flip on the light and start to browse. One of the first things I notice was that I have many more shoe racks than Jake does. There is nine pair of tennis shoes on the bottom two shelves on the right. White and black, white and blue, white and purple, white and pink, plain old white, white and red, white and green and a multi-color blue, and a black pair. Above those there were red high tops, yellow high tops and black high tops. I have always loved those.

There are also two shelves of different color walking shoes. Topping the walking shoes are loafers and Mary Janes. The top two shelves consist of different color flats to wear with jeans or dress pants. Wow, eight shelves of casual shoes. I never would have imagined it possible. To my left, there are another eight shelves of shoes. These are dress shoes and heels. Every style and every color that I could imagine are here. Some had low wide heels and some are stiletto heels. Man, Jake was not kidding when he said a little of everything. This is crazy. I'll bet I never wear half of these shoes. On the floor next to the heels are a row of boots. A couple of pair of cowboy boots starts the row and the rest are dress boots. A few pair are wide toe boots with wide tall heels. A few pair have low wide heels. A few pair are high heels with pointed toes. Now those I like. Those would be cool to wear with jeans and a tight black shirt at the Super Freak. Above the shoe racks on the right is built in shelving which holds an infinite number of scarves. They are neatly folded into small individual squares. A lot of them look like they are silk. It looks like there is every style and color of scarves as well.

Above the shoe racks on my left is more built in shelving but the shelves are farther apart than on the other side. These shelves hold purses, handbags and a few small back packs. There is a row of various change purses and lipstick holders as well. Further back on the left, on the top row I see skirts. Some long and some short. Some for dress and some were casual. Incredible. I cannot believe I'm seeing what I'm seeing. Jake somehow had managed to get my favorite patterns and colors. I walk over to the skirts and ran my hand through them. I stopped dead in my tracks. My eyes lock on a particular skirt that was in the middle of all the others. Could it be? I stand starring at my favorite casual skirt. It is a black slip bottom layer covered by a see through black layer. It is pretty much a straight narrow skirt but the bottom flares out just a little. I wear this skirt all the time. I have a pair of black slip on sandals I wear with this in the summer. I always keep my toe nails painted in my favorite red nail polish. I always wear a black and white snug top with a sweetheart neckline and three-quarter sleeves.

I love to go out on a warm summer night in that outfit. Guys always stop and stare. I always felt really sexy when I wear it. I have a lot of work to do before I feel sexy again. My hair's a mess. So are my nails. Not to mention my whole life! Once, I was out alone and got into trouble in that outfit. I remember it well. That was the night I met Brian. I had gone just around the corner to our neighborhood bar and grill. I had a really crazy day at work and needed to unwind. I remember I went home, changed and went to get a bite to eat. I sat at the bar first. What was I drinking? Oh, yeah. I think it was a long island ice tea. A sleazy guy from the end of the bar kept bothering me. He wasn't taking any of my hints that clearly said "Not interested" and "Get Lost". I was ignoring the guy and lost in my thoughts of the day and didn't notice when Brian came over. He sat near me acting like he knew me. He made small talk, insisting I let him buy me a drink. I let him because his presence made the other guy back off. We talked. I was shocked that I actually found him interesting. He was handsome. I am not the type of girl that just dates anyone, especially not guys in bars. Usually I'm very discriminating. I let him join me for dinner. Afterwards, we walked in the park and talked until almost midnight. I let him walk me home. After that, I don't think a day went by that I didn't see him. We started dating and that was the beginning of a terrific three years. After the first two years we moved in together. My breath catches in my chest and throat. Oh, I remember! We were going to get married!

Now my head starts spinning. Maybe it is the closet that started spinning. I can't be sure. A wave of sadness, fear, and anxiety overwhelms me. I sit down in the middle of the closet and cry. Flashes of my life with Brian rush into my head. I remember. Oh, God, no! This can't be! We were so happy. We were...so in love. I had lived with April for a while after high school. It seems like I went to college. I can't remember if I finished or not. I remember having to get my own apartment just to have peace and quiet in order to study. That was it. April always played her music too loud and always had way too many people over partying all the time. She was a regular party girl. I, on the other hand, like my quiet time. No, needed my quiet time. So I got my own place. April and I had a huge fight about it. Later we patched things up. She was happy I found a great apartment. When I told her about Brian she was hurt and jealous. Oh, no way. I remember!

I sobbed a little while longer and then forced myself to stop. I can't believe my life has turned out this way. I was such a grounded person. Not a weirdo or some party puke. No, I was on the right track. Had a great apartment, a great job that paid pretty well, and had fallen in love! Brian. Oh, Brian! I wipe my eyes on my pajama shirt. I lie down in the middle of the closet. I remember Brian! I put my head down and close my eyes. I remember him. I remember Brian! He was the guy I had dreamed about! Jake was right. I am getting my memory back! Brian was muscular and tan. Very fit. He had black hair and black eyes. Memories flood my brain now. He was perfect. Brian was perfect for me. He was my best friend. We of course had to get past the work of the day, but he made every night special. We'd go out to dinner or he'd cook for me. Often I'd come home to find a candle light dinner waiting for me. At least once a week he'd pick up my favorite bottle of wine and we'd just sit and talk for hours. There were nights of endless passion. Some nights we made love all night. We'd never even bother to get dressed. I remember touching his hair, his face. Oh, his back. How many times did I grab his strong back? Too many to think about! Oh, he was so good! We were so good together. And I loved him. Oh, yes, I loved him so much! I think that's the happiest I've ever been. He filled a place in my heart that no one else can ever fill.

Brian, what happened to you? I can't remember. I feel like my memory hit a brick wall. I sit up frustrated. I bang my hands on the floor, mad that I can't remember anything else. I just remember being so happy with him. He was everything to me. I can't believe I just remembered all that! It's hard to believe that looking at a skirt made me remember all that. I want more. I want to remember more. I want to know myself again. Not to wonder about me. Not to have to find out from some stupid pictures or paperwork. I want my life back. I am trying to keep an open mind and to understand all that has happened to me. I want to stay strong and not be too sad. But it's hard. All of a sudden I don't want to be alone. I want Brian. I wish he'd just walk into this closet and wrap his arms around me right now. Why can't I remember what happened to him? Why can't I remember what happened to us? My hands are shaking and tears roll down my cheeks now. I scold myself. I tell myself I've been through a lot. Also, that I am overwhelmed. It doesn't do any good. I want Brian back. I know I need to try to be logical about this. I know I probably won't remember everything all at once. I know it will probably come in bits and pieces like Jake said. But I'm impatient and petulant and I want to know now!

I sit for a long time with my head in my hands. Overwhelmed with what just took place. Is it real? Was that my reality with Brian? My life? Why in the world would I want to go to the deep freeze if I was so happy? There's more. I know there is. I just have to try hard to remember. I don't know how long I've been sitting here like this. I force myself to get up. Not up to the task I force myself to finish looking through the closet. Now I don't even feel like picking out anything to wear. *Jesse, focus. Just do what you have to do and get through the day. You can feel sorry for yourself later.* Past the skirts hang slacks, suit skirts and pants. Underneath them hang the matching suit jackets. The next row on the top is casual pants and jeans. A lot of jeans. Jeans on the bottom as well. Past the jeans are built in drawers. There are two drawers filled with different styles, colors and sizes of silk underwear. I don't miss the fact that there is a row of sexy silk panties on the left. *Nice, Jake. Really!* The third drawer is cotton briefs and the last two drawers consist of bras, bras and more bras. Again, a row of sexy bras are on the left in the first bra drawer. Of course, they match the sexy panties. Amazing. Something for everyday.

A whole section of summer dresses hang past the built in drawers. The whole back wall of my dressing room is a built in white vanity. Lights surround the vanity mirror. They are not on at the moment. A bench is neatly tucked underneath the vanity. I can see it is white as well with a gold cushion seat. A large oval mirror stands to the right of the vanity. It is encased in the same white wood but has gold trim. This closet is fairly the same layout as Jake's closet. I stand with my back to the vanity and look at the clothes on the other side. Incredible dresses hang to my left. Yes, evening wear. I probably will not even wear any of them. I don't see myself going to many parties in the near future. Some are really nice. They all looked expensive. Past these dresses hang less formal dresses. They are still very nice but slightly more casual. Next, silk shirts of every style and color imaginable it seems. Then there are more casual western style button down shirts. Some long sleeved, some are short sleeved. I walk toward the middle of the closet. Casual shirts are next. Different style tanks in every color caught my eye. There are some V-neck T-shirts mixed in with these. Another row of built in drawers is on this side. I quickly glance in the first drawer. Looks like nightgowns. I'll check those out later.

A row of jackets hang next. A black leather jacket immediately caught my eye. Nice. There was a brown suede jacket that hangs next to it. The suede was nice, too. Past the jackets are the shoes and scarves. I am now back standing at the front of the closet. I turn around and just looked at it all again. This is crazy. I don't think I've ever owned this many clothes in my whole life. I will probably never wear even half of them. My thoughts drift to Brian. I think about all I remembered. I can't wait to tell Jake I think I am getting my memory back. I go over and sit on my bed. The quilt that I had covered Jake with this morning still lay on his side of the bed. I see that Jake has quickly made the bed and put the pillows back perfectly. I lean over and hugged the quilt. It smells like Jake. I buried my nose in the quilt and took a deep breath. Jake. Dear Jake. I wouldn't be here now if it weren't for you. You saved my life! I can't help but feel guilty for remembering Brian. I don't want to hurt Jake. He said he thought he was falling in love with me. What if I am married to Brian? What if Brian is alive and waiting for me? Is that possible? Should I try to find him? Build a life? What if Brian and I were never married? What if? What if? What if? Ugh!

Jesse, stop it. Focus. You have to take it one step at a time. I stand up and neatly fold the quilt and lay it across the foot of my bed. I go into the closet and randomly grab a pair of stone washed jeans and a black tank top. I find a short sleeve western shirt that has black in it. I go to the built in drawers that held the panties and bras. I pick a black pair of sexy underwear and a black lace bra. I put it all on my bed and go into the bathroom to shower. After turning the water on in the shower I go to the cabinets and find a towel and wash cloth. In another section of the cabinets I find shampoo and soap, along with a body sponge. I do a double take and see a back scrubber. I lean back down and grab it as well. In the shower I can't help but think about my life. I can't believe this is all happening. It's like a bad dream. If I didn't have Jake right now I would be completely lost and alone. I make up my mind not to tell him about Brian until after we eat our lunch. At least we can have a few enjoyable hours before I tell him. I fear I'll hurt him. I can't stand the thought of bringing him any more pain. He's been through so much already. And he has taken care of me for five years! I mean, come on! *Who does that?* I think he has gone way beyond his job description.

The water is hot but it feels great. Even though I have sat near the fire last night and felt flush in the greenhouse, I still feel a slight chill deep in my bones. I think it's from the deep freeze. It could be my imagination but I don't think so. It feels real enough. Hopefully a day in the sun will help get rid of it. I take a few steps forward, turn and just stand under the hot water. It hits my shoulders and runs down my back. Oh, that's great. My thoughts now drift back to Brian. Memories of us showering together flood my mind. Sometimes it was so innocent. He'd wash my hair and scrub my back for me. Other times it was so hot and sexy. I admit to myself that we definitely had great shower sex. A smile crosses my lips just thinking of him. How long has it been since I've been with him? At least thirty-one years. Wow! That's a long time! That has to be some kind of record! It's no wonder I reacted to Jake like I did when I saw him earlier. Even though I may not have recognized it right away, my body knows what it wants... what it needs. My body remembers great shower sex.

I don't realize I am speaking out loud when I say softly, "Brian, what happened to you? Where are you?" The sound of my own voice startles me back to reality. I can't believe I just remembered more about Brian! If I keep remembering things at this pace I'll have my life back in no time at all! I know I should hurry but instead I think about this great sadness I feel. I have a sad, deep, hole in my soul. I feel like a piece of me is just gone. I'll never be able to get it back…ever. It bothers me to think Brian's out there somewhere. If I could find him I should. I feel an obligation to see him. I should apologize to him. What could I say to him though? I mean, really, this is not an everyday situation. There's no "sorry I don't love you anymore" or "sorry I slept with your best friend" line available here. This is unique. There's probably nothing I could say to make him understand. I don't even understand it myself. I've been standing under the hot water for a while and I finally feel warm. I think of the picnic and know that I'd better get moving if I'm going to pack a lunch. I wash my hair and scrub like there is no tomorrow. It feels so good to take a shower.

I turn the water off and towel dried my hair. This is a huge towel. I wrap it around me and step out of the shower. I stand in front of the mirror and evaluate my reflection. I run my fingers through my wet hair. What do I do with this mess? My hair is a light brown color and medium length. It looks like it's all one length. Even my bangs. If I had a hair clip I could put it back today. That would be all right for horseback riding. I'll really have to get a haircut and have a manicure. I will need to go shopping for some personal stuff it seems. Unless I can find what I need here. Nosing around the other cabinets in the bathroom I find a whole cabinet with just hair supplies. You name it and I found it. Hair spray, mousse, hair gel, hair clips, curl brushes, regular brushes and combs, and a variety of hair dryers. Ponytail holders and scrunches were in their own crystal container. Wow. I hit the jackpot. Some of the hair clips were really beautiful. There are some silver ones with something that looks like a silver ribbon flowing from the top. Gold hair clips of all styles were next to the silver ones. Some of the gold ones look like they have diamonds in them. Surely those are not real diamonds!

I dry my hair and pick a black hair clip that has a black see through bow draped over the clip. After several tries I just have to say it out loud, "I hate my hair!" I think most women have said that a time or two. Finally, I get my hair up in the clip and spray it. I fluff the top a little and spray it so it doesn't look so flat. It's ironic that I really hate flat hair and that's exactly what my hair is right now. Hair is the least of my problems. I'm thankful to be standing here fixing my hair right now. Thanks to Jake. I go to the bedroom to get dressed. While I am dressing I can't help but to think of both Brian and Jake. I think Brian would have liked Jake. I think they are similar in many ways. They are both strong, handsome men who seem to know what they want out of life. Both on the right track. Both have character and integrity. Well, at least I think Jake does anyway. I have to be honest with myself. I really don't know him at all. The only thing I do know is what he told me last night. Just the fact that he saved me says a lot about his character. Would Brian have done all that for me? I'm not sure, but I'd like to think he would.

These jeans are a little big on me. They are really comfortable. I inwardly hope they don't look bad. I think I like them. The black tank fits me pretty good. It, too, is a size too big. It's just as well though. I'm not in the mood for a snug fit today. I put the western shirt over the tank. I thought of buttoning it up but it looks good unbuttoned. I think I'll leave it like this. The tank barely hits the top of my jeans. Good. I thought I might have to tuck it in, but this works great. Now, I need some make-up and I'm ready. I head back to the bathroom and check all the cabinets. No make-up. I did, however, find all the personal stuff I might need. Pads, tampons, douches, a pregnancy test. Whoa, I hope I don't need *that* in the near future! I did not check this cabinet before when I got my towel and shampoo. Someone has stocked this bathroom with everything a woman needs. I'll bet Jake had it done. I do get the sense that he is always planning ahead. I know, I will check the vanity in the dressing room. I'll bet I'll find what I need in there.

I make my way back through the bedroom and into the dressing room. I head straight to the vanity and, bingo. Check out all of this make-up. A girl could get a little crazy in here. I turn the vanity lights on. They are so bright. They could light the whole dressing room on their own. They remind me of that bright light above me at the lab. I quickly push the thought out of my mind. I step over to the mirror to take a look at myself. Wow. I look pretty good for just getting out of the deep freeze. I turn around to look at my backside. Yes, these jeans make my butt look great. I'll have to wear these jeans more. I turn back around. All in all I did okay. I look casual yet a little sexy. I'm starting to feel like myself again. It's amazing what a good pair of jeans will do for a girl. I go over to the vanity and sit down. I want to look natural, not too made up. Leaning forward I look at my face carefully. Wow, my skin is really good. I can't believe that after going through the deep freeze I have a good complexion.

I want to get some sun on my face. I find a light moisturizer with sunscreen in it. I rub it over my face and throat. It's some brand I don't recognize but it feels and smells great. I lightly powdered my face and add a touch of blush to my checks. I put on just enough color to accent my green eyes. I quickly blend it all in and add a little mascara and my work here is done. I go back over to the big mirror to gauge my appearance. Wow. I really do look good today. I shouldn't be so surprised I guess. It really feels great to be dressed. It seems like ages since I've done my hair and make-up. I find a nail file, a strengthener and a base coat in the vanity. I flip the lights off and go to my bed. Quickly I file my toenails first. Then apply a quick coat of the strengthener. I let that dry while I file my fingernails. I brush the strengthener on them and then put the base coat on my toenails. By the time I am done with my toes my fingernails have dried. I brush the base coat onto them and quickly put it all on the bathroom counter. I'll do another base coat tonight and maybe a color and a top coat. This is sufficient for now.

I wonder what time it is? I don't have a watch. There's no clock on the bedside tables. I find a pair of black socks in the dresser. I won't put them on right now. I'll give my toenails extra time to dry. Now, what shoes will I wear today? I walk over to the dressing room again. Without putting much thought into it I grabbed the black pair of cowboy boots. They have a white design of a cowgirl swinging a rope on them. Not really my style, but they'd work for today. If they fit that is. I look inside to see they are a size six. It depends on how shoes are made but usually I wear six and a half or seven. Well, I'll carry them downstairs with me and try them. It can't hurt. If they don't fit I'll just come back up and get that black pair of high tops. With my socks and shoes in hand I make my way down the stairs grinning ear to ear. I am just happy to be alive today.

I go straight to the kitchen and look at the clock. I'm really cutting it close. It's eleven. I'll have to hurry in order to finish before Jake gets back. I quickly find the picnic basket in the pantry right where Jake said it would be. I realize that I have no idea what he likes on his sandwich. I find turkey and ham in the fridge. I pull out the mayo and mustard and put it all on the counter near the coffee pot. I find white, wheat and rye bread in the other side of the pantry. Now where in the world are the knives? I would put them in that long drawer under the coffee pot. Bingo, I've found them along with the forks and spoons. They were separated neatly in their own sections of an extra-wide divider made out of wood. The divider is lined with a thick off white lace. Nice. I make two ham sandwiches with mayo only. One on white bread and one on wheat. I make two turkey sandwiches as well. One on white bread with mayo only. One on wheat with mayo and mustard. I find sandwich bags in the pantry when I put the bread away.

I quickly put the sandwiches in the bags and sit them in the basket. What else? We can't just have sandwiches. I put the mayo and mustard back in the fridge and see the cheese ball. I pull it out of the refrigerator. I take four different kinds of crackers from the pantry and put a little of each kind in sandwich bags. I locate a small plastic container with a lid and put half the cheese ball in it. It fits perfectly in the bottom of the basket with the sandwiches on top of it. I put the crackers to the right side of the sandwiches. I include a few bottles of water I found in the refrigerator. My eyes fall upon a red can when I am searching for something else. Coke! All of a sudden I want soda like I've never wanted it before. The fizz! I yank the can out of the refrigerator and quickly pop the top. I murmur "bottoms up" under my breath and take a big gulp. Mmm. Delicious. The carbonation and syrup feel prickly and sweet in my mouth and throat. I think I use to be addicted to these! I swallow and take another big gulp. I look at the side of the can. Yikes, look at the amount of sugar in one of these! Twenty-seven grams! Add the caffeine...this will put a bounce in my step today!

I look in all of the other cabinets and search the fridge again but can't find a single bottle of wine anywhere. I thought it would be nice to bring one as a surprise but I'll have to ask Jake if he has one. I put napkins on the top of everything and close and latch the picnic basket. I notice it's eleven-thirty now. The only other thing I need is a blanket and we'll be ready for a nice afternoon outing. I leave the basket on the counter, walk past the formal dining room and into the hallway. I go to the bathroom and look in the bathroom closet. I do not find a blanket. This closet is small and only holds hand towels and a few wash cloths. As I step out into the hallway I notice a panel underneath the stairs that stands out from the rest because of a slight difference in color. I walk over to it and barely touched its top left corner. Nothing happens. I touch the top right corner. It swings open and bingo, she's done it again! Give the girl a prize! It is full of quilts and blankets. I grab one of the plain beige blankets and close the door. Now I think I'm ready.

9

I start to make my way back through the formal dining room when the front door swings open. Jake comes in and shuts the door behind him. He smiles when he sees me. "Wow, you look great" he says. He looks so sexy. I cannot take my eyes off him so I watch him put his keys and wallet on the empty pillar near the door. Ah, that's what that is for. Next he bends down and takes off his shoes. He sock skates over to me and gives me a big hug. The sock skating thing makes him look young and playful. I hug him back. The feel of his arms around me brings back memories of Brian. I actually feel guilty. I feel like I am cheating on Brian, which I know is silly, but I do. Jake leans into me to hug me tighter, holding me closer. Oh no! I can feel him getting hard! He takes the blanket from me and unfolds it. Jake takes a step back and puts the blanket over his shoulders while holding the ends of the blanket. He then comes back to me and hugs me again…wrapping me up in the blanket with him. He kisses my forehead. "Baby, I'm so glad to see you. I have thought about you all morning…and about our picnic." He pauses and looks at me. I am not scared of him at all. I feel quite comfortable in his capable strong arms. I do feel like I am betraying Brian. He leans down as if to kiss me but doesn't. He just stays like that for a moment. Wow, when I look up I see how amazing his eyes are. They are blue with flecks of green in them. A girl could get lost in those eyes.

Jake pulls back just a little and strokes my hair and my face with his blanketed right hand. "Stand on my toes" he says. I do as instructed and he begins to walk a few steps through the dining room. As he is going forward I am going backwards. We both laugh out loud. All of a sudden we lose our balance and start to fall. Jake holds me with his left arm and halfway catches us with his right. When we hit the floor we are still laughing. "Thank God I had this room carpeted" he says with a boyish grin. I am lying underneath him looking innocently up into those amazing eyes. I am so comfortable with him. A part of me just wants him to take me in his arms, carry me upstairs and make love all afternoon. The sane part of me knows that that'll never happen. Especially after I drop the Brian bomb today. Jake gets quiet and a serious look sweeps across his face. It is that longing look. It is also very sexy and the same look I saw before he kissed me last night. I realize that I do that to him. He slowly lowers himself down onto me and props himself up on his elbows. Oh, no! It feels good being this close to him. His weight on me is distracting. My mind is racing...what about Brian. He brings his face close to mine. We are nose to nose. He strokes the top of my hair again leaving his hand on the side of my head as he slowly and gently kisses me. The whole world seems to melt away. Brian who? I forget about all my questions and my guilt as desire stirs deep down in my belly and groin.

I kiss him back. Slow at first. Within a matter of seconds our slow kisses quickly become deep and more passionate. I stroke his face, his hair and his neck. His body feels so good under my guilty hands. I let them wander to his strong back. My head is screaming at me to stop but my body has a primal need. He slides off me on his left side and with his right hand, grabs my backside and pulls me onto my right side so I am facing him. He kisses me hard. His tongue is searching the boundaries of my wanting mouth probing everywhere. My tongue meets his and does its own probing with equal urgency. Unexpectedly, he stops kissing me and lets out a frustrated sigh. "Ah, baby, you're killing me" he says. We are both still breathing hard. He holds my hand and continues, "I want to be with you so bad. I'd like nothing more than to make love to you right here, right now. However, I want to be respectful of you and your situation. Like I said yesterday, I'm falling in love with you." His words hang heavy in the air between us. I don't know what to say to that so I don't say anything at all. I am sure I have a stupefied look on my face. Jake continues, "Well, hell. I'm already in love with you. I don't care about any faults or quirks you think you may have. I just want to be with you all the time. I want to get to know you. I want you to let me love you. Let me do nice things for you. Spend quality time together talking over a bottle of wine." He lets go of my hand and sits up. He runs his hands through his hair. I sit up too and we are face to face. He holds both of my hands in his and looks down.

I can see that he is disappointed in himself for letting it go that far. But, oh, he felt good above me. He does drive me crazy with his kiss and his touch. I can't stop thinking about the weight of his body on mine. I whisper his name but he doesn't look up. "Jake" I softly call out to him again. He still doesn't look up. I continue anyway, "I don't want you beating yourself up over this. Seriously. I'm a little shy so this is hard for me to say. I, uh, I...enjoyed it. Really. I mean look at you. You're handsome, smart and incredibly sexy. A girl would be crazy not to fall for you" He looks up and I see tears in his eyes. "No Jake. Don't do that" I say. A lone tear falls to his cheek and I wipe it away. I know I need to say something but don't know what is appropriate in this situation. Ugh...men! "Honestly, Jake. I think I want you more than you want me!" Surprise sweeps over his face. *That's the way to shock him Jesse.* I've sure got the whole shock tactic down. "At least you can say you love me. I barely know you Jake. I can say that I love that you saved me and that you've done all this stuff for me. But let's be adults here and face it. I think I hold the dry spell record. I mean, well, I was frigid for thirty-one years!"

With that we both laugh. "That is quite a record" he says. He is lost in thought for a moment and then he grins a shy boyish grin and says, "Incredibly sexy, huh?" Is *that* the only thing he heard me say? He gets the serious, all business Jake look on his face again. After a long pause he says, "It's just that I'm afraid you'll be disappointed in me. I am afraid you won't love me back and that you'll leave me all too soon. I've devoted the last five years of my life to you Jess. I know what I've read about you and I love the person I think you are. But I just want the chance to get to know the real you. I want to spend time with you. I've told you an awful lot of stuff late at night, in the lab. I've bared my soul to you. You were the only person I had to talk to, and you were unconscious. You, of course, had no response. I've often wondered what your responses might be. I know I can't expect you to fall in love with me Jess. But could you just let me get to know you? We have a lot to talk about and I need to fill in blanks for you. I'm especially afraid of when you get your memory back." He glances at me peculiarly. "And you will get it back Jess. Eventually. All the research shows it usually takes a few months, but you will regain you memory. I'm terrified of that day. I hope you don't walk out of my life forever."

At this point I feel like I'll never leave him. I see the lost boy again that his mother worried about. I have to be realistic though. I can't say that to him. Who knows what else I'll remember. Who knows what's going to happen to me, what's waiting around the corner! I hold his hands tight and look him straight in the eyes. "Jake. That's an awful lot of weight to be carrying around. I am here for you, because of you. I do want to spend time with you, too. I also want to unlock the mysteries of my past. I promise you this. No matter what happens in the future, I will take time with you, to get to know you. I promise that I won't leave you unless ... I absolutely have to. If something happens and I have to leave you, I just don't know ... I promise you we will explore my past together. Okay?" I run my fingers through his hair. He leans into my hand and slightly smiles. The next thing I know he stands up. I stand up too and pick up the blanket.

"Look, I'm sorry. I didn't mean for all that to happen." I finish folding the blanket. "Oh, Jake, you don't need to apologize to me." I step toward him and smile. I kiss his cheek and playfully say, "You know, this blanket is going to get us in a lot of trouble!" He smiles back at me. I am relieved that he is not tearful anymore. "Now that's what I like to see. Keep you're happy face on." I go into the kitchen and he follows me. I can still feel his lips on mine. I still want him and I know he still wants me. There is sexual tension in the air. I know if I turn around right now I'd catch him looking at my rear end. I have got to pull myself together. *Come on Jesse, get a grip.* I walk to the counter to get the picnic basket. "Jake, I packed our lunch. I tried to find a bottle of wine. I was thinking I'd surprise you with it but I couldn't find one. Do you have a bottle hiding somewhere?"

That boyish grin swept across his face. "Do I have a bottle?" He said. "Yeah, you bet I do, follow me." I do as instructed and follow him out of the kitchen into the hallway. The greenhouse is directly ahead of us. Jake turns to the left at the fork in the hallway.

We stop at the end of the hallway at a door to our left. A large wooden sign hangs above the doorway. Burned into the wood is all I need to see to understand. The sign reads "WINE CELLAR" in big bold letters. Jake opens the door and we step inside. It is vast. Rows and Rows of wine racks hold just about every kind of wine imaginable. "Do you remember what kind of wine you like?" he asks. Of course I can't remember. That would be way too easy. I'm not that lucky. I shake my head no and he laughs. "Okay, I'll pick a nice Riesling, a sweet wine for an even sweeter woman." Smiling I say, "Oh, you're good, I'll give you that." Grinning he heads midway into the room and stops in front of one of the racks.

Ever so gently he pulls the bottle of wine down and brings it to me for my examination. "Since I can't remember a thing about wine it works for me" I say as I shrug my shoulders. "You will like it, trust me" and I do for some reason I do not understand. I follow him back into the kitchen and he takes two crystal wine glasses from the cabinet on the far left. I watch every move he makes. He is so careful as he wraps the glasses in the napkins that I put on top of the sandwiches. He goes to the freezer and takes out an insulated wine carrier and slides the bottle of wine in it. He put the wine in the basket and puts the crackers on top of it. Jake asks if I know how to ride a horse. I guess I don't really know how to answer that either. He sees I'm struggling for an answer and so he says, "Don't worry about it. I'll carry this stuff on my horse and I'll lead your horse. We are not going very far today. I do have somewhere I want to take you. Once you've had a little practice riding, that is. It's about an hour's ride. The scenery is beautiful. That's for another day. Today we will only ride about twenty-five minutes to get to our prime picnic spot. Are you up for it?" he asked. I shake my head enthusiastically, "You bet I am" I answered. "Just let me get my boots on."

Jake smiles his great smile. "Jess, while you're doing that I'm going to head upstairs and throw on a pair of jeans. Be back in a flash." Earlier I had sat my socks and boots next to the table in the kitchen. I go over and sit down. I quickly slip into both my socks and boots. The boots fit me. That is a surprise. Maybe they're made big. I take the moment alone to use the restroom because I won't have access to one for hours. When I enter the kitchen Jake is standing in front of the picnic basket holding the blanket. He is wearing jeans and a black western shirt. He too is wearing black boots. "Great" he says as he picks up the picnic basket. "Let's go." I follow him out the front door. I think I would easily follow him anywhere.

10

The sun is shining and the sky is clear blue. A few white fluffy clouds float overhead. I spot his car in the circle drive. A four wheeler is parked near the front door. He winks at me out of his right eye and says, "I left my shades in the car. I'll be right back." I watch him walk over to his car and open the door. Movement to my left catches my attention. A man in a dark suit and dark glasses quickly walks around the side of the house out of view. I turn to look back toward Jake's car but he is now standing five feet in front of me. "Ah, don't worry about him. He's part of security" Jake said. "He's very good at what he does. Here's a pair of sunglasses for you." I close the distance between us and take the glasses out of his hand. He says, "We're going to take the four wheeler to the stables. It'll just take a couple of minutes to get there." He sits the picnic basket on top of the blanket in the back and we get in the front. It starts up immediately. Amazingly it is very quiet. I can hardly hear it but it jerks forward when Jake steps on the gas.

I didn't really notice the lawn yesterday. It is freshly cut and the landscaping is beautiful. There are enormous trees with rings of flowers around them. Tall colorful flowers surround the whole house. Shorter flowers are next. Short greenery is in the very front. It all looks so perfect. The land to the left of the house sloped upward. Jake drives right on the grass and up the hill. I glance back to see that the security guy has walked back to the front of the house. There he stands talking with another security guy. When we reach the top of the hill the land flattens out. I cannot believe my eyes. I see green land as far as my eyes can see. Not just in front of us either. I look back toward the house and am astonished to see nothing but green land far beyond the house. About a mile ahead I see a long building. I can't really make out anything else this far away. That must be the stables we are heading to. Jake is quiet. I wonder to myself if he is thinking of us kissing in the dining room this morning. I can't tell by the look on his face. "Is that where we are going? Is that the stables?" I ask eagerly. He nods his head but doesn't speak. I just look around in awe while he drives.

We pass through an open gate and finally arrive at the stables. The stables are very large. There must be at least thirty-five horses here. We are the only people around. I don't see any security. Jake parks and jumps out. With the sun beaming down on me I am again excited about the possibilities of the day. I stand up and stay still because I am not sure what I am supposed to be doing. Jake takes the blanket and picnic basket and starts toward the stables. I follow closely behind him. I can't help but check out his great ass because it is right in front of me. He is muscle everywhere. Damn. Jake tells me to stand in the shade of the stable overhang and he'd get our horses. He sits the blanket and basket at my feet. In a few short minutes Jake brings out two horses. They are already saddled and ready to ride.

Just then, a man rides toward us on a horse. It is like he appears out of nowhere. Jake sees me looking at the man and says, "That's Marcus, my stable hand. He's also part of my security team. He's a good guy. Loves the horses and takes great care of them. His father worked for my father for about twelve years. When his father died I offered him a job. That was when I was still living in my parent's house. After my dad died I was taking care of my mom and did not have the time to spend with the horses. I'll tell you what. He's the best stable hand I think I've ever seen. I think he's even better than his father. When I moved here I insisted he come with me. I hired his cousin to take over the work at my parent's house." In the short time Jake has been talking the man arrives at the stable. We watch him dismount his horse and tie the reigns to a stable post. He walks over to us.

Jake and Marcus shake hands. "Hey man, how are you?" Marcus asks. "Couldn't be better" Jake replies with a sly grin and Marcus looks curiously at me. Continuing he said, "Marcus, I'd like you to meet Jesse. Jesse, this is Marcus. He's one of my best and only friends. He knows about your situation. You can trust him. If I ever have to go out of town I'll have him check in on you. He lives here on the grounds and is here at the stables every day." I eye Marcus with curiosity. Jake's friend, huh? Marcus looks clean cut but has two day stubble. He looks like he's either trying to grow a beard or just hasn't shaved in a couple of days. He wore blue jeans and a navy button down shirt which was currently unbuttoned. He has on a white tank undershirt. Through the white undershirt I can see the definition of his abdominal muscles. He's built all right. What is it with all of these incredibly hot guys around here? Seems like a nice guy. He has on an old beat up pair of brown cowboy boots.

Marcus shakes my hand and says, "Nice to finally meet you Jesse. I'm glad Jake's helping you. If you ever need anything just ask. Any friend of Jake's is a friend of mine." He smiles a big crooked smile. "Take care of my friend here, will you? Keep him out of trouble and on the straight and narrow today. Jake, I see you got the horses. I was hoping to be back and have them out for you, sorry man. I did saddle them up this morning after I fed and brushed them. They've had plenty of water this morning but it's going to be a hot one today. Don't run them too hard and please give them more water later. Try to find shade for them. Well, you guys have a great afternoon. I'll be on three if you need to reach me." With that he goes over and unties his horse and leads it through the stable door.

Jake puts me on my horse first. He hangs the blanket across his horse near the saddle. He is still holding the reigns of my horse in his left hand and the basket in his right hand, and mounts his horse. "Don't worry about a thing, Jess. Your horse is a very calm old girl. She won't rare up on you. We'll just walk them this morning." Jake barely kicks the sides of his horse and it starts to walk at brisk pace. My horse follows dutifully. I can't believe I'm sitting on a horse. No, I am *riding* a horse! This is so great. This time yesterday I was freezing and confused and trying to escape that awful place. I shudder at the thought. The land is beautiful and the sun warm on my face and arms. We ride in silence. I take in all the beauty and listen to the birds sing. Twenty minutes pass quickly. A few times while looking around at the scenery I have caught Jake looking at me. *What is he thinking?* He smiles at me and says, "We're almost there. Just on the other side of that hill. " He points ahead of us.

When we top the hill I look across more green rolling hills as far as my eyes could see. Wow, the view here is amazing. To my left is a huge tree. It must be very old. Yellow and purple wild flowers flourish near it. On the right side of the tree a large wide swing moves a little with the breeze. The tree produces shade twenty feet past its branches in all directions. Also, there's some kind of old well or water pump to the left of the tree almost hidden in the wild flowers. "Jake, this place is huge. Look at all that land. I feel like we are the only two people on the earth!" He smiles a huge beautiful smile and climbs off his horse. "Right now, we are." He walks me on my horse over to the tree and tied both our reigns to a low branch. "May I?" he says as he holds his hands up to help me off my horse. I let him help me down and when both my feet land on solid ground he keeps his hands around my waist. Our eyes lock and for a moment I think he is going to say something.

The moment passes and we walk a few steps when he turns to me, "Jesse, you hold onto the basket and let me spread the blanket over there." He is pointing to a flat area to the right of the tree. I watch him walk over and pull the blanket down from his horse. In what seems like seconds he is done so I go over and sit down with the basket. Jake sits on the other side of the blanket. We don't speak at first. I take my time to enjoy the beauty around me. My stomach growls and I realize I am really hungry. "Are you hungry?" I ask him hoping he is. He is amused. I like the playful look he gives me because it makes him look young and carefree. He is young, but I have learned in this short amount of time that he has an incredibly serious side and he wears that serious, all business look often. "Baby, I'm always hungry! Let's dig in. What did you bring us?" I pull out the four sandwiches and the bottled water. He chooses the turkey on wheat with mayo and mustard. I know I better try to eat something soon because I am quite hungry now. The second I take a bite of my ham sandwich my stomach growls again. He finishes his sandwich and then eats the other half of my ham sandwich because I surprisingly can't finish it. We each sip our water. "Jake this is so nice. What a great way to spend the afternoon." He smiles at me.

"This place is huge. How many acres do you have here?" He thought for a minute and says, "Roughly about seven hundred and fifty, I think." I think I heard him wrong. "Did you just say seven hundred and fifty?" I asked. I gape at him with a surprised look plastered on my face. Now he just laughs at me. "Yep, that's what I said. What can I say, I like my privacy. I don't go out that much, so, I might as well enjoy myself at home." Wow, I guess that's one way to look at it. I don't remember much from before but I am sure I am not accustomed to such luxurious surroundings and this much space. I pack up our trash, put it in the basket, and scoot the basket to the edge of the blanket. Jake put the lid on his water and lays on his left side facing me. I follow suit and lay on my side too so that I am facing him. There are a couple of feet of empty space between us. I ask him if he got his loose ends tied up and he said he did. "In fact, Jesse, I have arranged it so I don't have to go into work for a while. At least three months, maybe four. I have a working office here at home and can do anything I might need to do here. I've talked to both the cryogenicist and nurse. They are closing up the lab. It will probably take them a full month to complete that daunting task. There's a lot they have to do with the research and equipment. So, what I'm saying is that I'm all yours baby. I am free to help you regain your memory and manage your situation."

I don't really know what to say to that. I am glad that I won't have to be alone. "Wow, you don't have to do all that. Thank you for all your help. I mean it." The sun's starting to fry my skin. Great! I don't want to burn. We've only been out here a short while. I think I always use to tan and get dark. I don't think I burned a lot before. Did I have to use sunscreen before? The answer evades me. "Jess, you don't need to thank me. I am doing what I want to do. It makes me happy to help you. Plus I do not have to be alone. At least the house won't be so empty now." He gets that brooding look on his handsome face. I look around. The wind blows his hair into his eyes. He runs his fingers through his hair to push it back. Damn, why does he have to be so sexy! "I hope every day is as enjoyable as this" I say. I am so relaxed and am enjoying this. He reaches over and takes my hand in his. "Jess, we should talk. We need to get started right away. Start working it out, I mean. I will need to monitor you medically, of course. You seem like you're doing fine. This evening though I would like to examine you...if that's all right?"

"I, well, uh, sure...I guess. What do you mean? What kind of exam?" I ask nervously. He senses my trepidation and tries to reassure me. "Oh it's nothing invasive. I just need to monitor your pulse, breathing, check your ears and throat. You know the usual stuff. I'll do a body scan. You probably don't remember having it done before. It is a quick and painless scan. It will tell me about any muscle deterioration or any problems that may be lurking under the surface." He smiles at me and squeezes my hand. "It's no big deal. I promise. I need to monitor you at least twice a week for two months. Research shows that any problems that may occur will show up within that two month time frame. After that, you're home free." I squeeze his hand back and tried to sound cheerful. "Well, all right then. You're the doctor. I trust you. Whatever you say goes."

Jake lets go of my hand and runs his fingers up my forearm. I get goose bumps. "You're so pale. Why don't you ditch the shirt and just wear your tank top. I'll rub some suntan lotion on your arms for you" he said. "That would be great" I say hesitantly. "I do want to get a little sun today." I sit up and take the western shirt off. He sits up and scoots over closer to me. I wonder if he is just being nice or if he just wants to touch me? Leaning across me he reaches into the picnic basket and pulls out suntan lotion. He must have put that in there right before we left the house. He definitely plans ahead. Is he always so organized? I sense he is. Sitting next to me Jake removes his shirt. He is not wearing an undershirt. His firm body is tan already. Still he rubs some lotion on his chest and arms. When he is done he looks at me and whispers "come here" in a low shy whisper. I scoot a little closer to him. I am now a little jumpy just being this close to him. I feel an energy exuding from every part of him. It is enticing. Addictive even. He squeezes a small amount of lotion onto his hands and gently touches the back of my neck. The lotion is a little cold at first. He slowly rubs the lotion in, allowing me time to become acclimated to his large hands on me. He is tenderly massaging my neck and shoulders as he does. He gets more lotion on his hands and begins to rub it in on the front of my neck and chest.

I close my eyes and just enjoy the feel of his hands on my body. His thumbs and forefingers playfully dip under the top of my tank as he gently rubs the lotion into oblivion. He takes a little more lotion and rubs it into my arms. I open my eyes when he is done. "Can I do your back?" I ask him. He quickly answers "Yes." Jake positions himself in front of me. I am really going to enjoy this. I squeeze some sun block onto each shoulder blade. I begin to rub it in slowly. I rub it up toward his neck in deep massaging circles. He moans with pleasure. "Ah, that feels great! Oh yeah baby!" Another moan escapes his lips. I note he is very tense. "Jake, you're so stressed. You're, tense. Here, try to relax" I say as I massage my way down to his mid back. I put more lotion on my hands and slowly touch his lower back. I gently increase the amount of pressure as I work my hands up and down, side to side in deliberate, slow motion. I hear his rapid breathing and take note of his silence.

I work my way up to his mid back and back down again. This time I slide my fingertips under the top of his jeans as I fiercely massage his lower back. He groans and then sighs a long, deep sigh. His back is perfect, strong and tan. My thoughts wander as I gently alternate rubbing and scratching his back. I feel him sigh again and physically relax under my hands. Now I am back up to his shoulders. He reaches back and grabs both of my hands. "Oh, baby, you're something else" he says and then pulls me around to him. I fall into him and he wraps his arms around me. I hug him back and can smell the mixture of his perspiration and sun block. It is a smell I like. It's a Jake smell and it is very sexy. I slide over and sit next to him and take my boots and socks off. I rub the excess lotion from my hands onto my feet. We sit in silence for a moment. "Jess, do you remember any of it? I have always wondered what caused you to make your decision to volunteer for the project. Your family life? Friends? Work? Anything?" I shake my head no. "Well, we've got our work cut out for us, don't we?"

I agree with him. I want to tell him about Brian right now but it is too late. Jake startles me as he jumps up. He grabs my hands and pulls me up with him. "Let's swing" he says playfully. He puts his arm around my waist and we walk over to the swing. He sits on the swing and motions for me to sit on his lap. "It's okay, you know, I won't bite." I giggle a little and sit down. "Jake, are you sure this thing will hold us? It looks pretty old." He wraps his left arm around my waist and says "It'll hold. Trust me." Jake pushes off just a little with his legs. We are barely moving and I wish we could stay like this for the rest of the day. I know I have to tell him about Brian. Oh, I don't want to hurt him. He's having a great afternoon. A gentle breeze blows and the scent of the wildflowers fills the air.

This close proximity to him has got the better of me. All at once I imagine us naked, sweating, and him slamming into me over and over again. Our naked bodies entwined passionately in each other, savoring the moment. *Oh, whoa – what the hell is wrong with me!* Why am I like this? Thinking about him like *that*? I know I am not usually so focused on sex. I have got to keep control of my emotions. "Jake, I have to tell you something. It's, well, it's, uh something I remembered this morning. I think I am starting to get some of my memory back." I want to see the look on his face. I turn as much as I can and see a surprised look cross his face. Stunned he said, "Jess, that's great. What is it? What do you remember? A person, a place? What?" I feel so guilty. I can't face him anymore. I turn away and look down at the wildflowers as we softly sway in the swing. "A man. Jake. I remembered a man this morning. His name is Brian and we dated for a couple of years and then moved in together. We were going to get married, but I don't know if we did or not. I did not remember a wedding."

I glance back at Jake who is trying to show his poker face but I think he's hurt. I probably should not have told him until I remembered more. "Well, Jess, I knew a beautiful woman like you would most likely have a significant other. A boyfriend or a husband. I was just hoping... Never mind. That's great news! You're getting your memory back! Come on. Let's break out the wine and celebrate a little. I want you to tell me everything and how you remembered it. Did something trigger your memory or did it come out of the clear blue?" he asks as we get up from the swing. He motions for me to follow him back to the blanket. I wait until after he opens the wine to tell him about this morning. I appropriately leave out the juicy details of our shower sex but Jake got the idea. He doesn't say anything. Both our glasses are empty. He poured us both more wine.

"Wow. That's incredible that one skirt provoked all those memories. You're going to get your memory back quicker than I originally thought." Thunder sounds in the distance and the horses clatter around next to the tree. Jake looks at me curiously. "Well, I guess we should head back now. I'd hate to get caught in the rain. Thanks for coming out here with me. It's been a perfect second day with you. I have really enjoyed today and just talking with you. I am glad you're starting to remember. I am sorry that I come on a bit strong sometimes. It's just that I am excited you are here."

I touch his face. "Jake, I'm sorry if I hurt you. I saw the look in your eyes when I told you about Brian. I never intended to hurt you. You know that. I'm anxious to remember more, but I meant what I said earlier at the house. I want to spend time and get to know you, too. I promise you that. I have had a wonderful afternoon." We put our shirts back on. I slip my socks and shoes on. I place the basket onto the grass and start to fold the blanket. Jake raises his arm and talks into his watch. "Marcus, you there buddy?" Within seconds Marcus answers. Jake told him we are on our way back and should be there in about thirty minutes or so. I know I must look ridiculous but I can't move. That is just bizarre. Jake looks over at me and asked if I was ready to go. When he sees the look on my face he laughs. "Oh, yeah. One of life's little conveniences. It's a watch and a radio. Has up to eight channels. Marcus is the only security person who has this particular one. That way what we say stays private. It's great for communicating back and forth on the grounds."

More thunder, closer this time. "We'd better go" Jake says. "Sometimes summer storms pop up out of nowhere. Jess, I have something to show you later tonight or tomorrow, okay." I nod my head yes and watch him pick up the basket and we walk over to the horses. He gets me up on my horse and then easily mounts his. He starts his horse and again mine dutifully follows. I glance back over my shoulder and see dark clouds approaching. We ride in silence the whole way back. Midway Jake picks up the pace and asks if I am okay with it. I told him yes and that was all we said. I look over at him several times and each time he is lost deep in his thoughts. I know he must be thinking of what I told him about Brian. We just make it to the stable when I feel the first drops of rain. It is cool on my skin. The breeze has picked up a little and I get goose bumps as a slight chill passes through my whole body.

Jake leaves the blanket draped over his horse and instructs Marcus to "keep it here for next time." Marcus takes the horses into the stable. Jake and I walk to the four wheeler. He puts the basket in the back and we climb into the front. As we drive toward the house I notice another security man. He is way down the drive in front of the house. I can't see anyone else near the house. I follow Jake back into the house. Being the gentleman that he is, he holds the door open for me. "Jake, if you'd like, I'll take the basket back to the kitchen." He hands me the basket without speaking. I turn to walk to the kitchen. "Jess, I think I'll go up and change. I'll be in the rec room when you're done." With that he quickly makes his way up the stairs. I watch him until he turns right at the top of the stairs and is out of sight.

Whew, I exhale loudly. I hope he's okay. I hate to see him like that. I turn around and carry the basket back to the kitchen. Slowly, thinking about Brian, I unpack the basket and put everything away. This has been quite a day. I think I'll go up and change too. As I trudge upstairs the house is silent. My legs and butt are sore from riding. I can't tell if Jake is still up here or if he's already downstairs. Outside my door I stand quietly in the hallway listening for any indication of Jake. Nothing. I change into a casual pair of khaki pants and one of the long sleeved casual shirts. It is navy with a V-neck and makes me think of Jake's bathroom. I put my jeans, tank and western shirt across the foot of my bed. I go into the bathroom and take the clip out of my hair. I run my fingers through my hair thinking about Brian. My hair is about shoulder length and full of body since I've had it up this morning. It's always a problem. Why is my hair always a problem? I can never seem to get it right despite trying every hairstyle known to woman. The only good thing I have ever been able to do is to pull it up off my face. Screw it, I am tired. I refuse to deal with it today. I run a brush through it quickly and head downstairs.

All at once I have to pee. Ugh. Why didn't I go upstairs? I make use of the hallway bathroom and wash my hands. There is a lotion dispenser next to the soap. I rub lotion on my hands. It smells like vanilla. I decide I like the smell of it and rub some along my neck line and upper chest. I go down the spiral staircase to the rec room. Jake is sitting at the bar drinking a cup of coffee. He has changed into a pair of jeans and a white T-shirt. He has on white socks. "Would you like some?" His voice is soft and sexy. "Sure" I answer. "I got chilled upstairs so coffee sounds great. It'll warm me up." He walks around the bar and pours me a cup. He leans down and retrieves the creamer out of a small refrigerator underneath the counter. I would have never guessed that *that* was a fridge. He's amazing. I can't believe he remembers that I like half and half from this morning. I mean, wow, here is a man that actually pays attention! This morning seems like years ago. It's been a full day.

Jake sits my coffee two stools down from his. He walks around and sits on his stool. I sit in front of my coffee and make no effort to move closer to him. "There's a refrigerator to the right of the sink and a dishwasher to the left. They are both hidden behind wooden panels that look just like the cabinets. I hang out here a lot so Fran keeps the refrigerator stocked with soda, juice, milk, half and half, cheese, olives and pickles. There's a lot of chips and crackers in the cabinets if you get the munchies." He is quiet for a moment. I sip my coffee and curiously watch him. "Jesse. Can you remember anything else? Try to remember. Think about the bar and grill you went to. Do you remember the name?" Sometimes he calls me Jess and other times he calls me Jesse? I wonder if he realizes he is doing it? When he is business Jake he calls me Jesse. I like it when he calls me Jess because it is sexy. I sip my coffee and try hard to think about it. "I'm not sure. It seems like it was Chester something. Chester Blake's, Chester Bongo's, Chester Buck's. I think the second word started with the letter b."

Jake sits his empty coffee cup down and looks at me. "I know I've been a little distant since we started back to the house. I'm sorry. I've been thinking though. In a week or so I think we will drive by your old neighborhood. That may jog your memory. I'm sure it will help you if you see it in person. I have your address from your paperwork and kind of know the neighborhood you lived in." I finish my coffee and he asks if I'd like more. I shake my head no. "Jesse, this morning while I was at the lab I boxed up your files. Anything related to you I packed up and put in my car. My trunk is full with your charts and information. So is my back seat. I was in a hurry so I may have missed something. I have instructed the cryogenicist and nurse that if they should find something specific in regards to you they should box it and call me. That I'd come down and pick it up." Jake looks at me and smiles. I am completely not following what he is trying to say. I am sure I have my stupid girl look plastered all over my face.

He somehow understands that I need further explanation. "I have to think of your protection, Jesse. If someone should break into the lab I don't want them nosing around your research and personal information. That's one of the reasons I told them to dismantle the lab. As I said earlier I have an office here. Tomorrow Marcus is going to help me unload my car and bring it all into my office. Marcus is the only person who knows where my office is. It's, ugh, let's just say it's well hidden. I know you may think I'm strange, but, there's something else you should know. I also have a small clinic here in the house. Not for patients to come to. Just for our use. In case anyone gets hurt. It's stocked with medical supplies. It's back there, behind the bar." He pointed to the wall where the lanterns and horseshoe hang. "There's also a secret underground level to this house. No one, not even Marcus, knows about it. It looks like a regular house and is fully stocked with food, water, the works. Anything and everything you need is down there. I had five generators installed for that lower level. If the power goes out the first one will kick in. When the first one runs out the second one automatically kicks in and the first one regenerates itself. So, really a person could live down there as long as needed."

I hear what he's saying but it's so weird. "Jake. Are you serious? That's crazy. You have taken all of these precautions. Why? For me?" I can't move. I can only sit and stare at him. I'm dumbfounded. It seems like every time we talk he is surprising me with something else. "Please, don't think I'm weird or crazy. The world is a different place now. Well, some of it is anyway. You checked out of a halfway safe place. You checked back into a not so safe place. Since the Millennium different militant groups have formed here in the good old USA. The government has a handle on most of them. Terrorism has flourished though. There's always a news story about places being bombed or broken into. It's still pretty safe for the public. Well, there are probably ten times the police on the streets now than before. But you can never be too careful. Besides... my father made me promise I'd protect you. So it's not something I take lightly."

Wow. This is really incredible. What other tricks does he have up his sleeve? "What else, Jake? Tell me all of it. I can see the worry on your face. What else should I know about?" He stands, leans over the bar and places our coffee cups in the sink. He walks a few feet away from the bar and then turns to me. "Jesse. I mentioned before that I've had threats. Someone in the government wants to stop your project dead in its tracks. I have my men working on it. We're trying to find out who's behind those threats. I will meet with whomever I have to and offer them the general research about the whole cryogenics process if need be. The success of your project has been phenomenal in many ways. You are unique Jesse. My cryogenicist is working on pulling all that info together for me as well as helping close the lab. I won't let them have your personal information. I've got some idea who may be behind the threats. I'm not sure though. My guys are trying to verify it." Wow, I am completely overwhelmed with all this information.

I take a deep breath and sigh. Jake continues, "Once they do, I will meet with that individual and his secret circle of goons that are involved from his company. Offer to turn over the information along with a handsome payoff. In return, I'll ask that they let you live a free and normal life." "Oh, Jake. This is just crazy! Do you really think that someone would hurt me? Or want me dead? If I'm dead the project wouldn't be a success, now would it? How can this be? This is just too much! I just can't imagine... that someone would try to kill me!" My eyes filled with tears and I put my head down on the bar. Is this really happening? Are the last two days real? "Baby, there's more, but it's not for now. It will keep for another day."

11

Jake wants to walk over to Jesse and comfort her. He knows he must keep some distance between them for now. He wants her so bad. Not just sexually but on an emotional level as well. He's been alone for so long. He also knows she must work out the past before she can think of her future. There is also the other thing to think about as well. If it is true, it makes her case even more extraordinary. However, it is going to be a huge shock for her. He hopes it's not true for her sake, and for his. "Jesse, just calm down. Take a deep breath. You're safe here, with me. I've got extra security out front near my car tonight. The regular guys are all over the grounds. Please just calm down and take it one step at a time. Okay?" She looks up at him and wipes a few tears from her cheeks. "I'm sorry, Jake. Usually I have total control of my emotions. This is all so overwhelming. It's hard, you know. I feel a connection to you Jake. I wish we could picnic every day and ride horses and have fun. Truth be told I know I have to figure out who I am and put the past behind me in order to move on. But, oh God! Jake, I feel like I'm losing my mind when I stop and think about it!"

"This is your awakening! Your new opportunity! Whatever you did not like about yourself before, well, you can throw it out and do something different. You can re-invent yourself, Jess and money talks. You can buy new clothes, get a new hairstyle if you'd like, get a manicure and pedicure. Hell, when this is over we'll go to my favorite spa for a whole month. They baby you like crazy. Yeah, Jess. When this is all over with that's what we will focus on. We will have some real fun then. We can take a year and travel if you'd like. Did I mention I have four huge luxury liners along with a fleet of private jets? We could do anything in the whole world Jess. Anything your heart desires. Just for now, let's stay focused on the work ahead of us. Be thankful you're alive and here with me. I am so thankful you're here with me. An awful lot of things had to go right in order for you to be sitting here right now. And usually, if I can be honest, my luck is not that good!"

Watching Jake I can't help but feel better. I fix my poor posture and smile at him. How did I get so lucky? This guy is amazing and really trying to help me navigate the mess of my life. I need to be appreciative, I know. "Thank you for keeping me from being a stick in the mud. You are absolutely right. I will continue to try to be positive about this. I *am* appreciative to be alive. I'll try to act like it from here on out. I'm sorry. It's been such a nice afternoon. I'd just hate it if I ruined it for you. And uh, hey, I may take you up on the traveling and the spa stuff." Jake grins an insane grin from ear to ear, "Now that's what I like to see and hear" Jake says. "Oh, by the way, tomorrow after breakfast I'll show you what I need to show you. By the time we have dinner and talk a little more you'll be worn out anyway. As your doctor I insist you get to bed at a decent hour this evening. Also, I was kind of hoping I could get your exam out of the way before dinner, if it's okay with you. How does that sound?"

Crap. Forgot about the exam. He said it was not going to hurt. Some sort of scan. "Well, I guess its ok. I trust you." "Great" he says. "Go lie down on the rug over there. Just give me a minute to get my bag and I'll be right back." I didn't know he means right now. "You mean now?" He winks at me. "Well, sure, why not. Let's get it over with so we can enjoy our evening." I do as instructed by the good doctor and sprawl out on the rug. I love this rug; it's soft and feels more like a bed than a rug. I'll bet he has slept down here before. I would. I watch Jake disappear into the door at the back right corner of the rec room. I don't think I noticed that door before. Or if I did I didn't pay attention to it. Jake reappears and sits down next to me. He is carrying a bag and also a thing that looks like a small suitcase but is some kind of medical equipment. "Okay, Jesse, sit up and let me get your temp and check your ears first. I have an old fashioned thermometer. I just want to check your temp this way too, just to make sure my machine's accurate on its numbers." He put what looks like a small weird shaped flashlight with a rubber stopper at the end into my ear. Seconds later it beeps. "Uh, huh. A slight temperature, but nothing to worry about I am sure."

Jake pulls out a small clipboard from his bag and scribbles something down on the paper attached. Next, he uses the tongue depressor and holds my tongue down and tells me to say 'aaagh.' "Just a minute. I can't see well enough." He searches his bag and pulled out a small flashlight and turns it on. "Okay, repeat" he says sternly. I do as instructed. Again he scribbles on his paper. "Okay, Jesse, flip your wrist over and let me take your pulse." I think he is going to use his fingers and am shocked when he rubs a cold jelly on my wrist. He pulls out what looks like a watch with Velcro on the ends. He centers the square part over my inner wrist and has me flip my arm back over so he can fasten it on. "Just like a watch or bracelet" he says as he flashes me a quick smile. He pushes a button. A minute passes and the thing beeps. Jake looks at the square part and scribbles on his paper. "Looks like it's pretty normal" he mutters under his breath.

"Okay, Jesse. This next thing is a body scan. You've probably never had one and if you have, you probably don't remember it. So, all you need to do is lie still. It's completely painless. It's similar to an x-ray but it tells me a whole bunch of things about pretty much everything else except your bones. Lie down for me please." I do as he asks. He turns the scan machine on and it beeps. Next, he detaches a wand or scanner of some sort and places it over my hair. "Jesse, I simply just slowly slide this scanner over your body little by little. It won't touch you. It is just directly above you. Just try to breathe normally. Don't hold your breath." Inch by inch he begins to scan me. When he is done with my face I turn my head to the opposite side and close my eyes. I am a little tired now that I am lying down.

The scan machine beeps occasionally. All at once it beeps a whole bunch of beeps that sound more like an alert or warning. I quickly opened my eyes and looked at Jake. "What is it? What's wrong with me?" Jake is pale. He reaches over with his free hand and turns the volume off. "Oh, nothing. Nothing at all. You're fine, now be still." "Well, what was it beeping like that for? And you're pale. Are you sure it's nothing?" Jake barely smiles. "I am positive there's nothing to worry about. If I am pale it's just because the last couple of days are starting to catch up to me. It's nothing that a good meal and some rest can't fix." Jake finishes his scan and puts everything back into his bag. He attaches the scan arm to the machine. "Just let me put this away. It will just take a minute. I'll be right back." I watch him leave through that same door.

Jake enters the pool room and quickly goes over to the table and chairs. His chest is tight and his knees are weak. He sits his bag and scanner on the table and sits in the nearest chair. Fuck! It's true! What the hell? Can't I catch a break? Just one fucking break! Damn. How am I going to tell her that! This is not fair. It's just not fair. Why, dear God,

Why? Jake's head is spinning and he is oblivious to the tears streaming down his face. His anger at the whole situation seethes and bubbles to the surface. He sits with his head in his hands for what seems an eternity. How can he go back in there and face her. Should he tell her now or wait until after she sees tomorrow's surprise? It's just not right that he should be the one to have to tell her this.

Why, God, Why? Why does it have to be this way and why can't he just be happy for once? Jake knows he has to pull it together. He doesn't want her to see him like this. He doesn't want to pull it together. He would feel better if he could beat the shit out of someone....and he knows who he'd like to hurt. The one responsible for all of this shit. He stands up and goes into the dressing room to his left. He splashes water on his face and dries it with a towel and blows his nose. He takes a cool washcloth and holds it over his eyes so they don't look puffy. Jesse, still lying on the rug, wonders what is taking Jake so long. The sudden urge to pee hits her. Oh, great. This isn't going to wait. She gets up and goes upstairs to the bathroom.

12

Jake is sitting on the leather couch near the fireplace when Jesse gets back to the rec room. He forces himself to halfway smile at her. "Sorry, I had to go upstairs for a quick minute." She hasn't eaten much since she's been here and he knows he has to get her to eat more. "Oh, that's all right. You know, Jess. I am starting to get hungry. I think I'll go upstairs and defrost a couple of steaks for dinner. How does steak, potatoes and salad sound to you?" I'm not that hungry now but by the time it takes to cook I'll probably be. "That okay with you?" I don't really care when we eat but I nod because he is trying so hard, "That's fine, Jake. I'll be starving by the time it's ready. Can I help you?" He said that would be great and we head back upstairs. Jake first and I follow closely behind him. As Jake walks up the stairs I can't help but notice that he has a really great ass. Again, I know I shouldn't, but I can't help but look. It's right in front of me. He is muscular... everywhere. "Hey. I think I'm going to start calling you Dr. Feelgood" and I laugh out loud. He laughs because I am and then he shakes his head. "Now where did that come from?" "Oh, I just think it's cute. I mean, I guess you're whole doctor impression back there made me think of it." I am pleased with myself because he is still smiling when we reach the kitchen.

"Okay, I want to show you this amazing piece of technology that I call my refrigerator. It does everything a normal refrigerator does and more. You ready?" Saying this he holds out his hands as if to showcase his fridge. "Sure, let me have it." Jake reaches into the freezer and pulls out a couple of steaks. He puts them in the very bottom drawer of the refrigerator, turns a dial and pushes a button. He takes out two bottles of water, closes the door and motions for us to sit at the table. "Here, drink this. It's good for you." He hands me the bottle of water. "Well, that was it. What did you think?" He laughs. I am confused. "I don't understand. All you did was move the steaks from the freezer to the fridge." He grins and holds up his finger, "Just wait another thirty seconds and you will." We both take a few drinks of water and sit quietly. A beep and then the refrigerator says "You're steaks are defrosted. Thank you Jake. Have a nice day." It has a woman's sexy voice and spoke slow and clear.

Jake smiles stupidly at me. I am surprised. What! A talking refrigerator. That's so great. "Now that's cool" I say with the ridiculous smile on my face. "Jake, I've never seen anything like it. I can't believe your fridge just talked!" "She does everything but the dishes" he says proudly, grinning ear to ear. He gets up and goes to the fridge. He takes the steaks out of the bottom drawer and brings them over to me. "See, completely thawed in a minute." He points to the refrigerator, "Her name is Faith. Short, for old faithful. She orders my groceries too. There are sensors on the inside of the entire refrigerator. The only thing is that you have to load your groceries in a certain way. That took some getting used to. The sensors tell it when you run out of something by the empty space. It's computerized, of course, and keeps a list of items I've run out of. Every night at eleven it updates the list. Every morning at six it automatically sends the list to my grocery store computer. Usually the store delivers my groceries twice a week. Fran signs for them and puts them away. However, if I've run out of something I use all the time, like milk, it instructs the store to make a morning delivery. The keypad on the front of the refrigerator is how I program it. If I want to add something to the list I use the keypad. If you think that's great you should see the stove!"

Jake puts the steaks on the counter. I just sit there. "Wow that's incredible. I swear I've never seen anything like it! And to think I was happy to get my four slot toaster. My mom gave it to me when I moved into my own apartment. She didn't like the color I begged her to buy. She did get the one I wanted though. It is red. I love red and everything in my apartment is red, beige and navy. Those are my favorite colors. The two slots on the right of the toaster are big so bagels fit." Jake jumps up and is apparently happy about something. With a gleam in his eyes he claps his hands together in front of his mouth. "What are you doing?" I ask, shocked that he jumped up like that. He sprints over to me and grabs my hands. "What. What, Jake. Why are you looking at me like that?" At that moment it hit me. I have just remembered more about my life! My mom, the toaster, my apartment! "Oh, Jake. I remember my apartment. Oh, I want to go home, Jake. I remember! My kitchen's navy with beige trim. All my appliances are red. The living room is beige with red trim and I have a huge leather navy couch with red and beige pillows. The rug is red with a pineapple design in it. The hallway is beige. The trim on one side is red and the other side's navy. The bathroom is navy with beige stars! I remember, Jake! I remember! My bedroom is multi-colored. The bottom part of the walls are navy. There's a beige middle border and the top of the walls are red! I have a huge navy frame with a beige mat hanging above my shaker style bed. It's a picture of beautiful magnolias mixed with hydrangea. They're my favorite flowers! Oh Jake, I remember. I'm really getting my memory back!" He pulls me to him and hugs me. We bounced up and down together. "That a girl, Jess. That's the way to remember! Here, sit down and take it easy. Do you remember anything else?"

I try and try but can't remember anything else. I blurted out "See Jake. See. That's how it happened this morning. I just saw that skirt and flashes, memories just flooded my head! Like just now. See. I remembered all that in just seconds! I'm so excited Jake. I am getting my life back!" He lets go of my hands and sits down. "Here, have a drink of water, Jess. Just clear your mind and try not to think of anything in particular. Just rest." We sit in silence a few minutes and then Jake gets up. He goes to one of the cabinets and pulls out a large baking pan. He opens and rinses the steaks and places them in the pan. He gets four potatoes out of the pantry, washes them and sprays something on them. He tosses them in the pan as well. Jake puts the pan in the oven. He turns a dial and pushes a button. I am starting to see a pattern here. Turn a dial and push a button. Hmm. Next he took out a salad and put a little in two bowls. He brings it over to me and asks if I'd like some dressing. "Uh, ranch will be fine, if you have it" I say, not wanting to sound too demanding. He gets the dressing and sits down with me.

We eat our salad in silence. I finish almost all of my salad. Jake demolishes his. The stove beeps. Jake takes some rolls out of the pantry and puts them on what looks like a plastic cutting board. He takes the pan out of the oven and put the rolls in. "Jake. That can't be done yet. It's only been in there a few minutes. It normally takes a good hour for baked potatoes" I say. "And that plastic will melt!" He smiles a crooked smile. "Well, that's the beauty of my high-tech stove. Dinner *is* done and the plastic won't melt. Trust me. The stove beeps again. Jake pulls the rolls out of the oven. They are steaming. "I can't believe that. You mean that's it? It's done?" I ask. "Yep" he says. "Even a lousy cook like me can be a gourmet chef with this stove. It's quick and easy and doesn't burn a thing."

I watch him fix two plates and carry them to the table. "Ketchup, steak sauce, butter, sour cream?" he asks me. I smile and ask for the last three. He quickly gets them and sits back down.

"Jake. That is amazing! You'll have to teach me so I can cook for you sometime. I do like to cook and I am pretty good in the kitchen." Jake can't help but think she's probably pretty good in other rooms too! He is just about to take a bite of steak. Instead, he lowers his fork and looks at me with a slight smirk on his face. "Now, Jess. Fran would have a fit it she caught you in the kitchen. This is strictly her territory. But, maybe we could convince her. Besides, I want you to use all your energy remembering and getting stronger and stronger with each passing day. We have our work cut out for us. It won't be easy baby." He ate the steak and digs into his potato. I pour some steak sauce on my plate. Next I butter my potato and top it with sour cream. The steak is very tasty and the potato perfect. "Jake, this is delicious. You're a great cook!" I chew on my steak and think about my apartment.

I offer to help clean up but Jake will not let me. He insists I either go to the rec room or go upstairs and rest or shower. He says when I come back down we can talk a little more and maybe watch a movie. I stand and so does he. I pick my plate up but he walks over and takes it from me. Our fingers touch and I am immediately affected. He is incredibly handsome. I can't look at him without staring at his square jaw... and those eyes! My throat is very dry and I feel shy around him all of a sudden. "I, ugh, I think I'll go up and take a nice, long, hot relaxing bath. I'd like to get the suntan lotion off of me. I am a little slimy and I think I smell like my horse!" I start up the stairs and Jake calls out "Don't get the water too hot. I don't want to find you passed out up there. I'll check on you shortly." I sigh and roll my eyes at him. *What am I, two years old?* I take that as my cue to leave the bathroom door cracked like I did last night. I don't mind. I somehow completely trust him. I don't think he's a pervert or anything. Well, then again, he is a man.

I start the bath water and use extra vanilla bubble bath I find under the counter. I go into my dressing room and get a white pair of bikini silk panties and a white lace bra. I look in the nightgown drawer. There are a couple of granny pajama sets that I wouldn't be caught dead in. The rest are pretty decent. There are a few that I really like. One is red and one is white. I choose the white one. It is a long white silk night gown that has a fitted lace bodice. With the spaghetti straps and plunging v-back it looks like it would be both comfy and sexy. I see it's got a built in bra so I put the other bra back in the bra drawer. Folded to the side of where the nightgown is I find a white silk matching robe. I lay it out on my bed and go check the water. Bubbles are almost overflowing the bathtub. I quickly turn the water off.

Ah, yeah. This is going to feel great. I strip and throw my dirty clothes in a heap in the corner. I get a clean towel and washcloth and sit them on the side of the tub. As I step into the hot water I think of Brian. I ease myself into the water and slowly lay back. Aaagh! This is the best. I used so much bubble bath that I am up to my neck in thick foamy bubbles. I think about Brian until I cannot think anymore. How did I ever get myself into such a mess? I lay still with my eyes closed enjoying the peace and quiet. Jake's voice startles me back into reality. "Jess, you okay?" Oh, now it's back to Jess. His voice is gentle and soft. "Oh, yeah, I'm fine. Just relaxing... and thinking. Wondering how I got into such a mess?" He pauses and I can hear him breathing quicker now. "Have you remembered anything else?" he asks. I blow bubbles away from my face. "No. Sorry. What have you been up to?" Jake says he quickly cleaned the kitchen and took care of the fire in the sitting room. He asks if he can start a fire for me in my room. The irony of his request is not lost on me and I roll my eyes again and think that one touch from him in just the right way and yes, he could start a blazing inferno. "Oh, yeah, sure. That would be nice." Suddenly I don't want to be alone. I am surprised that I am craving his close proximity. "Jake, I'm up to my neck in bubbles. Why don't you come in and talk." Silence and then I hear a log being added into the fireplace. "I, uh, well. I probably should just go back down stairs and give you time to be alone." I am frustrated and sigh again. Is he being obtuse on purpose? "That's just it, Jake. I don't want to be alone. Come keep me company for a few minutes and let's talk. Please. I promise I'll be on my best behavior." I hear him laugh. "Well, since you put it that way. Give me a minute."

13

Jake comes in and sits on the side of the tub near my feet. We just look at each other for a moment and then I smile. "Thanks again for cooking. I guess I was hungrier than I thought. Thanks for being so kind. There's nothing that says you have to be. I was just soaking and thinking of Brian. I don't know what happened or what caused me to volunteer for 'the project'. But I do know I have to find out if Brian's out there somewhere. He'd be old now. But if he's out there somewhere I feel an obligation to find him. To explain and let him know I'm okay. Can you understand that?" Jake looks down at my toes sticking out from the bubbles and is quiet. He sighs. "Yes, I can understand that. I just can't imagine how it must feel to be you right now. If you want to find out about him I'll help you. I just don't want you to be hurt. If he's alive and out there he's probably moved on with his life. He probably has a wife, children, and maybe grandchildren by now. I just don't want to witness your heart breaking. But, I know it's something you must do, so I'll help you. Do you remember his last name?"

"No, not yet. But eventually I think I will. Thank you for your support Jake. It means a lot to me. I am excited to go to my apartment next week. Oh, I can't wait for you to see it. Hopefully the neighborhood is still good. Maybe we could have lunch at that bar and grill." Jake looks up and I see something strange in his eyes. Maybe it's the look on his face. I can tell that his tight smile is forced. "Jake, what is it? Is it something I said?" He sighs, "Oh, no, Jess. Not at all. Forget it. No big deal. You just reminded me of something, that's all." Jake reaches over and grabs my wash cloth. He holds it in his hands and twisted it, untwisted it, and twisted it again.

I think he is nervous. "When you remember anything, anything at all, I want you to tell me, even if it's the middle of the night. Wake me up. I must keep a record for medical purposes. For the completion of the project, I mean. I have compiled a small statistical cryogenic transcript of your past four years. No personal information. It's all general medical information. In the transcript I call you Jane Doe so no one will know your real identity. I had planned to finish it and publish it for the National Medical Board. Basically, it would be in a book in a medically library that a medical student interested in cryogenics could read and learn the process. Only the top projects get published and that's always been a goal of mine. However, if it bothers you I won't do it. Just say the word and I'll forget it." I thought about it for a split second. "As long as my personal information's not mentioned I don't see why not. Besides, I've always wanted to be famous!" He laughs.

"Seriously, Jake, I don't mind. I want you to do it. I know you have put a lot of work into me the last five years. I know it's been your life and I know it will give you a sense of completion if you publish your work. You'll be famous, you know. Other doctors will call you for your advice." He nods his head. He is beaming with excitement now. "You know, Jess, I realize that thirty-one years seems like a long time for you. But in the medical world it's just a second. It is just a flash in time. This cryogenics thing is still relatively new and the process can always be improved upon. It is going to be widely used in the next hundred years or so. The next fifty years will still be a learning and upgrading process." I glance up at him because he has stopped speaking. He is looking at me in a strange way. I see various emotions flash across his face but I am confused. I am not sure what this is. Jake can do nothing else but stare at Jesse. God she's beautiful. His heart aches for her. His body aches for her. Does she even have a clue how he feels about her? He wants to scream he is so frustrated.

Instead he looks down and sighs again. He knows he cannot have a physical relationship with her right now. And the other thing still looms in the back of his mind. It's not going to go away. He just can't get it out of his head. "I started a fire for you. Your room will be warm and cozy when you retire tonight." There is a brief pause and Jake slowly smiles. "I want to thank you for hanging my towel up. I know I can be a slob. Fran and the rest of the staff take good care of me. I'm sure they hate that I'm a slob. I'm trying to do better though." With that we both laugh. A serious expression crosses his face. "Jess, can I wash your hair?" At first I don't know what to say. A million thoughts and emotions run through me. I want to be near him. I want to feel his touch. "Oh, Jake. I'd love it" drawing out the word love as I say it. He goes to the other end of the tub and sits down. The shampoo is at the front of the tub but on the left side. I sit up and lean forward to get it. I can sense his eyes on my back.

I hand him the shampoo and wet my hair. He pours a small amount into his palm. "Ready?" he asks. I nod yes because my voice escapes me. I realize I am holding my breath in anticipation of his touch. When his hands meet my hair I exhale and close my eyes. He slowly and gently massages the shampoo into my scalp. He touches my neck when he picks up my hair. I shiver at his touch. Jake lathers my hair and gently scrubs away the day. I savor every sensation he is giving me right now. He's good at this. I completely forget about Brian. He finishes scrubbing and lathering and I rinse my hair. I can't get all the soap out of my hair like this. I'll have to put my head under the faucet later or jump in the shower. Jake dips his hands in my water and rinses off the shampoo. "Feels great" he says.

In a soft sexy voice Jake says, "Come here baby; let me wash your back." I see the want in his eyes. I don't want to deny him. Who am I kidding? I want him for me. Selfish reasons withstanding, I bite my lower lip and nod my head yes because I am not able to form words when he is looking at me like *that*. I lean over to get the wash cloth. I see through some bubbles in front of me. My bubbles are starting to disappear. I know he may be able to see more than my back.

I hand him the wash cloth. He reaches over me and gets the soap. First he slides the soap up and down my wet back. His fingers brushing my skin as he does. I lock my hands around the back of my neck, look down and close my eyes. His touch is electrifying. Jake dips the wash cloth in the water to get it wet. He generously soaps it and then reaches over me to put the soap back in the soap dish. I breathe in and enjoy his scent. He touches my back with the soapy cloth. He only uses his fingers and gently rubs my back in small circles. He then uses his whole hand and applies a little more pressure. Yeah, his touch feels incredible on my bare skin, like I knew it would. I open my eyes and see my breast exposed and my nipples are hard. Patches of bubbles are scattered around them and I notice more of my bubbles have disappeared. Jake now plunges the wash cloth into the water and scrubs my lower back and the top of my backside. Can he tell he is driving me crazy?

A moment later he brings the wash cloth back up to my shoulders and neck. He reaches in front of me for the soap and I see his surprise when he sees my exposed breast. He stammers for a moment and then says "I just need the soap one last time please." He lathers the wash cloth and with his right hand massages my shoulders and neck. Next he goes around to the front of my neck and down to the top of my chest. He pauses and our eyes met. I know he is searching for an answer. I give him permission to continue, "Mmmm... Don't stop, it feels so good...Please...." I smile. He leans over and gently kisses me on the lips. With our lips still touching he says "You're incredible." Jake pulls back just a little. He begins to rub the lower part of my neck in small deliberate circles. Using bigger circles he lathers every inch of my chest. When he reaches my breast he slows down and uses his fingertips to make small circles. "Oh, Jake, that's perfect." I moan. Very gently he massages my right breast. I can feel his fingers through the wet cloth. He playfully circles around my whole breast without touching the tip. He does the same on my left breast.

He gently rubs underneath my breast and down my stomach. He pauses for a moment when he reaches the water and then keeps going. I moan again and say "yes." He's driving me crazy. He has to know it. Plus it shows on my face. I lean back in the tub and he scoots in closer. I stroke his face with my hand. Water and bubbles drip down his face and onto his white T-shirt. He is enjoying this as much as I am. He rubs my stomach and then slowly he passes over my left hip. He gently rubs my left thigh slowly moving to the inside. He brushes across my groin when he moves the wash cloth to my right thigh. I am full of anticipation. He massages my right thigh and then stops. Keeping his hand in place, he releases the wash cloth and leans over to kiss me, his hand still on my thigh. "I think I should go" he says with disappointment in his voice. I kiss him more passionately. "No, don't. Stay, I want you to stay. I want you..." His mouth is on mine, kissing me hard. I groan into his mouth. He strokes my thigh with his fingers. Slowly his fingers move to my clitoris and softly strokes and massages me with his whole hand. I moan again and closed my eyes.

"Oh, Jake" I cry out. I never want this moment to end. He continues to gently caress me, not making any effort to go further. I arch my back and push into his hand. He smiles. I lick my lips and then bite my lower lip. "You're driving me crazy" I whisper. Jake reaches over and releases the drain. He smiles at me. "No, baby, you're driving me crazy!" The water starts to quickly drain out. He kisses me again and brings his left hand up and touches my cheek and lips. Slowly his left hand drifts down to my breast. He slightly backs away from me. He takes his index finger and circles my right nipple. When he finally rolls my nipple between his thumb and index finger I feel it deep in my groin. With the fingers of his right hand he finds my clitoris and I am lost. He raised his hand slightly and barely grazes me now. I can't believe how much I want him. He applies a little more pressure and I breathe sharply, throw my head back and close my eyes. I am completely unhinged when he slowly slides a finger inside of me, then another. Oh, it feels so good, so right. Suddenly he withdraws his fingers and moves his hand away from me. There's a few inches of water left in the tub. I reach down with my hand and throw water and bubbles on him, and say "Hey...come back.'

Jake jumps back and stands up. "I can't believe you splashed me" he says through his laughter. His shirt is soaked through. I can see his erection just under his jeans. He leans over the tub searching for water to splash me with but it has all drained out. He turns on warm water and splashes me back. We splash each other wildly. It is the best water fight I think I've ever had. After we laugh ourselves silly the moment passes and I stand up, naked in front of him. He eyes me from head to toe and turns the water off. "Come here" I whisper, motioning for him with my index finger. He stands in front of me and gently puts his arms around me. I tug at his shirt and raise it. I run my hand across his firm chest. He is so warm and all muscle. He leans into me and his breath on my neck is hot. I lean back and pull his shirt up the rest of the way. He pulls it over his head in a swift and efficient move and immediately returns to me.

I unbutton his jeans and run my hands up and down his chest. As I do so he closes his eyes and revels in the pleasure of my hands stroking his chest. I think he's perfect. Suddenly he picks me up and carries me to the bed. He puts me down near the marble top table and turns the light out. I watch him in the glow of the fire. He pushes the pillows off the bed and yanks all the linens back at once. He gently lifts me onto the bed. I watch him slip out of his jeans and socks. He's not wearing any boxers. His erection springs free and I ache to touch him. He's long and hard and beautiful. I'm aching to feel him inside me. I scoot over and he lies beside me. Looking at me now he begins to stroke my hair and face. "Baby, you sure? If you want me to stop...to leave... I will." I see the want and need in his eyes. He is making it my choice...giving me the opportunity to change my mind. He needs this. Jake needs me. "Shhh." I put my finger over his lips. "You're right where you should be. Where I need you to be" and

I pull him closer to me. He kisses me softly. He kisses my neck down to my breast. I moan. He smiles and then glides his tongue gently across my nipple. All I can do is close my eyes and groan. He works his way back up and kisses me hard while his masterful hands are pulling and pinching at my nipples.

Oh, I want him to touch me. I want him inside me too. My hands travel over his face, shoulders and chest. He groans into my mouth as he kisses me hard. I reach down and finally take him into my hands. He is incredibly hard and long. It feels so good to touch him. I imagine all of him inside me. Jake pulls away from me and positions himself above me. I stroke his neck, chest and abdomen. He is perfect in every way. He rubs himself against me firmly and then positions himself at the right spot. He's killing me. I want him inside me and I am impatient. "Jake, I can't stand it. Please!" I beg. He leans down and kisses me gently and I pull him closer to me. He starts to slowly apply pressure and I cry out as he enters me. He is warm, hard and incredible. I gasp with pleasure. Through clinched teeth he says, "I don't want to hurt you." I have an uncontrollable urge to touch him. I stroke his handsome face. "You're not. Don't you dare stop!" He leans down and kisses the corner of my mouth. He moves to hold himself up with his elbows. I slowly acclimate to the sensation of him inside me. The feeling of fullness is incredible. He moves, slowly and rhythmically, driving me crazy. I move with him and we are meeting each other's thrust. I arch my back and press into him. I feel more of his fullness as he thrust deeper into my body and my soul.

Our bodies seem to fit perfectly. I needed this. I pull at his shoulders and back. "I've wanted this moment for so long" he whispers while we gaze into each other's eyes. He picks up the pace and before long we are thrashing wildly in each other's arms. It's a primordial instinct that takes over, and I feel the pressure building and building until I cannot stand it any longer. "Oh, yes, now. Please, now!" I scream at him. He's sweating and breathing heavy over me through clinched teeth. He has the most determined look on his face. I can't control myself and I orgasm and scream his name as I do. I feel him spasm deep inside me. The sweat is running down his face and he whispers my name over and over and collapses on top of me. Our bodies spent, all we can do is lie still and catch our breath. I gently rub the back of his head and neck. "Oh, Jake, that was amazing...you are amazing." I open my eyes and see he is staring at me. He shyly smiles his boyish beautiful smile and my heart melts.   He slowly rolls over and pulls the sheet and blanket up around us. He snuggles close to me with my back to his front and cradles me in his strong arms. I sigh and think 'this is heaven' just as my eyes are closing. I drift off to sleep very satisfied. I wake later with Jake wrapped around me. He is still holding me close to his chest and I am yet again amazed. I hear the crackling and popping of the fire. I never want to move from this spot. I want to stay here forever. I don't want to wake him. I yawn and drift back to sleep.

Jake wakes up. Jesse is still sleeping peacefully. He lies still watching her. She looks like an angel sleeping. He knows how fragile she is both mentally and physically. He frowns and reprimands himself.   *How could I have been so stupid? Why did I let that happen? Can't I control myself? Will she regret it when she wakes up?* He hopes she doesn't. He realizes he didn't even offer to use a condom. At the time neither of them seemed to care. The reason he didn't offer was because he knew there was no need. What if she realizes and worries about becoming pregnant. He could make up something. Maybe tell her that it takes time after what she's gone through before she could get pregnant. He could tell her that it could take a year or two. Well, at some point he *has* to tell her the truth. He doesn't want to. He knows it will kill her.

14

Jake decides to get up. He pees then decides he better clean up the mess and uses towels to dry the water on the floor and cabinets. He opens a new toothbrush and brushes his teeth. Jake evaluates himself in the mirror. He is relaxed and happy. He doesn't look like this often. He can't believe it has finally happened. Even though he knows he shouldn't have let things go that far, he enjoyed every minute of it. She was amazing. So soft when he touched her...and so responsive. So beautiful under him...calling his name. Yes, she is perfect for him. He gets hard just thinking about it. He often sat next to her in the lab and daydreamed about her. Their actual physical joining was better than any of his daydreams. 'She's the love of my life' he whispers to himself in the mirror. He goes into the bedroom intending to put his jeans on and go downstairs. Instead, Jesse rolls over and holds her hand out to him. Jake climbs under the covers and wraps his arms around her. *Will she love me in the end? Will she stay with me?*

I wake confused and think I am home in my apartment. It takes me a moment to get my bearings. I hear a shuffling noise and I quickly remember where I am and see that Jake is gone. When he returns he sees I am awake and climbs back in bed. I lay my head on his shoulder and sigh. I think to myself how happy I am with him. And no matter if I find Brian or not, the past is the past for me now. I'll have to move forward with my life when this is all over. I hope that Jake will remain a part of my life. There is so much to discover about him, yet lying here next to him, I know he is the man I want now. I know I'd love him for the rest of my life, if he lets me. I have only spent two days with him. We have a strange, strong connection and I feel like I have known him all my life. I feel very comfortable around him. Somehow I know he is the one man I am meant to be with. I look up to Jake and smile. "Thank you" I say. "No problem" he says with that shy boyish ridiculous grin. "I always like to help out where I can." We both laugh. "Jake, I need to get up for a minute. Please don't go anywhere." "Never" he says and he kisses my forehead. He watches me walk naked into the bathroom. 'She's magnificent in every way' he thinks to himself. I quickly use the bathroom and run a warm wash cloth over my face. I brush my teeth and get a drink of water. I notice that Jake has cleaned up the water off the floor. Briskly I walk back to the bed.

Instead of lying next to Jake I climb on top of him and kiss him. His body instantly reacts to mine. "Jesse, what..." "Shhh" I say, putting my hand over his mouth. I kiss him again and again. We take our time learning each other, touching each other and pleasing each other over and over again. Afterward, he puts his jeans on. I find my nightgown, panties and robe on the floor where they landed when Jake yanked the covers back last night. Jake said he was going to get a shirt from his room and then go to the rec room. I told him I'd meet him there. I quickly dress and, after finding my slippers, I go downstairs. Jake has started a fire in the rec room. He is sitting on the leather couch with his head in his hands. "Are you all right?" I ask as I quietly walk in. I immediately go to him and he puts his arms around me and hugs me. Smiling he says, "Better than all right. I'm with you." Oh, wow. He is romantic too. I smile as I run my fingers through his hair.

I sit on the couch next to him. "Jake. I don't want to talk anymore. I don't feel like it. I just want to spend some time with you tonight. I don't want to think of the past right now." He put his arm around me and squeezes me tight. "I know, shhh. Whatever you want. I want to just be with you too. Just us, here and now. We'll worry about the rest tomorrow. We've had quite a day. How about a movie?" He leans down and gets a remote out from underneath the couch. "Now you know my hiding place" he said grinning. He pushes a button and there is a slight humming sound. *What is that?* Part of the ceiling opens above the fireplace. A large object slowly descends. It is a huge television. *Okay, now that's cool.* He pushes another button and the TV turns on. The TV speaks in a woman's sexy voice and informs us of the date, time, temperature outside and the fact that it is on channel 10 out of 1998 channels. It is a different female voice than that of the refrigerator. I am amazed that he has nearly two thousand channels. "Whoa. I could watch this for two or three days and still not see all the channels" I say stupidly.

Jake grins and nods in agreement. "The crazy thing is that I only watch about eight or ten channels. I really never even watch the rest. My favorite channel is a news channel. It's like the CNN channel you will remember. The whole broadcasting system is set up different now. Instead of having different networks now there is just one in the whole world. It's called WIN, World Independent Nations. They all work together now. I mean, well, how can I explain this? Our local news is on at five-thirty in the afternoon but you can re-play it anytime that you want after it goes off. After the five-thirty news then it switches back over to the world news. The world news is on the rest of the day. So, it's really not that different from what you will remember. Just the way it's organized I guess is different."

He glances over and grins again at me. He says, "The coolest channel is the space channel. I've been following this one mission. They are almost to a small planet across the galaxy from Mars. I'm going to watch them land and explore next week. That will be really neat. They cloned animals and are going to leave them there to see if they will survive or not. I think that's really cruel personally. However, from a medical viewpoint I understand that they are trying to learn. That's about the only reality TV I watch. Oh, yeah, besides the medical channel. Almost forgot that one." I can't believe he only watches eight or ten channels. Well, he's not the couch potato type. He's definitely the outdoor type. Not so rugged. Jake starts to flip channels. I watch as the images fly by. "Jake. This is so awesome. I never would have imagined!"

He picks a movie channel. A love story was about to start. We sit quietly and watch the first half. A famous young American model moves to a remote jungle village to get away from his fame. He'd left a note that he would be back in three months and takes off without telling anyone where he is going. His agent is going crazy looking for him because he has a big shoot the following week. The young foreigner begins to understand that there are more important things in life than his pretty face as he helps the local village children learn to read. He also helps with the everyday chores and makes many close friends in the village. At this point the TV speaks and says it is time for intermission. I look at Jake and laugh. "Will I ever get use to a talking refrigerator and television?" I ask. "Oh, sure you will. Just give it a week and you'll think you've had them your whole life."

Jake stands up and walks over to the bar. "I'm going to fix a snack. What would you like? Popcorn, chips, pretzels, trail mix, chocolate? Also, pick a drink. Any drink." Jake is smiling a lot tonight. He is truly happy. It makes it nice to be around him. Brian had mood swings. If his day or week was going great he was happy. When things were going all wrong he always took it out on me. Never in an abusive way. He was just grouchy and not very pleasant to be with. When he was like that I'd have to steer clear of him for a day or two. I always hated it when he was in a mood like that because he'd dirty every dish in the house, leave them laying all over my living room and never clean a thing. "Jesse, do you know what you want?" I snap back to reality and see Jake waiting for an answer. "Oh, uh, I guess popcorn and water is fine." I can't believe I just remembered more about Brian. Why am I remembering about him so much and not about my parents, work or friends? I look back over to Jake and he is happily going about the business of getting our snacks.

He brings me a bottle of water and goes back to get the bowl of popcorn and his soda. I won't tell him just yet. I'll wait until after the movie to tell him what I just remembered. When Jake sits down he pushes a button on the remote. The TV says "intermission complete" as the words flash across the screen. The movie comes back on and we snack and watched the rest of it in silence. Turns out that the model gone good rescues a Baptist teacher from Florida when her plane crashes. Everyone else aboard dies. He takes her back to the village, nurses her back to health and they fall in love. She saw the need for both a church and school. After getting in contact with her family and friends and telling them she was going to stay a while, she arranged for her church to sponsor the small village and send missionaries to build both.

While they are in the process of building the church and school the model and teacher get married. The church sponsors the building of a new home for them as well and they lived there happily ever after. He never returned to modeling. What he didn't know is that his agent dropped him and took on another worthy model to fill his place within three weeks. Jake yawns and looks over to me. I yawn as well and drink the last of my water. He says, "Well, that was okay. At least it was a love story. That's one reason why I never watch TV anymore. There are a lot of alien movies and ridiculous war movies that are just so out there. I mean, really. They don't even get the guns and ammo right in the war movies anymore. And the equipment and vehicles they use is just outdated. I have not seen a Q-V in one single movie yet. And they were holding a Gomez blaster the wrong way in the last war movie I watched. It totally turns me off when they do that."

I know I'm behind the times but I say "Q-V and Gomez blaster? What are they?" He explains that a Q-V is similar to what I'd remember as a military vehicle called a Humvee. Then he went into this long story about how in the invasion of Mexico a Captain Gomez had to actually build a weapon from scratch when he and his men were pinned down. That he built a small rocket launcher and it worked. He immediately gave it to his men to start using and built two more. It was the turning point of the invasion. He and his men accomplished their mission because of his quick thinking. That it was never disclosed to the public because he had learned to build different types of weapons during special training. "Well, if it was never disclosed to the public, how do you know about it?" I asked. "And how did they include it in movies if it was supposed to be secret? It all sounds a bit farfetched to me." I arch my eyebrow at him. He shakes his head and laughs. Jake turns the TV off and sends it back to the ceiling storage. He finishes his soda and took everything back to the bar. I am still waiting for him to answer me.

After a long sigh he slowly begins to speak. "Well, baby. I guess now's as good of time as any. I left out a small detail about myself. Not only am I a good hearted doctor and loving son; I am also in a secret military organization. This organization evolved from what you will remember as Special Forces. Now we fight terrorist more than ever. I was there Jess... at the invasion of Mexico. I helped Gomez create and build his rocket launcher. So, I know what it's supposed to look like and how it's supposed to be held. I did not want any credit for my help because I try to remain as anonymous as possible."

I am gaping at him with my stupid girl look plastered on my face. He ignores me and continues, "He has a family and I knew he could use the accomplished mission to obtain the promotion he'd been waiting for. So, that was that. He got promoted and I retained my anonymity. However, somehow there was a government leak. I think one of the State Agents blabbed to his girlfriend or mistress. She was actually a spy for a cocky reporter. It was described on the world news. After that news story it did not take long for it to start showing up in movies. That happened six years ago. I was on my three week break from my medical rotation when I went to Mexico with their unit." I sit dumbfounded and try to process what he just told me. "Unbelievable" is all I can manage to say. After another minute I say, "Wow, you really know how to vacation" and his face relaxes and he grins. "Promise me that if we ever take a vacation that we'll go on one of those boats you mentioned. And that we'll stay away from invasions and weapons." He grins bigger and asks if I am mad. Dumfounded yes, mad no. "Oh, no. Jake. We have so much to learn about each other. I'm just surprised I guess."

I begin to tell him what I remembered during the intermission. He comes over, clasps my hands in his and kisses my cheek. "You see, Jess. It won't be long at all and you'll have your full memory back. You'll be stronger physically as well. You're getting there Jess. It's going to be sooner than later." He hugs me and I yawn again. "We have got to get some rest" he says. "We have a big day tomorrow." I have no idea what he's referring to. "I am going to cook you a great breakfast and then I have a surprise for you." He leads me out of the rec room and up the stairs. Whoa, another surprise? I think the army man thing was a biggie, surely tomorrow's surprise will not top that! I try to make him tell me now because I am impatient. "Come on, tell me. I want to know. Is it a big surprise or little surprise? Is it bigger than a bread box? Smaller than a Toyota? Groovier than tie-die? Come on, you have to tell me." He just shakes his head no and laughs. We reach my room and he says, "Here. Let's straighten it up before we turn in." He makes the bed haphazardly and then takes all of our dirty clothes. "I have a laundry drop in my bathroom. I'll just go drop these. I'll show you where it is tomorrow if you remind me."

He buries his face in my neck in a no arm hug. He kisses me gently. "Please try to get some sleep. Tomorrow will be quite the day, I can assure you. I'll sleep in my room so I won't bother you." "Oh, no you don't! Please!" I beg him. "Stay, with me. I don't want to be without you. Not even while I sleep." I see him weighing the idea. Smiling he says, "Well, why don't you come with me then." "Okay, just give me a minute." I rush into the bathroom. I've had a lot of water today. I've had to pee a lot today. I rush back to Jake to find him grinning at me. "What?" I ask. "Nothing" he says laughing. "What?" I ask again. "Well, if you must know. I have a bathroom in my room too. Or did you forget?" I playfully punch him in the arm and he pretends to be hurt.

I stand near his bed while he disposes of the clothes in the bathroom. I notice he's stripped and put on boxers while he was in the bathroom. He turns the light out on his way back over to the bed. He pulls down the linens and we climb in. I scoot back into him and he wraps his arm around me. "Now this makes me happy" I say just before I drift off to sleep. For a long while I sleep soundly in Jake's arms. Eventually, I begin to dream of Brian. We are at the park again. People all around us are having picnics, playing with their kids and dogs, and throwing frisbees. I lay my back against Brian's torso and he whispers in my ear as we watch the happy families around us. Then we start to have a heated discussion. That's when people start looking at us. All at once we are yelling at each other. People were now staring. He slaps my face and jumps up and walks away from me. I throw food at him as he walks. He was in those khaki pants and long sleeve black shirt.

I begin to sweat and thrash around the bed. In my dream Brian shakes his head no and throws his hands up in the air. I watch him walk past the sidewalk and onto the street to get into his car. He is looking down and does not see the truck coming. I yell at him but he doesn't hear me and it's too late. The truck hits him with a tremendous amount of speed and force before it slams on its brakes. I scream and run over to him. He is unconscious and bleeding. I hold onto him and cry. I yell at people to get a doctor and to stay away from him. "Jess, wake up. Baby. It's me. Wake up. Jess, it's O.K. baby, it's just a dream. Wake up!" I open my eyes and gulp down air. My nightgown is wet with sweat and Jake is shaking me and telling me it is just a dream. I try to catch my breath. "Take some slow deep breathes. Shhh, baby it's okay. You're okay." Jake takes me in his arms and holds me close for a long time. When my tears calm and I can, I tell him about my dream. "Oh, Jake. Is it real? Did that really happen? Is Brian dead?"

"I don't know, Jess. But we will find out. I can find out for you. I'll have my guys search through the past records to see if they can find out anything about the accident. I'll have them start tomorrow. Let me get you a wash cloth." He goes to the bathroom and quickly emerges with a warm cloth. I wipe my face and neck and feel much better. He takes it back to the bathroom and brings me a drink of water when he returns. He has left the bathroom light on and is going to go back and turn it off. "No, leave it" I say. He climbs into bed and I scoot my wet nightgown up and pull it over my head. I toss it on the floor and slide under the covers facing Jake. He moves my hair out of my face and asks "Better?" I nod and in a whisper I say "Yes."

He meets me halfway and gently kisses. His mouth is so wet and warm. I feel his firm chest up against my breast and get a sudden playful urge. I want to play with my new toy. I begin to playfully stroke his chest. Slowly I glide my hand down to his groin and feel him hard already. He smiles and closes his eyes when I touch him. Jake lets his hands wander over my body. We kiss again. We take our time and explore each other. We passionately make love, holding back nothing. He kisses me hard. We are both sweating and breathing heavy in the end. Through his clinched jaw he whispers, "Jesse, oh...baby." When he lies back he puts his arms up over his forehead. "I love being with you" he whispers. I glance up at him and he is smiling. He looks so happy. I slide over to him and rest my head on his shoulder. He brings his arm down and wraps it around me. "I love being with you too" I whisper back. It is the truth because even though I have only just met Jake I feel a really strong emotional connection with him that I cannot explain. I fall asleep in his arms and I do not dream about Brian anymore.

When I wake up Jake is not in bed. I miss him immediately. I go to the bathroom. I am surprised to see Jake in the Jacuzzi. "Good morning beautiful" he says and flashes me that fabulous smile. "Want to join me?" "Of course I do" I say enthusiastically. "Just give me a minute" and I walk past him to the bathroom. I walk back to the Jacuzzi and step up into the warm water. Jake holds out his arms. "Come here baby" he says. I quickly make my way across the Jacuzzi and straddle him. We kiss and slowly make love. The warm water makes it even more erotic. "You are spoiling me. A girl could get use to this" I whisper in his ear afterwards. "I hope so" he says quietly in my ear. He holds me and we sit quietly for another few minutes. "Jesse, did you dream anymore last night?" I move over to his side and turn to face at him. "Thanks to you, I did not" I reply with a colossal grin. "When I would sit next to you in the lab I would often daydream what you would be like. I never dreamed you'd be so naughty." "It's not so bad to be a little naughty" I say after running my tongue across my lips. I switch gears when the dream pops into my head. "Oh, Jake. It was a horrible dream. Maybe that's what caused me to volunteer for the project. I...I don't know. What do you think?"

"Jesse, I just don't know. I've already instructed my security team this morning. They'll let me know as soon as they find something. Jess, baby" he said taking my hands in his, "we have to work today. It's not going to be easy. There's the thing I have to show you after breakfast. I know you may need time after I show you so... please understand. I'll give you space and let you take your time with it. Just don't be angry at me."

I begin to ask why I'd be angry at him but he puts his finger to my lips. "Shhh. I promise you I did all I could do. Don't ask me any questions now. You'll understand after breakfast. I'm thankful to have had this morning and yesterday with you." He kisses me quickly then leans over and grabs his towel. "I'm going to start breakfast. Shower and come down when you're ready." I just watch him go quietly. *What the hell is that about?* Well whatever it is I promise I will not be mad at him because I know deep down he is really trying to do all he can to help me. It's just that my situation is screwed up and I am sure he can only do so much to help me. He can let me stay here until I get my memory back. Then what? I don't know what will happen in the future. I will worry about it later. I can't stop thinking about it...trying to imagine what the surprise could possibly be. I force myself to hurry because the suspense is killing me, and I am starving.

15

I shower quickly, make the bed and hurry to my room. Just before I enter my room my stomach growls. I smell a delightful aroma drifting up the stairs and spilling out into the hallway. I can't wait to eat. I'm unusually hungry this morning. I must be getting back to normal. I rush to my closet. I choose a pair of blue jeans and red casual button down. I slip on a pair of socks, find a red hair tie and tie my hair to the nape of my neck. I go to the vanity in the closet and use very little makeup. In one of the vanity drawers I discover jewelry. I put a pair of small hoop gold earrings on and a thin gold chain. I scurry downstairs in my sock feet. Jake has not only cooked but has also set a beautiful table. Our orange juice sparkles in the crystal stemware. He has used an off white table linen with matching napkins. The centerpiece is an array of burning candles on a silver tray. Behind the candles and off to my side is a huge spray of hydrangea and red roses. Some of my favorite flowers. He remembered! Nice. The place settings are china, I recognize the pattern but don't recall the name. There is a single red rose across my plate.

"Oh, Jake, it's beautiful. Thank you" I say as I walk over to him. He has his back to me and I hug him. "Can I help with anything?" Jake turns around and hugs me back. "No. You take your seat and enjoy your breakfast. We're having steak and eggs, hash browns and biscuits. Are you hungry?" I say I am as he motions for me to take my seat. "How about some coffee?" he asks. "I'd love some." The next instant Jake is filling my coffee cup and handing me creamer. I manage to drink half of my coffee before Jake takes my plate, fills it and sits it back down in front of me. "It looks great. If I keep eating like this I'll be fat." He looks at me and shakes his head. "Believe me; you have nothing to worry about. You need to eat to get stronger. You're so bony you can stand to gain a pound or two." Jake fixes a cup of coffee for himself and sits it on the table. He fills his plate and sits down next to me. He is pleased to see I finish all of my steak and over half of my eggs. After half of my hash browns and half a biscuit I am done.

Jake clears the table. I feel guilty not helping him. He won't let me do a thing. "Well, you can fix me dinner in the next few weeks. Don't worry about it" he says smiling. He pours us both another cup of coffee and sits down. Silence fills the air. "Jake what day is it?" I ask to break the silence. "It's Sunday. I ran across you Friday and brought you here. So it's our third day together. Fran will be back on Tuesday and she'll baby you like there's no tomorrow. There's no getting away from that woman." We both laugh a little and look back down at our coffee. "So, you said you wanted to show me something. What is it?"

Jake rests his hands over mine. "Jesse. When I started to work with you I did not know about what I need to show you. After my father died and I went back to work I nosed around. I found paperwork pertaining to your apartment. Rental payment stubs. Only, the rent had been paid up for the next ten years. I discovered that my father had been secretly paying the rent for you in case you were regenerated and needed your things. I am pretty sure that the other doctors involved in your project had no idea he was paying it. I also found a note from my father explaining that prior to his handling it that the government agency overseeing your project was taking care of it."

"Oh, Jake! Go on, tell me!" He squeezes my hand and continues. "There were some people he didn't trust. He thought they might sell off or take your things and give the apartment to someone else. Anyway, with a little persuasion and probably a lot of money, they let my father take over your estate management. I called the landlord to let him know my father passed away and that I'd be taking over for him. I instructed him to call me if he needed anything. A few years later I got a phone call saying the building had been bought and that all the residents had until the end of the month to find another place to live." I have been looking down. Jake lifts my chin. "Jess, are you okay?" He gives me time to start to digest what he's just laid out. My thoughts are racing again and question after question runs through my head. "Yes, it's just that I was really hoping to go home sometime. What happened with the building? With my apartment?"

"Well, it turns out they tore it down and built a new school there. That was about three years ago. I'm sorry Jess. But, don't be too sad because I had all of your things brought here. That's your surprise. I have your things. Follow me and I'll show you. I am hoping it will help you remember. Come, I'll show you." Jake stands and tries to pull me up. I can't move. My mind is racing, my head spinning. First, I can't believe that his father did that for me. I mean, wow, he did not even know me. Why would he do that for me? Did he suspect that I would be thawed out sooner than I was supposed to be? The fact that he paid my rent for ten years…that would be somewhere in the neighborhood of one hundred thousand dollars. Whoa! That is just insane. Why would he do that? Second, I can't believe that Jake had my stuff brought here. Put my things in his own home. He didn't even know me either! Why would he do that? Just because his dad told him to take care of me? There is more to the story and I need to find out what it is. Right now I am anxious to just see what he has here. "Oh, Jake. Your father did that for me? And you... had my things stored here!" He smiles at me. "I wouldn't exactly call it 'stored' but yes." I squeal in delight. "Oh, it's the best surprise ever! I am so excited. Hurry, Hurry. Show me!" This time when Jake pulls me up I jump and quickly follow him downstairs.

"Come on ... tell me more! What do you have? Any pictures? That will surely help me to remember!" He just shakes his head. "You'll see" he says smiling. We reach the rec room and I follow Jake through it and to the door in the right back corner. "I was going to show you this pool area yesterday and we just ran out of time." We enter into a huge room with very high ceilings. There is an Olympic size pool in the middle of the room. To our right there is a large Jacuzzi. Immediately to our left are a few rows of tables and chairs. The bathrooms are to the left of the tables. The pool is surrounded by large columns, planters overflowing with greenery and statues. In the center of the pool there is a low walkway across the pool about two feet above the water. As we are walking past the bathrooms I see what it is. There's a bar in the center of the pool. That is so cool. The pool is long and we finally arrive at the opposite end. The right side of the pool is occupied with lounge chairs and small tables strategically placed. There is a 'towel shack' behind the lounge chairs.

The roof is solid on the left side. However, on the right side it looks like it's a tinted glass or something. Jake is stopped in front of a door to our left. "Jake, this pool is incredible! I swear I've never seen anything like it!" He is pleased that I like it. "Promise me we'll swim later" I say. "I promise we'll swim sometime. I don't know if it will be today. But sometime." Jake's serious business look takes over his face. He holds my hand and then hugs me. "Baby. This is it. The end of the line for me. I'll hang out in the house in case you need me. I hope you like it." I stand still. Not understanding what he means. "Go on, Jess. Your life awaits you" as he nudges me forward. I take hold of the doorknob and open the door. Confused, I glance back and see Jake sprinting away from me. I watch him disappear into the rec room. *What the hell...?* As I open the door further and step inside I understand. I am in my apartment.

I take a few steps inside and close the door. My knees buckle in the foyer and I fall on my knees to the floor. I can't believe my eyes. How did he do this? I'm at home. I'm in my apartment! My eyes search frantically over the living room. My pineapple rug! My navy leather couch! I look past the living room and see my navy kitchen. There are my crazy red appliances! He's done it. I don't know how. But here I am, thirty-one years later, standing in my apartment. Down to every detail. A flood of memories fill my head. I jump up and run through every room, giggling and jumping and flailing my arms. As I go through each room even more memories surface. Home, home at last! I go to the buffet and slide the door open. Oh God. There they are. A long row of photo albums sit patiently waiting to be explored. Unbelievable! I can't wait to look at them. It's been so long since I have seen them. I'll look at every single one and when I'm done, I'll start at the beginning and look at them again!

Something catches my eye on top of the buffet. It's a picture of April and I standing next to our tent. We went camping on a long weekend. We were both off work and on the spur of the moment we took off. Mosquitoes were really bad and we had to douse ourselves in bug spray. We smelled terrible but we had the best time. We roasted marshmallows, talked about everything under the sun and demolished four bottles of wine. I pick up the picture and hug it tight. Tears fill my eyes as I stand there frozen like a statue. I just think about all the good times we had over the years. It's so hard to imagine her gone. I sit the picture down and pull out a stack of photo albums. I sit them on the couch and start looking at the first one. I laugh, cry and laugh again. After I finish I quickly look through the first one again. I go to the bathroom on official business and giggle when I see the toilet paper.

At first I don't remember doing it, but after some thought I finally do. I had written myself a note with a blue pen on a brand new roll of pink toilet paper. I read it through quickly and then re-read it slower.

Future Jessie
If you're reading this then you're a success
Don't be like me, I'm such a mess
My life is turned upside down
I've never been the princess with the crown
Now I have the chance to change it all
With one tiny, ity, bitty, phone call!
I've decided to do it, to go for the gold
Here's hoping I look young when I'm really old!
****

Future Jessie, don't be sad. Try to make friends
and keep a positive attitude. Look in the top drawer
under the silkies. I've put a long letter there explaining
a few things. And use J-E-S-S-I-E and not J-E-S-S-E.
You like the first one better even though the latter is on your
birth certificate.
Take care and good luck.
Love,
Past Jessie

    I open the bathroom cabinet where I have always kept toilet paper, and there it is. Jake has got it down to every small detail. I take off the roll that is written on and replace it with an unused roll of paper. I use the bathroom and turn the light out. Next I go to my top dresser drawer and find the letter. Ironic. From myself to myself. I jump onto my bed and begin to read the letter. Halfway down the page tears stream down my face.

16

Brian and I had broken up after the accident. There was another woman. Someone he had been working with. They planned to move to Pennsylvania where he accepted a job working on a big project. He never said what it was but that he would be helping do some kind of research. That it was his big break into owning his own company. My family would get paid a lot of money because of my 'project'. I spent a week mulling it over and found no reason why I should stay. My boss would not promote me because we were friends and did not want people to think she was playing favorites. On top of that I had to switch to a shift I didn't like and work an hour longer every day. My dog died and my car was vandalized. Thinking about all of this now, I wonder if Brian had anything to do with either of those. The biggest motivator, my dad had been diagnosed with the late stages of cancer and didn't have long to live.

Within two weeks my world had crumbled. I knew I could quit and look for another job, get a new dog, get my car fixed and try to help my dad as much as possible. However, I just didn't see the point. I was tired of working hard and struggling and never getting the payoff. At least if I enrolled in the project my family would be set financially. I was just sick and tired of it all. I wanted to check out. Take a break. Take a risk instead of playing it safe. I was tired of the what if's. I had no strings tying me down so I might as well do something different. That was how I felt and what I was thinking when I agreed to do 'the project'. At first my family and friends did not want me to go through with it. I convinced them that it was the thing for me. That I wanted to do it. After that, they supported me. They threw me a big going away party. It was like New Years all over again.

The rest of the letter was just me telling myself to check things out to see if they are still there. I had carved my initials into a tree in my parent's front yard. Past me wants future me to see if my initials are still there. Also, if our house is still there. Past me had buried a time capsule in the city park and instructed future me to dig it up immediately after finding this letter. That if I didn't I'd be sorry. I had written that it was of an 'extremely important nature'. Also, past me had written a letter to Brian and sealed it. It's in the time capsule. Past me instructed future me to find Brian if he is still living and give it to him. That it too, was extremely important and I am not allowed to read it. Man, I used to be really bossy, I think and I laugh at myself. I can't believe I wrote a letter like that to myself. How crazy is that?

I read the letter four times. Each time, looking to see if I missed something...searching for clues. I must have been pretty desperate to agree to do 'the project'. The letter answers some questions but only leaves me with more unanswered questions. I go to the kitchen and open my good old regular non-talking fridge. It is full of groceries. I know Jake did this for me. I check the cabinets and they too are stocked. I grab a sweet roll and a Coke. I go to the couch and start looking at the next photo album. I spend the rest of the morning and most of the afternoon going through all of my belongings. Memory flashes come and go. Mentally exhausted, I fall asleep on the couch. I wake to a knock on the door. "Jess, are you all right?" Jake asks cautiously. I wipe my eyes and yawn. I get up and answer the door. Jake stands on the pool side of the door, careful to give me my space. He looks tense. The look on his face is all business Jake and very flat. His lips are a tight line. I respect him for being such a strong person emotionally after all he's had to deal with.

"Jake, I...uh...Oh Jake...Thank you so much. This is the best! You've given me my life back. I'm remembering a lot! There's so much to tell you!" I hug him tightly. "How did you do all this? This is amazing! I can't believe you did all this for me!" He holds my hand. "Baby, I think I'd do anything for you." I pull him into my apartment. He is hesitant at first. "Jess, are you sure? I want to give you the time you need to digest this. To come to grips with it. I know it's a lot to figure out at once." While that is very kind of him I want him to stop being ridiculous and just come in and sit by me. "Jake, come in. Just hang out with me while I look at the rest of these photo albums again. It's nice that you are here. Have you already looked at these pictures?" I assumed he did since he had my stuff moved here. He shakes his head, "No. I haven't looked at anything in here. I had it moved here and put in its exact place. However, I felt it belonged to you and that it was private. I hoped that one day you'd want to share it with me."

I stare dumbfounded at him like he has three heads. "Are you kidding me? I can't believe you! Men are so...ugh...nevermind! You have entirely too much discipline! Of course I want to share it with you." He looks relieved. I lead him to the couch and we sit down. I start with the first photo album. Before I can turn to the first page Jake interrupts me. "Are you hungry? I came by to see if I could get you something." "Oh, no, I'm fine. I had a sweet roll and Coke earlier." He frowns as if my choice is not acceptable but he doesn't say anything. Instead, we look at the albums. The first one starts with baby pictures and pictures of when I was growing up. There are school pictures, sports pictures, birthday parties, Easter, Thanksgiving, Christmas, Fourth of July and Valentine's Day. We laugh at crazy teenager pictures, my first car, and my junior and senior proms. College. Everything right down to the acceptance letter from where I was hired at my last job. Jake gets to know me better as I learn about myself. Jake frequently asks me if I am okay when I get a memory flash. He says I stop what I am doing and stare off into oblivion for any length of time when they hit. I yawn several times.

Jake is so helpful. He has got me several glasses of water and juice so I don't have to stop looking at the albums. I know he is trying to do whatever he can for me. When I run across a fond memory I turn to Jake and thank him for helping me to remember. "Jess, I'm sure that there is so much more for you to remember. You're off to a great start. I'll do anything I can do to help you. The key is to keep working on it." I show him the toilet paper and the letter. "Well, I guess there are a few things you can help me with." When he is finished looking at them both he grins at me. "Okay. First thing in the morning we are up and at it. We will go to your parent's house to see if the tree and your initials are still there. Also, we will head over to the city park and see if we can find your time capsule. How does that sound? That will take at least three or four hours. We'll see how it goes, okay?" My stupid girl grin is plastered on my face and I hug him. "That's great. Thank you." He smiles and I can see he is tired. "Hey, what have you been up to today?" I ask him, hoping he hasn't worried about me all day.

"Marcus came by and helped me move the boxes from my car to my office. We hung out afterwards and talked. We ate pizza and drank a few beers. He informed me of some progress in regards to who was behind the threats but I'm not ready to share any of that information with you just yet.

Some things need to still be verified. I have to make sure I'm absolutely right about this." Oh, wow, there is some kind of progress. That is a good thing, I think. "I just want this whole thing to be over with. I don't want you taking any unnecessary risk because of me" I say. He shakes his head side to side, "Oh, you don't worry about that. I can handle a lot more than this. This person is just a two bit upper class criminal. He's a lowlife all right. He's got his hands in a bunch of different cookie jars. I intend to bust them all wide open!"

"I'm sure you'll do it too. He sounds like a real jerk." Jake's eyes flash with what I think is anger or hatred and he says "Baby, you have no idea! Yes, a real…jerk." I put the photo albums away and start going through kitchen drawers and then closets. Jake follows me around. Before we know it the time is nine-thirty. We walk back to the living room and are standing on my pineapple rug. "I can't believe I've been here all day. Poking around and rediscovering who I am. My whole situation is incredible, but you doing this for me…well, you're incredible." He kisses my forehead and asks if I'd like to stay here or walk back with him. "I'll walk back with you. I don't need to stay. I've enjoyed today and I'll hang out here a lot in the near future. I'm just happy to have my stuff and that I'm remembering my life."

"I wasn't sure how you'd react to all this. I was hoping it would help you to remember. I was afraid that you'd want to hide out here for a while. I was afraid that, in a weird way, I'd lose you to your past. I mean, I know that sounds stupid, but it's true. I was afraid of how you'd act once you remembered your life. I was really afraid you might not want to be around me…that maybe…I'd lose you to him." Jake sighs and turns away from me.

Whoa…wait a minute. He is afraid of losing me? Huh? I try to reassure him, "Oh, Jake. After yesterday, you thought you'd lose me?" I say in disbelief. "Look at me." I touch his arm to get him to turn around. Tears are in his eyes. "Jake. You have done more than any man has ever done for me. If it weren't for you I wouldn't be standing here right now! Don't be that way! I think you're stuck with me." He wipes his eyes and nervously forces a smile. "Besides, you're not just helping me get through this. I can tell that you're going to be my best friend now - and to be honest with you…well, I don't want to be without you Dr. Bradley. Don't ask me how, but I think I'm falling in love with you!" He stares at me as if the words don't register. I smile at him and the next second his expression says all I need to hear. He smiles, holds his arms out and scoops me up. He twirls us around and then lands us on the couch. "Glad to hear it baby" he says softly before gently kissing me. "I know you don't understand all that's happening, but just know that I do love you and I will protect you and take care of you for as long as you let me." He kisses me again and runs his hands underneath my shirt.

His touch has my nerve endings springing to attention and I tingle everywhere. How can one touch from him make me react like this? My stomach growls and interrupts us. *Oh, great. Now that's romantic.* "Come here" he says standing and pulling me up. He puts his arm around me and leads me to the door. "Let me fix you something to eat...then we can get back to...this... if you feel like it." Grinning a devilish grin he kisses me and runs his finger along the nipple of my left breast. *Oh yes, Jake, I will definitely feel like it.* He turns off the light and we walk hand in hand to the rec room. "There's some pizza in the refrigerator down here. Would you like that or would you like something more...like maybe meatloaf and mashed potatoes? A nice salad? What do you feel like?" he asks while moving a strand of hair that has fallen into my eyes. "Oh, no, don't cook this late. Pizza is fine. Water too, please." We go over to the bar. I sit and watch him warm up my food. One thing is for certain. I don't think Brian is like Jake, that's for sure. He never really treated me like this. Like I was... important. Like I was the center of his world. With Jake, that's how he makes me feel. "Smells great" I say as Jake puts my plate and water in front of me.

17

After I finish my pizza Jake asks me if I am ready for bed. He sees I am tired. After all that has happened today I just need to unwind a bit. Take a few minutes to slow down. Everything keeps running through my mind and there's no way I can sleep now. Jake suggests watching TV. "Sounds great" I say. I watch him turn the TV on and then arrange the pillows on the large rug. He turns off the lights. "We can watch it from here" he says as he lies down and props himself up on the pillows. "I do this all the time. I can't tell you how many times I've fallen asleep watching TV down here." He smiles and holds out his hand to me. I can't help but notice how good he looks. He showered earlier and changed into black casual pants, a pale blue light weight ribbed sweater, black socks and black dress shoes. I can see his muscles flex under his shirt when he moves. When he hugged me in my apartment I could smell his aftershave. It is a smell I definitely like. I think he has on cologne as well. I am touched that he wants to smell nice for me.

I take his hand and sit next to him. I have been in my socks all day. He bends down with his left hand, takes off his shoes and neatly sits them to his side. We lie back on the pillows and I am quiet as he flips channels. He can't decide what to watch and finally switches it to the news channel. "How are you feeling?" he ask sincerely. "Oh, I'm fine, just getting a little tired is all. It has been one big thing after another. Do you think that I will be back to normal soon?" I look over to see he seems to be struggling with what I think should be a simple answer. Finally he says, "I'm sure you'll be fine. I just need to monitor you occasionally, that's all. It seems you are doing quite well so far."

"I'm getting excited about tomorrow. I can't wait to see if my parent's house is still there. If it is, I'm sure it's run down by now. I'm not expecting much. I know it's most likely gone by now. Maybe the tree is still there though. And to think that we may find my time capsule. I wonder what is so important that I'd be sorry if I didn't find it?" He is quiet for a moment and then shakes his head, "I don't know. You're just full of mysteries" and flashes me his boyish, playful grin that is heart stopping beautiful. He continues, "One thing is certain...it's definitely going to be interesting." Suddenly an awful thought crosses my mind. "Oh, Jake. I just thought of something. What if the park is not there anymore? What if they built a school or something on top of it like they did my apartment?" I feel even more anxious and now frightened at the idea. "I guess it is a possibility. We just have to get there and find out. Just try to keep an open mind okay?" I know he's right but it's terrible to think that clues from my past could be gone just like that.

"You're right, I know. I'll try to be positive. I guess I'm just a little anxious about tomorrow." Jake wraps his arms around me and squeezes me tight. "You have every right to be. I can't imagine what it must feel like to be you. Surreal, I'm guessing." He glances over at me to see my reaction. I nod, "Yeah, it's been a little strange. I'd really be lost if it weren't for you. So, thanks...again." I smile and halfway hug him back. "Like I said before...I always like to help out when I can. And you, baby, need my full attention right now." He leans over and gently kisses me. "Is there anything in particular you'd like to watch?" he asks me. "Is there a scary movie on? I use to like to watch a good scary movie." He channel surfs and finds a murder mystery. I lay quietly next to him and we watch half of the movie. All at once fatigue washes over me. I gently nudge him, "Jake. I can barely keep my eyes open. Do you mind if we turn in now?" He yawns. "Not at all. Are you kidding? I'm tired too and we do have a big day tomorrow." He turns the TV off and I pay no attention to the slight hum as it retreats back to its hiding place.

We lay in the dark a moment longer. I hear Jake sigh. "Jess, were you happy with Brian? Do you remember if he was good to you?" A smile crosses my lips. I doubt that Jake can see it and am glad it's dark. I think the good doctor is jealous...of my past! I want to answer honestly but I don't want to hurt Jake. "I think he was...from what I can remember. It seems like we were really happy for a long time. Something happened to us though...around the same time we had that fight at the park. If only I could hear what we were saying in my dreams ... maybe that would help me to know what happened, why we broke up." "You'll remember in due time. Don't worry about it. I just want to protect you. I feel so lucky to have you in my life. I hate to think that he may have treated you bad. That's all."

"Jake, can I say something without you taking it the wrong way?"
Even though I can't really see his face I sense his lips are in a tight line now.
"Sure, Jess, I want you to feel like you can tell me anything." Well here
goes nothing. "Brian was good to me, from what I remember. But he was...
very...different from you. He never treated me the way you treat me. On
some level we did not connect. I loved him, sure. We were friends, sure.
We were not best friends though. It would have been a mistake if we had
gotten married. I know that now." I can hear Jake take a deep breath and
then exhale. "I know we've only spent this weekend together and I don't
even know you that well. I feel it and I know you feel it too. We connect
on every level. We're meant to be together. I hope that doesn't sound stupid to you. Do you understand what I'm trying to say?" Jake rolls onto his
side and gently touches my cheek. "Shhh... baby I know exactly what you
are saying. We're like old souls who have found each other again. You're
my soul mate. I *am* meant to be with you."

This time I lean up to kiss him. His lips are soft and warm. I feel
the love in his gentle touch and tender kiss. I know from this moment
on that I'll never be apart from him. I know that I will love this man for
the rest of my life. "Hey, let's go to bed" he whispers in my ear and kisses
my neck. My fatigue has disappeared and is now replaced with a stronger
urge for him. I want to be with him. I want to feel his touch all over my
body. Jake pulls me up and then picks up his shoes. We walk hand in
hand up the stairs. We pass my doorway and go to his room. There is a
fire burning and the crackling sound is soothing. He must have started the
fire earlier when he showered and changed. I see he already has the linens
turned down. He is such a boy scout and always thinking ahead. I like
that about him.

"I have something for you. It's special and I want you to have it."
He pulls a diamond and sapphire ring from his pocket. "Oh, Jake...I can't
accept that...you shouldn't have!" He shakes his head at me, "You can and
you will" he says vehemently as he slips the ring onto my finger. "And I
didn't. It belonged to my mother. My father gave it to her before they were
married. It's not an engagement ring or anything. I just want you to have
it. Every time you look at it I want you to remember how much I love you
now, and forever." *Wow!* The fire in the fireplace is not the only fire. We
are both burning with desire as we peel away each other's clothing and slip
beneath the sheets.

Our hands act of their own accord as we explore each other again and again. As my hands travel all over his tan, firm body I realize how much I love to touch him. He is such a strong man and yet so gentle. Jake slowly enters me and smiles his devilish smile. I smile back at him and pull him to me. "I love you" I softly whisper in his ear. "Oh, baby, and I you" he whispers as he kisses my neck. We drive each other crazy and when we can't stand it any longer we both find our release and orgasm together. "I promise you, Jess, I'll never leave you. From this day forward we'll never be apart." He rolls onto his side and wraps me in his arms. I drift off to sleep a very happy woman.

18

Bad dreams slowly creep into my peaceful slumber. I am with Brian in his car. We arrive at the park. He comes around and opens my door for me. I am carrying our picnic basket and a small blanket is draped over my arm. We find our spot. There are not many people here yet. It is still early. We have planned to spend the day relaxing. Things have not been exactly the same between us for months and I can't quite put my finger on the reason why.

He would never cheat on me. I know that for sure. We have planned to get married next month. There is a sense of urgency although I don't know why. I think something is going on with his new job. He never talks about his work anymore. We spread the blanket out and unpack the basket. We talk for an hour and more people arrive at the park. We take a walk and then head back to our blanket near a beautiful old tree. We come here often and usually just walk. It's nice to sit and watch all the families have fun. We start arguing about something. I can't hear what we're saying. People are starting to look at us. We are increasingly irritated with each other. He's had enough. He slaps my face and begins to walk away. I throw food at his back and burst into tears. I drop my head in my hands.

I look up and wipe my eyes. Brian is walking around to the driver's side of the car. I am focused on him and don't see the truck until it is almost to him. "Look Out!" I scream as loud as I can. Tires screech and Brian flies through the air and hits the pavement hard. I scream his name as I run over to him. "Brian, Oh my God! Brian. Answer me. Brian. Are you all right?" Tears stream down my face as I scream "Somebody call an ambulance!" He's bleeding. What do I do? Oh God, what am I supposed to do? "Get back! Everyone get back and let him get some air! He can't breathe!" I sob next to him on the pavement and hear sirens in the background. "They're coming Brian. Hang on. They'll be here any minute. Just stay with me Brian. Don't you dare leave me!" His eyes flutter and he barely opens them. His lips quiver and he tries to speak. I bend down close to his face to hear him. "Shhh, Brian, don't try to speak. You'll be all right. I'm right here." The ambulance has just pulled up.

His lips move and I listen carefully as he says "I love you Katy." I must have heard him wrong. The paramedics rush over and begin to evaluate him and prepare to transfer him to a gurney. They quickly put a hard neck collar on him. "Just for protection during transfer ma'am", the tall skinny paramedic says. I am standing right next to him the whole time. "I love you too" I say to him. "They're going to help you. Just hang on. You're going to be fine." He starts murmuring something under his breath I can't hear. The paramedics make me move back. Just before they put him in the ambulance he says "Katy, marry me. I love you Katy." I'm sure I've misunderstood. I shake the paramedics arm. "What did he say? I didn't hear him. Please, tell me what he said!" The paramedic moves me back and the other one closes the doors. "He says he wants you to marry him. He says he loves you." See, I did misunderstand him. The paramedic starts to walk away and then turns back to me. "Miss" I am in shock and do not really notice him speaking to me. "Katy. We're taking him to County General. Can you follow us in your car? Katy, did you hear me?" I nod my head yes even though my name is not Katy. I think I am in shock.

The ambulance left and a stranger picks up Brian's keys off the pavement and hands them to me. "Ma'am. Are you going to be okay?" I say "yes, thank you." Instead of going to the hospital I drive myself home. Who the fuck is Katy?

19

I wake up in a cold sweat. I sit up in bed and sob with my head in my hands. I can't believe it! He was cheating on me! Why would he do that? I just don't understand. I'll never understand. That would explain him withdrawing from me the last few months before the accident. Was it real? It seems too real to be just a dream. I'm sure it happened. Jake hears me crying and wakes up. When he sees me he quickly comes over to console me. I tell him about the dream. "It was so real Jake. It had to be real. It couldn't have been just a dream! It had to have happened." Jake, being the kind and loving man he is, holds me tight until I calm down. He goes into the bathroom and quickly comes out with a navy terry cloth robe and slippers for me. He has put on a matching navy robe with a pair of men's navy house shoes. "It's five forty-five. Why don't we go downstairs? I'll make some coffee and we can try to sort through this. All right?" I shake my head yes and wrap myself quickly in the robe.

Jake hands me my coffee and warms a breakfast casserole. We silently eat our breakfast. We both are thinking about the dream and what we might find at the park today. "I'm sorry baby, it *is* probably a memory. It sounds like it's real to me. The fact that you keep having the same dream over and over makes me believe it *is* real. And you dreamed more of it this time. Let's try to keep a positive outlook about today. If it's real then I'm so sorry Jess. But the reality is...that was thirty-one years ago if it did happen. Somehow, some way, we will have to find a way for you to go on with your life. I'll help you. You know that. Let's just see what happens today. Take things slow." He smiles and squeezes my hand. He stands up from the table and takes our dishes to the sink.

"Want some more coffee?" he asks. "No, I think I'm just going to shower and get ready. I'm anxious to see what we find." He forces a smile, "Okay, I'll do the same." He hugs me and kisses my forehead. "Meet me down here in forty-five minutes. That'll give me time to write down the address and get the map. It's approximately a forty minute drive from here.

I think I know where I'm going and don't think we will get lost. I want to be sure though because it's not the best part of town now."

Jake and I go upstairs to our separate rooms to dress. I quickly shower and dress in brown trouser socks, a brown pair of casual pants and a short sleeve V-neck light brown shirt. I don't bother with my wayward hair. I quickly dry it and push the front out of my eyes. I spray it and apply some powder and lipstick. I still have the hoop earrings and chain on from yesterday. I slip into a pair of brown flats and take off downstairs. Jake is sitting at the dining room table with some paperwork. He is dressed in jeans, a navy short sleeved shirt and loafers. "Ready baby?" he asks when he saw me come around the corner.

"I'm as ready as I'll ever be" I say nervously. "Jesse, it's not the best part of town. I've asked Marcus to come with us...just for added security. I know I should have asked you first. I'm sorry. I hope it's okay." I smile at him. "Sure, it's fine with me. No big deal. I hope he isn't too bored." He has a relieved look on his face. "Great, I was hoping you'd be all right with it. He's outside by the car. This will give you guys a chance to get to know each other a little. He's a great guy, you'll love him...well, I don't want you to love him as much as you love me...but you can like him" Jake grins and pulls me to him. We kiss and I wish that is all we have to do today. He holds my hand as we walk to the car.

"Hey Jesse, it's nice to see you again. How have you been?" Marcus asks extending his hand. "Oh, just fine" I say as I shake it. "Your boy, Jake, here has been taking real good care of me." In this moment I wonder what Jake has told him about me. Did he tell him we slept together? I push the thought out of my head before more like it can rush in. I doubt it because I don't think Jake would do that to me. "I knew he would, miss." We get in the car and Jake drives out of the drive. He pushes the button and we are out of the gate in no time. We drive down the hidden road, emerge onto the gravel road and eventually came to the main road. He turns right onto the main road and our journey to the past begins. "Here we go" Jake smiles and looks at me. We are in the front and Marcus is in the back seat sipping a cup of coffee. There are a couple of bags that kind of look like black gym bags on the opposite side of Marcus and a black briefcase sitting right next to him. He saw me look down at them but didn't offer an explanation. Instead he asks if I am busting out of my seat with excitement. I say, "I am, can't you tell!"

"I'll bet. It's not every day you get to find buried treasure" Marcus says and grins. I laugh and out of the corner of my eye I can see Jake smiling. "I'm sure it's nothing of value. Whatever it is it probably has sentimental value. I can't imagine there would be much in there anyway." Marcus continues, "Maybe its money. Or, maybe a collection of some sort. Maybe it's just your lucky rabbit's foot." He is clearly having a good time teasing me. "You're enjoying this way too much" I say. Jake speaks up, "All right, All right you two. Everyone knows that the rabbit's foot was popular in the 70's. That's obviously *before her* time." Marcus laughs but reaches up and playfully slaps the back of Jake's head. "Thanks for defending me" I say grinning from ear to ear. A quick naughty thought races through my mind and I can't resist. I scoot over in the seat next to Jake and whisper in his ear, "you don't have to try to win me over, you are going to get lucky tonight anyway." His eyes get wide and he arches his eyebrows and grins wildly at me. He grabs my hand and brings it up to his mouth and kisses it twice before putting our hands on his right thigh. He wants me to stay next to him...and I am glad because I am really nervous. They are both smiling. "You boys better behave on this trip or I won't take you anywhere else!" I say in my best threatening stern voice.

We ride in silence for the next twenty minutes. Jake stops for gas and Marcus gets a refill on his coffee. I sit in the car waiting for both of them to return. I decide I'd better find the bathroom before we leave. When I am finished I walk back around the corner to see them looking frantically around. "Oh, baby, don't ever do that to us again!" Jake says in a raised voice. "You had me scared to death. I didn't know where you were." He races over to me and hugs me tight. "Okay. I just went to the bathroom." *Jeez, guess I am not the only one who is nervous about today.* Jake does not let go of me until we reach the car. "Hey, I'm sorry for getting angry...I was so scared something might have happened to you. This is really the first time we've been out. I just want to keep you safe." He hugs me again and I get into the car. "Next time just tell us, okay?" I agree, even though I think they are both overreacting. I really didn't mean to make them upset. I don't like being treated like a two year old either. I'm a grown woman for crying out loud. I should be able to pee without testosterone involvement. *Come on, Jesse, you know they are just worried about you.*

I take a deep breath and sighed. "How much farther is it?" I ask nervously. "About ten minutes. Nervous?" Jake asks. "A little bit. I just want to get this over with. I just want an answer." I am quiet the rest of the way and I lean over on the window with my eyes closed. As soon as I feel the car stop I jump up. I quickly look around. Rows of dilapidated houses loom in the early morning sunshine. I look to the opposite side of the street and see it. Tears fill my eyes. My parent's house is standing, but in very bad shape. The windows are boarded up. I run across the street and start up the stairs. "Jesse, wait" Jake calls after me. "Jesse, I said wait." He catches up with me and I try the door. It opens and I take a few steps inside. The house is fully furnished and just like I kind of remembered. Everything is old and dirty. The furniture is falling apart. I don't remember everything about my life, but I do know my mother was a clean freak. She'd die if she saw the house like this. Instinctively I started putting things in the right place and wiping dust off pictures.

"I...I don't understand. Why is all of their stuff still here? Why wasn't the house sold after my parents died? It doesn't make sense." I slowly walk through the living room and into the hallway trying to figure it out as I go. My room! I hurry down the hallway. My foot went through a floorboard. Marcus steadies me and Jake helps me free my foot. "Jesse, please, be careful. There are probably snakes and God knows what else under the floor." Oh, gross. I hadn't thought of that. I have always hated snakes and creepy crawly things. I push the door open to my room. Dust covers everything. "I can't believe it. It's the same. It's exactly the same. My mom never changed a thing. I remember this house and my room. Oh, Jake, I remember my life here!" Tears stream down my face now. Jake goes to my dresser and touches my trophies carefully. He picks up my old pom poms and playfully swings them in the air. Dust flies off them and floats in the stale air. Marcus stands in the doorway laughing at Jake. He is very handsome and when he laughs he oozed charm. He must have a girlfriend. I'd probably be attracted to him if I were not interested in Dr. Feelgood.

An old perfume bottle sits on top of my dresser. I'd recognize the shape of the bottle anywhere. It's Sand-n-Sable. It was my favorite perfume as a teenager. I shake the bottle a little and remove the dust around the nozzle. I spray the nozzle and it still works. That's crazy. I take a deep breath and it still smells pretty good. I put some on. The boys pretend to like it although I know they really don't. I go to my closet and open the door. It is filled with a bunch of old uniforms and clothes that don't fit anymore. Shoes are haphazardly lying on the closet floor. The top shelf is overflowing with blankets and year books. Sunlight streams into the window through cracks in the boards and dust particles are flying around the air. I hate to see it like this. "When I leave here today I won't come back" I said matter-of-factly. "I'd rather remember the good times we had in this house. I don't want to see it like this again." I tell them about some of the good times I have had here. I point out where we use to put up our Christmas tree. I sigh a long sad sigh. "Jake, I'd like to take a few things with me... if that's okay?" "Oh, yeah, sure...you just tell us what you want and we'll put it in the car for you." I can tell by the look in his eyes that he understands why I want to take some things.

"Well, I know I want to take my year books and those pictures in the living room for starters. There is also a quilt that my grandmother made. She gave it to my parents the day I was born. She had my baby information sewn into it and had left four blank patches for additional baby information. In case my parents had more kids. They didn't though, just me. If I could find it I'd love to take it. If it's not ruined, that is." I walk to the doorway and Jake follows me. Marcus stands aside for me to pass and I smell a trace of his aftershave. He smiles at me and I think I see a twinkle in his eye. It must be my imagination. I go down the hall to the linen closet. I open the door and a rat scurries out from underneath a mattress cover lying on the floor. It startles us and we each take a step back. Once we are sure that no other creatures are going to pop out we search the closet from top to bottom. "It's not here. The only other place it would be is in my mom's closet. Let's look there" I say with disappointment in my voice. I go to the end of the hall and open the door to my parent's bedroom. Marcus and Jake follow me into the bedroom.

Dust has taken over everything in here as well. The lamp on the night stand has been knocked over and shattered glass is on the floor. The clock is hanging off the side of the night stand by the cord which is still plugged in. A lighthouse print has been knocked off or has fallen off the wall. It is upside down against the wall. The wood frame is cracked and the print is crooked inside the frame. "What a mess" I say as I make my way to the closet. I motion to the closet door. Jake comes over and opens the door. We hear a quick thump and then a raccoon jumps out at us and runs under the bed. It barely misses Jake when he quickly evades to his left. I look at my mother's clothes hanging neatly in the closet. I sigh again. "Okay, let's hurry up and get out of here This is way too depressing!" I say as I feel more tears forming in my eyes. On the shelf I see a long white box with my mother's handwriting on the side. 'For Jesse, the quilt, love mom' is all it says. On top of that box is another small box. It is enclosed in a large plastic storage bag. On the side of the small box my mother had written my name.

Jake and Marcus pull the long box down, careful not to drop the smaller box. They sit the boxes on the bed and puffs of dust rise up into the air. I open the plastic bag and pull out the smaller box. "It's a photo storage box" I say while I open it. "Oh, you guys. Look, pictures of my family. Look, here I am when I was six. That was my first day of school. And look, here's my first basketball picture. I was seven. Oh, man. Look at this one." I hold the picture up for the guys to see. "This was my best friend in the whole world when I was eight. She was the best dog a girl could ask for. I was getting ready to go to a football game to cheer. See, I'm in my cheerleading uniform." They nod their heads accordingly. "Is she a golden retriever?" Marcus asks. I nod my head yes. "She's beautiful" Jake says. "And I'm not talking about the dog!" I playfully punched his upper arm. "I love those kinds of dogs, they're hard to find now" Marcus says. "Come on, you guys. I don't want to get these pictures all dusty. I certainly don't want to open the quilt in here. Besides, it looks like mom had it preserved and sealed." I put the pictures back in the box and head for the door. Jake picks up the long box and they follow me to the hallway.

"Jesse, is there anything else you see that you might want?" Marcus asks. "No, this is it. There's nothing here for me now but memories. As long as I have these pictures and the quilt I'm happy. I am thankful to have these few things. I never dreamed the house would still be here. And still furnished! I haven't figured that out yet." We walk past the living room and out the front door. Jake hands the box to Marcus and heads back to my room to get my year books. By the time he comes out with them Marcus has already put the quilt box and pictures in the car. I stand on the front porch and look around sadly at the decaying neighborhood while Jake takes the year books to the car. I am lost in my memories when Jake walks over to me and holds my hand. He points to a tree near the crumbling sidewalk. "Is that the tree?" I gasp, "Yes, it looks pretty much the same, just a little taller and maybe a little wider." We walk over to it and I smile when we are two feet away. I see it from here. "I can't believe it! It's been about forty-five years and it's still there!" I drop Jake's hand and go over to the tree.

Halfway up the trunk and centered is the small heart I had carved into the tree with my dad's Swiss army knife. I run my fingers over the heart and then over my initials inside the heart.

Jake walks over to me and puts his arm around me. I can't help but smile. I can't believe what I'm seeing. Does Jake see it too? This is it. I can't believe it! It makes sense. Jake and I were meant to be together. All of a sudden I feel at peace with my whole situation. I stare at the initials JNB carved into the tree. My life has come full circle. "Jess, that's your initials?" he asks in amazement. I smile at Jake and shake my head yes. I bite my lower lip nervously. Jake is stammering over words and I am lost in the moment. Finally Jakes says, "But, baby...that's mine. I mean...your initials are exactly the same as my initials! I didn't see it before. That's really amazing!" I am proudly wearing my stupid girl grin now and I say, "We're meant to be together Jake." He sweeps me up in a bear hug and presses me against the tree. His face is less than an inch from mine. Our lips are almost touching. "What's you're middle name?" he asks. I smile and he smiles back at me brushing his lips over mine. "Come on, tell me. I've always wondered. You're paperwork only had your middle initial. What is it?" I finally cave and say, "Nicole. What's yours?" He grins his boyish shy grin, "Nicholas" he says before gently kissing me. "I love you, Jesse Nicole Birchfield. Please, do me the honor, make me an honest man, marry me?"

Somehow I know I have never been happier than this moment. "Jake Nicholas Bradley, I love you too. I'll marry you as long as you promise to always kiss me like that! Even when we're old!" He lowers his lips to mine and says, "Always". The world stops for us and he kisses me again. His mouth is warm and sweet. He puts me down and presses his body against mine. "Jesse, I'll never leave you. I want you with me forever. I promise you I'll love you for the rest of my life." Tears stream down my face and my lips quiver, "Oh, Jake! I feel the same way. I want to be with you forever." I gently touch his face and stroke his hair. We kiss again. "You're driving me crazy" he says. "No, you're driving me crazy! You'd better promise to make mad passionate love to me tonight!" He grins that heart stopping boyish grin. "Well, okay, if you insist!" We both laugh. "Hey, love birds. Think we can get out of here now?" Marcus shouts with an irritated tone. We've been caught and we laugh again. Jake kisses my forehead and backs away from me. We hold hands and walk to the car.

20

We are all quiet as Jake drives to the city park. It is just minutes away from my parent's house. The benches and tables are old and worn. The barbecue grills are long gone. The sun is beginning to shine brightly through the trees now. The day is shaping up to be quite beautiful. Jake brings the car to a stop. We get out and stand by the car. After only a few seconds and a quick scan of my surroundings I recognize this park. We are parked in almost the very spot that Brian had parked his car that day. This is where Brian and I use to come. This just proves to me that my dream *was* a memory. *That the accident really did happen.* I gasp, "Jake, this *is* the park in my dreams where the accident happened I'm sure of it." Jake and Marcus are both standing next to me now "What accident?" Marcus asks. "Baby, you go ahead and look around. I'll fill Marcus in on your dream." I leave them at the car and I walk toward a large clearing in the center of the park. Past a picnic table and on my right is where Brian and I use to spread out our blanket. To my left is the large tree in my dream. It looks pretty much the same. Just bigger and older.

I look back over my shoulder and see Marcus shaking his head from side to side. Either he's disagreeing with Jake or he feels sorry for me. Suddenly I'm overwhelmed with memory flashes. I feel faint. The world seems to be spinning. I make my way over to the picnic table and sit down. I have to close my eyes to try to regain control. I lay my head on my hands on the table. I feel the cool rough concrete texture of the table and it somehow soothes me. More memories fill my head. My temples start to pound. "Jesse, are you okay?" Jake shouts. I can't raise my head to look at him so instead I hold up my right hand. I hear his feet crunch grass, leaves and sticks as he hurries to my side. "Jesse, what is it? Are you all right? If this is too much we can leave. You've been through so much the last few days. We can leave, it's no big deal. We can come back another time if we need to." Jake sits next to me and holds me close for what seems like an eternity. Finally I look up at him with tears in my eyes.

"Oh, Jake. I just had more memory flashes. I remembered more. It's just so sad though. I was trying to change him. Change Brian, I mean. He was a good guy but he had a bit of a dark side. A bad streak, you could say. There was something he was going to do that was really serious. I just remember I did not want him to do it. It was a big deal. It would change our lives forever and I begged him not to do it that day. The day we had the fight here. Oh, Jake. I think it was my fault! I think I must have said something to him...something that made him so angry...that he just wanted to get away from me. I think that's why he walked away from me...I think that's why he got hit by that truck!" Tears stream down my cheeks. Jake squeezes me tight and wipes away some of my tears. "Shhh. We both knew this would be a tough day. That whatever we find it would not be easy. I know it's hard for you but you're really doing great. Just being here has helped you to remember. I'd understand if you want to leave though. What do you want to do? Shall I take you home?"

I force a smile. "No, Jake. I have to see this through. You know that. I am just tired, I'll be fine." He nods and motions to Marcus still standing next to the car. Marcus goes to the trunk and pulls out a small shovel. He slowly walks toward us. He looks back over his shoulder several times as if he were looking for someone. "Jesse, do you have any idea where we should start looking for your time capsule?" Jake asks almost impatiently. "Yes. I know exactly where to look. Or at least I think I do anyway." Jake wipes my face again. "You're going to be fine. No matter what happens or what we find, you're going to be fine. I promise you that much. I'm here to make sure of it." He kisses my forehead and pulls me up. "Come on, then. Let's get to it. Marcus saw some guys drive by earlier when we were at the house. When we were standing by the car we both saw them drive by here. They are up at the intersection. Instead of turning to come to the park they just slowly drove by. I think they are just checking us out. Trying to see what we are doing here."

"Who are they? Why do they care if we're here? It's a free country. We have every right to be here. It's a city park for God's sake!" I threw my hands up in a frustrated motion. "Jesse, things have changed. This is their territory now. I don't think they want any trouble. If they do, we can give it to them. I hope they are just trying to see what we are doing here and leave it at that. One thing's certain. We will find out either way." Marcus reaches us and hands Jake the shovel. "Come on. Where to?" Jake asks again. I point to the back of the clearing. "Back there, next to the fountain" I say. The back of the clearing is just dried up brown grass and weeds now. I motion with my hand, "The whole back part used to be a beautiful flower bed. I used to think that it looked like the fountain magically appeared in the midst of the flowers. They blended perfectly together."

The fountain is crumbled and decaying. Graffiti covers the gray stone it is made of. "That's about a half mile" Marcus says. Jake does not say anything but nods. "I tell you what. You guys go ahead. I need to stick by the car. I may just drive the car down there. There's plenty of room. Let's just see how it goes. Here, Jake. Take this, I'll get another." Marcus hands some type of gun to Jake. Jake instinctively checks to see if the safety is on and immediately tucks it into the back of his jeans. *That makes me nervous.* "Okay. Let's get a move on." Jake says. Marcus walks back to the car while Jake and I walk to the back of the clearing. As we approach the fountain I can see that several of the stone flowers had been knocked off. "It's sad to see this once beautiful place in such ruin. Why didn't they keep it up? They could have taken better care of the park." Jake shrugs his shoulders, "It's probably a matter of money. Everything seems to be these days. Show me where." I counted the flowers on the fountain. "The fourth flower. That's the one." I stand directly in front of it and take four steps out. "Right here. Try right here." I mark the ground with my shoe.

Jake starts to dig and I look toward the car. Marcus is standing near the car watching the intersection. Every few minutes he turns to look at us. I wave to him and he waves back. I look back at Jake just in time to see him plunge the shovel into the hard ground. His arm muscles flex as he continues. He is sexy. It doesn't matter what he is doing. He is always sexy. He always looks great, but it's the way he moves that gets me. Every move he makes is sexy. And the best part of all is that he doesn't have a clue. I watch Jake pull up three shovel mounds of black lumpy dirt. As he emptied the dirt off the shovel I realize my need and I can't stand it any longer. I have to kiss him. I walk in front of him until our chests are touching. "Jesse, what are you..." "I can't stand it anymore. I want you." I lean into him and give him a long hard kiss. He grins and shakes his head at me, "You're something else, Jesse Nicole Birchfield. And when this is all over with we're going to live happily ever after. I can't wait to make you my wife."

I sigh deeply. The sun is now beating down on us and we are both getting hot. "You're amazing" I say and kiss the good doctor again. "We'd better hurry" he says while he gently moves me out of the way. The next time he plunges the shovel into the ground it hits something. I feel like I am going to explode I'm so excited. Jake brushes away the dirt with his hands and there it is. A square metal box. "My time capsule!" I shriek with delight. Memories flood my mind again. I remember digging the hole and covering the sleek metal with the dirt. I was upset that day. I honestly thought I'd never live to uncover this time capsule. I fall to my knees next to Jake. "I can't believe it! That's it! It's still here after all this time!" Jake tugs and pulls and finally lifts it free of its lonely dark grave.

The edges are rusty and the top of the metal box is dented a little bit. Other than that it looks fine. I hope that water did not leak inside. Shouting catches our attention. At the same time Jake and I turn to see Marcus arguing with six gang members. They are standing all around him, circling him. "Oh, great!" Jake says. He firmly put the hard metal container in my hands. "Jesse, whatever happens, if I tell you to stay down you stay down. Get inside the car if you can. Got it?" "Yes" is all I can manage to say. I sprint after Jake. He is in a full run heading toward the men. I feel the contents of the time capsule shaking around inside it. I know I'm not back to normal and I'm definitely not in shape, but this little bit of running is killing me. I have to stop running and I briskly walk to the car. Jake is already there trying to assess the situation. Neither Jake nor Marcus looks in my direction. A few of the gang members watch me slide into the back seat of the car.

Marcus speaks first. "Look guys. Like I told you. We don't want any trouble. We are just out for a walk in the park. That's all. A little fresh air. So what do you say, guys. Looks like we are just leaving." In the back seat I notice that one of the black bags is open. I glance into it and see there are a few more guns and some ammunition clips. I am scared now and really don't like this whole situation. What if those guys go nuts and try to kill Marcus and Jake. Then what do I do? I see that the black briefcase is opened on the front seat. It is empty, but the foam on the inside of the case still holds the indentation of the weapon it usually held. I look to Marcus and see the bulge underneath the back of his shirt. Jake was not in the circle but standing beside one of the gang members.

"Okay, here's the deal" Jake says with authority. "You boys don't want to mess with us. We'll give you the chance to leave right now. If you choose to stay we can't be responsible for what may happen." The gang members look around at each other and start laughing at Jake. One of the gang busters is in all black and has gold chains around his neck. He has an empty machine gun clip tied around his waist as a belt. *That is not an attractive look for him.* He is a good looking muscular guy with a nice tan. He has blonde hair and brown eyes and a slight mustache. He does not look like a street thug or gang member to me. When he spoke it is clear that he is uneducated. He turns to Jake. "Why'n should we leave? This is ours park! Ain't it? What makes youz three soz special? What'n gives youz the rights to steals ours property?" "Steal your property!" Marcus shouts. "This is ridiculous. We are not stealing anything. We simply had unfinished business here. That's all. If you know what's good for you you'll leave us alone" Marcus says a little more agitated now. Jake chimes in quick, "Now, Now, Marcus. These fellows are just protective of their property. Look guys, I can understand how you'd be protective of such a prime piece of real estate in times like these. What if we pay you guys rent for the short time we have been here?"

The gang members look around at each other but say nothing. Blonde mustache speaks up, "How'z much 'rent' you'n willingz to pay?" he asks Jake. "Well, name your price boys. What do you need? I'm sure we can accommodate you." Blondie smiles. His two front teeth were actually silver caps. The sun makes them sparkle. Blondie looks at Jake and Marcus and then looks at the car. He looks back to Jake. "Youz pay us five-hundreds dollars and we'z lets youz leave." Jake takes a few steps toward Blondie. "So you're telling me if I pay you five-hundred dollars that you'll just let us leave. No fighting, no more questions?" Blondie takes a few steps toward Jake. They are approximately two feet apart now. "Yeah, sure'n will. Whyz not" he says smiling. "Well, here's the problem" Jake says. "We don't trust you guys. So even if you give us your word, how do we know you're not going to cause trouble?" "I'z guess'n youz don't. You'z twoz will'n just haz believe'n me. That's all. What'z little missy carrying when she'z got'n the car?"

"Oh, that's nothing. Just some private unfinished business" Jake says. He adds, "Pretty boring stuff. Really. I'd hate to waste your time." Blondie eyes him suspiciously and then says, "Why'z don't youz leave'n little missy anz the box here'n go bout yer biznezz." Jake shakes his head. "See now, I'm afraid I can't do that. She has to leave with us. That's how it has to be." I sit the metal box on the floorboard and I unzipped the other black bag. I can't believe what I'm seeing. Are those grenades of some sort? I feel like I'm going to be sick to my stomach. My mouth is watering and now I have no choice. I grab one of the grenades and hide it underneath my shirt as I jump out of the car and slam the door. The two gang members close to me turn to look at me. I manage to scoot in between them before I let loose. I violently throw up all over their shoes. The two thugs shake their legs and try to get the vomit off of their shoes but they don't say a thing. "You'z gross lady" Blondie says smiling at me.

"She's not feeling well. We really need to get her home. So let me pay you and we'll be off" Jake says. Marcus moves closer to me and asks if I am all right. I shake my head yes and he hands me a handkerchief. I cleaned myself up and just stand there not knowing what to do next. "You'z betz pay'z me'n evenz thouzand now'z, see'n I gotz to buyz the boyz new'z shoez." Jake smiles at me. "Marcus, you go ahead and help the lady to the car while I pay this fine gentleman." Marcus moves toward me. When he is close enough I unwrap the grenade and carefully place it in his hand. "Stay in the car, head down" he whispers as he helps me back into the car. While he is bent over he takes a small gun out of the black bag and tucks it in his waistband in the front. When he stands up I can't even tell it is there. Marcus shuts the door and walks over to Jake. "She's tucked away" he says. Jake hands the gang leader the last bill. "There you go, sir. Nice doing business with you. Now if you don't mind we will be on our way." Jake starts to turn to leave. "Notz soz fast. I'z glad to take youz moneyz'n all but we'z can't just'n letz youz leave like that." Blondie smiles a crooked smile and motion for his thugs to move in.

They are fast. All at once they are all over Jake and Marcus. I can hear punches and shouting. Blondie does not look at me. He is watching the slaughter enthusiastically. I guess we're the best entertainment they've had in a while. Marcus throws a guy off of him and within three karate moves has taken down two others. Jake gets a few good punches in before a guy jumps on top of him. He punches the guy again and throws the guy off of him. He takes a karate stance just when another guy comes at him. Jake spins around and kicks the guy in the face. He flies backward and lands with a thud. Jake still has two guys standing. He fights them until they are down. Two of the guys Marcus had grounded got back up and go after Jake. Marcus and Jake are standing next to each other. They look at each other, smile and nodded their heads in some unspoken communication. They each explode in a barrage of karate moves. Within seconds the rest of the men are down and do not get back up.

Blondie is now frowning. "You'z two fight'n purty'z good. You'z leave'n me'z no choice." He pulls out a gun from the left side of his pants. He aims it at Jake first, then at Marcus, then back to Jake. He means to kill them. I see that. But what can I do? Without even thinking about it I take one of the grenades, roll the window down, pull the pin out of it and throw it over their heads and it lands in the gang buster's car. Within seconds it explodes. The blast from the explosion knocks Blondie down, along with Jake and Marcus. Flames shoot out of the car in between clouds of thick black smoke. The other gang members start to get up. Jake and Marcus swiftly get to their feet. Blondie is still down but four of the gang members lunge at Jake and Marcus. Jake jumps out of the way and Marcus shoots them in the lower leg. They calmly walk to the car and get in. Marcus gets in the driver's seat and Jake gets in the back with me.

"You okay?" he asks me. "Yes." The car lurches to the side as Marcus spins out of the parking lot and quickly makes his way up the road and through the intersection. Once he passes the intersection he slows down. The area near the park has pretty much been deserted but now, just three blocks up, we are in normal traffic. Jake and Marcus are not even out of breath. "Nice aim" Jake says. He feels my forehead as if checking me for a fever. "You two were awesome! You guys fight awesome! I've never seen anything like that, except on TV!" Marcus turns to me and smile. "Oh, that's nothing. You should see us when we really get aggravated!" Jake smiles and shakes his head. "Forget about all that. How are you? Do you have a headache? Are you in pain anywhere?" I shake my head, "No, I'm fine, just really tired, and a little lightheaded and dizzy still. I guess it's just from running. You're fast. I couldn't keep up with you!" Jake leans over and whispers in my ear "I'll slow down later and let you catch me." He kisses my neck and we laugh. After all the excitement I have forgotten the metal box on the floorboard.

Once we are in a better part of town Marcus stops at a gas station. He quickly comes out with three bottles of water. He gets back in the car and hands me a bottle of water first. "Here, thought you could use this." I take it and say, "Thanks." I swish some water in my mouth and open the car door and spit it out. Once Marcus starts the car and we are back on the road I see the metal box on the floorboard. I quickly pick it up and run my fingers across the top of it. "Oh, Jake. I'm nervous." He puts his arm around me and squeezes me closer to him, "Go on, you can do it." I try to open the time capsule but the lid is stuck. Jake pulls out a small knife and runs it along the seam and pushes it in where he could. "Try it again" and he motions with the knife toward the container. I do and it slightly opens. I glance at Jake nervously. "Go on" he says gently. "Whatever it is, I'm right here. We are doing this together." I nod and open the box. The contents are double sealed in plastic bags. The first bag holds a large envelope. That must be the letter for Brian. I flip it over and it has his name and address on it. "There's his last name" I say to Jake.

We both look down and through the second plastic bag. I have to look twice to make sure I am seeing what I think I see. It is a used pregnancy test stick. The marks had faded over time. I could barely make out the two lines. "Oh, dear God!" Underneath it there is a picture of the marks up close. I pull the picture out and hold it up. Jake didn't say a word, he just stares at me. "No way!" Marcus stops at a red light and turns around. "What is it? What's going on?" All I can say is, "Oh, God! I'm... pregnant!" I look at Jake. "Unbelievable! How can I be pregnant? And I don't even remember taking this test! There must be a mistake!" As soon as the words leave my mouth my mind is flooded with more memories. I gasp. Memories of Brian and I fighting at the park. He doesn't want the baby and I do. He says he isn't ready for it and doesn't have time for it and that he has too much going on with his new job. Big things are about to happen for him. He can't be burdened with a wife, not to mention a child. In that split second I made my decision. It was a done deal. I'd do the project anyway. I couldn't stay now. "Jesse, what is it? Are you remembering something?" Jake asks and holds my hand. "I'm here baby, its ok, and you're safe." I hear Marcus questioning "Pregnant?" in the front seat just before I pass out.

21

I come to in the rec room. I am lying on the couch covered with a quilt. A large fluffy pillow cradles my head. I keep still with my eyes closed. I am spent. Both physically and mentally exhausted. I don't remember the events of the morning and I'm confused as to why I feel this way. It hits me like a ton of bricks. I play back the mornings events over and over again in my head. Can it be? Am I...pregnant? How can it be true? Wouldn't the deep freeze have hurt the baby? Surely they would not let me go through with it if they knew I was pregnant. Did I just not tell them? Did I hide it from them? I just don't believe it. They ran test on me. They would have found out, even if I did try to hide it. Well, Jesse, old girl. Your life just keeps getting better and better. You've certainly made a mess of things. Mom and Pop would really be proud. Not. How have I let this happen? What was I thinking? How could I be so stupid? Slowly I run my fingers over my belly. I've lost so much weight. My stomach is as flat as a pancake. I must not be far along because I'm not showing at all. A month or two, maybe. I couldn't be more than that. Talk about strange!

My whole situation is weird but this certainly brings it to a new level. I guess Brian must be the father. After that dream I had this morning he must not have wanted the baby. Was that a dream or a memory? Ugh, I have so many unanswered questions. It *must* have been a memory. When we were in the park today it was just like in my dream. When I was there today I recognized it from my dream. So it must be a memory. Sadness fills me. If it was a memory then Brian never wanted our baby. I never thought I'd be in that type of situation! I shudder at the thought of raising a baby on my own. Oh...No! I open my eyes and sit up on the couch. Oh, no. What about Jake? What will he think of this new development? He'll hate me for sure! What if he doesn't want anything to do with me? What if he sends me packing? Where will I go? What will I do? He's been so good to me. He's going to be hurt. Oh, God! What have I done? I know we are meant to be together! More so than Brian and I ever were. How will he react? How do I approach him? I have to talk to him right now.

I make my way upstairs to the bathroom. I splash cool water on my face and dry it with a wash cloth. Upon exiting the bathroom I hear dishes clanking together in the kitchen. I rush to the kitchen hoping to find Jake. Instead I find Marcus cooking a homemade vegetable soup. The aroma hits me as soon as I turn the corner. He does not hear me come in. I stand watching him hard at work. He is arranging crackers on a napkin that sits next to a bowl. I spot a tray sitting on the kitchen table. It has a bottle of water, a napkin, packs of salt and pepper and a spoon. He is startled when he sees me standing in the doorway. "Oh, hey, you're awake." He quickly rushes over to the table and pulls out a chair. "Here, sit down. You've had quite a morning." I walk over to the chair and sit down. "I was going to come down and check on you again. And bring a tray down to you. This is the best soup. There's nothing in this world that makes you feel better than a big hot bowl of this soup." He fills the bowl and carefully sits it down in front of me. In a flash he comes back with the crackers. "Smells great" I say and note that the rest of the house is quiet.

"Where's Jake? I really need to talk to him. Is he upstairs?" Marcus shook his head no. He pulls a large bowl down from the cabinet and fills the bowl with soup for himself. He grabs the rest of the pack of crackers and his water and sits them on the table. Next he picks up his soup and halfway to the table he spills it on the floor. "Shit! Fran would kill me if she knew I messed up her clean floor!" He quickly sits the soup on the table and wipes up the mess with a handful of napkins. He tosses them in the trash and sits next to me. Steam rises from our bowls. "Be careful, it is really hot" he says. "Marcus, I appreciate the soup but I really need to see Jake." He slurps his soup from his spoon. "I know you do but he's not here at the moment." My heart sinks. "What do you mean...he's not here? Where is he?" I am already nervous enough, I don't need this. Where could he have gone? He's mad at me. That's it. That's why he doesn't want to see me. I've ruined it! I have blown the only chance to be happy with the man I love! He eyes me over the rim of his water bottle. "He's out riding. Getting his thoughts together. Clearing the cobwebs. Figuring things out. He'll be back soon." I watch as Marcus slurps down more of his soup.

Tears fill my eyes. "Oh, Marcus! What have I done? He hates me now! I'm sure of it! We would have been so happy together! I know it sounds stupid because I've only known him such a short time, but I can't live without him! I know we are meant to be together! I know it! I love him and I fear I have ruined any chance of us having a future together. I've blown it!" I sob and wail with self-pity. Marcus does not say anything. He simply hands me a napkin and slurps up more soup. It takes fifteen minutes but I regain my composure. Marcus says, "Look, I know this has been tough on you. You're a real trooper to still be standing after going through everything you've been through. I want you to know this has been difficult for Jake, too. He's my best friend and I've watched him struggle with this so called 'project' for the past five years. He cares about you. It's been hard for him to see you in the past at the lab, partly because he's had his own demons to wrestle. He has overcome most of them. He struggled with what he should do with you for the past six months. He knew he had to do something."

I sigh and slurp a spoonful of soup. It is still hot but has cooled considerably. "I don't understand...what are you talking about? What do you mean 'he struggled with what to do with me'? What do you mean when you say 'he knew he had to do something'? I'm so confused!" Marcus moves his bowl aside and reaches for my hand. He gently holds my hand as he continues. "Jesse, he knew about the baby. Before today, I mean. He found the hidden notes two years ago. Plus your medical record. He put things in motion to try to get things ready for you. He had your stuff moved here and wrapped up some loose ends. He just finished last month. He confided in me, Jesse." Marcus sighs and looks down shaking his head. Then he looks me straight in the eyes. "What I'm trying to say is that it's no accident that you're here. He didn't know exactly how to do it, so he did what he thought was best. He unhooked some of the hoses, turned some knobs, ran a program or two and it was done. I'm sure it wasn't quite that simple. You get the idea. I'm trying to be honest with you here. Look, don't tell Jake I told you. Okay? I just want you to know. You're here because he wants you here. Baby and all. You haven't blown it."

I can't move. I'm shocked. Did I just hear Marcus correctly? *Does that mean that there is a chance for us after all?* "How long will he be gone? Do you know when he'll be back?" Marcus shakes his head no. "Oh, Marcus...Do you mean he defrosted me on purpose? That he wanted me to believe it was an accident?" This time he shakes his head yes. "Oh, God! Does he really still want me here? Is there really a chance for us?" Again, Marcus shakes his head yes. "Well, why is he out riding then? What's wrong? Is he all right?" Marcus sighs and shrugs his shoulders, "Jesse, I said he wants you here, but I didn't say it was easy for him. He honestly loves you. And that baby is not his. That's a lot for a man to deal with. Don't you worry. I know him better than anyone. He just needs a little time alone to get things straight in his head. He'll be back shortly and when he comes back, the past will be the past. It'll be fine, you'll see. I told him I'd stay with you until he gets back." I am lost. I feel helpless. I can only hope he is right about Jake. "Oh, Marcus...I hope you're right! I just hope you're right!" I finish my soup in silence.

Marcus clears the table. I notice the pictures, year books, the large quilt box and the smaller photo box at the opposite end of the kitchen table. "It's a beautiful day. Come on. Let's go sit outside and wait for Jake. Have you been out back yet?" I am anxious and I know I will not be able to relax until I talk to Jake. "No, I guess I haven't." "Well, you're in for a treat. Bring your water and follow me." We walk through the small hallway past the kitchen. We pass the green house door and keep to the left. The wine cellar is to our left. Marcus opens a door straight ahead of us. I am pretty sure I did not notice this door before. I am going to have to learn my way around this house better. We walk out onto a large patio area, me in my sock feet. We are standing under an enormous cabana. The canvas is navy blue, of course. It makes me smile because it reminds me of Jake's bathroom. White mosquito netting hangs down large wooden post. The navy blue canvas partly covers the mosquito netting. An exquisite wrought iron table is centered underneath the cabana. Eight matching chairs with navy cushions are neatly tucked under the table. A tall vase on the table holds a large arrangement of white and blue fluffy hydrangea interspersed with a mixture of greenery that makes it absolutely breathtaking. Large grapevine planters surrounded the patio. They hold beautiful arrangements of flowers I don't know the names of. Green spikes protrude up and out from behind the colorful flowers.

Marcus pulls out a couple of chairs and we sit quietly. On the left of the door we have just passed through is a wet bar, backed up to the house. A gardener's rack is on the right side of the door. It's filled with potted red and white geraniums, ferns, white petunias and a wandering Jew. On the bottom shelf there is a pair of dirty gloves and a small gardening shovel crusted over with dried potting soil. "Wow" is all I can say. Originally, I thought the house was in a valley. Now I see that the house is actually on a large hill. The area immediately following the patio is flat. However, in the distance, I see that the lush green grass slopes down and out to what seems like a hundred acres of rolling hills. As far as my eyes can see there are only trees, green grass and rolling hills. The immediate area following the patio is beautifully landscaped. A large fountain is in the center. Water is spewing up and out in all directions. Scantily dressed women hold urns from which the water is flowing and cascading down large flat stones. The water flows over the stones and adds to the wow factor of this beautiful space. The water is a soothing sound in my ears.

Flowers surround the fountain. A thick green hedge maze is directly behind the fountain and spans out six feet on both sides of the fountain. To the sides of the maze are beautifully landscaped pockets of flowers. To the left of the cabana in the distance are a gazebo and an arched trellis that is filled with red climbing roses. A large wrought iron bench with a navy cushion sits directly under the roses. "This is so beautiful" I murmur. To the right of the cabana is a large brick grill. It has four cooking areas built into the surface. The grill is situated in such a way that cooks can stand on both sides of the grill at the same time. Marcus sees me looking at the grill. "I'm sure one day Jake will host fabulous parties here. To date he has had none. Charlie and I did come by and have a couple of cookouts with him. Nothing fancy. A birthday bash for Charlie and a Fourth of July cookout last summer. As far as I know we're the only guests he's entertained here, besides you, that is."

I take a drink of my water and ask "Who's Charlie?" I listen while Marcus tells me about his girlfriend of five years. He smiles and looks happy when he talks about her. He says they would be married this year. That Jake and I would have to attend. He confides in me that he just couldn't get married and leave Jake alone. That he was waiting on 'me' for Jake. I am surprised to hear this and note that Marcus is a dear friend indeed. He does not want his happiness to contribute to Jake's loneliness. Wow. Marcus is truly a nice guy. No wonder Jake is friends with him. Marcus talks about Charlie for another ten minutes. I am thankful for the distraction. Two security guys walk around the maze and flowers. Once satisfied they walked to the far ends of the house and finally disappear around the corners. "Jake already has a security team tracking down this Brian. Now that they have his last name and a previous address they'll have him located by sunrise. Hell, quicker than that. Probably within the next two hours. Just thought I'd mention it to you." "Thanks" I say with my head lowered.

Marcus looks down quickly at his watch as it starts beeping loudly. He pushes a button and Jake's voice filled the air. "Hey Marcus, you there buddy? What's going on? Is she awake yet?" I hear the anxiety in his voice. Movement in front of us catches my eye. I look past the fountain and landscape to see Jake topping a hill in the distance. He rides down the hill and out of sight. Moments later he reappears topping the next hill. Marcus was talking into his watch, telling Jake we are sitting outside waiting for him. Marcus teases Jake, telling him lunch was delicious and it's too bad we didn't save him any. I hear Jake laugh through the watch. "You know I'll kick your ass" he says to Marcus and this makes me grin. "You guys sit tight, I'll be there in a minute." Marcus and I watch Jake ride up and over the last hill. As he quickly approaches us Marcus shakes his head. "I told him not to run'em like that. Now I'll have to walk'em to the stables and cool him down. Will probably have to give'em a quick bath to get the sweat off him." I look to Marcus and say "I hope you're talking about the horse and not Jake." We both laugh.

Jake is now just four feet away from the cabana. Once he stops the horse he looks at me, glances at Marcus and then locks his gaze back on me. As he climbs off the horse and walks the horse closer he does not take his eyes off me. He hands the reigns to Marcus, who mutters something about Jake running the horse too much. "I need to cool'em down and clean'em up. I'll be in the stable if you need me." He walks the horse around the corner and out of sight. Jake never takes his eyes off me. Not knowing what to do I stand up and walk over to him. We stand looking at each other for what seems like an eternity. What do I do? What can I possibly say to him? I see he's hurt. All at once Jake smiles at me and pulls me to him. He gives me a long tight hug and then takes a step back. "Shall we sit?" he asks. He leads me to the table and we sit in the same chairs Marcus and I occupied moments before. He reaches over and holds my hands. "I'm sorry I wasn't here when you came to. I needed time to get my thoughts together. How are you feeling? Better?" I nod, "I'm fine. How about you? How are you...with all this?" I am not sure I'm ready for his answer. He sighs.

"Well, I did a lot of thinking this last hour and a half. Mostly about you. I thought about my parents too. About how everything finally fits together in my life. Here's the thing. I know there are still some things to work out, but I've made my decision. I still want to spend the rest of my life with you, if you'll let me." Tears fill my eyes. "I do love you and want to be with you. The baby's father will obviously not be a part of his or her life, and he or she will need someone to look up to. Someone to teach him - or her - about animals, about cooking, about picnics, about baseball, about sports in general, about life...about love." Jake pulls some tissue from his pocket and wipes away my tears. "I have made my decision. I want to be that person...if you let me. Will you still marry me Jesse? Will you let me be a father in every sense of the word?" I am amazed again by this handsome and humble man sitting in front of me. "I don't want to lose either one of you. What do you say, Jesse? What's your answer?" I think those are the most beautiful words I have ever heard. I am bursting with happiness and for a moment cannot speak.

"Oh, Jake. Yes, I want to be with you. I think you'll be an incredible father. Are you sure it's what you want to do? I just want to be sure... I just want us to be happy." He squeezes my hands, "I have never been more sure of anything in my life!" I get up and sit in his lap. "You are an incredible man, an incredible lover, and now my best friend." We kiss and Jake presses something into my hand. I look down at a small ring box. I gasp when I open it. A large diamond ring with a gold band sparkles in the sunlight. Jake smiles at me. "Now, that *is* an engagement ring" he says with his heart stopping beautiful grin getting bigger. I sit still, shocked. After the initial shock wears off, I move the diamond and sapphire ring that was once his mothers to my ring finger on my right hand. He takes the engagement ring out of the case and slips it on my ring finger of my left hand. In this moment I think I am the happiest I can ever be. "Oh, Jake! It's beautiful!" His eyes are locked on me, "No...you're beautiful. I want to spend the rest of my life waking up to your beautiful face. We will never be apart from this day forward." Tears fall to my cheeks and he gently wipes them away. "Thank you. You've made me the happiest woman alive! Thank you!" I hug him tight and throw my arms around his tan neck.

"Well, I wouldn't say that" Jake says. I just look at him not understanding what he meant. He nods toward the stables, "Now Charlie will be the happiest woman alive. Marcus will finally marry her. She's been after him for the last two years to get married. I know the reason he hasn't already married her. He felt bad about leaving me alone. He'd never admit it to me but I know that's it." I shake my head yes and kiss Jake. "You're right. He just told me about her...and that he didn't want to get married until you had me. So you wouldn't be alone." "I knew it! He'd never admit it to me, but I always knew it!" I kiss his neck and corner of his mouth. "I think this is his way of admitting it to you". Jake hugs me tight and nuzzles my neck. After snuggling a while he puts me on my feet and stands beside me. "I think you're right. Now come and talk to me while I eat a bowl of soup. I'm starving; then again, I'm always starving. And we have a wedding to plan." Beaming, I follow him to the kitchen.

22

We sit for a good hour at the kitchen table talking about Marcus and Charlie, planning our union, and also about what needs to take place in the immediate future. We both agree that if I can get in touch with Brian it would be best. Possibly bring some closure to past me, allowing present me to move forward...to live happily. "I have my guys working on finding Brian. We should hear from them tonight or tomorrow. Last I heard there were three or four possibilities. Two of them right here in town. One in the next town over. Another one in Aspen. So we'll see which one is our Brian, and then we'll go pay him a surprise visit." Marcus didn't mention that they had the search down to four guys. "Wow" is all I say. I don't know if I should mention that Marcus had already told me that the search was on. I watch Jake carry the dirty dishes to the sink. He turns and stares at me. "Sometimes I feel overwhelmed by my love for you." Huh? What? That may be the sweetest thing anyone has ever said to me. "Oh, Jake...you don't have to..." He walks over to me, takes my hands and pulls me to him. In my ear he whispers "Oh baby I do, I am never going to waste a single minute with you. I am going to enjoy every moment of our life together. I watched as work and politics forced wedges between my parents. It wasn't often, just three or four times. They always made up... they were really never apart anyway. But you see they could never regain that lost time. I think it's something they both came to regret in the end. The what if's. That will never happen to us. I will never take you for granted...I love you now and forever." He lifts my chin and gently kisses me. My hand in his, I follow his lead to the rec room.

We sit on the couch and Jake flips channels. There's really nothing on that either of us want to watch. "All these channels and you'd think something good would come on!" Jake tosses the remote on the floor. "What do you feel like doing?" he asked. "I don't know" I say as I lie on the couch and put my feet on his lap. He slowly rubs my sock feet and I close my eyes. This is much better than hanging out down here alone, I think to myself. Despite the events of the day, I am full of energy. Not really tired now. Maybe it's just adrenaline from all that's happened today. I don't know, but I need to do something physical. "Jake, what do you want to do?" He shrugs his shoulders. "I don't know either. I guess we could just sit here and talk." My mind starts to wander to the possibilities. "What do you do when you're here by yourself?" "Sometimes I lie on the rug and read. Sometimes I have one too many drinks and fall asleep on this couch with the TV on. Sometimes I play video games. Often times I sit here in this very spot and wonder about you...about what it would be like to hold you in my arms...to kiss you." I grin shyly. "Do you really...think of me like that?" He grins his shy, boyish grin and my breath hitches in my chest. "Yes, I can't tell you how often...but not anymore, now that I have the real girl!" He squeezes my legs and climbs on top of me, careful not to put all of his weight on me. He hugs me and then smiles ear to ear saying, "I know exactly what we can do! Let's go for a swim!"

He jumps up and starts stripping, leaving a trail of clothes behind him on the floor. I can't help but laugh at him and join him. It does sound like fun to me. By the time he reaches the pool he is gloriously naked. I am three feet behind him. I watch his lean body dive into the water. I am a little slower at undressing than he is and I go to the dressing room to finish undressing. All the while I can hear him splashing around. I walk out and to the edge of the pool. He stands still and watches my every move. "You are beautiful, you know. Brian was a fool!" I smile at him, thinking of my sad past. Jake stays put, as if to give me my space. I slowly lower myself into the water expecting it to be cold. Instead, it was warm, a nice surprise. Jake does some laps while I paddle around and do a side stroke to the deep end. The bar is just two feet to my left. "Oh, Jake. Let's have a swim party here after we're married. That would be so much fun!" Jake laughs at my enthusiasm.

"Well, I don't know anyone to invite" he blurts out. "The only people I really know are Marcus and Charlie. I mean, the guys that work for me and their families...I don't really know them...personally." "Don't you see?" I splash toward him now. "It would be a great opportunity to forge new friendships. I want our child to have so many friends that he or she never gets bored!" I am now standing in the warm water in front of Jake, who is as still as the surrounding statues. I do not realize what I said to bring tears to his eyes. Jake smiles and I wipe a tear from his cheek. He draws me in with his left arm and puts his right hand on my belly. "Our child" he says softly. I finally understand. "Thank you, Jess. I promise to become this child's father in every sense of the word. He or she will never feel unwanted or unloved. I promise you..." I hug him. He is a wonderful man. "Come on" Jake says. "I'll race you two to the shallow end." His words ring in my ears. 'Two' is correct. I guess I'd better start thinking of myself that way. It's weird though. As I stand here mulling it over in my head Jake beats me to the shallow end.

He gets us towels and we sit and talk a while longer. He is going to make arrangements for a small wedding, yet very lavish, as soon as we finish this business with Brian. In addition, he will offer the use of the grounds and also pay for the wedding for Marcus and Charlie. Our gift to them. We dress and go back to the rec room. I sit at the bar and watch as Jake pulls out some chips and dip and a couple bottles of water. The TV is still on and I watch a baby kangaroo climb into his mother's pouch and get comfortable for the night. The phone rings and Jake answers it behind the bar. I didn't even realize there was a phone back there. I listen while trying not to listen. I feel like I am eavesdropping even though Jake knows I am here. "Uh huh, okay...I see...when and where? How much does he know? That, we can do...yes...it's a done deal, thanks. If I need to change anything I'll buzz you. Later." Jake hangs up the phone and sighs. I know something is wrong by his expression.

"Jake, what's wrong? Who was that? Was that about finding Brian? What is it? Jake, tell me...please." He comes around the bar and sits next to me. I watch him pop a chip in his mouth and chase it with half of his water. He turns to face me. "Jesse, here's the thing. I had my suspicions but had to wait for proof. There's no easy way to say this so I am just going to say it. You're not going to believe this, but...Brian is behind the threats...Jesse, Brian is the one that wanted the whole project terminated!" I can't move. I gulp down air and hang on to the side on the bar as my head spins. "It can't be, Jake...it just can't be." I feel weak all over. A shudder runs down my spine. I'm sure all the color has left my cheeks. "There must be some mistake...Jake, how can this be? It has to be a mistake!" Could the father of my baby be so ruthless? He gives me a minute to process it all. "I am sorry but there's no mistake. I am so sorry baby." He takes me in his arms and holds me until I can compose myself. I look up to him with red eyes "Are you sure Jake?" He nods his head. "Yeah, baby, I'm sorry but ... I'm sure." I run my hands across my face and wipe my eyes. If there's one thing I've learned about Jake, it's that he is a careful and deliberate man. I know he'd never say a thing like that unless he had proof and there was absolutely no doubt.

As I study his face it is clear that there is more. I am a determined and stubborn woman. I say, "Okay, then...that's just one more thing I need to address with Brian. I will not be fearful of him...I just won't. You and Marcus will be with me, right? What else is there?" Jake remains silent and I shake my head. "Come on, Jake. Just tell me. Let's get this over with. When do we meet with him? Is he the one you need to speak with... about me? How do we go about it?" Jake leads me to the couch and turns the TV off. It hums quietly as it retreats to its hiding place. I sit and listen, dumbfounded, as Jake explains the rest to me. Turns out he's known about Brian for years. Every since he found the 'hidden notes' as Marcus had put it. He's been tracking Brian for a while. He thinks Brian found out about it and had a couple of his men killed. After their deaths Jake lost track of Brian. He's been looking for him every since. He'd get good leads and then Brian would disappear again. Jake said it seems this time that Brian wanted to be found. Probably, because of me. "Listen, Jess. Don't get ahead of yourself. First I will need to meet with him alone. Marcus of course will drive me. I need to negotiate the specifics with him. He is a dangerous man. I know it's hard for you to believe, but that's what he's become. Really dangerous."

Deflated but still angry I want more answers. "So, how will this work? When will you meet with him? Will you offer him a payoff like you mentioned before? When can we put this whole thing behind us?" Jake tries to reassure me and repeatedly rubs his thumb across the back of my hand. "I know you're anxious, as am I. I shall meet with him tomorrow afternoon at a popular cafe downtown. You will remain here, under the watchful eyes of my security." I throw my hands up in the air in a frustrated gesture. "Why Jake, I should be there!" He quickly shakes his head no. "I only have your safety in mind. Once I meet with him and see what he wants and what he agrees to, then I'll arrange for you to meet with him. You can give him the letter and discuss what you need to discuss. This will be the one and only meeting between you two so get your thoughts together. Write them down if you need to. Just know what you're going to say ahead of time. He is a cunning and talented debater from what I'm told. He uses words to his advantage. With ease he changes people's minds and opinions with a few words. He's slick, I'll give him that. He will probably be nothing like the guy you remember."

"It's so hard to believe that he is 'dangerous' as you say. I mean... the guy I remember was kind and generous. I know I wouldn't have been with him if he wasn't. Although he did cheat on me and I did at times see what I considered to be a dark side to him. Everyone has their own personal demons. I just assumed he'd work through them and we'd be happy together. I guess I'm still in shock about this whole thing." Jake nods yes. "How did he rise to such a position to be able to make threats to my project? Do you know what happened to him? How he got this way? And which of the four possibilities did he turn out to be, by the way?" "He's been living in Aspen I'm told. You remember the new job he had just before your project began?" "Yes." Indeed I do. He wouldn't be strapped down with a wife, much less a child because of his new job! He didn't want to be burdened with us. He was about to begin work on some big thing that would require most of his time. Deep rooted anger seethed in my heart and soul. When I see him I'll give him a piece of my mind!

Jake continues, "He worked on numerous special projects to learn the ropes so to speak. In a short time he became very good at what he did. I don't know what he told you when you were uh...dating, but he actually worked in a cryonics lab. He worked his way up to a project manager on numerous small, insignificant projects. All very successful by the way. Then he hit the big time. They were going to offer him the position of Operations Chief on a human cryonics project. Turns out, he was the one who took over your particular project!" I become dizzy. How can this be possible? The room starts to spin. "Jess, are you okay? You look like you're going to pass out!" I take some deep breaths. "No, I'll be okay. I thought he worked at a nursing home when we were together. I don't remember the particular name. He was a doctor. I think he wanted to study Alzheimer's disease. It seems that he was fascinated with it. That he was doing a lot of research on it. He told me he wanted to find a cure. To help people. Never mind. Just, go on. I need to know."

"If you're sure you're okay." I take another deep breath and nod. "Yes, please continue." "Well, he didn't exactly lie to you. He was involved in Alzheimer's research. The first couple of projects he did were along those lines. He took a job at another lab. An entry level position on an animal cryonics project. This lab had many more research projects in progress around the same time. Often times he'd question employees working on other projects. Word got around that he was doing so and many of those project managers questioned him. He'd always tell them the same thing... that he was just trying to learn as much as he could and he wanted to head a project of his own someday. He said he was just trying to prepare himself. The top scientist in that company took notice of him. They watched his progress over the next few years. They watched as he successfully completed four projects as project manager. They saw great potential in him. They offered him a training program for a human cryonics project. It took him about three years of non-stop on the job training. You see, he had already read so much on the subject that he was pretty knowledgeable prior to his entering the training group. At the end of his three year training he was allowed to be a part of the team that worked with that young girl I mentioned to you before."

I don't really remember what he's talking about. "Jake, all of this. Are you sure?" He stands up and stretches his legs. "I'm positive." "What young girl are you talking about? So much has happened, I'm sorry, I don't remember. Give me a refresher." "The first night you were here, in front of the fire, I told you about that nineteen year old girl that was a test subject for a year. Two years later she married her boyfriend and the next year she had a baby. Remember?" "Oh yeah, I do remember you telling me about her. The no side effects girl." "Yeah, you got it." Jake stands still in front of the couch. Thoughts rush through my mind. If I agreed to my project after that nineteen year old girl's project, then that means Brian was working in Cryonics when we were together! Is that possible? He was always home in the evenings. Well, most of the evenings, anyway. I know some nights he worked late, but it wasn't that often. How did he do it? I didn't notice anything back then, did I?

"Jake, I'm trying to figure it all out. So, if he was involved in the young girl's project...and mine was after hers...then he was already involved in this when I knew him. Is that what you're telling me?" Jake lowered his eyes and shuffled his feet. "I'm afraid so." My mind is racing and I am still confused. "But, Jake, how can this be? He was young himself. Just six years older than me, I think. There has to be a mistake. How could he have pulled that off?" He nods as if indicating he knows what I am getting at. "He is very smart, Jesse. Incredibly smart. He has a mind that is leaps and bounds ahead of normal people. He graduated High School young and finished two Master's Degrees in college at the age most normal people graduate High School. On the side, he invested heavily in numerous different companies and they all did well. He saved and invested more and more each year. Before long he was a millionaire." I sigh, confused and hurt.

"So, you're saying that during the three years we were together, he was working on that young girl's project?" "Yes, that's what I'm saying." "I don't think I knew about any of that. In fact, I'm positive I didn't. I know I didn't know anything about the money. I remember we both worked every day...to make ends meet!" "Jesse, I hate to say this, but he made millions when he was with you. The numbers don't lie." Okay, now I really hate him even more. How could he do this to me? "That bastard! I hate him!" I stand up and pace around the room. If this is true...how could I have been so stupid? "Jake, I do remember he spent a lot of evenings on the computer. He said it was an internet thing. I read a lot or watched TV. That was his time and I never bothered him. I entertained myself and considered that time to be 'my time'. So do you think he might have been actually working...from home? Is it possible that he was working on that girl's project from our home?" I pace faster back and forth in front of the couch. God help me! I am just realizing the totality of my pathetic situation!

"Yes, it is possible. Come on, Jess. Don't beat yourself up about not knowing. I told you...he's smart. Look on the bright side. The more we talk the more you seem to remember." I stop dead in my tracks. I had blurted out my last words so naturally. "Oh, Jake...you are right! I did just remember more!" He comes over and hugs me. "Now, Jess. You'll remember more. I'm sure of it. For now, just know in your heart that he's a snake. He lied to you. I do think he loved you in his own way. I mean, how could he not! And I'm not sure that his involvement in cryonics has anything to do with your volunteering for your project. Honestly. It could be two totally separate things. It may just be a coincidence. However, it is my belief that once your project was well under way, when the Operations Chief suddenly passed away...suspiciously I might add...when Brian was picked to take over your project...it was all very dubious. You had been frozen for nearly twenty years when Brian took over your project."

"Whoa, that's a long time. What was he up to in those twenty years?" "Well, best I can tell is that he worked on different projects doing different things. He finessed his rough around the edges approach. He became a worldly man, living abroad and helping other countries with their pro-grams. He speaks four or five different languages. He grew wealthier and more powerful as the years progressed. He always kept tabs on you though, no matter where he was or what he was doing. I'm sure of that." I know that this will take its toll on me later tonight. I am numb to it right now. Later when I have time to actually stop and think about it...well, I hope I don't have a nervous breakdown or something. I feel nauseous and weak now. I need to just sit down and breathe. It would be really gross to throw up my soup. I shudder as chills travel from my head to toes. I am not cold. Instead I know its Brian's ruthlessness and what he's become that caused chills down my spine. I go to the other couch I had been lying on earlier. I wrap the quilt around me and walk back in front of the couch where Jake and I have been sitting. I bounce down in disgust and just stare at the stitching of the quilt.

"I thought the government was in control of my project. How could Brian have gotten involved if the government was supposed to be in charge?" Jake laughs. "Well, that's the answer. The government always seems to mess up everything...or so it seems these days. Fact is that Brian was working with them in the beginning. All of the politicians knew about him. He was famous at that point. However, after threats and too many payoffs to trail, he got control of the whole thing. For at least the last ten years there has been no government involvement. I am just thankful that my father was involved for a while. He helped to protect you, along with a few other scientists. In the end, when everything fell apart, I knew I couldn't leave you...I knew I had a duty to protect you...so, that's what I've done." I take a deep breath. Wow. "This is all so crazy. I never would have guessed my life would turn out like this. I should be a happy old lady by now, tending to my garden and grandchildren. You know, baking and helping in fund raisers or working with charities. Not this life now. How bizarre. And the baby! It's just the icing on the cake. In a way I'm disap-pointed in myself."

Jake sits next to me on the couch and lifts my chin. "Oh, Jess, this baby will be a gift of a lifetime. It doesn't matter who the father is or even when you got pregnant. God is giving you your own special angel to look after for a while. Enjoy it while you can. He or she will be gone all too soon. When you are a beautiful old lady, with time for gardening and grandchildren, I'm sure you will have incredible memories to look back on.

And I better be part of them!" He smiles and I can't help but smile back at him. I really don't deserve him. "I promise, you will" I say and lean over to hug him. "Jake, I have all these thoughts going through my mind. It's overwhelming. It's so hard to believe that Brian was involved in all of this when I knew him. I guess I read him wrong. I never suspected a thing. I was so stupid!" He shakes his head no, "Not at all. He has always been good at what he does. Lying is a big part of what he does. He has people all over the world fooled. And the ones he can't fool he pays off. He's built an impressive scientific following along with a not so legitimate delinquent following. He has criminals of all levels willing to do his bidding. Mostly because he pays them well."

"What I find amazing is that you were able to find all of this out. Your guys must be really good to find out all of this stuff. And you could have just left me frozen and things would be a lot easier for you." Jake squeezes me to him. "I didn't want easy...I wanted you...and the baby. You're right though...my guys are really good. You're learning about this all at once but remember, it took me years to piece all this information together, little bits of information at a time. Sometimes it was really frustrating for me." I imagined Jake sitting next to frozen me in the lab, getting reports from his men about a sighting or a payoff. I imagine his men busting through doors when they thought Brian was there only to find they had been evaded yet again. "I guess it has been. Thank you, for hanging in there. For not giving up on me." He shoots me an annoyed look. "Oh baby, I never have given up on you and I never will." We share a warm smile. "I'm not angry with you. For not telling me sooner, I mean. I do understand why you didn't want to drop this bombshell without the proof to back it up. Is that it? Do I know everything now? Or is there more?" Jake turns to face me on the couch. "That's it. You've heard pretty much everything now. I'm glad you're not angry with me. I've worried about that. I had visions of you never forgiving me. To be honest...I just couldn't handle that. I know you may not understand it now, but I need you Jess. Probably more than you need me." He kisses me softly and I melt into him. I sit quietly next to Jake and I know I do need to prepare myself to see Brian.

"Listen. If you don't mind I'd like to go hang out in my apartment for a while. Just to look at my stuff. Who knows, maybe I'll remember even more about my life. Do you want to come with me?" I sense his trepidation. "Uh, no...you go on. I need to tie up some loose ends and get ready for tomorrow.   You should start going over in your head what you want to say to Brian. I have some paperwork to finish up in my office and then I may take a walk. There are some remarkable walking trails in the back. Ask Fran tomorrow and she can point them out for you if you'd like to try them. Fran will be here in the morning bright and early. Don't be shocked if she wakes you with a smile and a breakfast tray. She's notorious for that." His grin shows he has experience regarding the subject. "If you decide to stay in your apartment tonight I understand. If you decide to stay in the house, that's fine too. Just look for me...I'll be around." "Okay. Thanks for understanding.   I just want to process all of this and rifle through every- thing again." With that I stand and leave him. As I pass the pool I smell the aroma from the flowers mixed with a slight chlorine smell.

Upon entering my apartment I go through it one room at a time, looking at all my stuff and touching items as I pass them. I go through all of my photo albums again. I think a lot about the meeting that is to take place the next day. I really want everything to go well so I can meet with Brian. I decide to make note cards with my questions for Brian, in case I forgot them when I am face to face with him. I find a notebook in a kitchen drawer and write down my list of questions. I have seven questions in all. Not too many, yet just enough to find out what I need to know. I will need to make it quick. The thought of being in his presence for very long disgusts me. I hate him. I hate him for doing this to me. I hate him for wanting to destroy me and our child. I hate him for hurting me, for being a liar. I hate him for being rich. I hate him for slapping me. I hate him for not dying in the accident. I hate the thought of him existing. In the secret confines of my mind I pray that he will be the one who is destroyed. How can I get even with him? What could I possibly do to repay his thought- fulness? Somehow, someway, I will have my revenge on him. I don't have criminals at my service so I'm at a disadvantage. What can I do to him? I'll keep working this little problem in the back of my mind, where it's well hidden from the world. Maybe dwelling on it a while will produce some sort of action I can take. There must be something...some plan I can put into action that will cut the cord and kill the monster!

23

I fix a sandwich for myself and wash it down with water. Glancing at the clock I see it's already ten o'clock. Wow, the time flies when you're having fun...or planning revenge! The thought of sleeping here crosses my mind but I quickly think about Jake and I change my mind. I need to move on with my life. I can't hide out here all the time. I must think of Jake. I admit to myself that among my things...this *is* where I feel the most comfortable right now. With my past surrounding me. Yet I know I must forge ahead. I fold my list of questions and tuck it into my pocket. After I turn out the lights I go into the main house. Jake has left a light on over the bar for me. I walk over to turn it off and that's when something catches my eye. At the very front of the rec room, to the left as you enter, where the games are, I see something peculiar. I rub my eyes thinking I must be seeing things. Nope, it's still there. The pinball machine is moved forward and to the left. There is a small door that is actually the back of the pinball machine. The doorway itself is only about four and a half feet tall and maybe two and a half or three feet wide. Soft light spills out onto the floor and illuminates a small wedge of hardwood.

As I draw closer I see Jake slumped over at his desk with a banker's lamp on. The desk is centered in the room and is large. There are four bookshelves behind him that are full of books about the medical field, cryonics and computers. Peeking around the corner I see on the right wall bookshelves full of American Medical Association magazines. I walk over to them. He's got them in order by date, the first of which dates back to early 1990. The most recent is this month's issue. I see his diploma proudly matted and displayed above the bookshelves behind his desk. Above the magazine bookshelves there is a large print of a hunting scene. There are a few more prints of hunting scenes on the two side walls. These prints are much larger. The frames alone must have cost a fortune! I see boxes all along the side wall that I'm nearest to. They are stacked three high. A couple on top are opened and they are filled with files and papers that are bound together. There are two boxes next to Jake's desk. He has half the contents of the top box spread out on his desk. His head rest on them and he is fast asleep. He is so adorable when he sleeps. I could stare at him forever. It looks to me like he does this often, which makes me very sad. He deserves to be happy. Well, so much for his well hidden office!

"Jake...hey...Jake, wake up" I whisper so as not to alarm him. I get no response so I go over, lean across his desk and gently shake him. He stirs. Finally, he lifts his head and rubs his eyes. "Oh, hey baby, I guess I fell asleep." Rubbing his eyes makes him look like a young boy just waking up. I grin because I love it that he looks like that. "I am just going up to bed. Are you ready to turn in?" He looks at the papers spread out on his desk. "I guess I am...I didn't realize I am so tired. This is not the most exciting reading either. It's enough to put anyone to sleep." He smiles as he stands and stretches. He looks very academic behind his desk. "Go ahead and exit and I'll turn off the light" he says. I do as I am told. When he turns off the light a red light at the top of the pinball machine comes on. He steps out of the doorway and runs his hands under the belly of the pinball machine. About midway he finds what he is looking for. "Here's the button" he shows me. He pushes it once and the pinball machine slides back into place against the wall. Whoa...that's amazing. I can't even tell where the doorway is. It's completely covered by the game and invisible to the naked eye. "Wow, now that is so cool! You're right, it is well hidden. No one could ever tell there's an office back there." He smiles looking quite proud of himself.

"Yeah, I like it down here. I'm right here by the bar, so, if I get hungry I don't have to go far. Also, if I decide to just hang I'm right here by the tv, and the bathrooms." What? I didn't know there were bathrooms down here. "What bathrooms? You know, I've been going upstairs this whole time. I didn't see any bathrooms down here." A stunned look spreads over his face, "I am so sorry. I guess I forgot to show you. When you enter the rec room to your right there are two sectioned panels right there. I keep them closed and they do blend in nicely with the wall. You have to really look to see them. Anyway, the left is the men's and the right is the women's. I had them built separately for entertaining purposes. So far, they haven't really been used for that yet. Each bathroom has six stalls, two rows of sinks and computerized paper-right machines. During parties though, I shall have attendants in both offering dry warm towels along with mints or chocolates." What? I can't control myself and I laugh out loud.

"Jake, you never cease to amaze me! I just have one question. What is a paper-right machine?" I watch him shake his head at me and grin in the glow of the red light. "Oh baby, you have a lot to catch up on! I'll show you later. It's like the paper towel dispensers of old. Except it's a computerized machine that dispenses just the right amount of paper with a wave in front of the sensor. Except it doesn't dispense paper, it rolls out a more absorbent and anti-bacterial cloth like towel that stays attached to the roll. Once it's used it gets rolled onto a second roller at the back of the machine. It's also more sanitary because when the roll's been used up it drops that one out of the back of the machine to be discarded and immediately lowers the next roll for use. It's great because you never have to manually refill the rolls. When the machines are installed they are filled with twenty-five rolls. When the machine is down to the last four rolls, it automatically notifies the company. They come out within a week and refill the machine. I am still only on my third roll since I've moved into this house."

"Wow, that's crazy. I guess you're right. I will need to learn all of these new gadgets." He takes my hand, "All in good time" he says. We walk out of the rec room and head up the stairs. I look back and see the red light go out by itself. To keep from tripping on the stairs I hang onto Jake's waist. We make it to the main floor and my legs protest as we start up the second stairway. "All these stairs kill me" I say, trying not to sound out of breath. Jake turns and scoops me up in his arms. "I'm sorry. I guess I'm just use to them. Where to? Your place or mine, ma'am?" I flash him my best devilish grin, "Definitely yours, Mr. Bradley." He slightly grins and starts back up the stairs. He carefully sits me on the edge of the bed. "I'm going to take a quick shower. You just make yourself at home and do what you need to do. I think you have a sense of where everything is now. I'll be out in about ten minutes." While he is showering I go to my own room and I put on a nightgown and quickly brushed through my hair. I run a warm washcloth over my face and brush my teeth. I quickly retrace my steps and go back to his room. I climb into his bed and pull the covers up. Who would have guessed my life would turn out this way? Not me. And certainly not my family or friends.

I am almost asleep when I feel Jake get in bed and put his arm around me. I start to turn over and he whispers "Shhh, go back to sleep" in my ear. Before I drift off to sleep, I smell his soap on his skin, masculine and delicious. The day has taken its toll on me and I am exhausted. I sleep hard for hours. Like a rock. In the wee hours of the morning, Brian somehow finds a way into my dreams and it is there that he torments me. In the beginning of my dream I am in my apartment alone, cleaning. I am straightening up Brian's papers he's left spread all over the living room table. I organize them as best I can and then put them on the computer desk, where more papers are strewn about. I try to organize them as well. At first I don't notice it. Just as I am about to complete my daunting task I see it...the article that would change my life forever. It is about the contest and how they would have to scrap the whole thing if they couldn't find someone in the next two weeks.

I read on, very interested. Sounds like something I might have done before, but not now. I just can't now that we're having a baby. Brian doesn't know yet. I'll tell him today at our weekly lunch at the park. He'll be so surprised. I can't wait to see his reaction. We'll just need to move the wedding up a couple of months so I can fit into my dress. That's what I'm really worried about, his reaction to *that*. I know he's been working so hard lately and he has been somewhat distracted. I know there's something big he is going to start soon. I guess I'd better approach him with all this before he starts on his new project. So, I guess today's as good as any. The article goes on about how the process has been perfected and it's completely safe now. How medicine will change in the next twenty-five years because of this new emerging field of study. Several of the involved top scientists are listed as some of the best minds in the world. They are described as being honest, caring men with a passion for science.

The first one is quoted, "I got involved in this particular field of study because I was curious. Now that I have grasps these concepts, I only want to serve my country in its efforts to surpass the technological advances of other countries and keep our great nation in the front of the race. These applications hold great hope... not just for the field of cryonics, but also to fight disease and help our aged citizens lead more full and happy lives. This information must be guarded. Terrorist must not get their hands on this technology, for it would prove to be most devastating!" The article concludes with an address of who to contact if a person is interested in finding out more about the particular program and how to apply. I close the magazine and put it on the top of the neatly arranged papers. I dust the living room and vacuum my pineapple rug, and notice I am running late. Shit.

I rush into the bedroom to change. When I emerge I look like a totally together woman, ready to picnic. I pack our lunch and head downstairs. The exact moment I descend the top stair Brian pulls up. I jump in and we drive to the park. We talk about going to see a movie over the weekend, although we can't agree on which one. We decide on Mexican food Friday night and Italian Saturday night. At the park things go well at first. We spread our blanket out and have gone for a walk. We sit watching families play together. Frisbees fly in the air every which way. Both dogs and kids catch them. The heated discussion begins and we are under heavy scrutiny from the other park dwellers. Then he slaps my face and jumps up. He throws his hands up in the air as he walks away. I throw things at him. The truck, my scream, the accident. Brian flies through the air, landing with a thud. I rush over. Soon the ambulance, the paramedic... and who the fuck is Katy? I get in Brian's car and follow the ambulance to the hospital. Turns out he has more than a couple of broken ribs, some of which have punctured his right lung and damaged the left one. They think he may have a bruised heart to go with his fractured right leg and a broken right arm. There is a strong possibility he'd have a concussion and they are worried about brain damage from the impact to his head. At the moment, he is unconscious and they have him in intensive care.

I sit next to his bed for a while. Talking about the things we'd do once he gets better. How this will be a small setback but in the end, he'll get well and we will get back to normal. I tell him I'd call his family in Delaware. I promise I'd take time off work to nurse him back to health at home. I sit quietly for a few minutes, thinking about how the future may be. What if he does have brain damage? What if he is a vegetable and I have to work and take care of him and the baby? What if he has to be in a wheelchair the rest of his life? There's no way I could manage to care for him that way. I'd be horrible at it anyway. And besides...did I want to spend the rest of my life taking care of a liar and a cheater. Damn it...Who is Katy? Why doesn't she take care of him? I'll gladly let her. She can have him. I could always send him packing with his family. I have always liked his mother and three sisters and I know they'd be upset by the news of his accident. I will not tell them about the baby. Maybe, if things work out and we make it through this. Maybe, if we do get married. Chances of that are pretty slim now. The nurse comes in and adjusts his machines and his tubing.

She informs me they are short staffed today. Three other nurses are out sick. That she's trying to run the desk and visit all the patients at the same time. Two or three nurses from a couple of other floors are coming up to help her as soon as they can get away from their other duties. She says she needs to go get a cup of coffee and run to the little nurse's room. "Go ahead" I tell her. "I'll sit with Brian. If anything happens and you're not back I'll track down a doctor or someone." She thanks me quickly and walks out. Without thinking about it I squeeze his oxygen line until it is closed off. The light begins to flash and the machine starts to beep. Either the volume is turned down or it is just a quiet beep because it is not that loud. I doubt if anyone passing by would even be able to hear it.

At first nothing happens. He gasps a small gasp for air. The next gasp is larger and the next one even larger than that. His face turns red and then blue and gets puffy. He never regains consciousness. When the horrible gasping and choking sounds are over I calmly let go of the tubing. There is no mark in the line. No one will ever know what I have just done. I sit with Brian for about two minutes while the machines beep. When I do search the hallway I don't see anyone. I have to get in the elevator and go down to the floor below to find a doctor. He runs to the elevator and I frantically try to explain that all of a sudden he starts gasping and choking and the machines start to beep. I want to explain that I tried to find someone on our floor but everyone was gone or busy. When we reach Brian's room the doctor turns the beeping off and quickly checks the machines and Brian. The nurse reappears at that moment. They try to save him but it is too late. The doctor turns to me. "I'm sorry ma'am. He's gone. There's nothing more we can do."

I wake up in a cold sweat. I must have been tossing and turning because all of the blankets are on the floor on my side of the bed. I wipe sweat off my forehead and throw my legs over the side of the bed. My chest heaves a little as I catch my breath. So, that is it. That's how I find out about the project in the first place. If it were only true. If Brian were dead I wouldn't have to worry about him anymore. I scold myself...*Stop it! You're not thinking clear.* I try to stand up and almost fall to the floor. I have to grab the side of the bed and pull myself up. Jake stirs at the movement but then rolls over. Good, at least I didn't wake him up. I put on a robe and slippers and go downstairs. The coffee pot is already gurgling. My eyes halfway adjust to the dim light and I see it's ten after six in the morning. Today is the big day. Jake will meet with Brian downtown.

24

I fill a coffee cup with creamer and stand impatiently in front of the coffee pot. I know the last part of my dream couldn't be real. I know Brian is still alive. Why would I dream such horrible things? A chill sweeps through me and I cross my arms. The coffee finishes brewing and I pour myself a cup and sit quietly at the kitchen table. A small light under the cabinet near the coffee pot is the only light on. It dimly lights the room and I can barely see. My dream haunts me. I hope to God I never tried to do anything like that to Brian. I'm sure I didn't. In my other dreams I had simply got in his car and gone home. I didn't even go to the hospital. I get a second cup of coffee and make my way to the sitting room. A fire is roaring in the fire place. My mind stays focused on Brian even though I try to think of other things. What will he say to Jake today? What will they discuss? What will be the outcome? Will Brian accept Jake's terms? Will I be allowed to live my life in peace? I don't want to feel like I have to look over my shoulder all the time. I don't want to be fearful for my life and the life of my child. Please, God...let this all be over with soon. Wouldn't it be great to be able to get on with my life? There's so much for me to catch up on and so many things I'd like to do. I could learn to really ride horses. I want to learn to quilt. I would like to see an opera or a ballet. I want to throw huge birthday parties for my child. I want to have years to love Jake. Have more children and watch them grow. Maybe even help him with his work, if that's at all possible.

I stare off into the fireplace, watching the flames lick up and over the wood. I am not sure how long I sit there thinking, but my coffee is cold. I shuffle back to the kitchen to get another cup. As I walk into the kitchen I see a woman and a man in an embrace. The man speaks to the woman, "Good morning, Frannie. Shall I cook you a luxurious breakfast? Maybe an omelet and sausage. Now how can you resist that?" The hug ends but they remain close. The woman laughs at him. "Oh, please, Sherman, we both know you can't cook worth a flip. Do I dare mention the hot cakes incident?" He shakes his head, "No, no...no need to drudge up past indiscretions. You've made your point." He gets a cup of coffee and sits at the table. I recognize him to be Sherman, the man I met the first day I was here. The woman, I believe, is Fran, Jake's housekeeper. After all, he did call her Frannie. Her hair is down and she's in a sweat suit. Sherman is in jeans and a checkered shirt. She looks totally different from how I saw her before. He looks the same, but then again, I saw him in regular clothes. I wonder if they are a couple. If not they must be really good friends. They seem very close.

Fran notices me first. "Oh, Jesse, dear, you're awake. Sit, please." She waves me over to the table. Sherman quickly rises and pulls out a chair for me. I sit down and Fran turns the light over the stove on. "Did you have coffee dear?" I shake my head yes. "I was just coming to get another cup. Sorry, I didn't mean to interrupt you two." Sherman motions with his right hand as he spoke, "No, no...don't be silly. We're glad to see you today. It's Monday and we are usually off Mondays but we both had things we needed to do so we decided to work today. So, tell us, how are you feeling?" He smiles kindly at me. "Oh, I'm fine. Jake has taken good care of me." They both smile at me. I see them flash a quick glance at each other and then they both focus on me again. I'm not stupid. I know what that's about. They probably are wondering if anything happened between us this weekend. If I've noticed how handsome Jake is. Fran pours me a cup of coffee and asks if I'd like creamer or sugar. I ask for just the creamer and she nods her head as if in approval. Within seconds she pours creamer in my cup and puts it down between Sherman and myself. "Well, dear, we knew that Jake would take great care of you." She goes to the refrigerator and begins pulling out eggs, sausage, cheese, milk, onion, green onion and both green and red bell pepper. By the time she is finished she has a large stack of items sitting on the counter next to the stove.

Sherman and I look at the stack, look at each other, look at Fran and laugh. "Well, you guys laugh, go ahead. But Sherman knows how Jake eats. That boy's a bottomless pit. How he stays so thin I'll never know. He's always especially hungry on Tuesday mornings because he usually eats junk food over the weekend and barely cooks anything that'll do him good. You'll see, he'll eat at least two omelets. Jesse, dear, don't let this old man fool you. Sherman eats as much as Jake. I keep thinking one day he'll slow down, but it hasn't happened yet." Fran goes to the pantry and retrieves vegetable oil and a large fryer. She begins to cook. "Is there something I can help you with?" I ask. "No, dear, you need to rest. You just sit there and drink your coffee." Sherman reaches over and grabs my hand. "So, tell us, what have you two been up to this weekend? Anything interesting happen?" He raises his eyebrow on the word "interesting. "Oh, Sherman. Leave her alone. She's not use to us yet. We're strangers to her." Fran shakes her head at him as she cooks.

I sip my coffee and say. "Oh no, I don't mind. In fact I want to tell you what's been going on. It's been such an amazing weekend. And there's something big happening today that you should probably know about. I just hope it turns out the way Jake wants it to, for both of us." I give them a brief summary of all that's happened. Stressing the parts where I remembered things and leaving out the more personal details. When I am about halfway into everything, Fran refills both our mugs and places a large steaming omelet in front of me. It looks absolutely delicious. It is very colorful. It is full of red and green peppers and onions. Cheese and sausage is in the middle and more cheese oozes over the top. She brings salt and pepper shakers to the table along with napkins. Next she sits a large omelet in front of Sherman. Fran goes back to the counter and fixes a plate for herself. Only now does she fix herself a cup of coffee and start a fresh pot.

She walks over and sits at the table with us. "It's almost seven-thirty. Jake will be along any minute. He's a morning person and usually always gets up before seven. He must have been tired." She takes a bite of her omelet and exchanges a look with Sherman. I eat half of my omelet and am stuffed. "Is that all you're going to eat?" Fran asks. "Oh yes, it is wonderful but I'm full." I drink down the last of my coffee. Sherman is still working on his omelet and Fran is halfway through hers. They both take a drink of coffee. "Well, go on then. I want to hear the rest" Sherman says as he waves his fork in the air. I continue from where I left off. Often they shake their heads or look down sadly. When I tell them about the fight in the park they are both on edge. "Our boy Jake is tough. There's no doubt. He does more to help this country than we'll ever know" Sherman says. Then he looks at Fran for a moment. "We both worry about him though. One day he just may meet a guy tougher than he is. I hope that day will never come. We have tried to get him to quit this particular group he is involved in. He says it's his way to contribute and help his friends. But we both hope and pray he gives it up. Maybe now he will." Sherman smiles at me.

They both know about my apartment already. They have been instrumental in helping Jake, from what they tell me. "Jesse, I know this is tough for you" Fran says. "You're in the best of hands dear. Jake is a fine doctor, a great protector, and a gentleman, if I may add. Sherman and I have both helped raise him from when he was a young boy, and well... we just want the best for him. We treat him as if he's our own. You see... we're married. Been that way for twenty-two years now. We couldn't have children of our own. So, naturally when Jake's mother passed we stayed on with him. We love him like our own, we do." Sherman clears his throat, "So, this Brian guy...is he really that dangerous?" I shrug my shoulders, "I don't know. I guess he is. I have only known Jake a short while but I trust what he says. His guys have tracked Brian for a while now. I am anxious to have this day over. I just want to be able to get on with my life." Fran nods her head at Sherman. He speaks up, "Well then, it's settled. I'd best go with Marcus and Jake today."

Fran clears the table and starts an omelet for Jake. She walks over to me and hugs me. "Jesse, dear. Thank you for telling us everything. I know it's hard for you, but we do appreciate it. Jake is quiet. Sometimes he doesn't tell us...everything. He keeps everything locked up inside. I hate that about him. I know he feels like he doesn't want to burden us, but sometimes I wish he would." Sherman takes a deep breath. "Now, Frannie, you know a man has to keep to himself sometimes. You know Jake's always been a very private guy even when he was little. Remember how he'd sit and play with that train town I built him. If he ever had a problem he'd sit in front of it for hours until he figured out the answer. He's always been like that. That's just his nature." I immediately think of his ride to 'clear his head' and it makes sense he's been that way his whole life. Fran goes back to the stove and the sizzling omelet. "Well, that may be, but knowing how he is doesn't keep me from worrying, now does it?" Sherman gets up and walks up behind her. He hugs her tight. "Now, Frannie, don't you worry. Your boy will be fine. You'll see, this too, will work itself out. I've got to get changed." She patted his hand and he walked away.

As if right on cue as Fran was scooping Jake's omelet onto his plate he walks into the kitchen. His hair is ruffled and he is in a pair of navy sweat pants and an undershirt. Barefoot. He has long skinny toes. He goes over to her and hugs her. "Morning honey" she says to him as she hugs him back. "I missed you" he says taking the plate from her. He walks over to the table and sits down next to me. "I know you did sweetie. I'll bet you missed my omelets more" she said smiling. While she was pouring him a cup of coffee he smiled at me. "Good morning. You disappeared on me." I stare down at my hands, "I know. I had another dream. I didn't want to wake you. This one was even more bothersome. Eat. I'll tell you later." Fran looks from Jake to me and back to Jake as she sits his coffee down in front of him. She smiles at him but he doesn't look at her. He takes a bite of his food and eyes me curiously. "I hope you don't mind but I sort of filled them in on what's been happening." Sherman walks back into the room but now he is completely dressed in his work uniform. Black pants and a long-sleeved black shirt. I can barely see a white undershirt. He has on clean, shined black shoes and what looks like black socks.

"Wow. You didn't have to go and get all dressed up just for me" I say playfully. He grins at me. Fran is hovering over Jake, "Well, now. Jake, do you need anything else? How about some toast?" He shakes his head, "No thanks, this is fine. Thanks. I'd hate to ruin my lunch." She laughs at him. "I need to go change. Be right back." Sherman says "I too have a few things to attend to. I'll check in with you later Jake." They both leave the room. I sit in silence and watch Jake finish his breakfast. "Are you nervous?" I ask him. "Nervous?" he repeats, sounding confused. "Oh, you mean about today, meeting Brian?" I nod my head yes. "Not at all. He's a scoundrel, but I'm not nervous. I'll go do what I need to do and we'll see what happens." I shrug my shoulders. "Well, I am nervous and anxious. I can't wait to see what happens. I mean, this could determine the rest of my life!"

He put his dirty dishes in the sink, refills his coffee cup and comes over and puts his arms around me, careful not to spill his coffee. "Now let me properly tell you good morning." He gently hugs me and kisses me with his soft coffee lips. "Come on. Let's go to the sitting room." I follow closely behind him. Neither of us speaks until we sit down. "Jake, all this morning I've been thinking about what you two will discuss today. I am more than a little anxious. I mean, I know you'll do the right thing and all. I just want it to be over soon. You know..." He shakes his head yes. "Baby, I do know, that's the thing. I want it to be over with too. For both our sakes. For the baby's sake. I know it's been hard on you, but hang in there. We're almost there, Jess. I'm positive I'll be able to make him see things my way." A shiver runs through me. "I don't know how you can be so confident. I'm worried." I sigh. "Just trust me Jess. Okay." We are quiet for a moment. "Well, tell me about your dream." I sigh again. How can I tell Jake about my dream without sounding like a monster? There's no way around it. I should have never mentioned it.

His eyes never leave my face as I tell him everything. I am not even sure if he blinks. "Wow, that's quite a dream" he says. I search his face for an answer. When I don't find one I blurt out "What do you think it is? Just a bad dream? I know I didn't kill Brian. He's still alive. The question is, 'did I ever try?'" Jake's face grows less ridged. "Oh, baby, is that what you're worried about? Oh, no! Don't you dare and waste another minute on thoughts like that. It was just a bad dream, that's all. I am absolutely sure you did not try to hurt Brian. You are the good guy...uh, make that gal...remember?" It seemed real enough to me. Jake's reassurance barely makes me feel better. I force a smile. "Did you think of what you'd say to Brian when you see him?" "Yes. I made a list of seven questions; I think that'll do it. I'm pretty sure if he answers those questions that all my questions will be answered." "Great. He's ruthless, just remember that." I am having a hard time with that, but I am sure Jake is right about it. "I will" I say.

"Well, since I'm not leaving until this afternoon, I thought it would be nice if I personally show you around the gardens out back. The walking trails are nice. I'd hate for you to be lonely. Unless you have something else you want to do."

The thought of exercise doesn't appeal to me at this particular moment but I know I need to do it. And any time I spend with Jake is a plus. "Honestly, I really don't feel like walking. However, after Fran's omelet I know I need the exercise. Besides, it will be good for the baby. So, I guess you've got yourself a date." This makes him happy. "Great. I'll go up and shower and dress. You can come up with me." Jake grins his devilish grin. I love to see that grin. He is so sexy this morning. If I wasn't so nervous about today I'd take him up on that offer. "I'd love to go with you, but I think I'd better hang out here for a few minutes." He is clearly disappointed; I see it in his eyes. "Oh, come on, why?"

I get up and sit in his lap. He puts his cup on the table and wraps his arms around me. I lean over and whisper in his ear, "You drive me crazy, you know that. It's just that, I'm nervous about today." Jake pushes back a strand of wild hair that has fallen into my face. "Well, all right, have it your way." I stand up and take a step back. Jake gets up and starts heading for the door. He stops, turns around and just looks at me and I see he's thinking hard about something. I immediately go to him. "Jess" he holds my hands tight. "I want you to know I love you so much. I will always protect you. No matter what. Okay?" All I can say is "Okay." He makes me feel like a giddy school girl. He lets go of my hands and leaves. I watch him walk up the stairs and around the corner. Wow, what was that about? I think he *is* nervous about today. I pick up his cup and I take it in the kitchen.

Fran has finished cleaning the kitchen and is now mopping the floor. I walk on the part she has not mopped yet. Luckily it is the side that the sink is on. I put the cup in the sink and ask "Are you sure there's nothing I can do to help?" "Don't be silly, dear. I've got it under control. It escapes me how the floor gets so dirty, so fast. Anyway, no matter. We'll have a clean floor for dinner." I giggle inwardly thinking about Marcus spilling his soup on the floor. With nothing for me to do down here, I might as well go up and shower myself. I head up the stairs. Suddenly my stomach cramps. I stop dead in my tracks and double over. I try to take a deep breath. It is not letting up and actually seems to be getting worse. In my mind I run through the possibilities. Am I dehydrated? Am I going to be sick from breakfast? Did I eat too much? It grows stronger and stronger with each passing second. The cramps are so bad now I have to sit down on the stairs. I immediately break out into a sweat. I grab the spindles of the staircase and squeeze them as hard as I could. *Oh God! What is this? What's happening?* The pain is so bad I clinch my teeth. It starts to subside and then quickly returns. I can be silent no longer. I let out a blood curdling scream. I need help. Fran gasp with horror when she sees me. "Jesse, dear, what is it? Jesse, hold on..." She screams for Sherman. The pain is so intense now that it's making me light headed. *Oh, please don't let me pass out.* That's the last thing I need, especially today of all days. Sherman comes up from the rec room in a full run. "What's wrong?" He sees me sitting on the stairs and rushes to me. "Frannie, go get Jake. I'll take her up." Fran darts past me. I can hear the ruffling of her skirt as she passes by me. Sherman takes a clean handkerchief from inside his jacket and wipes the sweat from my brow.

The pain slowly starts to disappear. "Jesse, I'm going to pick you up and take you upstairs. Just put your arms around my neck, okay." I do as instructed and he lifts me up. He manages up four stairs and then the pain comes back and is more intense. I try to focus on Sherman's face. "Take some deep breathes Jesse. Come on. Breathe girl, breathe." I take a few deep breathes and quickly blew them out. It's not working, I feel myself losing consciousness. I look down and see a growing red spot on my beige robe. It's the last thing I see before everything goes black. Sounds linger in my ears and then there's nothing.

25

Sherman lays Jesse carefully on the bed. Jake, in only an undershirt and boxers, rushes in with Fran close behind him. "Jake, I brought her up as quick as I could. What can I get? What do you need?" Sherman asks with a calm head. Fran rushes to the opposite side of the bed and tucks pillows behind Jesse's head. "Sherman, go get my medical bag, there's one I keep under my bathroom cabinet. Hurry." Jake begins to examine Jesse. "Oh, Jake, dear. What's wrong with her?" Jake shakes his head. "I don't know. I hope she's not losing the baby!" The color drains out of Fran's face. "Baby? What baby? Dear lord! Is she pregnant?" "Yes." Sherman reappears and hands the medical bag to Jake. "Sherman, I need you to go down to the pool area. Get my scanner; it's on the table out there. You can also bring that other medical bag. I might need it." Sherman was gone before Jake finished his sentence. "Oh, Jake. Hurry... hurry" Fran said frantically. Jake inserts a needle into a clear bottle of medicine. He quickly measures it and thumps out the air. Within seconds he injects Jesse. "This will stop her from having a miscarriage... if it's not too late." "Oh dear. This is terrible." Fran said as she looks at Jake. He listens with his stethoscope and takes Jesse's pulse. He tries to remain professional but tears fill his eyes.

With a wavering tone he shouts, "Fran, go get five large towels and roll them up cross ways. Hurry." Sherman comes in as Fran is headed toward the bathroom. Jake takes the scanner and quickly runs it over Jesse. The red light flashes. The volume is still turned down so they do not hear the rapid beeping. Fran reappears with the towels and frantically rolls them up. Through clinched teeth Jake says, "This has all been too much for her. Too stressful." He finishes examining her. "Everything else looks okay. Her body is still weak. I...I don't know if she'll keep the baby. Also, looks like she could possibly have a fibroid tumor" A confused look floods Sherman's face. "Baby?" he asks. Fran nods her head yes. "The next eight hours are critical" Jake says as he places the folded towels under Jesse's hips. Trying to sound calm, Jake says "Now, Fran, please get that old blanket out of the armoire, bottom shelf. Roll it long ways." Fran moves quickly.

Sherman pulls the chair away from the desk and sits it next to the bed for Jake. He sees Fran struggling to quickly roll up the blanket and grabs the other end. Together they roll it tightly. Jake rolls Jesse toward him and they placed the blanket behind her. Fran shakes her head. "I don't know Jake...she looks uncomfortable." "I know it looks that way, but she's fine. It will help with her blood pressure...it will possibly help with the baby, but there's no guarantee...we will have to wait now. If you two will step out I'll clean her up a little." Sherman takes Fran's hand and leads her out into the hallway. "We'll be right out here if you need us" Fran said. With tears in his eyes Jake nods and shuts the door. He immediately goes into the bathroom and makes a cleaning solution at the sink. He takes a small container used to hold hair accessories and washes it with hot soapy water and fills it with the cleaning solution. Jake gets a wash cloth and drapes it over the side of the container.

He quickly grabs a dry towel and a maxi-pad. In his right hand he carries the solution. Jake sits it all on the table next to Jesse. He chooses a clean gown and robe and puts them across the chair. Carefully Jake takes off Jesse's robe and gown. After wiping her down with the soaked wash cloth, he towel dries her and gently position the maxi-pad. After slipping the gown over her head and shoulders he covers her with a blanket from the armoire. "Please God...let this medicine work...let the baby have a fighting chance!" Jake doesn't know what to do next so he sits in the chair and cries. A while later when he is able to pull himself together, he goes to the bathroom and splashes cool water on his face.

When Jake opens the door Sherman and Fran stand up. They have placed two chairs in front of Jesse's door and have been patiently waiting. Jake does not give them time to speak. "I will need to re-check her in an hour or so. Fran, I want you to stay with her for now. I've got to finish getting dressed and get a few things ready in the clinic, just in case. Sherman, come with me. Fran, yell for me if you need me. We'll be back." They close the door behind them. Fran sits in the chair and holds Jesse's hand. "Oh, you poor child. I had no idea. You've been through so much. Please get well...not just for yourself, but for Jake's sake too." Fran begins to pray.

Jake throws on a pair of jeans and a button down shirt. He grabs his socks and shoes. "Come on, Sherman. We will get everything ready. If that medicine doesn't work in the next hour or so, I only have one last option. If it doesn't do the trick, I may need to do a laser procedure on Jesse. So, we have a lot to do. I'll need your help. We've got to sterilize everything." They quickly dart down the stairs. Once in the rec room, Jake goes behind the bar and pushes a button. Part of the wall behind the bar slides to the left. The doorway to the clinic stands open. Jake rushes in and Sherman follows him. "Here, put these on" Jake says as he hands a pair of white gloves to Sherman. He put a pair on himself. "You know, Jake, I've never been in here before" Sherman says.

"Yes, I know. I think Marcus is the only one that has been. Him and that other guy...Oh, what was his name? Well, it doesn't matter now...he's dead. It was after that bombing in Australia. Remember how banged up we were when we got back? Well, if you thought that was bad you should have seen us right after it happened. It was bad. But Marcus and I recovered quickly. I only hope the same's true for Jesse." Sherman watches as Jake prepares a sterilization machine. He pulls open a drawer lined with white cloth. Surgical instruments are lined up neatly inside. Next he retrieves a tray and spreads some of the same white cloth over it. He places the instruments of choice on the tray and after inserting the tray into the small square machine, he touches a few buttons on the number pad. The green light on the outside of the machine comes on but the machine itself is quiet and Sherman can't even tell it is running. Jake opens some sterile cleaning pads and wipes down the exam table. The stirrups pull out without a hitch. The bottom of the table looks like a walnut wood but is actually a new type of steel. There are two deep wide drawers built into it. They contain surgical scrubs and patient gowns.

"Sherman, do me a favor. Open that large cabinet on the left, next to the wall, and pull out the large and small lamps. Also, I'll need you to grab the laser gun out of the cabinet next to the lamps." Above the sink are rows of cabinets. From these Jake takes out gauze, antibiotic ointment, long q-tip swabs, alcohol and a tall plastic see through container that is wrapped in a clear sterile wrap. He opens the plastic container and fills it a little over half full with alcohol. "Where shall I put these?" Sherman asks. Jake turns to see Sherman standing near the table with both lamps. "If you don't mind, please plug them in behind the table and just sit them there, next to the wall. You can sit the laser gun on that counter for now" Jake says, motioning to a counter against the wall near the entrance. Jake finds a pop-up tray table and assembles it. He pulls out a tray from underneath the sink. It too, is wrapped in the sterile wrap. He unwraps it and snaps it onto the assembled tray table.

Jake quickly looks until he finds four small metal bowls also covered by the sterile wrap. Once he unwraps them and places them on the tray table, he fills the first one with the 4x4 gauze he opened. Jake squeezes half the tube of antibiotic ointment in the next bowl. He opens the sterile q-tip swabs and places them in the third bowl. Jake covers everything with a sterile towel. Sherman sits the laser gun on the counter as directed while he watches Jake. He doesn't want to know what the empty bowl is for. "Next, Sherman, please get an IV pole out of the tall cabinet by the door." As Sherman retrieves the pole, Jake opens what looks like a regular cabinet. Sherman is surprised to see six full bags of fluid hanging by individual hooks. Hanging to the right side of the cabinet are empty IV bags in the original packaging. Jake takes out a bag that is full of fluid and hangs it on the pole. He parks it near the head of the exam table. Next he pulls out a sealed package of tubing for the IV. Instead of opening it, he just hangs it on the other side of the pole.

"Okay. I think we're getting there. I just have to check for blood" Jake says as he squats down and opens up a refrigerator. There are three shelves stacked with bags of blood. Jake moves the ones he may need to the front and pushes the others back. He stands and gives the room a quick glance. *'Is there anything I'm forgetting?'* he thinks to himself. Satisfied that he has everything out that he needs, he connects the laser gun to an extension cord and plugs it in a plug that is built into the exam table. "Oh yeah, I almost forgot...Sherman, open that cabinet above where you sat the laser gun and hand me one of those small nozzles. They are in a clear blue wrap." Sherman quickly locates the nozzle and hands it to Jake. Jake opens it and attaches it to the end of the laser gun. "Okay, that should do it." Jake stands and throws away the blue wrap from the nozzle. He takes off his gloves and motions for Sherman to do the same. They throw away the gloves and Sherman follows Jake out of the clinic.

Leaving the lab door open, Jake says, "Let's go check on Jesse. I think we've been down here about an hour. Hopefully the medicine is working by now. I don't want to do surgery on her, but, if I need to, at least it's all set up." Sherman follows Jake briskly up the stairs. When they enter the bedroom Fran is still sitting next to Jesse, who has come to and is lying still with her eyes open. As soon as he sees her Jake rushes to her. He knows she must be scared. "Jake...what is it? What's happening? Is it the baby? Am I...still pregnant?" Jesse looks pale and very frightened. "Shhh, don't use up your energy by talking. Just be still and try not to talk. Your blood pressure was a little low and you had cramps and a little bleeding. I examined you and gave you a shot. The medicine I gave you will hopefully prevent a miscarriage. There is the possibility you have a fibroid tumor too." Fran stands up and Sherman goes immediately to her side. He holds her hand. "I need to scan you again. I want to see if the medicine has started to work yet."

Jesse keeps still as Jake runs the scanner down her body. She can't tell by the look on his face if it is good or bad news. Jesse tries to see if the light is flashing on the scanner but it is facing the wrong way. She nervously stares at him. He put the scanner down and checks her pulse and her breathing. Jesse, Sherman and Fran are all three anxiously looking at Jake when he looks up. "Well, the good news is that the medicine is working...but the bad news is that it's not working fast enough. We can wait a little while longer to see what happens, but I think I may need to perform the laser procedure." Jesse sighs and tears fill her eyes. Jake reaches into his medical bag and pulls out another syringe and a different bottle of medicine. "Jesse, I'm going to inject you with this medicine. This cocktail helps augment the first medicine I gave you." Jake tries to be gentle when giving Jesse the shot but he winces when she does. "As far as medicine goes, it's pretty much our last resort. I'll need to check you in another two to three hours. If this does the trick, then great. If not, I will have to do the laser procedure."

Jake can tell Jesse is scared and he wants to comfort her. "Don't be nervous. You're doing great. The baby is fine from what I can tell. Jess, there's a procedure called a hysteroscopy that I may need to do. That's where I can go in with a camera and light and look around to see what is going on. Going by the information I got from your scan; you may have a submucosal fibroid. That means a benign tumor growing inside your uterus. I may need to do a myomectomy, which is the actual procedure to remove the fibroids. It's an easy fix and the baby will be fine. So, let's wait to see how these meds do. A lot of women have fibroids and have these procedures. I have no doubt that if we need to do them you will tolerate them just fine. Don't panic, okay. You just need to rest for now." He takes her hand and she nods. Jake forces a smile. He feels guilty about this.

Maybe if he had not been so physical with her. Maybe if they had not made love this wouldn't have happened. He knows there is no medical basis for his internal dialogue, but he can't stop himself. Jake looks down for a few minutes. They are all quiet until Fran ask, "Jesse, can I get you some water or juice? Or how about a nice cup of hot tea?" "Water please" Jesse answers in a small weak voice. "Sherman, why don't you call Marcus for me and tell him I need him here as soon as possible." Sherman does not ask questions and immediately he knows what Jake is thinking. He and Fran leave the room. Jake sits next to Jesse, holding her hand. Neither of them spoke.

Fran comes back with Jesse's water. "Fran, I need to tend to some things. Please watch over Jesse. If she has cramps like earlier or starts bleeding, call me immediately. I don't think you should run into any problems, but if so, just call me." Fran nods her head. "Jake, what are you going to do?" Jesse asks. "I'm going to contact Brian and move our meeting up. Nothing to worry about baby. I promise." Jake leans over and kisses her lips gently. "I love you" he whispers. She smiles and grabs his hand as he stands up. "Hey, I love you. Please be careful." Fran is overcome by the exchange between Jake and Jesse. Her heart is overflowing with emotion. She is so happy that Jake and Jesse are really together now and Jake won't have to be alone anymore. She is so proud of the man he has become. "Yes, please, please be careful dear" Fran adds. Jake walks into the hallway and shuts the door, leaving Fran and Jesse alone.

26

Jake hangs up the phone and finds Sherman sitting at the kitchen table. "Did you catch Marcus?" "Yes" Sherman answers. "He's on his way. Should be here any minute." "Good, I want to get this over with so I can get back and take care of Jesse. If I can time this right, it will be time for me to examine her when we get back." Sherman shakes his head. "Jake, I'm coming with you." Jake gives Sherman an obstinate look before saying, "No, Sherman, I can't let you. I need you here...to take care of Fran and Jesse for me. I don't have any choice. You and Fran know what to do if Marcus and I don't come back." Sherman's eyes widen and his lips form a tight line. "Yes. But come on, reconsider, Jake. You know I can help you if you get into trouble!" Jake walks over to Sherman and pats him on the shoulder. "You're a good man, Sherman. You and Fran are my second parents. You two must keep Jesse and the baby safe if something happens today. I can't do this unless I know you're here with them." Sherman understands what Jake is saying, he just doesn't like it. "Oh, all right, you win. Just be careful. Make sure it all goes your way. Don't give in an inch to him. You hear me. Let him know you mean business right up front. No playing around with this one...he's too dangerous."

"I know, I know." Jake runs his hands over his face and gets a drink of water. "Look, we will be careful, but if it comes right down to it we'll kick ass too! You know me. I am not putting up with this...at all! I didn't bring Jesse here so we can live in fear. I'm putting a stop to this...today! We are going to start living our lives together. We are going to be happy and I am going to make sure of it! I have waited so long to be happy." His voice cracks, "I love her Sherman." By the tone of his voice Sherman knows Jake means business. "I know you do...we both know you do. We just want you to be safe. And if taking care of Jesse is how we can help, then that's exactly what we'll do. Just keep some back up handy." "You know I will". Marcus rushes in, "How is she? What about the baby?" "They're both fine for now. However, we have to get this over with. I need to be back here in a few hours to see if the medicine has worked. If not, I'll have to do the laser procedure." "Did he agree to meet us early?" Jake shakes his head yes. "Well, okay then, let's move" Marcus says as he waves good-bye to Sherman.

They step outside and Jake laughs as soon as he sees what Marcus is driving. "Oh, come on, you brought the tank!" Jake refers to the limo Marcus is driving as 'the tank' because it is a bullet proof fortress stocked with guns, RPGs, grenades and ammunition. The tinted windows give it a foreboding look. Marcus grins, "What? You never know...she could come in handy if we get into trouble." Jake shakes his head at his buddy and smiles. "The whole point is to NOT get into trouble today" Jake says sternly. They quickly get in the car with Marcus in the driver's seat, posing as the chauffeur. Jake continues from the back, "Are the teams in place? And did our guy make the pickup?" Marcus looks at him in the rearview mirror and nods. "Yes and yes. The first team completed the sweep and the other two set up shop. One's directly in front of the cafe, the second one is on the corner. Griffin's got the cash and is waiting for you." Jake nods his head. They clear the gate and finally make it out onto the main road. Neither of them speaks until they reach the busy downtown area and Marcus begins to park. "You are doing the right thing" Marcus says as he turns the wheel to the right and then back to the left.

"I know. I just wish I didn't have to do this. I just wish this guy would fuck off and leave Jesse alone. We've both read his bio though and know that'll never happen. So, I'm left with no choice. I just want to get this done...hopefully with little resistance." Marcus turns the car off and they get out. Jake sighs and looks across the street. Next to the entrance to the cafe he sees Griffin waiting for him. Jake rushes across the street and Marcus follows closely behind, scanning the crowd on the sidewalk. Immediately he sees Brian's four goons mixed in with the crowd and watching the cafe. Griffin shakes Jake's hand, "Hey, man, it's been a long time. Good to see you." Jake nods, "Good to see you too. Thanks for doing this for me. I appreciate it" Jake says as he takes the briefcase from Griffin. "Listen, Griff, once this is all over I want you and the girls to come by for a visit. It'll be like old times and I want Jesse to meet Gina. We'll do dinner or something. What do you say?" Griffin smiles, "Sounds great. We'd love to. We'll catch up then. See you." A car pulls up and the door pushes open. "That's my ride" Griffin says as he steps past Jake. He gets in and within seconds the car is gone. Jake walks into the cafe and Marcus waits at the door where Griffin had been standing.

The cafe is full of people. An old couple shuffle past Jake and stop at the counter to pay the old fashioned way - with cash. A young couple gaze warmly at each other over the rim of their coffee cups while at the next table a set of twin boys punch each other in the legs. They make faces at each other and are caught by their mother just as Jake walks past them. A row of teenagers sit at the bar drinking milkshakes. Jake looks past the hustle and bustle and scans the back section. In the last booth on the left sits an old man. He wore an expensive suit and although it is June, he has an overcoat draped over his left arm. Jake immediately knows that it is Brian and is irritated that he has brought a gun. Brian's temple area is a little more silver than what Jake recalled, but it is definitely him. Jake walks over and sits opposite him. "Hello, Jake. It's nice to meet you face to face after all these years. I must say, you are as handsome as they said you were" Brian says. He extends his hand but Jake does not shake it. Instead he gives Brian an icy cold look that says 'fuck off asshole'. "Let's make this as quick and painless as possible" Jake says. Brian smiles an old man's crooked smile. His top row of yellow teeth protrudes over his bottom lip. "Jake. So tell me... have you two fallen madly in love or what? She's irresistible, you know. If you don't love her by now you will soon."

Jake sighed. "I have something for you." Jake slid the briefcase across the table to Brian. The waitress approaches Jake and asks if he'd like to order. Jake smiles at her and politely declines. She pauses and stares at him, giving him a sexy smile. Jake is irritated that her flirting is wasting his time. He flashes her a cold, harsh look and she gets the picture. Once she leaves Brian opens the briefcase just enough to glance inside. He quickly shuts it and glares at Jake. "Do you think that you can offer this to me and expect me to forget about her? About my child?" Hatred wells up inside of Jake. If he wanted a challenge Jake would be happy to give him one. Brian looks at Jake with contempt. Jake growls at Brian, "That's exactly what I expect...if you know what's good for you." Brian gives Jake a malicious grin, "I won't be threatened by you, young man" and shakes an old wrinkled index finger at him. Jake shakes his head. "Look, Brian, we're going to do this my way or no way. You take your payoff and go. You will leave Jesse alone and you are never going to see the child. Is that clear?"

Brian is amused, "Now, why would I want to do a thing like that?" he asks through his laughter. Jake is growing impatient and is tired of this game. "I'll tell you why...the information...that's why. If you agree to this, I'll give you the research from the project. Even the documentation you tried to steal from my father during the last botched robbery. I won't however, give you her personal information. So, take it or leave it." Jake rises from behind the table. "What's it going to be, Brian? You've had plenty of time to mull it over. I want an answer." "Sit down you foolish boy." Jake does not move. Brian motions for Jake to sit with his shaking wrinkled right hand. Again, Jake does not move. "Sit down, people are starting to stare." Jake is firm in his stance and his eyes are ice cold and locked on Brian's. "What's it going to be, Brian?" The two men size each other up, ignoring the looks from the other customers. Brian clasps his hands and rubs them in a circular motion. The movement causes the overcoat to open. The bottom of the automatic rifle is exposed briefly and then covered by the overcoat again. The table blocks Jake's view and he does not see it, but he knows it is there. "Can it be that I underestimated you, Dr. Bradley?" Jake holds his ground, "You may have old man" Jake says in an even cool tone.

They watch each other in silence through clinched teeth. Finally, Brian throws his hands up in the air. "Oh what the hell! It was never about her anyway. I'm an old man now and growing tired of all this nonsense. What could I possibly do with her now?" A terse grin crosses his chapped lips briefly exposing yellow, stained teeth. He continues, "Not what I'd like to do, that's for damn sure!" He lays his head back and laughs heartily, exposing dental work and more yellow teeth. Jake is repulsed by Brian. He physically grimaces at the thought of this disgusting scumbag ever being with Jesse. In a low, quiet voice Brian says "She has such a sweet ass. I'd like to have that one more time. I don't know if I like her ass better or her tits." Jake's blood is boiling and he is about to blow. He looks again at his surroundings and tells himself to calm down. In his ear he hears Marcus telling him "not yet buddy, soon, but not today." Brian evaluates Jake one more time and wisely, finally says, "She's been a burden on my conscious far too long. When will you turn over the information?" This small victory pleases Jake. "I'll have someone meet you here next week, same day, same time. He will give you keys to an old beat up blue beamer. Look in the trunk. You'll find four boxes of documents. Once you're goons have unloaded the boxes you will park the car in the parking garage at the corner. Park in the first level, near the elevator, and leave the keys in the car and walk away. Easy as pie. You stop keeping tabs on her, never try to contact her again and you never attempt to see the child. Understand?"

"Well, of course I understand. I didn't get where I am today by being stupid." Jake grins. He is far from stupid, that's for sure. "Oh, I know that. All too well, don't I? What good does all the knowledge do you if you can't live and be happy? I feel sorry for you, old man. You'll never be happy. You've blown it and for what? Money? The thrill of discovery? Different women? You will never know true love. Even I know that love is the only thing that matters in this world!" Jake turns to walk away. He takes three steps and is reminded of the letter. He turns to face Brian once again. "Oh yeah, there's one more thing." Now Brian stands and steps out from behind the table. The overcoat hangs down past Brian's knees. He was about the same height as Jake yet somewhat thinner. "Well, what is it? A man of my age doesn't have time to wait!" "Jesse will meet you here, in three days. Meet her here Friday, same time. She has some questions to ask you and a letter to give you. I'm warning you, one wrong move and my men *will* shoot you. Understand?"

Brian shakes his head yes and watches Jake walk out of the cafe. The prospect of seeing Jesse again thrills him. The young man is wrong. He did love Jesse then and still loves her now. His wife of thirty years, Katy, has just passed away. He never loved her the way he loved Jesse. She was great in bed and loved to party and they had a lot of great times together, but Brian has always known that Jesse was his one chance at true love. Sometimes his guilt got the better of him. When his son was young, often he'd come home after midnight and sit beside his bed and watch him sleep. He'd think of Jesse and her child and what their lives could have been like together.

He'd think of how he'd traded their happiness for research and wealth. He has made some bad deals and many mistakes in his lifetime. Now his soul is riddled with regret. Sadly he sighs and tells himself he can't change the past. Jake's young. He'd never understand the pain of regret and the 'what could have been's'. All he sees is an old man. An old and dangerous man. Brian begins to walk out of the cafe. Things haven't really changed. He made up his mind before he reached the cafe door, he will go ahead with his original plan to kill Jesse. He knows it is the right thing to do. Four days from now he'd never think of her again.

27

Two hours have passed and I can't stop worrying about Jake. Where are they? What happened? Fran tries to make small talk and keep me busy, but it's not working. My mind is in overdrive. It makes it worse that I have to lay here like this. I'd feel better if I can get up and walk around. "Jesse, dear, I know you're worried. I am too, but please, for the sake of the baby, try to relax" Fran says as she sighs. "Fran, there's just no way I can relax now. Besides, I feel fine physically. It's just my mind that's tormented now." Fran gets up and paces the floor next to Jesse's bed. Occasionally she'd look out the French doors to see if they are back yet. "Fran, if it's not too much trouble, I'd like to run a warm wash cloth over my face and put on a little make-up before they get back. I should run a brush through my hair too. Would you mind getting it for me?" Finally, something that Fran feels capable of doing. "Not at all dear. I think that's a great idea." Fran quickly returns with the warm wash cloth. She hands it to Jesse and disappears into the dressing room. When she comes back she hands Jesse a small basket of make-up and takes the used wash cloth back to the bathroom. She grabs a brush, hair spray, mirror and a hair clip and placed them on the bed next to Jesse.

"Great, thanks" I say as I picked up the brush. It takes about ten minutes but I feel better about the way I look. At least I won't look sick. Fran puts everything away and sits in the chair. At first we don't talk. The events of the last four days ran through my head. I think about everything that's happened until I cannot think anymore. Finally, I break the silence. "You know, it's weird." Fran has a blank stare on her face, "What's weird dear?" "All that has happened. I mean, I could still be frozen at the lab. I should not even be here now." Oh, Fran understands and wants to comfort Jesse. "Now, now, you must not think that way. You can't worry about the past... you must focus on the future." Fran smiles warmly. "I know, but it's just hard not to think about it. Jake's told me everything I guess. Although Marcus is the one who told me that it wasn't an accident. That Jake defrosted me on purpose." Fran gets up and walks to the French doors.

She pulls the curtain back and shakes her head. "They should be back any minute" and I think she is trying to reassure herself more than me.

She comes back and sits in the chair. "Are you worried about it?" she asks frankly. "Worried about what?" I question her, not understanding what she is asking. "About it not being an accident. About Jake... initiating the process so you could be brought here. Does it bother you that Jake 'defrosted' you so to speak because he wants to 'be' with you?" She's blunt, I'll give her that. "No" I said shaking my head side to side. "Not at all. I am thankful to Jake. If he hadn't done it I wouldn't be here now. I just wonder...why did he wait so long? Marcus said he struggled with the problem of what to do with me. Why not do this in the beginning, when he first found out exactly what was going on? I just wonder, that's all. I am not mad or hurt. Just so confused, that's all. You have to admit, it's a confusing situation." She nods her head in agreement. "I know it's confusing for you dear. Marcus should never have told you anything. Seeing as how he did, he should have told you how difficult it was for Jake. I wish you could know how it killed him to have to wait. He has grown into such a strong man, Jesse. He gets that from his father."

She straightens her back and lifts her chin. "Go on" I plead. "I really should not be telling you anything either. But, Jake's the son I never had and I don't want him hurt. I'll tell you what I can... just so you'll understand him better." I am anxious to hear it, "Please, tell me. Fran, you can't imagine what it's like for me. I have left everyone I've ever known and loved and am now here, thirty-one years later. I know that you and Sherman and Jake are here for me, but it's so strange. Any information will help. Please." Fran sighs. "Well, I'll tell you that Jake did struggle with what to do. He wanted to get you out of the lab as quickly as possible. But he didn't want to bring you here until he had everything ready for both you and now I understand, the baby too. He had your safety in mind too, dear. You have to know that every morning I saw him as he struggled with it. It was all he could do to not rush to the lab and defrost you right then. Sometimes we'd talk about it. When he brought you here he wanted things to work out. He wanted to find out for sure and finish this thing with this Brian fellow. He wanted a relationship with you and desperately wanted it to work out."

With that I look directly at her, searching her eyes to find out exactly how much she knew about our 'relationship'. She doesn't give away anything. I can only guess she knows we've made love. Probably by the way Jake's acting. "Jake loves you Jesse. He has felt a strong connection to you for so long. My only fear is that if your relationship doesn't work out that it will be devastating for him. I just don't want to see him hurt. He deserves to be happy Jesse. So, please...don't break his heart. I'm not sure he'd ever take a chance on anyone ever again if you hurt him." I know she is being protective but I am offended, "Fran! I would never do such a thing! I *do* love Jake...and not just for what he's done for me. There's something about him. I... I feel a strong connection to him too. I am going to marry Jake and he will become the father of this child. This baby will know nothing but love. I swear on my child's life, I would never hurt Jake. Never!" Fran reaches over and pats my hand. "Now, now. Don't go getting yourself all worked up. Calm down. I am glad to hear you want to be with Jake. We see the way you two look at each other. It kind of reminds me of Sherman and me when we first fell in love."

I squeeze her hand. "Now, that sounds like a story I'd love to hear." I hear what I think is the muffled sound of a car door slamming. Shortly after the first slam I hear another. Fran rushes to the French doors. She clasps her hands together and bounces up and down. "That's them. They're back!" She hurries to my side and holds my hand. "Jesse, please don't mention anything I told you. Jake's really kind of shy and I don't think he'd like it if he knew." I nod, "Oh, don't worry about it Fran. Mums the word. I promise." She sighs, "Thank you dear" and she bends down and hugs me.

Jake rushes in and smiles when he sees me. I hold out my hands to him and he takes them and holds them tight as he leans over me. We are nose to nose. "Well, it seems like things went well, judging by that smile on your face. Or - are you just happy to see me?" "Both" he says and gently kisses me. Oh, his lips feel so good. He kisses me again, this time harder. I wrap my arms around his neck and pull him to me. Jake sits on the bed, leaning into me and kisses me again. We both feel the passion between us and don't want it to end. Jake forces himself to pull away from me.

"How are you? How do you feel?" he ask as he sits holding my hands. "Oh, I'm just fine now that you're back." Fran smiles quietly next to my bed. Jake blushes when he sees her. "Well, dear, tell us how it went" Fran ask. Jake stands up and paces beside my bed. "Well, there's not much to tell. He has agreed to take the information and leave us alone. I told him Jesse will meet him in three days at the cafe. The following week I'll have one of my guys take him the documentation and that will be that." A broad smile crosses his face. He looks me square in the eyes, "Then we'll be able to begin our lives together...as husband and wife." "Oh, Jake! That's what I want. To be able to be with you! To try to get back to a normal life! To put all of this behind us!" I hold out my hands to him. "Whoa, wait a minute. Don't get too excited just yet" he says as he holds my hands again. "I still need to examine you. Let's worry about Brian later. I don't trust him at all. We'll have to see what happens. For now, tell me, have you been a good patient? Have you stayed in bed?"

"Yes, Dr. Bradley, of course I have. Fran hasn't left my side and she is my witness." He smiles. "Great. Now, if you don't mind, let me check you out." He takes the scanner and runs it over my body from head to toe. I see the light flashing but I keep quiet. Next he puts his stethoscope to his ears and listens to my breathing and checks my pulse. When he is done he looks down and sighs. "Oh come on Jake...tell me. What's going on? Did it work? Is the baby okay? What?" "Now, Jesse, stay calm. The baby's fine. The medicine hasn't worked completely though. I'm afraid I'll need to do the laser procedure. It's just a quick five minute procedure. Completely painless. You might feel a warm sensation, but no pain. I'm sorry, Jess. I need to do it as soon as possible." I try to process what he's saying but it's hard to focus. I feel lightheaded. Jake asks Fran to get Sherman. She leaves the room immediately without asking questions.

"Jesse, are you okay?" he ask as he bends down and kisses me. "Yeah, I'm fine. Just shocked I guess. I mean, I just thought the medicine would work and you wouldn't have to do anything else. I mean, I feel fine physically now. I haven't had any more cramps. Oh, Jake, are you sure you need to do this?" He gently hugs me. "Yes baby." I look down and run my finger across the sheet. "Is it...dangerous?" I ask with a wavering voice. "No, not at all. I promise. It's quick and painless, and a much better option than the old way." "What is the 'old way'?" He gives me the all business Jake look. "Well, to be honest it's surgery on your uterus and the top of your cervix. It takes hours and patients used to have to undergo anesthesia. That process is bloody, takes too long and the recovery is painful." "How long will this recovery be?" Jake squeezes my hand. I guess he can tell I am more than a little nervous. "Baby, I promise, a quick five minutes and that's it. You will have to rest a lot today. But you'll be up and walking tomorrow, no restrictions. Although I do want you to take it easy until you meet with Brian. What do you say, Jesse?"

"Okay. I trust you and I know if you say it's necessary then it must be necessary. Well, when do we do it?" Sherman walks in with Fran on his heels. "Well, I was thinking right now." Jake leans over and hugs me. He softly whisper "Don't worry; I won't let anything happen...I won't let anything go wrong." He sits up and brushes his right hand over my cheek and into my hair. "There's no time like the present" he says, slapping his hands on his knees as he stands up. "Sherman, please carry Jesse to the clinic. Fran, I'm afraid the only thing I can ask of you is lunch. Marcus is going to stay with us until after dinner." Fran nods her head. "Is there anything in particular you boys would like for lunch?" "No, just something hot. Whatever is easy for you. Don't go to a lot of trouble." She laughs, "Oh, you boys are never trouble! It'll be ready and waiting for you when you finish. Jesse, Jake's a fine doctor. Don't you worry. You're in the best of hands." She smiles kindly at me and then turns and walks out quickly. Sherman comes over and instructs me to wrap my arms around his neck like earlier. I do so and he carries me downstairs. He is still strong and burly for his age. I can only imagine how handsome he must have been when he was younger.

28

Jake follows behind us. He holds the medical bags in his right hand and the scanner in his left. I watch him over Sherman's right shoulder. He mouths 'I love you' and it warms my heart. I do the same and then giggle. Jake smiles and shakes his head. When we reach the rec room the first thing I notice is Marcus standing near the couch. He gives me a thumbs up and smiles at me. Next, I see the clinic door is open behind the bar. Sherman gently places me on the exam table and turns to go. Just as he is about to leave he turns, looks at me and smiles. "Don't worry, you'll be fine. Fran and I will be right here when you are done. We will all take good care of you and the baby." With that he leaves the room and Jake shuts the door. I watch him scrub his hands and put on gloves.

He asks me to don a paper mask then lie back and put my feet in the stirrups. I do as he asks though I feel a little embarrassed. I remind myself that it's nothing he hasn't seen already. If anyone else besides Jake were doing this I would be far too embarrassed. "Now Jess, I am going to run a sterilization program. It kills the germs in the air and around us. It is perfectly safe for us. You'll smell the slight smell of bleach the last few seconds." Jake enters a code on the keypad on the wall and immediately I hear movement above us. I look up and see four ceiling tiles slide open and sprinkler heads drops down. At the same time a see through door drops down and completely covers the door to the clinic. It looks like glass but seems more flexible, not as heavy as glass or Plexiglas. Okay, this is strange. Impressive but weird.

A slight hissing sound fills my ears. It reminds me of air being let out of a balloon. After a minute and a half I do smell the slight bleach smell. The hissing sound stops, the sprinkler heads folds themselves back up into the ceiling and the tiles close. Jake walks over and squeezes my hand. "Okay, we're going to get started." He grabs the IV pole and rolls it a little closer to us. I watch him connect the tubing together and then to the IV bag itself. He cleans my arm and inserts a needle. I gasp a little but the pain from the stick quickly goes away. He is quick and efficient. Once he sees it is patent and flushing well he tapes the IV firmly to my arm and smiles. He connects the IV tubing to my newly acquired IV site. "There is pain medicine in your IV, along with necessary fluids your body needs. You are probably a little dehydrated too. So, we'll just give it a minute to start working. Are you okay?" "Yes, just a little nervous, that's all. I trust you though. I just want to get this over with." He nods, "I know baby, just hang in there. It'll be over with before you know it." Jake takes the scanner and runs it over my whole body again. He moves it from side to side around my pelvic area. Once he gets the information he wants he turns it off and sits it on the counter. Jake turns on the big lights near my feet. They are so bright they blind me. I have to squeeze my eyes shut and when I open them I see spots.

"Sorry about that. Just try not to look directly into the lamps, I know they are blinding." I watch Jake position the stool at the end of the exam table, in between the stirrups. He steps past me and I hear him open a drawer and pull out something wrapped in plastic. He opens whatever it is and tosses the plastic in the trash. He walks past me and sits on the stool. I laugh when I see him. He is wearing a hideous pair of clear safety glasses. The kind I had to wear in chemistry lab in high school. "Nice fashion statement" I say. He sneers at me. "Yeah, yeah...glad you like them. You know...if they would have told me I'd have to wear these things I probably would have dropped out of medical school." After a shared laugh Jake gets serious.

"Well, they do serve a purpose. They are magnavision. The dials on the sides control the level of magnification. They actually work really great, especially for this type of procedure." God he looks good, even in his ridiculous glasses. How handsome can one guy be! He's got the brains to match his looks. I shake my head and smile. "Okay, now you're starting to scare me. You're beginning to sound like a real doctor!" He smiles back and then dons a face mask himself. "Enough of the wise cracks already. Okay, now, lie back and keep still. Do not move your feet...and please... don't kick me in the face." "I promise I won't" I say as he rolls the cart closer to him. "Ready?" he asks me. I shake my head yes.

Jake takes something off the tray and with his empty left hand he raises my gown. "Lift up" he says. I do so and he pushes my gown up until it is in the middle of my stomach. My whole bottom is exposed. He tosses the pad in the garbage and places his left hand on my right thigh. "Okay,

Jess, I'll talk you through this whole procedure. Just relax and lie still. Close your eyes if you'd like. Whatever makes you feel comfortable. I have to insert the clamp now. It might be cold and you'll feel a little pressure" he says as he slowly pushes the clamp. Oh, men doctors always say that. They don't know how this thing feels. I feel the sting and then a slight twinge as he clamps it in place.

"Just let me clean this up a bit and then I can start the actual procedure." I look down and watch him take one of the long q-tips and dip it in the ointment bowl. He pulls it out and it's covered in goo. He scrapes some of it off into the bowl but keeps a large amount on the swab. "Okay, here we go" he says as he focuses on the task at hand. He gently swabs the area. It's not painful, but the stinging is increasing to the point of almost being painful. I need a distraction. "So, tell me Dr. Bradley. How many of these 'procedures' have you done?"

He pulls the q-tip out and drops it into the empty bowl. Long strings of dried blood are wrapped around the q-tip and a bloody goo oozes from the stem itself. He puts ointment on another q-tip swab and continues his work. "Oh, let me see. I guess I sat in on about four of these in school. I have performed four others. One just months ago in Australia. That one was definitely interesting. She's the one that kicked me in the face." Nice. "Sounds like a great experience" I say. "Australia, what were you doing there?" Jake reaches up with his left hand and adjusts the dial of his mag-navision fashion glasses.

"It's a long story. Her terrorist boyfriend got scared and she panicked a little. Other than that, it all went as planned. Once I completed her procedure and made sure that both she and the baby were okay, they let us go." He pulled out the second goo covered swab. It too had strings of dark dried blood mixed in with bright red blood. "Let you go?" I ask him. "Yes, they were holding us hostage until they could hide the nuclear and biological arsenal they've managed to build up. They claim that we were trespassing on private property, which we were of course, but that was no reason to hold us. I mean, really, we were just carrying out our mission. A guy's got to have a little fun!"

Jake was quiet for a moment. I urge him to continue. "Our mission there was to get the proof of their terrorist build up, but also to destroy what weapons we could destroy while in country. Needless to say we destroyed very little, because while I was doing a procedure on Natasha, the pregnant

girlfriend, her thoughtful boyfriend hid the rest of the weapons and anything relating to the weapons. They have huge underground labs, bunkers
and warehouses that hold all of their weapons. The scientists that work
on the weapons live in those bunkers and work in the labs. Some of them
haven't been seen for years above ground. It's their own underground city.
They've given a new meaning to the term 'down under'."

Has the world changed that much in thirty-one years? "But, I don't
understand. I thought that we were friends with Australia. I mean, I
didn't think they were a threat to us and I certainly did not think they had
weapons like that." Jake put ointment on a third swab and quickly went
back to work. "How are you? Is this okay?" he asks. "Yes, I think I am
use to the stinging now, or maybe it's the pain killer in the IV. Either way,
I'm fine, keep talking."

"Well, they didn't have weapons like that. It's a changed world Jesse.
You wouldn't believe it but Russia is our greatest ally now. All the fighting
between Israel and Palestine finally stopped twenty-two years ago. Both
had been ravaged by the war. There is not much left. A group of allied
countries, England, France, Germany, Russia, Spain, Italy and the United
States got together and decided to do away with both regimes and start
fresh. Give the people of those countries all the monetary help and hands
on assistance they need to rebuild their countries. It took seven years, but
we did it. The government implemented a volunteer program that was
simple. If you volunteered your time for a year, they would pay your family
your yearly pay upfront. So that families here did not suffer while trying
to help. Also, a family member had to step in and learn and take over the
job of the volunteer while he or she was gone. Volunteers had to have a two
year break in service before they could volunteer again."

"Wow, that's different. Sounds like a neat program." Jake with-
drew the third swab. It was much cleaner than the previous two. He
took a fourth swab and dipped it in the ointment. He continued talking
while carefully working. "All the different church groups got involved and
signed up thousands of volunteers. The church leaders were instrumental
in getting clothing donations, food donations, materials for the rebuilding
of schools, churches and single family dwellings. Our allies were doing the
same in their countries. It was a huge undertaking, but it worked. The
church leaders had the foresight and wisdom to know that in order for it

to be successful the spiritual needs must be met, along with the incessant physical needs."

Jake put the swab in the bowl with the others. "Okay, now I'm going to start your procedure. Just breathe steadily. You may feel a warm sensation but it should not be hot or painful. If it is then tell me. This part takes about five minutes, depending on the person." Jake picks up a piece of equipment and holds it up. It looks like a silver water gun. "This is the laser gun. It is a very precise piece of machinery and is very easy to manipulate. Just stay still and don't make any sudden movements." I am no fool and he doesn't have to tell me twice. "No problem here. I'll be still." Jake quickly goes to work. Within seconds he stops and adjusts the magnification of his goggles and re-calibrates the laser gun. He hunches his shoulders down a little, leans forward and gets back to work.

My pubic area is reflected in his goggles. Since I don't want to stare at myself I look up at the ceiling. Still confused, I asked "So, in just seven years we rebuilt two countries? And how does Australia fit into all this?" He glances up at me and then returns to work. "Well, we were not completely done in seven years. They both had solid governments of their own. Both democratic too. There was still a lot to be done though. We implemented training programs in both countries and are still helping people there today. Our churches have scaled back their programs, but they are still very active. In the beginning, Iraq teamed up with Iran, Pakistan, Saudi Arabia and Syria to try to take over Israel and Palestine. The press nick-named them 'The Radical Five'. Immediately, T-shirts popped up with 'Kill the Rad 5' or 'Rad 5 Slaughterhouse' on them."

"Now, I have never been one to keep up on foreign policy but even I know that something like that is huge" I say, taking a deep breath. Jake nods and continues working. "Keep in mind the allies that helped rebuild Israel and Palestine had not intended to fight a war. All were in agreement, however, that the aggression had to be stopped before the progress was lost. So... they committed their military forces and won the battle. Iraq and Iran were virtually leveled." *Well, it's about time* I think to myself. "Good. I have hated Iraq since the Gulf War." Smiling, he continues. "The infrastructure of Pakistan and India were basically destroyed and Syria lost the majority of their population in the battle. To make a long story short, the 'Radical Five' put their differences aside and joined to create one aggressive force. They salvaged what they could and moved to Australia. They had terrorist in place in Australia for years prior to this. The majority of the terrorist were working in important jobs that required high levels of education. Some worked in highly technical fields while others worked for the Australian government."

This makes no sense. None. It would have taken years to get those people in place, in those jobs. I guess the world has changed a lot. And not for the better from what it sounds like. "So, you mean that they just went to Australia and took over? Wasn't there some kind of resistance? How did they pull it off?" He explained that there was resistance, but not enough to get rid of the 'Rad Five'. Once the violence started, the rich citizens of Australia simply just moved away; leaving the poorer citizens alone in the fight for their freedom. The Australian government could not protect itself from the terrorist. The allies got involved, but much too late. It was no use. Terrorism was rampant in Australia. "It's been that way for the last ten years or so now. The group I'm in... we fight terrorist in Australia on a regular basis. We're getting there. Eventually we will win this war against terrorism once and for all."

Jake finishes and sits the laser gun on the lab table between my legs. "Well, that's it. You're done. I told you it was quick and painless. How do you feel?" I sigh with relief. "Fine, I guess. So, is everything okay now? With the baby?" Jake gently reassuringly pats my right thigh. "You bet it is. Everything should be fine now. The medical precedent shows no further problems after having this procedure. Well, that is as long as the patient is healthy prior to getting pregnant. I don't think you have anything to worry about. I need to clean you up a little bit. I'm going to remove the clamp now." He does and I grimace without cause. To my surprise it is not painful at all.

Jake sees my surprised expression and grins. "It's a new type of clamp. It's not the hard metal of the old days. It's a type of plastic that softens while in your body. It keeps tightly clamped and is a bit more pleasant for the patient, especially during removal." "I'll agree with you on that, Dr. Bradley." Next he uses some of the gauze and gently cleans up the ooze and blood. He puts away the stirrups and hangs my legs over the edge of the lab table. After Jake turns off the lamps and moves them aside he stands and moves the stool out of the way.

After a moment of searching in the cabinet near the door he finds what he wants, quickly turns and hides it behind his back. Jake steps over to the lab table and pushes a button. The top part of the table lifts, making it easier for me to stand up. I feel pretty good, but can already tell I'll be sore tomorrow. Jake rushes to the end of the table and holds me firmly with his left hand. Once I am on my feet and stable he grins. "That a girl. You're doing great. I have one last thing I must ask you to do." He pulls his right hand from behind his back and dangles a disposable granny diaper in front of me. He smirks. I think he is enjoying this part way too much. "Oh, that's just great. You mean I have to wear that!" I say in disbelief. "Hey, I wore magnavision for you!" he says grinning. "Okay, okay...you're the doctor. Whatever!" He helps me slip the granny diaper on and pull my gown down.

We face each other and all at once I feel humiliated again. Jake gently hugs me. "Jesse. Don't worry about it. It's no big deal. Honest. I'm glad I could do this for you. You retain your privacy with me. Besides...I love you." He lifts my chin and gently kisses my lips. "I know, it's just a humiliating position to be in, that's all." "Forget about it. I want you to focus on recovery. I am going to have Sherman carry you back upstairs. Would you like to sit at the dining room table with us for lunch, or do you prefer your room?" Thinking about how sore I will be, I quickly answer, "Oh, my room, definitely."

"All right, it's settled. Sherman will carry you up and Fran will bring your lunch. You just have to take it easy today and tomorrow. If you need to get up to go to the bathroom that's fine, but stay in bed the rest of today if you can. Can you be a good patient for another day?" I know I am a terrible patient. For Jake, I will try to do what he asks of me. "I think I can. As long as you hang out with me so I'm not bored." He slightly nods his head. "Oh, I think I can manage that" he says.

Jake punches in the door code and the clear door lifts and goes back into hiding in the ceiling. I look up and can't even tell where it came from. The lab door opens and I see Sherman, Fran and Marcus all sitting at the bar. Sherman jumps up and comes into the lab. "Where to?" Jake asked him to carry me back to my room. With the grace of a man half his age, Sherman lifts me up and makes his way just past the bar. As he stands there Jake tells them all that it was a successful procedure, that there were no problems and that both baby and I are fine. Fran and Marcus give each other a high-five. "Well, I need to clean up a little. Fran why don't you go ahead and serve their lunch. I'll be up shortly."

Fran follows Sherman up the stairs and heads for the kitchen. Sherman carries me up the next set of stairs and gently places me in my bed. He covers me with the quilt. "You lie here for a moment and I'll help Fran bring up your lunch." I nod my head and watch him leave the room. 'Thank God that's over with' I think to myself. 'Thank God for Jake' I whisper, just before drifting into a light sleep.

29

A shuffling noise catches my attention and I open my eyes. Fran has brought a vase with fresh cut flowers while Sherman carries the lunch tray. I sit up and arrange the pillows behind me. Sherman carefully sits the tray over my legs and smiles. He turns and quickly leaves the room. Fran arranges the vase on the desk then stands next to the bed. "I want you to eat because it will help keep your strength up. I'll send Jake up in a few minutes to get the tray and check on you." She smiles and rubs my arm gently, then quickly leaves the room. She left my door open when she exited and occasionally a maid would walk by on her way to accomplish a task. Only one of the maids acknowledges me with a kind smile. The other two keep their eyes straight forward as they walk past my door.

As I finished up lunch I hear the distant sound of a phone ringing. Not long after that, Jake comes in and sits next to my bed. He smiles at me but I can immediately tell that something is wrong. "Jake what is it? What's wrong?" Jake holds my hand and looks down. He sighs and when he looks up his eyes lock on mine. "Jesse, I'm afraid I have some bad news. I have to go out on a mission. Marcus has to go with me. A group of our closest friends have been killed...just this morning...in Australia." His expression is grim. "Oh, Jake, I'm so sorry. That's horrible." I motion with my hands for him to come to me. He picks up the tray and sits it on the floor. He leans into me and I hug him tight. He sits back down in the chair and holds my hands again. He is quiet for some time.

When he looks up at me he forces a smile. "Jesse, I know you are looking forward to seeing Brian and getting some type of closure to your situation. I have arranged for two security teams to take you to see Brian. I don't think you should put it off just because I'm gone. It wouldn't be fair to you. Also, I have to tell you...every time I go on a mission it's with the understanding that I may not return...this particular mission may be the last thing I ever do." The words seep into my brain but I can't comprehend their meaning. It just can't be so. "Well, can't you just tell them that you can't do it? Can't you tell them that you quit and you just won't go?" A lone tear rolls down my left cheek. He shakes his head no.

"Jake, what do you mean? Don't go Jake! Please, don't leave us like this! We are so close to being happy! And the baby...she'll need you! You have to help me raise this child!" Now I start to shake as the meaning of his words sink in and fear rushes through me. "Jess, I can't back out. I *have* to go. My friends died over there doing what *we all* promised to do. Their mission went badly and we are being sent over to fix the problem. I can't and won't go into details, but please know this is an extremely dangerous mission. And know that I love you with all my heart and if I can, I will find a way to return to you...and the baby." I squeeze his hands tight. He has made his decision and I have to respect it and try to be supportive. "When do you have to leave?" I ask with a heavy heart. "Now" he says.

"Physically I'm sure you'll be fine. I'm leaving a phone number of a doctor you can trust with Fran and Sherman. If anything goes wrong, anything at all, don't hesitate to call him. He's a fine doctor. His name is Logan Eblin. He worked with my father for years. I worked with him for a short time during one of my internships before he opened his private ob-gyn practice. He is an honest and moral man. Very trustworthy and very good at what he does. If I don't come back, please contact him to follow you through the pregnancy. I'm not sure when this mission will be over with. Some missions take anywhere from a few hours to a few days. Others can take weeks. I've got to go eat a bite of lunch myself. Marcus left to say goodbye to Charlie. He'll be back within the hour and we are going to leave. As soon as I'm done with lunch I'll be back."

I watch him through blurred vision as he walks out of the room and my heart breaks. I throw myself down on the bed, landing face first into the pillows, and sob. I can't believe he has to go. Why? Why now? This is cruel. Is this my punishment for being happy? Is this my punishment for doing the cryonics project in the first place? Is this God's way of paying me back for messing where I shouldn't have messed? I pray over and over again that God would let Jake come back to me. I pray that this whole situation with Brian will be over soon so Jake and I can be happy. Desperate, I beg God not to take Jake away from me. I know now that I was stupid to take myself out of the equation. I missed out on precious time with my father and mother, and now I can't get that time back. April was right. I should have listened to her. "Dear God, please, please don't take Jake from me!

Not now. Not with the baby coming. Please find it in your heart to put an end to all of this and let me raise this child and be happy, with Jake." I swore I'd be a good wife; a good mother... that I'd never do another wrong thing in my life. Bargaining...that's what this is. I roll over, pull the quilt up and let the tears stream down my face. Resolved to the fact there's nothing I can do. Jake's leaving and he might not be coming back.

I lie there a while feeling sorry for myself and then realize that this may be the last time Jake lays eyes on me. I force myself to get up and go to the bathroom. I don't want him to remember a pitiful sight of a woman when he thinks of me. I wash my face and quickly brush through my hair. I use a gold hair clip and put my mane back. I go into the closet to the vanity and turned the light on. I sit down and find the bottle of liquid make-up in the top drawer. I dot the make-up on my face, rub it in and cover it with powder. I quickly put on a rose lip stick and rifle through the drawer until I find the blush I want. I accent my cheekbones with blush and then pick a plum colored eye shadow. After checking myself out in the mirror I realize what I forgot. I chose taupe eyeliner and quickly apply it. The finishing touch was the black/brown mascara. I sit still and look at myself again. There, now I look and feel a little better. I choose some diamond stud earrings and quickly put them on. I have to hurry. Jake will be here soon.

I slip into a loose fitting sleeveless summer dress made from a floral pattern. My granny diaper doesn't show through and I am pleased with my overall appearance. As soon as I turn the light off and sit on the edge of the bed Jake walks in. He comes over and leans down and kisses me on the cheek. "Jesse, I've been thinking over lunch. If anything happens to me I want to make sure you and the baby are taken care of. I want you to know that you are welcomed to live here for the rest of your life, if you want to. More than that, though, I have been thinking of the legal aspect of it all. I want you to marry me, right here, right now. Marry me, baby?" I gasp, shocked at his sudden proposal. "I'm sorry for the brevity, but we have to do it now. Marcus is on his way over and I have to go. Please Jess, will you marry me?"

My heart takes over and I don't have to give it any thought. "Oh, Jake, of course I will!" Carefully, he leans over and hugs me. He whispers in my ear, "We can get married with the whole lavish ceremony when I get back. I thought we could keep this private for now. I don't want to ruin the surprise or ceremony for everyone else. As soon as I get back we are going to have the best wedding you can ever imagine. I want you to get with Charlie and start making arrangements for our ceremony. Spare no expense. I want it to be incredible. Schedule it for two weeks from today at 2:00 p.m. I'll be back, I promise. Charlie will know all the right people to contact and will help you with your dress. She's great, just trust her. If something does happen and I don't return, then tell Fran and Sherman about our private ceremony and that they will need to contact my attorney for you. I will leave them a letter in my grey suit jacket pocket. Only give it to them if I don't return. Got it?" He pulls back from me and opens the door. A man enters and Jake shuts the door.

"Jesse, this is Mr. Mark Bowling, a Justice of the Peace. He will marry us now, and in a week he will hand deliver a copy of the marriage license to you and only you. Understand?" I shake my head yes and stand up. Jake walks over and stands next to me. Once we are still, Mr. Bowling eases closer to us and begins to speak his simple yet binding words. Within minutes the ceremony was over. Jake lifts my chin and gently kisses me. As tears fill his eyes he says, "Now at least I can go with joy in my heart, knowing that you and the baby will be taken care of if anything should happen to me. If I don't return, please tell the baby how much I loved him or her, and that I'm sorry for not being there."

Clearing his throat, Mr. Bowling says, "It's customary for me to take a few pictures of the happy couple. May I take some pictures now?" Jake turns around, wipes his eyes and runs his hands over his face. He turns to face me and takes my arm in his. We smile for our pictures; neither of us wants the moment to end because we know he has to leave. Jake thanks Mr. Bowling and asks him to let himself out. "Jesse, I need to do this, please understand. However, I have already spoken to my commander about quitting. No one else knows I talked to him about it, not even Marcus. I was kind of keeping it quiet. I did not want to get your hopes up and then not have it happen. He's checking out some guys to be replacements for the ones we've lost over the past six months and he said he'd look for a replacement for me as well. It may take a few months though."

"Oh, Jake, that's the best news. Well, besides our wedding, that is!" He pulls me close to him and kisses my neck. I feel his warm breath on my shoulder and wish we could be together one last time before he leaves. "Jake, please be careful. Please come back to us, please!" "I'll do my best" he says and pulls away from me. "You lie down and rest today and tomorrow. Promise the good doctor again that you will be a good patient and take care of yourself, as the doctor ordered." I hold up my hand as if taking an oath of office and say "I promise." "Good, now try not to be upset because it may adversely affect the baby. I promise I'll send word as soon as I can. If I'm not here the day before the wedding don't worry. Go ahead with everything as planned and I'll be there, I promise, 2:00 sharp! I love you." He kisses my forehead and walks out of the room. I can only hope he's not walking out of my life forever. I dash to the window.

Oblivious to everything around me I am lost in my sorrow. I sob and cry and pray while I watch as Sherman opens the limo doors for Jake and Marcus. They disappear inside the limo and Sherman shuts the doors. He gets in the driver's seat and within moments the car drives out of the circular drive and past the open gate. Paralyzed with fear I can't move. Oh god...this could be it. This could be the last time I ever see Jake. I pray it's not. I close my eyes and lean my head against the wall. I stand there for what seems like an eternity. I jump when a hand touches my shoulder. I open my eyes and quickly turned my head, hoping that it was Jake but knowing it couldn't be. Instead I am looking at a blonde petite woman with green bloodshot eyes. The streaks her tears made through her make-up were just as good as a name tag. I am face to face with Charlie.

30

Charlie hugs me and we cry together. Our sameness in this unique situation coupled with the fear of the unknown, of what may come, makes us fast friends. I believe it is the fear that somehow bonds us, the way that airplane crash survivors are forever bonded. She pulls out a handful of tissue from her purse and hands them to me. I quickly accept it, knowing that my make-up is running like my nose. She digs around and pulls out another handful of tissue and uses them herself. Once composed, she motions for me to sit on the end of the bed. I do so and she sits facing me. "Marcus asked me to stay here this week and help you with whatever you may need. He told me about the baby and about the problems you have had. You look great for someone that just had surgery this morning."

"I feel okay" I say, still thinking about Jake. A terrible thought crosses my mind. What if Jake comes back and Marcus doesn't? Oh, no, that would be devastating not only for Jake, but for this woman sitting across from me. I quickly put the thought out of my mind; maybe if I don't think about it, it won't happen. Charlie smiles warmly at me. "Now, I know that doc says you have to rest today and tomorrow. Fran said one of the maids would bring my bags up. I packed lightly because I didn't know how long I'd need to be here. Marcus and I practically live just around the corner, so to speak. I can run home and grab something else if I need to. Fran's putting me in the suite on the left end of the hallway. So, I'll be close if you need me, or just want to talk. I thought I could hang out here with you today. Maybe we could play cards or read or something. Talk a little, get to know each other. Maybe even gossip a little. What do you say?"

She smiles at me again and I can't help but notice her teeth, white and lined up perfectly. Not one out of place. They really make her warm smile. All in all, I size her up to be a warm, caring person. I think we will be really good friends. I could use a friend now. At least she's more my age. It's different with Fran and Sherman because they're older. What am I saying - so am I! A chill runs through me. I force a lame smile and say, "Sounds great. I'm going to change." I find a pair of loose fitting beige slacks and a short-sleeved navy button down in the closet and quickly change. I kept the earrings on and left my hair up. A few light brown strands of hair came loose and they now frame my face. I fluff my bangs and realize the mascara I used earlier must be waterproof because it is not all over my face as I expected. I cover my tear streaks with powder, walked out and shut the door. Charlie was gone. I go to the bed, make it and arrange the pillows. I just don't feel like being in bed right now. I choose a book I've never heard of from the shelf and sit in the chair near the desk. I take a deep breath in and the fragrance from the fresh cut flowers in the vase on the desk fills my nose.

As I read the jacket I learn the book is a love story about a single mom who finds the man of her dreams in the most unlikely of places, a DRMO site, which is an old scrapyard for military furniture and office equipment. I close the book and throw it onto the desk. Maybe I'll read it later, who knows, it could be a good escape from my current situation. Restless, I get up and head to the bathroom. The granny diaper has dried blood in it. There is a small patch of fresh bright red blood directly in the middle. I will keep this thing on for tonight, but tomorrow... it goes. As I wash my hands my stomach growls. Wow, I guess I am hungry. I wonder what time it is as I dry my hands.

I slowly head back to the chair and sit down. I casually prop my feet up on the desk. I have always liked to sit this way. If I knew how much the desk cost it may deter me from putting my feet on it; but since I don't and since I don't have any shoes on, I figure the desk will be fine. I am lost deep in thought when Charlie comes in. A man follows behind her carrying a Queen Anne chair. The baby blue upholstery is a damask pattern, one of my favorites. She orders him to sit the chair near the desk. He does and quickly leaves the room. Charlie sits down and smiles. "Well, I have some great news. There's nothing that makes a woman feel better than a haircut, a manicure and pedicure. I called my spa and they are sending over my two favorite stylists and favorite nail technician in the morning. By late afternoon we'll be beautiful!"

"Oh, Charlie, you didn't have to do that!" She pats my arm lightly. "Oh yes I did. I am desperate for a haircut and my nails are awful. The distraction will benefit us both. If...when... Marcus comes back I want to look extra-special! So, I will hear no arguments from you. Just enjoy it! Besides, I'll bet Jake hasn't thought of setting up a hair or nail appointment for you, has he?" I shake my head no. "Well, no...I guess he hasn't. We really haven't had time to worry about stuff like that yet. I mean, so much has happened...I haven't even really given it much thought myself!" She grabs my hands and holds them up for inspection. "Yes, yes, we will get you a manicure. You really do need one. Your nails are a nice length though. They seem strong. What color do you like?" I laugh out loud. "Well, I really don't know. I do remember that I use to wear a red nail polish during the summer. I always kept my toenails painted and wore sandals all the time. "A lady after my own heart" she says. "Don't worry because they'll bring every color under the sun for you to choose from. You can pick and choose the color that inspires you in the morning."

She released my hands and they flopped down into my lap. I remove my feet from the desk and sit up straight, facing Charlie. "Thank you" I say and try to smile warmly at her. "Thank you for just being here. For keeping me company. I know it's difficult for you, too. I just want you to know I really appreciate you being here and helping me. Okay?" She smiles back warmly at me but I see the sadness in her eyes. "Okay. I wanted to get over here and meet you sooner, but I've been gardening a bit and Marcus has told me how busy you guys have been. So, I figured I'd wait a week or so before barging in on you. You know, give you a week to get your bearings."

"Thanks, I needed time I guess. Speaking of, do you know what time it is?" She shakes her head yes. "It's almost five-thirty. I saw Fran a minute ago. She said she fixed a huge salad and was going to send us some hot steak-n-cheese sandwiches up for dinner to go with it. Also, she fixed a peach cobbler and a fruit bowl for desert." The thought of a steak-n-cheese sandwich takes my stomach growling to a new level. "That sounds great, I'm starving!" She nods, "You'd better eat while you can. After you have the baby you'll be back to watching what you eat." We laugh about it a little. "This cryonics trip has had one benefit...I lost something like fifteen or twenty pounds!" Charlie's eyes widen in surprise. "Wow, that's great... but what a way to lose it!"

A man knocks, doesn't wait for an answer, and comes in and sets up a silver table. Another man follows him and sets up two silver chairs with navy cushions and places them on opposite sides of the table. A maid comes in and puts a white linen table cloth on the table, arranges a small assortment of flowers tied together with silk ribbons and lace in the center of the table, and sets the table with crystal goblets, plates, bowls, napkins and silverware. She is efficient and quickly leaves the room without speaking a word. Charlie and I look at each other and laugh. "They are certainly professional" I say. Next, a couple of waiters enter the room. The first is carrying a large round silver tray with a rounded silver top with a handle. Balancing the tray with his left hand, he carefully opens the lid by the handle, revealing two delicious looking steak and cheese sandwiches. The second waiter places the sandwiches on our plates and quickly leaves the room. The first waiter replaces the lid on the silver tray and follows the second waiter out. I look at Charlie and say, "I swear, I don't think I've ever seen anything like this before!" We both grin.

Fran comes in next with a couple of helpers, one carries the salad, the other carries the deserts. Fran carries a pitcher of water. A man follows them in with a silver tray he quickly sets up. Fran motions for the girls to sit the salad and the deserts down. They do so and immediately leave with the man. Fran sits the water pitcher down and turns to face us. "You girls enjoy your dinner. If you need anything tonight I'll be here. Jesse, how are you feeling?" she asks directly looking at me. "Oh, I'm fine" I say. "Fran, is Sherman back yet?" I ask, curious. "Yes, he got back an hour ago. He went to the stable to check on the horses. He'll have dinner with me in the kitchen tonight. I have a long list of jobs to supervise and a few to finish myself. So, you two enjoy yourselves, but don't hesitate to come get me if you need to. Jesse, I've got the doctor's number. Please let me know immediately if you need me to call him." With that she left us and closed the door.

"It never ceases to amaze me...how she keeps this house running so smoothly. She has only been kind and warm to Marcus and me. Yet, I get the sense that she's a drill sergeant when it comes to her employees." I nod my head in agreement and we get up and sit at the table. Charlie pours our water. "I guess I get that too" I say. I watch Charlie dish salad into our bowls. I add, "I sense that the girls know their place; however, they look up to her. She might run the house with stern precision and maybe even a sharp word here or there, but I really think they probably love working for and with her." Charlie took a bite of her salad. "You are right" she says. We ate in silence, each lost in our own thoughts.

After dinner, we watch the precision of the staff as they take away the dishes and dismantled the tables as quickly as they had set them up. Sherman came in and started a fire for us. "Did they take off okay?" she asks him. Sherman nods his head yes. "Were they in one of those planes like before, or did they leave in one of those new-fangled X-52 choppers?" Sherman turned to look at us as if debating what he should tell us. "They left in the plane. They will fly until nine tonight and then, at an undisclosed location, they will land and get on the X-52. That's the only stop they have. From there it will only take them three hours to reach their target fly zone. I'm sorry ladies, that's all I can say...for your own protection."

Charlie smiles at him. "That's all right Sherman, we understand. I just wanted to know that they took off okay. Thanks for the fire, and the update." He winks at her and smiles at both of us. His gaze lands on me. "Jesse, how are you?" I shrug my shoulders, "Oh, I'm fine, thanks. As well as can be expected." "Well, ok, good. I'll be downstairs with Fran if you need me." As he left he closed the door behind him. We sit and talk for hours. Charlie takes care of the fire, moving the logs around a couple of times. She asks me a lot of questions about what I remember and how I felt about it all...and especially how I felt about Jake. She points to the rings on my fingers and ask if Jake gave them to me. I do not feel guarded with Charlie. I really feel that I can be completely honest with her. Therefore, I answer all of her questions and tell her everything about Jake and me, even revealing that we have already slept together many times and that it was wonderful.

Charlie discloses the most intimate details regarding her relationship with Marcus, swearing me to secrecy. Some of that stuff I could guess about him. He definitely looks like the kind of guy who likes to take control in the bedroom. By the end of the night we look and feel like old friends. Charlie had thrown her purse on the desk earlier. She got up off the side of the bed and got it. She dug around until she found her watch. "Nine-fifteen" she says out loud. "They are getting on the X-52 right now. I always get nervous around this time." I feel like I should say something to try to comfort her. "I don't know much about this mission stuff, but I do know Jake and Marcus. They wouldn't take the X-52 unless it was a good helicopter. I am sure they will get to their destination safely." She is distracted by my statement. "Yes" she says, "the X-52 is the best for troop transport. It's top of the line. It replaced the Blackhawk UH-60's." I gawk at her in amazement. How the hell does she know that? She grins sheepishly at me. "Well, that's what the guys say all the time." I watch her pace the floor next to the bed for a few minutes. I keep quiet and leave her to her thoughts, as I have my own worrying to do about Jake. Finally, I interrupt the silence. "Charlie, thanks for spending the evening with me. I want to talk more tomorrow, and we need to start planning my wedding, but for now I'm beat. I'm going to bed."

"Oh, Jesse, you're tired! I'm so sorry to have kept you up. I should have realized you'd get tired quickly, I mean, with your surgery today and all. I'm being counterproductive! I promised I'd make sure you get your much needed rest and here I am keeping you up!" She drops her watch back into her purse and heads for the door. "Don't be silly" I say. "I really enjoyed talking with you tonight. I am glad we are getting to know each other. It's been so long since I've had a friend...literally!" We share one last laugh. "Besides" I say, "I would have run you out sooner if I needed to." Still smiling she waived a quick goodbye. "Get your beauty rest. I'll swing by and get you on the way to breakfast in the morning."

I change into a pair of flannel pajamas and shuffle my way to the bathroom. I take my hair down and run my fingers through it. I wash my face and brush my teeth. While I use the bathroom I am pleased to see that the fresh spot of blood has not grown. In fact, it looks like the bleeding has slowed considerably. I pick up the book off the desk as I walk by. I climb into bed and prop myself up on the fluffy pillows. I read three chapters but cannot focus. My mind keeps drifting to Jake. Where is he now? Is he safe? Finally, I sit the book on the round table next to the bed and turn the light off.

For a long time I lay in glow of the dying fire, thinking about what may or may not happen in my immediate future. Just before I fall asleep I wonder about my meeting with Brian. How will he look? How will he act? Will I be in any physical danger from him? If so, why would he want to harm me? Will he want to see the baby once it's born? It's completely out of the question as far as I'm concerned. No way in hell will I let him near the baby! Does he regret his decision so long ago? Did he ever really love me? Did he have anything to do with me volunteering for the project in the first place? Did he kill Jake's men as Jake suspects? Does he regret any of it? Who is Katy? How'd he meet her and was he with her while he was living with me? Too many unanswered questions loom in my mind. My brain is numb. I slowly doze off to sleep searching for answers.

31

I lie in bed awake for a long time. I have not slept well. I have tossed and turned and thought of Jake and Marcus all night. I hope they come back to us. I hope their mission is successful. I am afraid of what Jake will have to do, but I know he must be trained well or he wouldn't be on a team like that. I tell myself that he and Marcus are the best, are well trained and that soon they will come back home. When I see the first signs of daylight I figure I may as well get up. Charlie did say she would come get me on the way to breakfast. I am guessing I have an hour to get ready. I slowly get up and head to the bathroom. I toss the grannie diaper and quickly shower. It feels great to wash my hair. I let the hot water massage my back and I think of the first time Jake and I had sex. I only miss him more and try to think about the baby instead. I am blown away by the fact that Jake is willing to raise this child as his own. I wonder if the baby will be a boy or girl. Girl, I hope. I don't want a boy that will look like the rat bastard. I don't want to ever have to look into Brian's face ever again. But I know I don't get to choose and I suppose I will be happy as long as the baby is healthy. As I dry off I find and use a pad so I can monitor any further bleeding. I want to make sure I know if it gets worse. I dress in loose fitting jeans and a brown silky tank top that ties behind my neck. I wear socks but no shoes. I apply a little bit of make-up and mascara. I dry my brown unruly hair and push it back into a large brown and silver hair clip. As I am making my bed Charlie comes in and smiles, "Good morning. Just leave that. Come on, Fran has breakfast ready." Will I ever get use to having other people in the house clean up after me? I don't think so. "I am almost finished" I say as I hurry and finish. We go down to breakfast. While sitting at the large table in the kitchen, Charlie and I are both quiet. I am thinking of Jake and I am sure she is thinking of Marcus. Fran is busy at the stove. She has cooked eggs, bacon, and pancakes this morning. She has already put large glasses of orange juice in front of us to go with our coffee, and now she is sitting down plates full of food. It looks delicious. We eat in silence and only occasionally glance at each other. When Sherman walks in we both look at him expectantly. "Sorry ladies. No word yet." He comes over and hugs us both in a fatherly way. "I promise to let you know as soon as I hear something." He smiles kindly at us but I think I can see the worry in his eyes. He goes to Fran and wraps his arms around her and hugs her too. She nods her head and keeps a determined look on her face. He says he has to work in the stables today and later will bring in more fire wood. He takes his plate from Fran and sits at the table and eats in silence. She places a cup of coffee in front of him and doesn't say a word. Fran eats standing up at the stove in thirty seconds flat. She washes her hands and then takes more things out of the refrigerator. I guess she is starting on lunch or dinner already.

When I can't stand the silence any longer I look to Sherman and ask, "When do you think we might hear something?" His eyes are flat and hard, he sighs. "There is no way to know. If all goes well maybe by lunch or dinner we may get word. Or it may not be until tomorrow. No way to really tell with these things." His face is not giving anything away either. "Oh, okay" I say, and resolve myself to the fact that I can't bug him every five minutes. I will just have to busy myself today and rest, like Jake wanted me to do. When I am finishing my juice Charlie glances over to me, "Hey, let's go to the sitting room for a few minutes." I grab my coffee cup and follow her there. There is a fire popping and cracking and the room is gloriously warm and cozy. I picture Jake sitting where Charlie sits and then I shake my head like I can shake the thought out of my head. She looks down at her perfectly polished toes, "You worried?" she asks me.

"Worried? No, I am going fucking nuts! What about you?" She doesn't look up, "Yeah, I am really worried this time. This is a rough one. I just want them back home in one piece!" We sit in silence for a while near the warmth of the fire. My insides are numb and I feel frozen all over again, despite the heat of the fire. This time I know it's the fear of the unknown. I refuse to let my thoughts wander down a dark path. I must remain positive for the baby and for Jake. I stand to take my coffee cup back to the kitchen and hear the front door open. I hear voices I don't recognize. Two men and a woman quickly prance into the sitting room. I have never seen them before. Charlie jumps up and hugs all three of them. She nods in my direction, "Thanks for coming on short notice. This is a well needed distraction for both of us. And we want to look really great when our guys get home." She introduces me to Reggie, Paul and Lorie. I cordially shake their hands and thank them as well. It is decided that we need to go downstairs to have our beauty treatments and we all turn to head in the direction of the staircase.

32

The team has worked through lunch and into late afternoon to make us incredibly beautiful. We have received haircuts, highlights, manicures, pedicures, facials, and have been waxed every conceivable place they could find to wax. The Brazilian wax was a little painful and I have never had it done before. They were consummate professionals and I am surprised it didn't take long. I am not sure of everything that pleases Jake, and can only hope he likes it. Apparently Charlie has it done all the time and says Marcus loves it. Afterwards, they completely applied our make-up and styled our hair. Since they worked through lunch Fran actually sent lunch down for all of us. Charlie and I barely nibbled at our food, and we left most of it sitting on our plates at the bar. I have been mindful to drink plenty of water because Jake says I need to. I trust him. I can't tell if I am dehydrated or not.

Charlie goes to the bathroom and I am lost in my thoughts worrying about Jake when Reggie and Paul go to their vehicle to retrieve the outfits they brought for us. Charlie sits next to me and we are silent. I take her hand in mine and am so thankful she is here with me. If I were alone I wouldn't know what to do with myself. She shakes her head, "I hate the waiting." I nod but don't respond. "They are good Jesse, the best of the best. They will come back!" I sigh. She has gone through this before, but I have not. I really hope Jake quits and soon. I do understand they depend on him, but we are now depending on him. Reggie and Paul enter the rec room laughing and Reggie is shaking his head about some private joke they are sharing. Reggie is boisterous and I wonder how he can be after working all day on both of us.

He hands one garment bag to Paul and unzips the other one. He lays it across the bar and pulls out a silver short dress that looks like it will barely cover a behind. There is no back to it and it has thin straps and a plunging v-neckline. "This beautiful piece of fabric is for Charlie. You will be absolutely stunning in it I know. I have also brought you matching shoes and earrings. You like?" She hugs him tightly, "I love it!" He smiles and is pleased that she is happy. Paul puts the other garment bag on the bar, unzips it and takes out another stunning creation. It is a shiny black short dress with narrow straps and also a plunging v-neckline. I gasp because it is beautiful but I can't imagine myself in such a dress. Paul says proudly, "You will look better than his favorite fantasy in this dress. You will be so beautiful his heart will have to burst open to let the love he feels for you out!" I tear up and hug him. "Thank you so much" I murmur and wipe my eyes so I don't ruin my make-up.

Reggie chimes in, "We also brought a silver silk gown and matching robe for Charlie and a black silk gown and matching robe for you, Jesse. In case you ladies want to get a little more comfortable." Charlie nods, "Thank you all for working so hard for us today. You have been the best help. We appreciate all you have done. Do you want to stay and eat?" Reggie and Paul both shake their heads simultaneously. Reggie says they must get going. They help Lorie clean up the few items left to claim and then they are ready to leave. We escort them to the door. Another round of hugs and they are gone. It is late and Fran informs us she will have dinner in the dining room in five minutes. We rush back downstairs to put our new dresses on. Upon returning to the dining room both Fran and Sherman do a double take. "Wow" Sherman says as he stares at both of us. "Wow, you two are stunning. Just absolutely stunning!" Sherman hugs us both and says again how beautiful we look. Fran hugs Charlie first and then me, telling us we are incredibly gorgeous and that she is proud of both of us. The table is formally set with an elegant beige table cloth. Candles and a large floral arrangement are exquisite as the centerpiece and there is stemware and china on the table. "This table is beautiful" I say to Fran. It looks like she has been keeping herself busy as well. I know her nerves are frazzled too. Fran and Sherman both join us at the table. They don't eat but they sit with us. Fran has been so kind to me. I glance over to her, "Are you sure you don't want to eat with us?" She nods. "I am sure. We have eaten a lot today." Sherman keeps looking at us but doesn't say anything else. I can tell he is thinking about Jake and Marcus, and probably wishing he was there to help them.

Charlie is the first to question Sherman, "Any news?" Sherman shakes his head no but I think he is holding something back. Why would he do that? I can't figure it out but my brain is over stimulated and I have to concentrate hard on eating the food in front of me. Of course I can't eat it all even though it is delicious. We try to help Fran afterwards but she will not hear of it. She sends us back down to the rec room to rest. We decide to watch a movie. That way we don't have to talk about anything and we can both rest and get lost in our own thoughts. Halfway through the movie I can't keep my eyes open. I can't stop worrying about Jake and Marcus. I look at Charlie and she is looking down at her hands. "Hey, I'm tired. Let's lie down and rest. They'll wake us up if we fall asleep." She nods and then yawns. We are both trying to be strong for the other but it is difficult. When we are lying on the large rug and have our pillows and blanket positioned perfectly, I take her hand. "Charlie, thank you so much for helping me get through today." She squeezes my hand, "I don't want to be anywhere else except here with you. We will do this together! Okay. Think positive. I am sure they are on their way back to us this very moment." I let her words sink into my numb brain as I drift off to sleep. Charlie yawns and also drifts off to sleep worrying about Marcus.

As soon as the wheels touchdown Jake and Marcus grab their packs and gear and stand in front of the door. They are both impatient for their own reasons. Jake knows the ache in the pit of his stomach will not go away until he is back with Jesse. He knew he loved who he thought she was. Once he started to get to know her, he knew he could never love any other woman. He knew he would never want to be with another woman. Somehow, she makes him the man he wants to be. A better man. A complete man. A happy man. Yes, she makes him very happy. When he is with her he feels satisfied. It is enough for him. He shakes his head in awe of her. She is truly a remarkable woman. She doesn't even realize her strength and power over him. He looks down and sees the dirt mixed with dried blood on a few of the knuckles of his left hand and recalls the fight. He closes his eyes tight and tries not to think about the close call. If it weren't for Marcus...No! He doesn't want to think about that now. He takes a deep breath and tries to center himself. The mission was successful even though it almost went to shit. They did what they had to do. It was difficult. The fighting was hard and there was bloodshed. Neither liked to be brutal but they knew they had to take care of business once and for all, and so they did. They lost some of their friends in the fight. With heavy hearts they rush out of the plane as soon as the doors open. As he descends the stairs Jake takes another deep breath and revels in the cool fresh air hitting his face. He immediately heads to the waiting limo where Sherman is standing and grinning at him. Marcus is lost in his own thoughts. He was glad Jake is back on safe ground with him. If it went the other way, and Jake wasn't here with him now, he wouldn't know what he would do. Truth is, Jake is his best friend and he hoped to always have Jake at his side. A guy doesn't get many friends like that in life. They mirrored each other in stance, fighting, and in all their actions just because they spend so much time together. They are more like brothers than best friends. They also think alike. Marcus knows it is killing Jake being away from Jesse. For Marcus, Jake's pain is almost palpable. Once they reach the limo Sherman slaps them both on the back. "It's good to see you boys." They nod at Sherman and quickly throw their gear in the trunk. Jake gives Sherman a quick run down of the mission. In turn, Sherman tells them what the girls have been doing to keep themselves busy. Marcus grins wildly, "Drive faster; I can't wait to get my hands on her!" At that, Jake grins his own devilish bad boy grin. He was just thinking the same thing. He runs his hands over his dirty face and through his hair. He knows he needs to shower but he has to see her first.

As always, Fran sent food and water with Sherman. Jake and Marcus are starving and eat it in the limo while Sherman races home. He knows their hearts are about to burst. He knows it firsthand because he used to be in their situation. He shakes his head thinking of a time long ago when he couldn't get back to Fran fast enough. A broad smile crosses his face as he thinks about the night they had. It was one of the best nights of his life. One of his best memories. He knows Jake and Marcus have their own memories to make tonight. He loves them and wants them to both find true happiness, the way he has done with Fran. He knows life is too short, and it can be plain miserable without the love of a good woman. Sherman glances in his rearview mirror and tells them, "Boys, there is nothing better than coming home to your woman." Neither one of them can wipe the grins off their faces. Jake is wrought with anticipation, "Sherman, please, hurry." Sherman's heart hurts for both Jake and Marcus. But especially for Jake with all he has been through the past five years. "I am son. You will be with her soon."

Fran is in the kitchen pacing. She always worries the most in these last few minutes. She decides to clean the countertops again even though they are spotless. She then paces from the refrigerator to the table and back for what seems an eternity. The girls are fast asleep downstairs. Fran is thankful for that. At least they are not miserable right now. Finally, she hears the door open and she runs to it. Jake and Marcus slide into the doorway as they try to slow down from their full out run. Jake hugs Fran. When she is satisfied that he is okay she lets go of him and hugs Marcus. "Oh thank God! I was so worried!" is all she can say. Jake hugs her again and says, "I know, we are fine. I will tell you about it tomorrow, okay?" She knows he is anxious to get to Jesse. "They fell asleep downstairs" she says smiling ear to ear. Jake hugs her once more; "Thanks for the food, we devoured it already" and then he and Marcus take off like a bolt of lightning running to the rec room.

Tears filled Fran's eyes. They are back. Her boys are really back. She didn't care that they were dirty and stinky. She didn't say a word about the mud or the blood or the rips in their uniforms. She will be able to sleep tonight because her boys are home. She wipes her eyes and goes outside to help Sherman. He is carrying some of their gear up to the house. He recognizes that look and he drops the bags and gear and takes her into his arms. "Oh Sherman" is all she can get out before bursting into tears. He holds her tight and comforts her for a long time. When she regains her composure, she helps him carry the gear into the house, careful to sit the bags down gently. She knows there are weapons in them. When they are finished, Sherman puts his arms around Fran and hugs her tight. "I guess they will be busy for quite some time" he says with his own devilish grin. "Why don't we head home? I feel the need to take care of you tonight." She could only smile lovingly at him and nod her head.

33

Jake and Marcus stand frozen side by side staring down at the two beautiful women snuggled close together and holding hands. After a long pause, Jake halfway glances at Marcus, "You two stay here tonight. We'll sleep in and have a nice leisurely breakfast in the morning. It will be nice...and I am sure they will want details. We should talk in the morning. Ugh, before we talk to them, I mean." Marcus slaps Jake on the back but doesn't say anything. He knows what Jake is getting at. He understands what Jake wants him to do. "Hey, it's ok buddy, I won't say a word." Jake nods at his best friend, thankful they are cut from the same cloth. Marcus smirks, "You know, men would pay good money to see this!" Jake has to laugh a little and shakes his head. "Yes, Marcus, we are lucky men!"

Jake kneels down next to Jesse. She is the most beautiful woman he has ever seen. He gently sprawls his hand across her abdomen. He swears again to himself that he will be the best father this child could ever have. In his periphery vision he sees Marcus going to the other side of Charlie. He gently lies beside her. Both men reach to the clasps hands of the women and slowly untangle their fingers. The men put their hands into Jesse's and Charlie's hands. Marcus slowly turns Charlie to halfway face him. Damn, he is a lucky man indeed. Charlie stirs and snuggles closer to Marcus. When she reaches out and touches a large solid man her eyes fly open. Marcus grins wildly at her and holds a finger up to his lips, "Shhh...let's go upstairs." Tears fall from her eyes and she kisses him long and hard before getting up and walking upstairs with him.

Jake lies next to Jesse and slowly, softly strokes her hair and then her face. He runs the palm of his hand down her shiny black dress along her curves. She stirs a little, nudging herself closer to him. He is amazed that even in her sleep her body recognizes him and responds so well to his touch. He slides his palm past the edge of her skirt and rests his hand on her thigh. He slowly strokes her thigh in small circles as he leans his head down to smell her hair. She smells heavenly. No... she smells like home. He plants feather light kisses on her neck and jaw line. Her mouth curves up in a smile and she stretches out before him with her arms over her head. He kisses the curved up edges of her mouth and then looks down at the phenomenal view of her breast that are barely contained by the shiny black dress. His growing erection is now almost to the point of being painful. He trails kisses down her chest and onto her breast not covered by the dress. "Mmm" is all she manages to get out. Jake smiles and wonders if she really knows how she affects him.

Jake is home and he is kissing me. Thank God! My heart is filled with joy. I want him to move the dress down and continue ravishing my breasts and am disappointed when he doesn't. Instead he climbs on top of me, holding himself up on his forearms, and kisses me gently and sweetly. I groan into his mouth and understand the depth of his need for me. I know we will talk later. This is all I wished for. That he would come back home safe, back to me in one piece. I kiss him back wildly and stroke his face and hair. Jake takes a deep breath and sighs, "Come on baby, let's go upstairs. I need to shower." He slides off me and gently picks me up. Without hesitation I wrap my arms around his neck. As he walks up the stairs he slides his right hand under my dress. He strokes my thigh and then moves his hand higher to feel the dampness of my small black lace thong. His grin is wicked. When we reach his room he has to contain himself so he doesn't kick in the door. He is hard and throbbing and by the look on his face he wants me now. But he also knows he is filthy. He kisses me and gently puts me down. Deciding he needs to kiss me again he immediately pulls me closer and kisses me up against the wall until we are both out of breath. He quickly pulls away from me and leads me to the bathroom. "I'll just be a minute" I say and he knowingly nods and smiles. He turns on the hot water in the shower. Walking across the bathroom he strips as he turns on some orchestral music, leaving a trail of camouflage clothing in his wake. He quickly enters the shower and washes his hair, face and body by the time Jesse stands before him. Relieved to get the filth and blood off of him before she notices too much. Jake is gloriously naked and sexy, scrubbing every delicious dirty inch of his body when I appear before him. I am still in the black dress. Jake looks like he will drool any moment. He steps forward to kiss me. His mouth kisses my neck and when he whispers in my ear, "Turn around, slowly" I feel his heated breath on the nape of my neck.

I do as ordered and am rewarded by Jake sliding his hands up and down my breast and stomach before reaching for my thighs. He kisses my back and reaches down to unzip the dress. He helps me shimmy out of and then step out of the dress. He tosses it on the floor, pulls me into him with my back to his front and continues to kiss my back and neck. He greedily strokes every inch of me that he can reach and then brings his hands up to stroke my breast again. I can't help but to moan with pleasure. The feel of his hands on me makes me even more impatient. I want him now. He tugs and pulls at both my nipples and the sensation shoots straight to my waxed bare groin. He slowly runs his hands over the lace thong. "This is… nice" he whispers in my ear and then strokes my bare bottom. His hand reaches around to my front and he strokes over the lace of the thong. I tense, remembering the wax, and immediately worry. What if he hates it?

Jake feels me tense under him, "Hey" he softly whispers, "what's wrong?" He pivots me until I am facing him. His jaw tenses and releases and I melt inside. He is so sexy. I wonder why he wants me. I am embarrassed to tell him about the wax. I know it's ridiculous to be embarrassed in front of him but I am. He kisses me softly and continues to stroke the lace thong. "It's a surprise." He arches an eyebrow at me. Jake kisses me gently and against my lips he grins his devilish bad boy grin and murmurs, "I really like surprises." He pulls me further into the shower and then trails gentle kisses down over my breast, this time taking his time on my nipples, nipping and sucking at each one. The want of his mouth and the hot water combined is almost more than I can take. I throw my head back and gasp. I can barely stand the pleasure of his mouth there. He grins and continues to head south. He loves driving me crazy. I can see it on his face. I think it makes him want me more. Slowly he removes the thong. I hear his breath catch. "Ah, I like my surprise" and he lowers his mouth and starts kissing my newly bare skin. He continues to stroke me. Just when I think it can't get any better he pushes his tongue between the delicate pink flesh and I gasp loudly. The pleasure is almost too much and I feel my legs almost give out. I don't think I can do this standing up. The feeling is incredible. He grins, gets up and carries me over to the bench. He strategically positions me so my knees are bent and my feet are on the edge of the bench.

Jake grins and kneels in front of me. "Wrap your legs around my shoulders." I do as instructed and he slides me down until my bottom is hanging off the bench. He is hard and throbbing and wants to bury himself inside me, but he wants this too. A primal instinct takes control and he dives into the warm pink flesh, licking everywhere, and then making the small circles I love so much. It is an exquisite feeling that I will never get enough of. I know I will never get enough of him. When he licks and then softly tugs on my clitoris with his lips I almost come apart then. He slides a finger inside of me slowly and then another and I groan loudly. "Jake, please" I beg him. He continues to lick and suck on my swollen sensitive bundle of nerves until I uncontrollably clinch and shudder and come in his mouth. He smiles against my newly bare skin. Jake thinks to himself, 'Yes, she makes me very happy.' He stands up and turns slightly so that he gets a mouthful of water and then spits it out. I stare at Jake and think he is the most beautiful man I have ever seen. It makes my heart hurt looking at the bruises on the back of his left thigh and on his back. He is scraped up and bruised but he is back in one piece. He came home to me. He now sits next to me and gently lifts me into his lap. The want is almost unbearable and I return his kisses and stroke his chest. I feel safe in his arms. This is home for me. This is where I belong now.

Jake whispers "I want you Jessie Nicole Bradley." My breath catches in my throat at the sound of my new last name. Oh, I haven't thought about it because I was so worried, but this incredibly sexy man is my husband. "Oh, Jake" I say and kiss him wildly. When we are both breathing heavy and out of breath I ask him, "What about the surgery? The baby? I mean, is it okay...?" He gently brushes his lips across mine and then traces my lower lip with his tongue. "Yes, it's okay. This will not hurt anything." Boy am I glad to hear that, because I think I want him more than he wants me, if that is even possible. And everything seems to be working as it should. I reposition myself with my back to his front so he can enter me. I slowly sink down his impressive length and the fullness is incredible, breathtaking even. He is amazing. Oh, the things he does. Oh, the things he makes me feel for him. He holds me still and kisses my neck. Against my neck I feel him smile, "Jess, I love you. You make me so happy." My heart wants to explode with love for this man. "Oh, Jake, I love you too." Jake and I are a perfect team as we work together for our pleasure. He thrust and I move myself up and down over him, loving and enjoying every sensation he gives me. He is so deep this way, it's not long before I shudder and cry out above him. He climaxes with me and I feel his hot breath on my neck as he calls out my name over and over.

I cannot move and lie back on his chest. We sit like this for a long time and let the hot water run over us. I feel myself drifting off to sleep. I turn to face him and he kisses me gently. "Jake, you make me really happy too. I love you." He smiles but I can tell he is exhausted. "Come on, let's go to bed and snuggle" I whisper to him. I stand and take his hand to pull him up. He stands but doesn't move. Slowly I dry his hair, back and chest and then hand him the towel to finish the job. I grab my own and quickly dry myself off. While he brushes his teeth I head to the bathroom. I am not used to having to pee so much. It's ridiculous. I quickly brush my teeth and we crawl into the safety and warmth of our bed. Once I snuggle into Jake's arms I am out. The last thing I remember before slipping into the blissful realm of sleep is Jake intertwining his legs with mine.

34

I wake reluctantly and see Jake lying on his side watching me. His hair is a glorious mess and I instinctively reach up and rearrange it into place. I am amazed that this ridiculously handsome man is my husband. I will share every morning with him for the rest of my life. I smile shyly, "How long have you been watching me sleep?" He shrugs his shoulders, "Oh, I guess since the sun came up" he says softly. "You should have woke me up." Jake smiles and snuggles closer and kisses me. "No way, I have been enjoying the view. You are lovely in the morning light. I love you... my beautiful wife." He kisses me again and I can only melt in his arms. Wow, he can say the most romantic things. "How long have you been awake?" I ask curious. I am sure he has been thinking about the mission he just completed. I think it must be hard to do the work of it, and then just... not talk about it. I don't know if I could do that. I am weak in so many ways and know I'd have to talk to someone about it. I guess he uses Marcus as a sounding board about those things. Thank heavens they both came home. "I woke up about four this morning. I have been lying here thinking ... About how lucky I am to be here with you. How lucky I am to have you in my life now. And the baby. I promise to be the best father I can be." Oh, no! Has he been worrying about becoming a father? I hope not because I know he will be a great father. I have no doubts he will raise this child as his own, the best he can. I try to reassure him, "Hey, stop. You are going to be a great father. I won't let you be any other way!" I kiss him and stroke his bare chest. "It's going to be okay. We are going to be okay now." He smiles and kisses me once more. "Are you sore? Hurting? I saw the bruises on your back and leg last night." He shakes his head no and pulls me close into a bear hug. "No baby, I'm fine. A little banged up and sore, but fine. Don't worry." I can't help but worry. Even though he got in the shower quick I didn't miss the filthy state he was in when he got home. He looked rough.

He playfully tugs at the edges of my hair. "I have also been thinking about last night. You were amazing. So sexy...that dress. I wanted to rip it off you, but then thought I might take you to dinner in it sometime, so I didn't." He kisses me passionately and I savor every second of it. Yes, I am so thankful he is home safe. He grins his best devilish grin and adds, "Hey...I liked my surprise...a lot." He playfully kisses my lower lip, nipping and biting at it. Now I am all shy again. Why do I feel shy in front of him about stuff like this? He's seen every part of me. I tell myself it's stupid to be shy with him. "I liked it so much I want to see it again...are you up for the Jacuzzi this morning?" I feel him and he is already hard. "Mmm...I think I like waking up this way...You are spoiling me!" I kiss him quickly and then scoot away from him, "Can you give me a minute?" He smiles, amused, I think. He knows right where I'm headed. I brush my teeth and use the bathroom. When I am done he is already sliding his firm glorious nakedness into the Jacuzzi. He holds his arms open for me, "Come here." I gently lower myself into the water and slowly make my way to him. He sits me on his lap and I lie back against him. "Ah, this is nice" I tell him. He wraps his arms around me and kisses the back of my neck and then sighs. "I wanted to talk to you before we go down for breakfast, but what I want to tell you, well, it'll be tough to hear. And I want you to keep it to yourself. I don't want to tell Fran and Sherman. They don't need to know." Okay, now he's scaring me. I try to turn to look at him but he holds me in place, "Shhh, it's okay. Just let me try to tell you a quick version okay." I nod without saying a word.

"I won't lie Jess, it was bad. So bad, that, well...I almost didn't make it home to you." I gasp loudly and before he can stop me I turn around to face him. I search his face and he quickly kisses me and holds me tight. "It's okay baby. I need to get this out. Please." I nod, "Yes, of course, go on." He is tense and his lips form a tight line. He grimaces as if he's remembering something horrible. Tears fill my eyes. "I will spare you details, the bottom line is that Marcus and I always watch out for each other. If it weren't for him..." tears form and start to fall down his cheeks into the hot water. I kiss him and wipe his eyes, and snuggle up to him. "Oh Jake, I was so worried about you! I couldn't think straight. I tried to be strong, you know, for Charlie. But I was so scared." He pulls me to him and hugs me tight. He sighs. "The fighting was hard. We were pinned for a while. We had to do what we went there to do, but there were some tense moments. I...ugh..." He closes his eyes and sighs and shakes his head. His eyes are tearful when he opens them. "You know I am not a bad person Jess, you know that, right?" I run my fingers through his hair, down his cheek and down to his mouth. "Of course I know that. You are a good man Jake. A caring, loving man."

He holds my gaze and tears fall freely down his cheeks. His voice is soft, "I want to be honest with you Jess. I don't want to hold anything back, so I won't. But I am afraid of what you will think of me after I tell you." It is ironic that I am the strong one now. I work hard to reassure him, to give him whatever it is he needs from me. "Jake, it doesn't matter. None of it. Do you hear me? I don't care what you had to do to come home safe. I am just glad you are back safe." He sighs and closes his eyes. "I knew I had to do whatever it took to come home to you...and the baby. So I did. The fighting was intense. Some of the worst that Marcus and I have been in lately. I fought a lot of other soldiers. Marcus and I are good together. We are trained well. When we were done, we were just about the only ones left standing. Hell, we were just about the only ones still alive. We killed a lot of guys over there. ..I killed a lot of guys over there."

I want to cry out for him. I want to take his pain away. The pain he is struggling with. I cannot imagine what he and Marcus must have had to do to get home safe. I am just glad they did whatever it took. I take his face in my hands and gently kiss his lips. "I love you Jake. I know it was hard to do, but ... thank you for doing what you had to do to come home to us. If you ever want to talk about it I will listen. If not, I understand that too." He nodded, "I can't really say too much about the details. Can only tell you pretty much what I've told you. We lost some good guys, some close friends. That will weigh heavy on our hearts for a while but we will be ok. This is the bad part about this job we have, and why I know I have to quit soon. For you and the baby. But I am torn because I can't leave Marcus behind." He shifts me off his lap into a standing position, leans forward and gently takes my left nipple into his mouth. I gasp as he rolls his tongue around and I immediately want more. When he pulls away he says, "Look, I am not telling Fran and Sherman everything. Well, I gave Sherman a quick run down but left out just how close it was. He could guess by the look of us and our clothes I am sure. He didn't say anything though. He didn't ask me about it. I don't want to scare Fran. I am not sure what Marcus is telling Charlie, so – let's keep it just between us okay." He trails kisses up my chest and neck and then to my mouth. This powerful, strong, lethal man kisses me so sweetly and softly and then whispers against my lips, "Turn around baby." It is a command and not a request. I do as instructed without hesitation. I know he would never hurt me. He reaches around and down to stroke me with his right hand while his left hand tugs and pulls at my nipples. All I can do is gasp and moan with pleasure. He continues his assault on my wanting body. I am all emotion and sensation and before I know it I am begging him to make love to me. He does so ever so gently in the Jacuzzi and then once more, not so gently, sitting in the chair next to the magnificent fireplace. Finally, we lie down and drift off to sleep holding each other tight.

35

We casually stroll into the kitchen at 10:35. Marcus and Charlie are sitting at the table holding hands, talking to Sherman and Fran, and drinking coffee. We sit at the table with them and Fran gets us coffee. There is already fruit on the table as well as a stack of pancakes. Fran looks to Jake, "You guys go ahead and eat. I am going to cook you some omelets while we talk." She walks over to Jake and hugs him briefly and then heads toward the stove. "I am just so glad you are home", she murmurs. "We are glad to be home" Jake replies and nods. We fill our plates and start eating the fruit and pancakes. I am like a kid in a candy store and put an extreme amount of syrup over my pancakes. I am famished and my stomach growls loud enough for all to hear. Jake grins and squeezes my thigh as Fran puts a glass of orange juice and water in front of me. Within minutes Fran is plopping down a nice size omelet in front of Jake and me. Jake cuts it in two and we share it. She then gives Marcus and Charlie and omelet to share. On her last trip to stove she produces an omelet in front of Sherman. Fran is a great cook. I can tell she enjoys being in the kitchen. "Oh, Fran, everything is delicious" I say to her. She smiles at me and sits at the table with her own cup of coffee. She is more than pleased to have both Jake and Marcus home. She sits and watches them both eat and is clearly proud of them both.

I am stuffed and put my fork down. Everyone else finishes their food while I drink the rest of my orange juice. When we are all stuffed Fran pours another round of coffee and Charlie and I help take the dishes to the sink. Fran complains over us doing so, "No, No, you girls sit back down. Let's talk, we will do it later." We take our empty chairs next to our men who can't seem to take their eyes off of us. It makes us both smile. Jake immediately takes my hand as I sit next to him. I don't think twice about letting him have my hand. My head spins as I think that just a short time ago I did not know him. Now I can't seem to get enough of him. I look lovingly at him and think that he loves me perfectly. Off to my side Marcus steals a chaste kiss from Charlie and they both laugh. Sherman puts down his coffee cup. "Okay, please tell us everything you can tell us about your mission. Well, I know you gave me a brief run down last night, but Fran wants to know and I'd like to hear the rest." Jake squeezes my hand and then releases it. "I need to talk to Marcus first. We will be right back." On cue, Marcus gets up and follows Jake out of the kitchen. Sherman watches them leave the room with a suspicious eye. A moment later he gets up and paces around the kitchen. I think he wants to follow Jake and Marcus but he holds back and remains in the kitchen with us instead. He knows what they are talking about, what they are doing.

Charlie moves down to sit next to me. She hugs me, "I told you they would come back." She is glowing with happiness. Fran frowns at Sherman pacing around the kitchen, deep in thought. Shaking her head she looks back to us. "Well, girls, seems we can all relax now that they are home safe. Charlie I know you know, but, Jesse, Jake usually clears his schedule and stays at home for a while when he gets back from a mission. Especially one as difficult as this one was." Her eyes dart from me to Charlie, back to me, and then she looks down and sips her coffee before continuing. When she looks up her expression is cheerful. "I am thinking we should have a party. I would like to have a big cookout and invite everyone we know, all the other staff and security teams and their families. You know, before it gets cold. We haven't had a cookout for a while. I don't think we have ever had one here, in this house. Everyone loves Jake and Marcus so much and it would be so much fun getting everyone together. But, of course, I will need a lot of help with a party like that."

Charlie is the first to chime in, now she is the kid in the candy store, her eyes beaming. "Oh, Fran, of course we will help. You just let us know what we need to help with. Do you want us to invite everyone? We can help with the food if you want. We can decorate, set up tables, whatever you need from us. Right, Jesse?" I shake my head in agreement. Seeing the excitement in Charlie's face gets me excited about it too. I smile at the thought of our first party together. I would love to meet all the people Jake knows. "I would love to help. I think it's a great idea. And I do love to decorate." I can't contain my smile and it takes over my face. Just as I think my face will split from smiling too much, Jake and Marcus come back into the kitchen. They sit in the chairs opposite us at the table. Fran dutifully ask them, "Would you boys like anything else to eat?" They both shake their heads no but then Marcus pops a strawberry into his mouth. Fran laughs and shakes her head lovingly at him.

Sherman sits at the table on the other side of Charlie and looks from Jake to Marcus and back to Jake. He is waiting for them to start talking. Jake knows Sherman realizes there is more to it than the short briefing Jake gave him last night in the limo on the way home. After all, Sherman has "been there, done that" so to speak. He is shrewd and tough and smart. Jake knows he will have to tell Sherman the truth eventually, but not here, not in front of the girls. And not today. All Jake wants to do is take Jesse back upstairs and get back in bed and pull her close. He knows Marcus is probably thinking the same thing about Charlie. He knows Sherman will be chomping at the bit until he gets the full briefing. Jake sighs. Now it's time for full disclosure about everything else. They all need to be on the same page starting today. Jake nods, "Yes, okay. You guys know this was a tough mission. We switched safely from the plane to the chopper and it took a little under three hours to get to our targeted destination. We did not meet resistance as we landed. However, once our boots hit the ground it wasn't long before we met a lot of resistance. Suddenly surrounded, and knowing we still had a good stretch to go on foot, we fought our way through the first wave of soldiers. They were not trained as well as we were. Even though we were outnumbered, we got through this first group fairly easily. We quickly hiked in the rest of the way, without another firefight. We reached the perimeter of our destination and started to execute our mission. We met heavy resistance, heavy fire, and intense hand to hand combat. The fighting was...very intense." Jake paused, closing his eyes and sighed. Jesse knew he was mentally thinking about what they had done to survive, what he told her in the Jacuzzi. Jake got up and started pacing back and forth near the kitchen table. Marcus was looking down at the table with a blank expression on his face. He closed his eyes, took a deep breath and harshly scrubbed his hands over his face. When he brought his hands down his face was red and blotchy in places, he eyes red and wet with stinging tears. Charlie got up and went to him, wiping his eyes and gently sitting in his lap. He nuzzled into her hair and quietly listened to Jake continue.

Jake stopped pacing and was standing at the end of the table when he next spoke. "Things were blowing up all around us. Literally... bombs, old RPG's, gunfire... hell, even tear gas, the old version." He gave Sherman a knowing look that spoke volumes. "Oh, the old GM 94's worked like a charm, just like we knew they would. We only busted a few of them. We brought the rest back with us." Sherman nodded for him to continue, "We held firm. Our team was executing our mission flawlessly, meeting goal after goal, never failing to achieve our next step. As guys went down, others took their place to continue the mission, as we were trained. Things were good until we got pinned down for a while. That's when it went to shit. We had neutralized the main target and they were pissed. We were determined to get out safely and they were determined that they were not letting us leave. Marcus and I knew what we had to do. So we did it, and that's that. We got back to the chopper and left as soon as we could."

We all sat quietly at the table. Sherman eyed Jake, as if trying to hear what Jake wasn't telling him. Jake shook his head side to side as if saying "no" to Sherman. Jake paced around the kitchen a few more times and then he rushed to me, pulled me up out of my chair and wrapped his arms around me and walked me backward a few steps until I was up against the wall. With his hands on both sides of my head firmly planted on the wall, he pulled away from me slightly to look at me. When our eyes locked I saw his pain, his fear, and his raw need for me. He lowered his mouth to mine and kissed me passionately, as if he wanted to devour me, as if he couldn't get enough of me. I kissed him back just the same. He leaned in close to my ear and whispered "I was so scared I wouldn't see you again." I held him tight and then kissed him gently. "Shhh, it's okay. You're home." He nuzzled into my hair and neck and took a deep breath. He wrapped his strong arms around me and I felt him physically relax into me before he pulled away. He held my hand and led me back to my chair. He sat down and pulled me onto his lap.

No one spoke. I looked up to see Fran wiping tears from her eyes. She laughed through her tears. "Oh, this is the worst part. I think I want to know, and then when I do know, what little details you can tell me, well…I always get too emotional…but especially this time, with Jesse and the baby and all." Sherman took her hand in hers, his face flat and his expression giving away nothing. Sherman nodded at Jake in some unspoken knowing way that Jake clearly understood. Fran sighed, "Well, okay, that's that. I am going to clean up and fix a picnic lunch for you guys. Sherman and I were going to check on the horses and I know Charlie and Jessie would love a picnic later." Charlie's eyes lit up and she now sported a face splitting grin. She jumped in Marcus's lap and he wrapped his arm around her waist and quickly adjusted himself with his other hand. "Easy baby" he said with a sly grin. Jake and Marcus exchanged a devilish look and I knew they were both thinking the same thing I am. Of course my smile is ridiculously huge and I say as innocently as I can, "A picnic sounds lovely." Sherman clears his throat, "Okay, you guys go get ready and meet me at the stables. I will get the horses ready for you." He leaned over and planted a sweet kiss on Fran's forehead and then stood to leave.

Jake stopped him abruptly, "Wait, there's a few more things Marcus and I wanted to share with you. Sherman, Marcus, later this afternoon we need to go over our plans for tomorrow, when Jesse meets with Brian. I want it all solid. I want to get it over with, but I want her safe tomorrow." Sherman, surprised, sat back down. Jake looked at Marcus and right on cue Marcus began to speak. "Jake and I are both a little older, both more settled in our lives now, and we have come to an important decision. We've considered it for a while, but after this mission I think we agreed without needing to discuss it further. We are both going to leave the team. It may take a few months to get it accomplished, but it's time." Fran gasped and covered her face with her hands stating "Oh this is the best news!" Sherman smiled and quietly mumbled "Hell yeah it's time!" Huge crocodile tears streamed down Charlie's face. She sniffled and hugged Marcus tightly, "I am so proud of you...and you know I have wanted this for so long!" He hugged her back, "I know, babe, I know." Marcus ran his fingers through Charlie's hair and gently kissed her. It was clear he loved her. Marcus turned Charlie around on his lap so she faced everyone else. "Oh yeah, by the way, Jake and Jesse beat us to it, they got married before we left yesterday!" Praise and laughter erupted in the room. Before I knew it, Fran and Sherman were on us, wrapping us up in their loving arms, telling us how happy they are for us. Fran exclaimed happily "Now we really have a reason to throw a party!" Fran and Sherman danced around the room and then Sherman took Fran in his arms and said softly to her, "Can you believe it, our boy's married!" Her grin said it all and he kissed her softly. She melted into his arms. I can't help but think how sweet it is and I hope we are like that when we are their age. Marcus and Charlie stand up. "Hey, can you two love birds be ready in 45 minutes?" Jake shakes his head yes, I stand and let him take my hand. Fran says to us, "You guys get ready and I will have lunch ready for you when you come back down." Jake and I follow Marcus and Charlie upstairs to get ready.

36

We meet downstairs and we all match in our jeans and boots. The guys are wearing t-shirts; Jake's is white while Marcus sports black. I definitely notice that they are tight and show off the wealth of muscles as the guys move effortlessly toward the kitchen. Charlie has on a leopard print spaghetti strap tank top that displays her perfect breast for the entire world to see, including Jake. Surprisingly though, he doesn't pay her any attention and only looks at my breast which are conservatively spilling out of the top of my own peach colored tank top. He doesn't try to hide the fact that he is lustfully looking and I can't believe it, but I actually like him looking at me in that way. I am bringing a short sleeved white shirt that buttons to wear over my tank in case I get cold. I thought about the wind blowing and then about Jake keeping me warm. I wonder if we will go to the same spot that Jake and I went to last time, near the tree with the swing.

Fran was true to her word and left us not one but two fully stocked picnic baskets. The guys rummage around in them to see what she has packed. Marcus says, "Looks like its turkey and ham subs, fruit, cheese, crackers and wine...only one bottle." Jake went to the refrigerator and pulled out bottles of water and added them to the picnic baskets. After pulling me in close for a much too short kiss he says "I'll be right back." I miss him already and am shocked at how fast my need for him has grown. He is addicting. Better than anything I have ever had before, or anyone for that matter. As I turn to say something to Charlie I am taken aback by Marcus and Charlie's open display of affection. Marcus has her backed up against the kitchen counter and they are kissing passionately. She is running her hands down to his backside. He is running his hands up her leopard print to their final destination. He already has her pinned with one leg between hers, but he quickly slides her legs open more and steps in between them with both of his. It's like a wreck and I can't look away. I admit to myself that they are sexy and fit perfectly together. It is clear they know each other's bodies well. I am so caught up in their foreplay that I didn't hear Jake sit down the wine he'd brought in. Instead I am shocked when his arms wrap around my waist and his hands start to move smoothly up my tank. I feel his warm breath on my back and neck as he repeatedly kisses me. I shudder as his chin stubble grazes my skin, and oh god, it feels so good. He is amazing. I turn my head to tell him I love him but his lips cover mine. We are both breathless from the kiss. He sits in a chair and pulls me down on top of him so that I am straddling him. I am reminded of our lovemaking in the chair by the fireplace. It was perfect. I glance nervously over at Marcus and Charlie. Marcus has Charlie sitting on the counter now with her legs wrapped around him tightly. They are oblivious to us.

Jake slowly caresses my sensitive breast and when he reaches my nipples he expertly squeezes and pulls them. I gasp and moan his name softly. I have the intense urge to kiss him. I want to lean down but he stops me with his left hand. His right hand is pulling down my tank top and he pulls me close to take my left nipple into his mouth. "Come here baby." The wet warmth is exquisite. I shudder with pleasure. The noises coming from the other side of the room only add to my excitement. When he swirls his tongue around my nipple and playfully sucks and nips at it, I completely loose it. I start writhing over him, rubbing myself on his jean clad erection trying to get some relief. He runs his hands through my hair, pulls me down to his mouth and kisses me so sweetly. With his lips pressed against mine he mutters "Christ you're killing me." As his words hang in the air his large strong hands press down on my thighs and squeeze them. He lovingly fixes my tank top and pushes me up into a standing position. We both know if we don't go now we are not going to make it to the picnic. Jake stands and gently kisses me. He softly whispers in my ear "I cannot wait to make love to you. I need to be inside you." He quickly adds the bottles of wine to the baskets. Holding one of the baskets in one hand and my hand in the other, he barks "Let's go" at Marcus and Charlie. They don't pull apart immediately and in his frustration Jake says "I will leave your horny asses if you are not outside in five!"

They finally meet us out front by the four wheeler. We get in and Jake drives us the short distance to the stables. Marcus took a blanket from the stables and put it across his horse. I recognize it as the one Jake and I used on our previous picnic. Once on our horses we follow the same path we took before. Again, I am lost in the beauty of the land. It takes us approximately thirty minutes to reach the spot of our last picnic. Jake tells Marcus that we are going to picnic here. "You guys go ahead, just meet back here by three o'clock, okay." Marcus nods, "Three if you need me" and then he takes the lead and he and Charlie ride off. I smile because I now know that comment means channel three on the watch radio. Jake dismounts his horse and helps me down. He ties up the horses the same way he did last time, by the tree. He quickly spreads out our blanket and sets the basket aside.

Jake pulls me close for a kiss. "I've got to have you baby, right now." As he pulls off his boots, socks, t-shirt and jeans his words bore into my brain. He needs me and it sounds like it's as much as I need him. Wow, his beauty blows me away. The sunlight shines on his hair and skin and I suddenly can't wait to be in his arms. I force myself to wait the few seconds it takes me to take off my boots, socks and jeans. Jake takes off my white button down, tank top and my peach colored lace thong. I am bare to the world. I am bare to him and he loves it. He motions for me to lie down. I quickly comply while he strips off his boxers and he is immediately over me, his warm firm body covering mine. I force myself to take a deep breath and relax. Oh, this skin on skin contact is heavenly. His warmth and scent overwhelm my senses. Jake kisses me so sweetly. He trails kisses down to my breast and then lower, slowing down to swirl his tongue around my belly button. His mouth on me is such a sweet sensation. My skin is sensitive and every stroke of his tongue burns me up.

I close my eyes and enjoy him worshiping my body. He strokes my legs and I love the feel of it. He barely brushes his fingers between my legs and I tense and wait for more. He surprisingly doesn't accommodate me. Instead he crawls back up my body and kisses me softly as he gently slides into me. I gasp and moan my pleasure into his mouth. His voice is a strained whisper when he says "Jess, I need you baby, so damn bad" and on some unconscious level of my soul I understand he is not just talking about a physical need. My heart explodes for this man. I am warm and tingling all over. My head tries once again to figure out how, in such a short time, have I fell in love with him. There is no rhyme or reason to it, but I unequivocally love him. Shit. I didn't see this coming, especially not the first day he brought me here.

There is a strong pull between us that I cannot explain. I am addicted to him. We are like magnets drawn to each other. That's it. That is the only way to explain it. I have to be with him. I never want to be without him. "Oh Jake" is all I can manage to get out as he picks up the pace thrusting wildly into me. I gasp again as he reaches down between us to stroke my clitoris. It's almost too many sensations at once. I cry out, "Oh yes, right there…Oh yeah…Mmmm…Jake!" I squeeze my eyes shut tight and hold my breath. "You are so beautiful like this" he says to me in a raspy low voice. "Come for me baby!" As I do I have to keep my eyes shut to handle all of the sensations and shudders tearing through me. I cry out again and then still under him. He positions himself on his forearms and nuzzles into my neck and hair and kisses me over and over again. I am spent. I suck in a deep breath and exhale slowly.

Jake quickly slides over and pulls me into a spooning position and trails kisses along my back and left shoulder. I am so relaxed and feel so safe in his strong arms. His warmth is exquisite against my skin. The gentle breeze teases my sensitive nipples and the feeling is amazing. I quickly drift off to sleep. I wake to Jake's kisses on my back and shoulder, "Baby, wake up" he whispers near my ear. I don't want to ever move from this spot. I wish we could just stay here forever. I open my eyes when I have a sudden urge to pee. Damn. I have to get up. I turn to face him and he has his bad boy grin on. Oh wow, he is beautiful when he smiles. I don't think I will ever get enough of that smile. He kisses my lips gently and then slaps my bottom. I can't help but giggle. "I am sorry, Jess, the only privacy is the other side of the tree" and I wonder if he can read my mind. "I will go in this direction and you can go on the other side of the tree. I can't stop my stupid girl face splitting grin. He kisses me softly once more and then he quickly gets up and starts walking out into the field, away from the blanket. I can't help but stare at his muscles as he moves. He is breathtaking. Does he know how beautiful he is? How sexy he is?

I hurry to put on my tank top and grab my thong. I quickly walk a good distance past the swing and tree. I squat and pee in a very unladylike position. The release is heavenly and I actually sigh and think how good it feels. With my tank and thong on, I adjust the blanket and open the basket. I pull out a bottle of water and take a drink. I get up and go past the edge of the blanket and pour water over my hands to clean them. I shake them off and then wipe my hands on the back of my tank top. No sooner as I get back to the blanket and start pulling out lunch Jake comes back. He quickly puts on his boxers and jeans and sits near me. I know he stayed gone longer than necessary to make sure I had time to do what I needed. He is a true gentleman. We eat and laugh and I don't think I have ever been so happy. I am in awe of this gorgeous man sitting next to me...my husband. Wow. Didn't see that coming either. I can't think of any place I'd rather be. I smile at the thought.

We haven't given any thought to the time. We are finishing off the wine and out of nowhere hear Marcus. "Jake, you there buddy?" We laugh, knowing they have undoubtedly been doing the same thing that we have been doing. Jake answers him, "Yeah, I'm here, what's going on?" There is a pause and then, "We are going to start heading your way. ETA ten." Jake looks at me and I nod. "Yeah, sounds good, see you then." The whole watch radio thing still amazes me. It's just cool. I can't help but grin. We pack up the remnants of lunch and I quickly put my jeans, white t-shirt and boots on. I know I must look like a mess. I try to run my fingers through my hair. Jake walks over to me and kisses me gently, "Don't worry about it, you are absolutely beautiful." I smile at him. How does he always know what I need? He is incredible.

We gather up the blanket and basket and head to the horses. As I walk I feel my jeans rubbing against my swollen clitoris, and it feels great. This is going to be an interesting horseback ride home. I laugh at myself and try to get my thoughts out of the gutter. Jake puts the blanket over my horse and helps me up. As he is walking over to his horse Marcus and Charlie ride up. Hmm...they look...relaxed...I think to myself. Better than in the kitchen. I can't say anything because we were just as bad. Marcus and Jake take the lead. Our horses follow closely behind theirs. Sherman meets us outside the stables. He waves and smiles but his eyes silently assess us all and I can't help but wonder why. Jake and Marcus help Sherman with the horses. Charlie and I walk to the four wheeler and wait for them. Her enthusiasm is sweet. "I can't lie. I love being out in wide open spaces with Marcus. Oh the things he does to me!" I nod and laugh. "What about you guys? You two lovebirds have fun?" "Fun, are you kidding! It was incredible!" I tell her. She smiles her perfect smile and says, "I told Marcus you would love it. There is nothing better than spending time with him and I knew you would feel the same about Jake." I shake my head and say "Yes, I do." The guys get into the four wheeler and we head back to the house. Once in the front door Charlie and I take the picnic baskets to the kitchen, discard the trash and put the baskets back into the pantry.

Charlie looks at me and I can see she is worried about something. "What?" I ask her. "Marcus and I are going to get my things and go home. I hope you don't mind. I thought after dinner we could hang out with you guys for a couple of hours downstairs. Is that okay with you?" I hug her. I can't believe she is worried about hurting my feelings. She has been really sweet to me. "Yes, of course it's okay. Thank you for staying with me. The fact that you were here, going through it with me, was really something. Thank you and I really enjoyed spending some girl time with you. I had fun." She smiled her best Charlie smile and said, "Okay then, I'll see you later." I watched her go upstairs to get her things together. I don't know where the guys are so I go find them. They are in the sitting room. As soon as Jake saw me he stood up, walked over and kissed my cheek. "Where's Charlie?" he asked. "Oh, she is getting her things together. She said she was going to go home but that after dinner that she and Marcus would hang out with us for a couple of hours, in the rec room." Jake looked over at Marcus who said, "Yeah, sure, sounds good." Jake walked me over to his seat and motioned for me to sit down. I did so and he stood next to me, his hand on my shoulder. His thumb made small circles on my back.

"Marcus and I were talking about tomorrow. Working out some details about when you go meet Brian." When I look up at him I can see he is thinking something and his lips draw tight into a straight line. He runs his fingers through his hair. He is ... what? Mad? Frustrated? I am not sure. I smile at him, "Oh, okay. Is there anything I should know?" He squeezes my shoulder. "You don't need to do anything special. Just go in, take the letter you want to give him, ask your questions, and get out quick." Marcus nods his head and adds, "Yeah, we will take care of the rest. Of course, we will have a high level of security. Don't be scared when you see the vehicles and guys. Just know we will do what it takes to keep you safe." I gasp. "You don't think that Brian will try to hurt me, do you?" Jake sighs and says, "We are not sure what his game is. We just need to be careful. Okay." I nod my head. I know he is right. I have a bad feeling in my gut but I don't tell them. I don't want them to stress over it anymore than they are doing. I just want it all to be over. Jake pulls me up so that we are standing within an inch of each other. He holds my hands, "Hey, we'll get you through this, okay." I nod my head but he sees the fear and anxiety in my eyes.

Jake presses his lips to mine in a gentle, sweet kiss. "Marcus was just about to go, and I was thinking how great it would feel to get in the Jacuzzi. Especially after riding horses today. You in?" Why does he have to be so damn sexy? I smile, "Of course I am." Marcus watches us and smirks. He doesn't say anything. Instead he stands and says "Okay, well, we need to talk to Sherman about some of the details for tomorrow. Other than that I think we are set. I am going to help Charlie. You two have fun." I can't help but notice him laughing as he turns and walks out of the room and heads for the stairs. There is obviously a private joke between the two of them. Whatever. If Jake wants me to know he will tell me.

37

Jake sits in the chair and pulls me down so that I am straddling him, my back to his front. I lean back and relax into his firm chest. Oh, wow, he feels so good. He wraps his arms around me and I love it. He slowly kisses the nape of my neck. "Mrs. Bradley, I want you naked and sitting just like this in the Jacuzzi." I have the warm tingling sensation all over again and I know it has nothing to do with the promise of the hot water. I know it is from hearing my name fall from his delicious lips. Will I ever get tired of being called Mrs. Bradley? I don't think so. I turn my head to the side and whisper, "I can't wait, let's go." He smiles and kisses me gently before getting up and leading me upstairs.

We start peeling our clothes off as soon as we reach the bedroom door. He is faster than me at stripping down and is gloriously naked now. It takes me a little longer to get my jeans and socks off. I am wearing only the thong standing near the doorway. I think he is going to race me to the Jacuzzi, but he grabs me, kisses and walks me backward until he has me up against the bed. I am breathless from our kisses. I think he is going to strip off my thong and make passionate love to me but instead, he says "Now, I've got you right where I want you Mrs. Bradley!" His eyes are wide and he laughs. He tickles me until I cry uncle. When I am exhausted from running from him and he is exhausted from chasing me and tickling me, we fall together onto the bed and laugh.

He is so much fun to be with. I think how my life has turned out, and really, it is for the better. I am happy, even though I know I still have things to work out. That leads my thoughts to meeting Brian tomorrow. Should I tell Jake I have concerns and am worried? I don't want to add to his stress and he is already worried about it, and about keeping me safe. I look at him smiling next to me. He looks so happy that I decide not to say anything.

Jake is in awe of this woman. Look at all she has been through, and she is going forward, picking up the pieces of her life and this time, putting them back together the way she wants them. He wonders if she has any idea how badly he needs her? Would it scare her to know? Would it make him look weak if he told her? He wants to be seen as a strong, dependable husband. He wants her to know he will always be there to love her and protect her. He's been alone for so long. Somehow he has to make her understand the depth of his need for her. Sometimes words fail him. He hopes that his love and actions will be enough to make her understand his need for her and his unconditional love for her. He can't stand it another minute, he has to touch her, has to kiss her.

Jake pulls me close and kisses me softly. With his lips on mine he says sweetly, "I'm so glad you are here. I was so lonely without you" and my heart breaks for my beautiful husband. He continues, "I was always the odd man out when Marcus, Charlie and I did anything. I got sick of it. That's one of the reasons I stayed with you at the lab so much, besides wanting to make sure you were okay." I kiss him gently and hug him tight. He takes my hands and pulls me up. "Come on, Jacuzzi."

Once we are up to our necks in the swirling warm water, with me lying back against his chest as he wanted, I finally relax. The skin to skin contact is exquisite. With his eyes closed he alternates stroking my thighs, my stomach and my arms. We talk about a lot of things, but say nothing about tomorrow. Jake asks if I have had any more bad dreams. "No" I quickly answer. I am surprised I sleep so well with him. Somehow I know I didn't get much sleep in my past life. I think of them as my previous life and my current life. I know in my heart and soul I am much happier in my current life, with Jake.

I swish and play with the water, popping bubble after bubble. Jake runs his fingers through my hair in a very sensual way. I still beneath his hands to enjoy the sensation that is so loving, so intimate. I think about tonight and wonder what we should do. Movie night? Card night? Board games? "Jake..." He has his head leaned back with his eyes closed. "Hmmm?" "What do you normally do when Marcus and Charlie come over?" He shakes his head side to side without opening his eyes. "Oh, I don't know...talk, eat, and watch TV...why?" I sigh. "I just don't want you guys to feel like you have to entertain me. I will be ok with anything. I just don't want to be a burden..." Opening his eyes he shifts me so I am halfway facing him. "Never think that Jess. I am so glad you are here. We all are." I nod, "Yes, and everyone has been great to me. I just want you to be able to relax at home. You have worked so hard for such a long time. I don't want to cause stress for you." He closes his beautiful hazel eyes, laughs and shakes his head before opening them again. "Oh, baby, you don't! You, being here, is the only reason I can relax at all." And there it is. My suspicions are verified. I feel awful that he stayed in the lab with me so much. At the same time, it's comforting to know I wasn't alone.

I try to drive the topic of our conversation back to what we can do tonight. "Does anyone play a musical instrument? Does anyone have a favorite game? Do you want me to make some homemade Chex mix?" Jake smiles until it turns into full blown laughter. The sound of his laugh is precious to me. Intoxicating. I don't get to hear it near enough. "Oh, I know, we can play charades." He continues to laugh at me. I rewind and think about what I just said. "Oh, I guess I made it sound like we were all back in seventh grade, didn't I?" He strokes his fingers slowly up my arm. "You don't have to worry about doing anything, really. We will just hang out for a few hours. Fran will cook. But, I have a confession to make..." he says as he playfully splashes water my way. "What" I ask with my stupid girl face splitting grin. "You may find it hard to believe, but I have never had 'Chex mix' before. I have always wanted to try it. Will you make it for me, another time?" Oh wow, first I realize I remembered more useless information about my life. Apparently I like to play games and eat. The second thing is that I play piano. I quickly think back to the rec room. Was there a piano in there? I think so. "Yes, of course I will make it for you sometime. I love to cook. Hey, I just remembered that I think I know how to play piano!" His expression changes yet again, to a look of genuine happiness. "Really? That is great! I play piano and guitar. We should play tonight." He kisses me on my nose and lovingly says, "Come, let's get out before we cook the little one" as he sprawls out his hand on my belly. His hand covers the whole area from the underside of my breast to the top of where my thong would be. Jokingly I gasp in horror, "I am thirsty, now that you mention it." He helps me out and we dry off. Jake gives me water and I drink it all without hesitation. For what seems like an eternity we sit naked, wrapped up in a blanket in the chair next to the fireplace. Before I realize it I drift off to sleep in the comfort and safety of his arms.

Jake holds Jesse close to him and takes in every feature of her lovely face. She is stunning. So damn dazzling. He doesn't understand how she doesn't know this. A woman like her deserves to be told everyday how beautiful she is. He wants to make up for every bad thing that's ever been done to her in her life. He knows it's ridiculous to think that and knows it's impossible, but he wishes like hell he could do it. He wants to take away the pain and replace it with joy and happiness from now on. He thinks of Brian and how bad he treated her. Jake wants five minutes alone with that asshole. That's all it'll take to put him in his place. Hell, probably less time than that, considering his age now. However, the fact that Brian was carrying a weapon last time he saw him tells Jake he must remain diligent, and be careful. The last thing he wants is for someone to get hurt, especially not Jesse.

Jesse stirs in my arms. Her eyes flutter open and she yawns. In a soft voice so as not to startle her I ask, "Do you want me to tell them not to come over tonight after dinner?" She shakes her head no as best she can lying against my chest. "No, I'm okay. Just needed a nap." I smile and kiss her forehead. "I know you must be exhausted. I knew this would be hard on you. Wrap your arms around my neck." She does and I gently carry her over to the bed. I climb in next to her and hold her close, occasionally brushing the hair out of her eyes and off her cheek. "Shhh, it's okay baby, just rest. I am right here. I've got you, just close your eyes." Does she realize I need to be here, like this, holding her, as much as she wants and needs me to be? The one thing I know for sure is that I am done wasting time with Brian. I will go with Jesse to ensure her safety and to finish business. After tomorrow, we will never have to deal with that cheating scumbag bastard again. "Jake" Jesse mutters sleepily. "Yeah baby." "This is home for me now. You are my home. I love you." There are no sweeter words. I smile and kiss her lips, "I love you, too, now rest baby." Tears overflow my eyes and quietly trail down my cheeks. Oh god. How long have I wanted to hear words like that fall from her beautiful lips? For the next hour I hold her in my arms and watch over her, never wanting to take my eyes off of her. I am so damn thankful for every minute I have with her.

38

Fran looks lovingly at them all sitting around the kitchen table. She could not be happier. She was really pleased when Marcus and Charlie fell in love. She has, however, always worried about Jake. She did not want him to be alone. She's not getting any younger and neither is Sherman. It is so good to see Jake laughing and joking with everyone else tonight. He's usually so quiet, deep in thought. Tonight, he looks young. He looks like a man in love. He looks happy. "Dinner was excellent, as always, Fran" I say to her. Marcus and Charlie are ready to go downstairs. I get up to help her take the dishes to the sink but she refuses my help and tells Jake and I to go downstairs to the rec room. "You kids go have fun, Sherman and I have got this." Her stern tone tells me not to push my luck.

Jake takes my hand and leads me out of the kitchen. When we walk past the hallway bathroom he pulls me into the doorway and lifts me up so that I am sitting on the counter. Instinctively I wrap my legs around his waist when he walks in between my thighs. His lips touch mine and we are enthralled in a deep, ravenous kiss. We are like a drug to a drug addict or like food to a starving person. We take everything the other is offering and then search for more. His tongue is wanting and warm, and it meets mine over and over again in the most delicious and seductive kiss. I have always loved kissing. It thrills me to know he does too. He has mad kissing skills and it never fails to leave me wanting more. Breathless, I say, "Wow, what was that for?" He smirks at me and answers, "Just because I can baby." Oh. Okay. I won't complain. He can kiss me like that anytime, anyplace. I have the most ridiculous smile on my face. "I just wanted to kiss you, that's all." I swear...I love this man!

When we finally get to the rec room, Charlie is beating Marcus in a game of air hockey. We stand and watch them finish the game. Charlie beat Marcus and he is feigning a wounded look. She leans over the corner of the table to kiss him, "There, does that make you feel better?" Before she knows what hit her, Marcus grabs her around the waist and pulls her to him, and kisses her passionately. When the long kiss is broken he says,

"No, but that does." They laugh together. They take their turn and watch us play a game of air hockey. Jake won by a landslide. He is incredibly pleased with himself. He leans over to kiss me, telling me it's to help me feel better and I can't help but laugh.

Charlie and I play a few games of Galaxy Quest and Frogger. She is much better at it than I am. I resolve myself to practice so I can have the mad skills to beat her next time. The guys fix us a glass of wine and stroll over to us, like two men on a mission. The lights go dim and soft music comes on. We sit in the leather chairs across from the video games and talk until our wine is gone. Jake puts my glass down and says softly, "Dance with me", holding his hand out to me. I do not hesitate because I want to be in his arms. He envelops me in a strong embrace and his heat is heavenly. I instinctively snuggle closer to him. As we dance slowly he nuzzles into my neck, kissing my ear first and then my neck. He works his way around to my mouth and we kiss until the song is over.

I see that Marcus and Charlie are also dancing and kissing. Another song comes on and Jake leads me over to the big rug and gently pulls me down with him. When he holds me close and kisses me I completely forget that Marcus and Charlie are in the room, until they walk past us and say they are going for a swim. Jake pulls me in to kiss me again, but this time he lets his hands wander all over my body. I crave his touch and the feeling is incredible. He looks me in the eye and says, "You know I can't get enough of you." I nod, "I can't get enough of you either." He lets his hand wander down between my legs. His experienced fingers find just the right spot to make me squirm beneath him. "I can't get enough of this" he says. I gasp. Oh wow. He knows just what to do and say to send my head spinning. I worry about Marcus and Charlie coming back in. "They'll be out there for hours" Jake reassures me. He pulls my shirt up over my head. I am panting, shaking with raw need for him. I have never wanted anyone so much. I am his and he knows it. We both stand and strip off the rest of our clothes. He quickly grabs the blanket from over the back of the couch. We take our time and explore each other, pleasure each other, until we are completely spent and out of breath. We are lying wrapped up under the blanket, catching our breath. "Baby", Jake says in a husky, breathy voice, "you are incredible." I turn my head to plant a soft kiss on his chest, "You too."

We are still naked and snuggled under the blanket when Marcus and Charlie stroll back through the rec room. They both have wet hair and

Charlie's is stringy across her face. They both are sporting ridiculously big smiles. They don't stop to talk. Marcus is clearly in a hurry to have Charlie all to himself again. He is holding her hand and leading her through the rec room as fast as he can. When they pass us Marcus growls to Jake, "I'll meet you in the morning" and then they were gone. We giggle at them because we understand their raw need for each other. I don't mind that they saw us snuggled under the blanket together. They were not paying us any attention at all. Instead, they were just getting the hell out of here as fast as they could. I am happy for them. I am very happy that Jake has a friend like Marcus. I am happy that Jake has someone that he can depend on, who is trustworthy and, is more like a brother than just a friend.

We are both yawning now. I can't keep my eyes open and, before I fall asleep right here, I say, "Come on, let's go upstairs." It's late and we know we have the house to ourselves, now that Marcus and Charlie have gone home. With our clothes in hand, we walk upstairs naked, hand in hand. As we snuggle in for the night, I cannot help but think how lucky I am. I also cannot help but worry about tomorrow. I know that whatever happens, Jake will do what it takes to protect me, and that's exactly what I am worried about. I don't want anyone to get hurt, especially not Jake.

39

I stare at my sexy husband. He is so gorgeous while he is sleeping. His face is completely relaxed, even that space on his forehead that gets furrowed when he is worried or stressed about something. He looks so much younger like this. He is usually awake first so I haven't had the opportunity to just gaze at him in the early morning light. I am amazed to realize that I've only known him a week but it feels like I've known him all my life. A week. My life has changed dramatically in a week. Every day since Jake brought me here, I have physically grown stronger. I continue to have mini-flashes of my past. Some memories are more in depth than others. Jake says this will go on for a while. He is confident that I will regain my full memory soon. I hope so. Each time I remember something else it's a small personal victory for me. He rejoices with me every time I remember something. He has been incredible this past week. He has never pushed me or made me do anything I didn't want to do. He has given me my space but yet, been there for me every time I have needed him. What an incredible man. I gaze down at his muscular bare chest. Oh yes, incredible indeed.

The next time I look up at him he stretches and opens his beautiful hazel eyes. When he sees me watching him he smiles. "Good morning beautiful" I say to him, returning the words that he usually says to me every morning. He smiles bigger, "Morning baby." He pulls me close, holds me and kisses the top of my head. "Big day today" he says. "You okay?" I nod my head yes, "I just want to get it over with" I tell him. "Me too" he says. "I want you all for myself. I want Brian out of our lives forever." I nod in agreement, lying against his chest. He moves to sit up against the headboard and pillows and I scoot up and lean my head on his shoulder, wrap my arm around his chest and I throw my leg over his. "Jesse, we have to talk about today. There's something I need to tell you." Oh shit, what now? This doesn't sound good. It's the ominous tone of voice he uses. He continues, "The last time I met with Brian he had a weapon on him. I don't want to scare you, but it's important that you know I will do anything, everything I have to do to protect you and the baby." He is quiet for a moment to let his words sink in. "I know you are not used to seeing that side of me, the harder more militaristic side of me. I don't want you to be scared of me today, when I am taking and keeping control of the situation. My personality will be... different... harder. Baby, this is the real me. You know the real me. I just don't want you to think you don't. But I can, and will, take care of business."

With his words I realize I haven't given the meeting today enough thought. In my gut I know he is right. I need to let him handle the details and I need to do what he says so that we can all come home safe. That's all I want anyway, is for us to get it over with and come home safe. "I won't be scared of you Jake. I know you will do whatever it takes to keep us safe." He looks at me for a long time, searching my face to see I completely understand what he is saying. "Jesse, I am used to things blowing up around me. I worry how you will react, if it goes bad. Look at me baby" I lift my eyes back to his. I see he is clearly worried. "We are going to have a lot of people there today. Some you will see and some you won't. If that bastard even thinks about hurting you, not only will I protect you, but I will take him out." His words and tone are both sharp now. "Do you understand what I am saying Jess?" I just stare at him, unable to move, unable to answer him. My thoughts are racing. Oh god, he means he'll kill Brian. My stomach is queasy and the reality of the situation lands hard on my chest and it's hard for me to breathe. I take a few deep breathes before attempting to speak. I nod my head, "Yes and I will do whatever you tell me to do today. I trust you Jake."

Marcus is already in the kitchen eating breakfast with Fran and Sherman. It seems that no one can sleep in this morning. I eat my omelet in silence and sip my coffee. I hope today goes well. I silently pray, please God don't let anything go wrong today! I have the unopened letter in my purse along with my list of seven questions. My mind is in overdrive and I realize I have seven questions and I have known Jake for seven days. How crazy is that? I am wearing jeans and a silk sleeveless brown top with a light sweater over it. I am not wearing much jewelry, just the rings Jake gave me. My shoes are black slip on flats that I can move easily in, and quickly, if I need to. I did not feel like doing much this morning with my unruly hair. It hangs like loose silk around my shoulders.

After breakfast I sit and wait in the sitting room for a long time. Sherman, Jake and Marcus are downstairs. I assume they are discussing today's meeting one last time. I have just come back from the bathroom when they finally come upstairs. They are dressed in military garb and boots and the only coherent thought I can manage is their black boots will mark up the floor and Fran will have to spend extra time cleaning it. Earpieces in and pockets bulging with items of various shapes and sizes, they look very official. They all have web belts on with various weapons and pouches on them. Guns hang on their side. Jake sees me looking intensely at his gun. "Not to worry Jess, it's a CZ-75, one of the most accurate and lightweight pistols, that's why we use it." Jake walks over to me and takes my hands in his, trying to gauge my reaction. "Are you okay?" I nod my head yes and he briefly kisses me. With a firm command he says, "Okay then, let's go."

When we step out of the front door I expect to see Jake's vehicle and am shocked to see a small convoy of nine black vehicles outside. Fear grips me as I look at them. Jake means business. He leads me to a vehicle in the middle of the convoy. Sherman is driving our vehicle and Marcus is sitting up front with him, an unzipped black bag at his feet. I notice other packs and equipment in the back of our SUV type vehicle. Oh, this is really happening! My stomach is in knots now. I hope Brian doesn't do anything stupid. If he knew what was coming toward him, the manpower and equipment we are bringing, he wouldn't dare try anything. Maybe he has changed. I try not to hold my breath. Jake is quiet next to me. He is holding my hand and his thumb is slowly making small circles on the back of my hand. We drive the approximate half hour or so it takes to get to the café in silence. We are all thinking and worrying about what will happen next.

When we arrive, the first three vehicles pull forward and completely block off the intersection up ahead. One pulls up farther than the other two, turns and has a complete line of sight down the street toward us. The last three vehicles in the convoy back up and block the intersection directly behind us with one vehicle further back with a complete line of sight toward us. We are in the middle of three vehicles parked outside the café. Jake and Marcus exchange a look that is different from any look I have ever seen them exchange. It's an all business, get it done look that says they are taking no prisoners today. They will not hold back. They have just communicated without words, said all they need to say to each other.

My blood runs cold and I shiver at the thought of what is about to take place. God help us all. Jake has a firm hand on my thigh now. We are waiting for something. Jake looks at me and speaks in a slow, deliberate manner so that I understand him, "Jesse, when I tell you to, we are going to move quickly. Get out of the vehicle and I will very quickly guide you into the building. I will be right behind you the whole way. Got it?" I nod my head yes because I don't think I can speak right now.

When we get the go ahead, we quickly get out of the vehicle. Jake's guys are posted at various places along the street, side walk and in front of buildings. Within seconds we are in the café and heading to a table set up in the middle of the room. An old man stands up and I gasp and freeze where I stand when I recognize Brian. He smiles an ugly grin that shows off his yellowed teeth. His hair is gray and sparse. He is wrinkled every-where. I recognize the cold look in his eyes immediately. I steel myself for our encounter. Jake guides me to the table and motions for me to sit down. I do as instructed and Brian sits across from me. Jake stands next to me in a protective stance which boldly says he will jump on Brian if he tries to harm me in any way. Brian clearly gets the message and holds his empty palms up and says "Relax, we are all friends here."

Jake's muscles in his jaw jump. "Let's get one thing straight asshole, we are not friends. Jesse is here to do what she needs to do. This is the only time you will meet with her or see her. Got it?" I look around the empty room. Where are all the customers? How are we here alone at this time of the day? Shouldn't they be getting ready for the lunch rush? I see Marcus standing inside near the door, gun drawn and ready, fully focused on Brian. I take a deep breath and look at Brian. Holy hell, let's get this over with.

Without words I hand him the unopened letter and then the piece of paper with my questions on them. He looks me up and down a few times and smiles wickedly at me. "Christ you look good. You're still sexy as hell. It's too bad I'm an old man. Remember when we"... "Watch it asshole!" Jake growls at him, cutting off the rest of his sentence. Jake wants to lunge at him but somehow manages to stay in place. The thought of him touch-ing me is disgusting. Not because he is old and wrinkled with yellowed teeth, but because he is Brian. I hate him. After a week with Jake I can't believe I was ever with this asshole. He is just looking to start a fight. Why is that? I know him well enough to know he doesn't do sporadic things. He usually has a reason for the things he does or says and I am sure that hasn't changed. What's he up to?

I clear my throat and try to make my voice sound as strong and as steady as I can. "I would appreciate it if you would open that letter in private. Please just read and answer the questions I have written down for you." His eyes narrow and he is trying to see what I am thinking. I try not to look scared or nervous. "So, Jesse, how have you been? How are you feeling? You are pale and too thin. You must be, what, two or three months pregnant with our child now?" A sardonic grin forms on his wrinkled and parched lips. I want to throw up. Jake looks like he is going to kill Brian right now. I take a deep breath, "I am not here for pleasantries Brian. Just answer the questions" I say dryly.

The look in his eyes tells me he is surprised by my comeback. He's amused, I think. Instead of reading and answering the questions individually like I want him to, he reads them all at once. He looks up at me and sighs. "Oh all right. I'll answer your silly questions." He looks from me to Jake and then back to me. "Anything for you, dear." Jake is pissed and growls again at Brian, "I'm warning you!" Brian snaps back at Jake, "Oh don't threaten me, I'm an old man for Christ sake!" Jake hisses back, "You're not fooling anyone old man!"

I shake my head, "No, Jake, it's okay. He's always been an asshole. Some things never change. Go ahead Brian, answer the questions." I see surprise and, maybe hurt, in his eyes now. I am not sure what the other emotions are, but he is definitely surprised. Brian is angry that Jesse is treating him this way. Why is she being so cruel to him when she is carrying his child? And this fucker standing next to her is really pissing him off. Brian decides the only thing that will make him happy is seeing them both dead on the sidewalk outside. He is biding his time. He looks at the clock and then looks directly at Jesse. "Oh, where to start? Of course I loved you. Still do in fact. You were the one and only love of my life. I knew I would not be happy with anyone else and I haven't been. No, I didn't have anything to do with you joining the project. You did that all on your own sweetheart" he says, smirking and pointing a slender arthritic, wrinkled finger at me. Brian continues, "It's not my fault you chose to take the easy way out!"

I narrow my eyes at Brian. He is getting me angry. So damn angry. I try to keep my composure. "I did not take the easy way out! You think it was easy to leave my family and friends? You think it's easy to go through this now?" I shake my head in disgust at him. "Tell me; did you kill Jake's guys as he suspects you did?" Brian lets out an old man laugh, "Why the hell would I answer a question like that?" Brian eyes Jake and then focuses his gaze back on me. Pointedly he says, "No, I don't regret a single decision I have made in my life, including Katy." That bastard. I should have known he would do this. He is trying to push every button I have and avoid answering the questions.

I decide to try another approach. Instead of getting pissed, I try to put on my sweetest, sexiest face to try to draw some answers out of him. I run my fingers slowly through my hair, and then toss it back over my shoulder. As I meet his eyes I make it a point to lick my lips several times. I think I see a break in his composure but can't be sure. I sit up straighter in my chair and point my breast at him. I fan myself. "Oh wow, is it hot in here? I am, hot, all of a sudden." I shrug out of my sweater and untie my tie at the top of my silk shirt, allowing more cleavage to be easily visible. I cross my arms and squeeze my breast together. I definitely see a break in his composure now. I avoid looking at Jake because I know he will be angry. Brian's hands are folded on the table. I reach out and hold them in my own. This move surprises both Brian and Jake. "Brian, tell me what happened that day in the park, the day of the accident." He is the one who looks confused now. "What the hell are you talking about? You were there, you know what happened." I slowly lick my bottom lip and smile sweetly at him. "I want to hear it from your point of view. Oh please Brian." I make sure to say the last part in a sexy, breathy voice while I rub his hands. He is clearly frustrated and, without pulling his hands away, finally says "Oh for fucks sake! What do you want to know?" Ha! Nice. Now I have to get him to tell me what I want to know and I hope it won't be that hard because I am ready to get the hell out of here. "As much as you can tell me" I respond sweetly, licking my lips and gazing at him as innocently as I can.

He has a permanent scowl on his face. "I picked you up and we went to have a picnic like we always did, in the park. You told me you were pregnant. I told you I didn't want a child because I had too much going on with work. You had no idea I was fucking my assistant. We argued. I left

and that's when the truck hit me." I am pissed but I try to keep an interesting look on my face. "Oh so, was Katy the assistant you were fucking?"
I rub his hands and spread them out on the table. "Oh Brian, your hands
are so dry. Here, let me rub some lotion on them while we talk." Before
he knows what hit him I pull the lotion out of my purse and start to rub it
on his hands and forearms. He closes his eyes and says, "Oh that feels good
Jesse. You know, you were the only one that ever really took care of me." I
force a smile at him. His guard is down and he answers me without thinking, "Yes, Katy was my assistant. We eventually got married. She just died
recently." I try to sound empathetic, "Oh, Brian, I am so sorry." I allow a
long pause and then say, "Brian, it was all so long ago. Think back, and tell
me, why did you cheat on me? Was there a particular reason?"

He looks at me, stares at my breast for a long while, and then looks at
Jake before looking back at me. He is now holding my hands and rubbing
them. I don't look at Jake because I know he is even madder now. Brian
smiles a yellowed tooth smile and I can smell tobacco on him. I scoot up
in my chair to make my breast shake and he watches me carefully. He says,
"No particular reason, other than I was a horny bastard and fucked every
woman I could. You were different Jesse. You actually cared about me. I
think you actually loved me. I still can't figure that out. I was not... good
to you. Why did you stay with me?"

I realize I have all of my questions answered probably as good as they
are going to be answered, except for knowing if he really is trying to kill
me. It takes all my determination but I force myself to smile lovingly at
Brian. "Oh Brian, I'll make you a deal. I will tell you that, if you answer
a question for me first." I pull my hands away from his and squirt some
lotion onto my hand and begin to vigorously rub it into my arms so that
my breasts shake again. It works like a charm and he agrees to answer my
question. "Sure, anything" he says with a wavering voice. I smile sweetly
at him. "If you knew I was carrying your child then why would you want
to harm me? Why terminate the project? Unless Jake's guys have the
wrong information about you?"

"Don't you get it Jesse? You were a huge problem for me. I married Katy and moved on, had a family. I became well known and wealthy.
Respected even, in some circles. Hell, I couldn't have a pregnant woman
from my past popping up unannounced now could I? She didn't know
about us. Katy didn't know about you." It took a few minutes of me sitting

quietly to process what he just said. Both Brian and Jake were watching me to see what my next move was. So, he was going to have me killed to protect his reputation. Fucking asshole rat bastard! So, Jake's information was correct. Great, just great! This fraternizing with the enemy is over! I don't say another word to him. Instead, I stand and put my sweater back on. I walk to Jake and kiss him seductively and say, "Come on, let's go home. All this talk has made me horny. Let's go home and have sex, a lot of sex, first in the chair by the fireplace and then in the hot tub." Jake is grinning, "Whatever you need baby" and then he turns to give Brian an 'eat shit' look.

When I turn to walk away I see that Brian is fuming now. More pissed than ever at me. Jake signals to Marcus who comes immediately to Brian and says, "Let's go old man." Marcus, who is considerably taller and larger than Brian, walks Brian out the door in front of us and pushes him up against the wall. I think I hear a bone crack and then Brian cries out in pain. As Marcus is pushing him up against the wall, none of us realize that Brian is signaling with his hands. Jake doesn't see it because he is trying to direct me back to the vehicle. Marcus is busy holding Brian down and is distracted by Brian's fighting underneath his hold and therefore doesn't look his hands.

We are not quite halfway to the vehicle when shots ring out. I can't tell which direction they come from. I instinctively start to duck but Jake immediately has both his arms wrapped around me and swings me around in a full circle and throws me back into the café. On the dive back into the café Jake spots a man with what looks like an RPG on a nearby rooftop. He quickly radio's Marcus, "RPG cover, cover, cover!" Marcus, in one smooth motion uses his sidearm to shoot Brian in the leg and then dives head first into the open door of the first of the three nearby tactical vehicles parked outside the café. A huge explosion rocks the front of the café. Glass shatters and flies everywhere, along with dirt, dust and metal. The air is thick and dark from debris. Jake has me on the ground and is shielding me with his body. I feel glass and debris crunch around us and I think I have glass in my hand. As soon as objects stop landing near us I hear Jake calling Marcus. "Marcus, you copy?" He must not be getting an answer because he repeats it twice. Finally, Jake says "Copy that, yes, okay."

Jake is getting up onto his knees now to assist me when the back door to the café flies open and an armed gunman runs in shooting at us. I have never seen anyone react so fast. Before my brain can even assimilate what is happening, Jake has his weapon drawn and, with one shot, has shot the guy dead. A second gunman runs in behind the first and starts shooting at us. Jake still has his weapon trained on the door and immediately takes down that gunman too. Jake grabs me and pulls me up to my feet. We exit the café and Jake gets me into the vehicle we arrived in safely. He uses the door of the vehicle as a shield and returns fires in the direction of the RPG fire. When we ran out of the café I did not spot Marcus anywhere. I keep low to the ground as instructed. Hell, you don't have to tell me twice! I want to go home. I am not made for this shit! Fuck, it's not even lunch yet and I'm being shot at!

Gunfire erupts on the opposite side of the street. I hear it but I have no way to know if it's us shooting the enemy or if they are shooting at us. I keep my head down and hope this will be over soon. Out of nowhere, the door on the other side of the vehicle opens and Marcus jumps in. He doesn't seem concerned with keeping his head down, although he tells me too. "Jesse, you are doing great, just stay down" he says to me before reaching into the back of our vehicle and pulling large, long bags over so he can reach them. Jesus! Did he really think I was going to move? The next thing I know he's pulling out all sorts of weapons and loading them. He gives Jake what I think is a long fat gun of some sort through the open car door. Jake takes aim at the second story window where he believes one of Brian's goons is located, shooting at us. I hear a loud popping sound and then an explosion in the distance. Jake fires numerous other weapons that Marcus hands him through the open car door. Within approximately thirty seconds the street is silent. Marcus and Jake stay put for another fifteen seconds or so and then, when they have the okay from some team member in their ear, Marcus exits the vehicle to stand with Jake. They halfway shake hands and halfway hug. I smile because they are both okay and can't help but think how unbelievably sexy they both are. Pure male beauty while saving the day, I smile bigger.

Jake is at my side within seconds. "Hey, Jess, you okay?" he asks me but I see he is already doing a physical assessment of me. "I'm okay, except I think I got glass in my hand." I hold up my left hand for him to see. It's at this point Sherman appears from across the street with the rest of the team. Everyone quickly gets into vehicles. Like before, Sherman is behind the wheel, Marcus is now in front with him, and Jake is at my side. The doors are closed and our convoy is moving. Except, of course, the vehicle behind ours that got blown to smithereens. Jake says, "Don't worry, we will get the glass out and clean it good. We won't let it get infected." Is he kidding? The glass in my hand is the last thing on my mind right now. We were just shot at for crying out loud! I have to remind myself he is used to this and I am not. I close my eyes and take a deep breath.

I keep my eyes closed. I am dazed and lean over onto Jake's shoulder. He moves to wrap his arm around me. "I am so sorry Jesse. It's okay, baby, everything is fine now. We will be home soon." He kisses the top of my head and I finally relax a little and exhale. I realize that hearing him say the words 'we' and 'home' warms my heart. Finally, when we are home, Jake carries me into the house and straight to the clinic downstairs. Marcus and Sherman head to the kitchen to talk to Fran and let her know that we are all home okay, plus they are hungry and want lunch early. Jake quickly picks the small shards of glass out of my hand, cleans the area, covers it with antibiotic ointment and then applies a sterile non-adhesive dressing, then wraps the whole thing with a gauze wrap. When he looks up I think he is relieved to have the whole ordeal over with. "Jesse" he says to me, "I am sorry about Brian." I don't understand what he is saying and I ask, "What are you talking about?"

"I am sorry he didn't give you better answers. I am sorry he was such an asshole. I'd like to say I'm sorry he's dead, but I'm not because that uncomplicates things for me." I gasp, "Dead? How do you know? Are you sure?" Jake sighs, "Yeah baby, I'm sure. I saw him on the sidewalk, near where Marcus had him against the wall. He was hit by flying debris when the RPG hit the vehicle behind ours. I'm sure he was killed instantly." Oh, wow. I am not sure how I feel about that. I don't feel sorry for him at all, I know that. "Well, he brought it on himself" is all I could manage to get out.

With my hand taken care of, and a once over check from the good doctor, he has determined I am not injured anywhere else. I could have told him that, if he'd just asked me. Well, as a matter of fact, I did tell him that earlier. Ugh, men! Jake runs his hand through his hair and sighs. Dirt and debris fly out of his hair and drift to the floor. "Jake, do you want to go upstairs to talk to Sherman and Marcus?" I am hoping he will say no because at this moment, I feel like I am on the verge of panic. I want him to stay with me. I feel like I am in a daze. Is this shock? Am I in shock?

Is it adrenaline? Maybe I just need to rest. "No baby, I don't." My brain is having a hard time understanding his answer. I crinkle up my nose and say, "You don't?" He shakes his head no. "What do you want to do?" I ask him, unable to figure out what our next step should be.

He pushes my hair back behind my ears and smiles a heart stopping loving smile that sends me reeling even more than I am already. "I am going to take you upstairs and wash your hair and scrub you from head to toe. I am going to climb into bed with you and hold you for as long as possible and let you rest. You are exhausted. I will have lunch brought up for us. Do you like that idea?" I smile with relief. Thank god! He is not going to leave me! I smile bigger at him now and manage to say, "Yes, I like it a lot."

40

I slept so hard that I have drool running down the side of my mouth. I am still half asleep and, with my eyes closed, I reach up and wipe the spit off my face. A few seconds later I realize that I am lying on a firm, bare chest. Jake's chest. Oh crap. Is he awake? Did he see what I just did? Did I drool on him? Double crap! I slowly stretch and open my eyes. I hope when I look at him he will still be asleep. I look at him and nope, he's awake. He grins his ridiculously sexy grin and hands me a washcloth. I sheepishly take it from him and wipe my mouth and hand off. "How do you feel?" he asks softly. "Better" I say, grinning stupidly back at him now. I look around to see the room is dimly lit, there is a roaring fire in the fireplace, and the sun is either going down or coming up. What?

"Oh no! Jake, what time is it? Have I slept all day?" A scowl replaces my grin. He pulls me in for a sweet hug and, in my ear, says, "It's almost eight pm. You were exhausted. You needed to rest. We hung out here today. It was nice." He trails kisses down my neck and when he reaches my mouth, he kisses me sweetly. He says, "I love watching you sleep." He draws it out and emphasizes the word 'love'. It completely grounds me. I am so thankful to have him in my life. I think of the day, about Brian, about the gunfire and the explosion. We were lucky. There could have been a different ending. I pull Jake closer and kiss him back with even more fervor. He is right there with me, deepening the kiss. When he pulls away he smiles at me and runs his fingers through my hair. With a serious look now he says, "If anything would have happened to you..." and then shakes his head no, trying to eliminate the thought. After a long pause he continues, "Oh God! Baby, if anything would have happened to you it would have been my fault...for taking you there in the first place!"

I scoot up further to lie next to him, so we can have the skin on skin contact I crave. "No, Jake, stop it! None of this is your fault! I wanted to see Brian, I needed to do this! I just couldn't reconcile that he was the way you tried to tell me he was." I sigh and stroke his face and run my fingers through his hair. "You were right. Your information was right. He is, was an asshole and he deserved what he got! He brought it on himself. He had every opportunity to do the right thing, and look at the life he chose!" Jake kissed my forehead. "Yeah, I know he chose that path. I just hate that it intertwined with your path. I am so sorry, Jess. I just wanted to make you happy. Let you do what you needed to do. At the same time I desperately wanted to protect you. If I would have tried to hold you back, tell you that you couldn't meet with him, you would probably resent me. Just the time we have spent together this week, has made me realize how strong you are. I know I need to let you do things on your own. Jess, you have shown me this week just how tough you are, and I am so damn proud of you!"

Wow. He is proud of me? When was the last time someone was *proud* of me? A warm tingle runs through me. I don't know, but hearing him say the words makes me feel like I am ten feet tall, like I can do anything. "Thanks for saying that. I'm not" I say firmly. He looks at me strangely, not understanding what I mean. "I mean, that I am not sorry our paths intertwined because I would have never met you!" With his finger under my chin he lifts my face up to kiss me. Just when I think it isn't possible for him to kiss me any sweeter, he does. There is so much love and respect, and need, packed into his sweet kiss. I think again to myself how much I love this man. I love my husband. I grin my ridiculous stupid girl face splitting grin. Now he grins too, "What?" he asks me. I don't answer and he playfully spanks my bottom, "Tell me!" he says in his best authoritative tone while he is laughing. "Oh, I was just thinking how much I love you. How much I love my husband." He nods, "The whole time you slept, I have held you close and thought how thankful I am to have you here with me, and how much I love you, wife." He kisses me gently again but then says, "Now, how about we go downstairs for a few hours? Fran and Sherman have left already, but you need to move around a while and you need to eat. I don't want you to be too stiff and sore from lying in bed all afternoon." I raise an eyebrow in a questioning look and say, "Just a few hours?" He responds by nodding and saying, "Because I want your full attention, here, in our bed, in a little while Mrs. Bradley." Oh! I melt right there in his arms. The anticipation of what he will do to me later awakens all of my nerve endings. "My full attention huh?" I say with a wicked grin and trail kisses down his neck and chest. In between the kisses I tell my gorgeous husband, "Anything for you Jake."

Fran has left me food wrapped up on top of the stove. "I am starving!" I say as I shove another bite of mashed potatoes in my mouth. I have devoured my pork chops and broccoli already. I am sitting on the kitchen counter where Jake put me while he warmed up my food. He smiles and says, "I love to see you eat. I am sure that baby is hungry too" and he spreads out his hand on my flat belly. Oh God! I am going to have to take better care of myself. I keep forgetting I am pregnant, except when I need to pee that is. That always reminds me. I need to drink more water and make sure I eat and rest. Suddenly it dawns on me that I have no idea what to name this baby. "Uh, Jake?" He is still smiling and now rubbing my belly. "You know, I really haven't given much thought to a name. Will you help me name him or her?" As I run my finger down my empty plate and lick my fork clean, he laughs at me and says, "Yes, of course. I am glad we have some time, it's going to be hard to decide."

I scoot off the counter and head to the sink with my plate. Jake trails closely behind me. I don't even know if it is a boy or girl. Do I want to know? Yes, I think I do. "Hey, Jake, when you can tell, I think I'd like to know what it is, a boy or girl, I mean." He can't stop grinning at me. He is absolutely beautiful and all mine! How the hell did I get so lucky? "Of course baby, I should be able to tell soon." He makes me quit cleaning, takes my hand and leads me downstairs. We sit on the couch in silence, just enjoying being with each other. Out of the corner of my eye I see the piano. Oh, I haven't got to play it yet. I force myself to leave the safety and warmth of my husband's arms and sit down at the piano. I strum the keys and listen to the notes fill the room. I can't help but smile. I try not to think of any particular music. I start to play a song that I think I know. Jake is sitting on the couch watching me curiously. I play the whole song without so much as even one mistake. Wow, I really can play the piano! I don't even know the name of what I just played, but it was pretty. He laughs and claps loudly, clearly impressed.

As he watched her play the piano, Jake's only wish is that his dad could see Jesse now. See how beautiful she is and how well she is doing. He knows his dad would be pleased with her outcome. Jake thinks of his dad's hard work that has made this outcome possible. He doesn't want to dampen her happy playful mood so before she catches him deep in thought he says, "Very nice, Mrs. Bradley." I watch him as he picks up the guitar and plucks at the strings. I watch him more intensely as he repositions it just so on his right thigh, his arm draped around the guitar oh so carefully. I can't believe it but I am jealous of that damn guitar. I want his arm around me, so I can feel his soft touch and his warmth. I cannot deny he plays me like an instrument too. I watch as Jake plays a song. Now I'm the one impressed. He is good…really good. He didn't tell me he could play like *that*. I guess we still have a lot to learn about each other. I marvel at my husband's many talents. I grin wickedly as I think about just how talented he is, especially in the bedroom. Yes. I am a lucky woman.

"Jess" he says. When I look up he continues, "Do you know what the great thing is?" I shake my head no, unsure of where he is going with this. "You got some of the answers you wanted. I had my belief's about Brian confirmed. It's over. We are free to live our lives as we want." I am elated because I realize he is right. It's sad that Brian is dead. I only feel relieved. I feel like a huge weight has been lifted off my shoulders. I feel like I can finally breathe. Jake puts the guitar back and I move to sit next to him on the couch. Once I snuggle up to him and he wraps his arm around me, pulling me closer, I look at him. He has such a serious expression. He is worried about something. Is there something he is not telling me? I know Jake and, he will tell me if he wants me to know. I know if he doesn't want me to know, that there's no way I can drag it out of him. After a brief pause he ask, "Jess, are you happy?" Oh no, is that what he is worried about? Is he worried if I will be happy here, with him?

I quickly answer to reassure him. "Yes, I am happy, here, with you." I lean over and kiss him. He responds with worry in his eyes, "I want you to be. I wanted you here so badly. I was so lonely but, I'd never forgive myself if you are not happy here. I could only hope I was making the right decision." I shake my head and run my hands through his hair and glide it over his cheek. I pull his face to the side to look at me. "Jake, *you* make me happy. So stop this! I am so thankful for all that you have done for me! But my feelings for you … the first day you brought me here, I never expected to have any of *this* happen. I love you Jake. I know we still have a lot to learn about each other, but I know you, the real you, enough to know I love you!" Jake pulled me closer to him and hugged me hard. He kissed the top of my forehead sweetly. "Let's go upstairs Mrs. Bradley and I will show you just how much I love you." He trails kisses down my ear and neck as he quickly runs his hands up and down my body. I am putty in his hands. I whisper in his ear, "Okay…thought you'd never ask" and smile back at him.

41

Jake knew he'd have to do this eventually. He put it off as long as possible. Now there was no getting out of it. He smiled when he thought of how great it's been, being home with Jesse these last seven months. He loved her so damn much it hurt. He would spend the rest of his life making sure she was happy. He wanted to give her everything she needed and more. He also loved working with the horses and with Sherman and Marcus on the many acres of land. There was always a fence that needed repair, or a barn to either build or fix, or a trench to dig. Sherman had a keen sense of just how to keep the farm in tip top shape. Jake didn't mind the hard work. Sometimes it was back breaking and he would come dragging in bone weary. Once he walked through the front door and saw Jesse, he was instantly recharged. Marcus and Charlie were amazing together. Jake knew that their relationship would last forever, just like he knew that he and Jesse are forever. He sighed deeply. Sherman slapped him on the back, "Looks like you're on" he muttered quietly. Jake nodded and stepped onto the stage and toward the podium and microphone that was set up at the front entrance of the hospital.

Immediately he was blinded by the camera flashes and bright lights. The crowd of reporters and curious on-lookers seems to be growing bigger by the second. Jake waited a few minutes for some of the chaos and noise to settle before reading his short speech he had prepared. Fran was at home, making lunch and snacks because she knew that they would all be starving before too long. Marcus and Charlie would be here soon to pick it and her up. When she saw Jake step up to the microphone she turned the volume up. She hated the way the reporters and crowd were invading Jake. Vultures! They were nothing but vultures! They are rude and nasty people. She hated this part for Jake. She wanted to protect Jake from this but knew she couldn't. At least Sherman was there with him. It's as if the reporters were trying to suck the very life out of him with each flash. She knew the flashes of light must be nearly blinding, and knew Jake would want to get this over as quickly as possible. She saw Jake wince a time or two at the bright flashes. He raised a hand to the pulsing, loud crowd and began to speak. "Good morning. As most of you know, I am Jake Bradley, the doctor who assisted with the continuation of my father's cryonics project. There are many things I could say to you this morning. I know you have many questions. I want to be as brief as possible. I will tell you that yes, it's true, the subject…uh…patient, Jesse, and I are indeed now married." The crowd cheered wildly. Jake smiled and held up his hand again. He saw that many of the reporters had their hands up indicating they, no doubt, had a question to ask him.

"It is also true that this was a special cryonics project in the sense that this was the first time a pregnant woman has ever participated." A hush fell over the crowd. He could hear a low murmur as people quietly discussed this last statement among themselves. How the hell had the fact that she was pregnant not have been leaked? Jake was pleased that it had not been, after all, he had taken great measures to prevent it. However, he had assumed that at some point Brian would have talked. Standing there he couldn't help but wonder if Brian didn't leak it because deep down he did love Jesse. It doesn't matter now. That bastard is dead and Jake refused to waste time thinking about him. "I am happy to report that she is doing fine and has fully regained her strength over the past seven months. She has no physical complications from the cryonics process and has, in fact, done very well. Probably better than what was originally hoped for. It is also true that we are here at the hospital today to deliver a baby."

The crowd goes wild again. There are non-stop flashes of light and shouts from the crowd, from both the reporters and the on-lookers. Various whoops and whistles shoot out from the crowd. Jake waits another moment for some of the noise to subside. "I want to keep this brief, as you can understand. I will take approximately a year off work. At this time it is not clear what I will decide to do after that. I will have to make that decision when the time comes. For now, I fully plan to enjoy being at home with my family. I would like to ask that you respect our privacy. I will take a few questions." Jake watched the crowd, annoyed to see just about every hand shoot up.

He was determined to pick the least obnoxious people with questions. It was their reward for not being so cut throat, he thought to himself. Jake honed in on a young blonde woman in a navy skirt and a tight navy and lime green sweater. It was a V-neck sweater and the first button was unbuttoned. Her breast bulged beautifully out of the top of the sweater while the rest of the sweater hugged the rest of her curves nicely. It was a warm January day and her breasts looked warm enough in that tight sweater. He couldn't help but notice them. Christ he was a man! Jake knew everyone would think he only called on her because of her breasts. However, it wasn't her breast that drew him to her. It was her face. She was young and had an innocent, sweet look about her. She reminded him of Jesse in a weird way, although they looked nothing alike.

As he called on the woman, her eyes gleamed brightly. She put her hand down and began to speak, "First, doctor, let me offer my congratulations" she said with a strong confidence in her voice. She smiled sweetly at Jake. He nodded to her in acceptance. "Could you speak briefly on the science and the process of it all? I mean on the actual thawing out process? I wonder how many years did it take to perfect the process? Were there glitches or did things go smoothly?" Jake nodded again in understanding of her question. "Its regeneration, not 'thawing out' he explained to her. I am not going to get into specifics. I will tell you that I have worked tirelessly, very closely with an incredible cryogenicist, one of the best in the field, and I have a wonderful nurse who has assisted me with a lot of the hands on stuff. Without them, the project would not have been the huge success it is! There were some minor glitches, but nothing that we couldn't handle ourselves. The science of it, the actual process has been evolving over the past eighty years. I am sure it will continue to evolve as new techniques and equipment are developed and the field is advanced."

Jake smiles at the crowd looking for the next question. Jake picked an older man in a tweed jacket. The man lowered his hand and adjusted his glasses before speaking. "This project success is incredible. There are many people paying close attention to what you do next with this knowledge. Will you work with the government or will you continue to work in the private sector? There are many people who would like to volunteer for a project like this and want the same successful outcome as we see here." Jake shook his head side to side and smiled. He knew this question was coming. "As I stated before, I am not sure at this point what I will decide to do after this next year. I will cross that bridge when I get there. I do think I will continue to work in the private sector. I don't think I could have the control I want if I worked with the government." This answer seemed to satisfy the old man. It was only a matter of time before the press hounded him about it and Jake knew it.

Next Jake picked a middle aged woman wearing black pants and a floral silk shirt and black jacket over it. She seemed harmless enough. "Yes, Mr. Bradley, I would like to know about the baby's father. Does he know about the baby? Is he still alive? What role will he play in the life of the child? What can you tell us about him?" Jake had prepared himself for this question too. He knew someone would ask it. "The child's father is not alive; therefore he will not play a role in the child's life. That is all I am willing to divulge on that topic." The woman scowled at him but didn't say anything else. Again, there was a low muttering among the reporters and on-lookers. The crowd watched as a man in a medical scrubs and white jacket stepped up onto the stage and headed toward Jake. Jake took a step back away from the microphone and leaned over so the man could tell him something in his ear. Jake nodded his head, responded briefly and then stepped up to the microphone.

"I am sorry folks. Looks like I have to cut this short. I will keep you informed of my official decision that I make in the future. As for now, I am needed at my beautiful wife's bedside for the arrival of our first child. She's watching from upstairs, "Hold on baby, I'll be there shortly." Jake spun around and practically ran off the stage. Sherman followed close behind him. The crowd went wild with cheers. Jake heard them through the closed front doors of the hospital. It was only when the elevator doors closed that he could no longer hear the cheers of the crowd. Sherman was standing next to him fidgeting and looking pretty nervous. Jake looked over at him and grinned, "You nervous?" Sherman stepped from foot to foot, unable to be still. "Hell yeah I'm nervous! The waiting...this is the worst! It'll be over with soon I hope. I can't stand the waiting!"

Now it was Jake slapping Sherman on the back. "Don't worry old man, she'll be fine! She's in good hands." Jake had tried to make his voice strong and confident, to reassure Sherman. He had to take a deep breath and exhale. Yes, he knew she was in good hands, but it didn't matter. Jesse, the love of his life, the woman he would do anything for, the woman he wanted to protect and hold and love the rest of his life, was upstairs alone, with strangers. He knew she was probably scared and needing him. He didn't want to admit it, but he was nervous too. Sherman knew Jesse was not just in good hands; she was in the best hands. Jake made sure of that. Jake had insisted that his best obstetrics specialists handle the birth, in case any complications should arise. He wanted it over with and wanted the peace of mind of knowing they were both okay. He'd promised his best friend, Jake's dad, he'd take care of his only son. He had promised him that he'd watch over Jake like he was his own. Jake was lost in his own thoughts next to Sherman. He wanted to be in the room and focus all of his attention on Jesse, and not have to be working and maybe miss something. No way. He wanted to be present for it all and completely available for Jesse. They stepped out of the elevator and before Jake could run to Jesse Sherman stopped him by putting a hand on his shoulder. "Jake, I have watched you grow into a fine young man...a respectable and honest man. You are a hard worker. You are a loving husband. You know your dad was my best friend. I know he'd be so damn proud of you. I just want you to know that I am proud of you too." Sherman pulled Jake into a big bear hug and squeezed him tight before letting him go.

Jake knew that he and Fran loved him like their own son. They had always treated him like he was, and he had always felt it. He had always known how much they loved him. But hearing those words from Sherman, especially now, meant so much to him. He hadn't known he'd needed to hear them. He didn't understand it but Sherman's words made him feel somehow healed and complete. Those words broke apart something deep within him. Maybe closure was the word he was searching his brain for. Hell, he didn't know, couldn't pin it down now, but he understood somewhere deep in his soul that he had needed desperately to hear those words, even if he didn't understand why.

A little choked up, he had to pause and clear his throat before speaking. "Awe, thanks Sherman. You've been so good to me. You are a second father to me, you know that. You and Fran are my other parents. I am so glad you've been here with me, through all of this. I truly appreciate everything you have done for me, and now for Jesse too." Sherman hugged him again and then slapped Jake on the back, "Okay, off you go then, you've got a baby to meet!" Jake smiled nervously at Sherman and took off down the hall. Sherman was so proud of him. He watched Jake leave and then stood there for a long moment gathering his composure and wiping tears from his eyes. He knew Fran would be here soon and he didn't want to be a blubbering fool when she found him.

As soon as Jake was dressed in the appropriate sterile scrubs he was ushered into the room. He immediately rushed to my side. I smiled and reached for him when I saw him. "Hey baby, how are my girls?" Jake leaned down and kissed me softly. "Your girls are fine. Let's talk about the navy and green sweater!" Jake's face went flat. Oh shit! He didn't think she'd be mad about that! "Oh, baby, you know, it was nothing, really. She was sweet. She reminded me of you." I smiled at Jake groveling and said, "Uh, huh, really?" Jake ran his fingers through his hair, "Come on baby, don't bust my balls" he whispered, aware there were others in the room. I couldn't help but laugh at him. He was nervous and I knew it, although he didn't want to admit it. He was so cute when he was nervous. I marveled again at how much I love my husband.

I smile at him and pull him down for another kiss. "As long as you are coming home with me, that's all that matters" I manage to get out and then the next contraction hit. Jake was right there with me, helping me get through it. Jake leaned closer and whispered in my ear "Baby, home with you is where I want to be, always, forever." He kissed me chastely, again aware of others in the room. Jake was so proud of her for everything. Today, he was especially proud of how she was handling her labor. She wasn't screaming in pain and becoming unhinged. No, instead, she was in total control. He knew it from the first moment he entered her room. As the contractions got closer and closer, he stayed right next to her, helping her as best he could from the side of the bed. He tried to keep her focus on the beautiful, healthy baby she would be holding soon. He tried to distract her from as much of the pain as he could. He knew he couldn't take the pain away, but he damn sure would if he could.

He had delivered babies before, and had seen more than a few women in labor. He knew a lot of women didn't handle it well, but Jesse was amazing. She remained focused and determined, talking and working with the nurses, bringing her legs up and pushing when she needed to. Her control made the whole ordeal somehow organized and orderly. Approximately forty-five minutes later, Jesse was handed a beautiful baby girl. Jesse looked at her precious daughter for a long time. She did the ceremonial counting of all fingers and toes, and then had to get her naked to look at the rest of her. When all parts and pieces were accounted for she quickly wrapped her little princess back up and held her close. Jake held them and kissed them as best he could from the side of the bed.

When I reached a point where I thought I could let Jake take a turn at holding the baby I said to the happy, warm bundle sleeping like a rock in my arms, "princess Jenna Nicole, I'd like you to meet your daddy. You are a very lucky girl because he is a special daddy. He saved us both and he is going to be the best daddy ever!" A few tears rolled down Jake's cheek and he quickly brushed them away. Jake had never heard sweeter words. He arched an eyebrow, "Princess Jenna Nicole?" We had narrowed it down to three names, but he wanted me to choose a name. He had liked all three and said he'd be happy with any of the names. I nodded, "Yes, Jenna Nicole, unless you want a different name." He shook his head no, "It's a perfect name for our perfect little princess." His heart grew bigger in his chest, and his stomach flip flopped. All Jake knew was that he was going to love and protect them for the rest of his life. He would never let anyone hurt his girls. He loved them so much that he had no words to describe it. He would do anything for them.

Jake did not hesitate and quickly nodded yes when I asked him if he was ready to hold Princess Jenna. He gently took her from me while carefully supporting her tiny head with his hand. The moment the baby left my arms I felt cold and empty and wanted her back. I was filled with an overwhelming love watching Jake hold Jenna for the first time. That love was what allowed me to resist taking her from him. Jake had held other babies before. This was different. This was incredibly special because the baby was his now. As he leaned down to kiss his new daughter, Jake felt the huge weight and responsibility of being a father.

As he held her close to his chest and stroked her hair and cheeks, he wondered to himself, how in the hell did Jesse's father let her do the project? If it were his daughter, this daughter, he'd never let her do a thing like that. In the past he had wondered if Sherman felt responsible for him, and had known all along that he did. His words at the elevator had confirmed what he already knew. He was so thankful to have Sherman in his life, as a second father. Sherman was even more special to Jake because of the connection with his dad and the fact that his dad trusted Sherman. Jake thought of his dad and wished like hell his dad could be here to see this! Another tear or two escaped before he regained his composure. He quickly brushed them away. When he looked up at me, I had tears in my eyes as well. It was such a beautiful moment.

"You okay?" I asked him. "Yeah, was just wishing my dad was here to see her." I squeezed his arm reassuringly, "I love you, and I know you will be the best dad!" Jake smiled because he knew I wouldn't let him be anything else. He held his daughter for a long time, lost in his thoughts. When he looked up at Jesse he saw that she wanted the baby. He knew he would have plenty of time to hold her later and reluctantly handed Jenna back to Jesse. After kissing them both once more, he finally was able to go out and talk to everyone while they were moving his girls to a larger room for tonight.

Jake told them everything. Fran couldn't help but cry and then Charlie started crying. Charlie said, "Oh, it's all so beautiful, isn't it" to Fran, who just shook her head and blew her red nose. Marcus grinned at them, knowing he shouldn't laugh, but couldn't help himself. Sherman slapped Marcus on the arm, a direct warning that he'd better straighten up. Marcus and Jake exchanged a look and then busted out laughing at the crying women. After a moment, Sherman shook his head and started laughing too. After another moment, both of the previously crying women were laughing with them.

When it was time they all entered the room to find me sitting up in bed holding Princess Jenna. Immediately Fran and Charlie rushed over to us, hugging us first and asking if I was okay and then wanting to know everything about the little princess who already had us all wrapped around her tiny finger. I was all too happy to tell them and show them every inch of Jenna Nicole. As Fran and Charlie took turns holding the baby, I took the opportunity to go to the bathroom, with Jake's help back to the bed. Next I ate one of Fran's delicious steak and cheese hoagies with chips and water. I can't believe how hungry I am. Sherman, Marcus and Jake ate too. Reluctantly, Fran laid Jenna down in my arms and let her rest contently there. Everyone left at approximately midnight. Since Jake owned the hospital we could do what ever we wanted and didn't have to abide by visiting hours, which was really nice. I loved all the visiting but admitted that I was tired and needed to rest. As soon as they left, I made a final trip to the bathroom, nursed Jenna once more, and then crashed hard for four delightful hours.

At approximately four thirty in the morning I heard Jenna squirming and making quiet sounds in her bassinette. I sat up in bed and looked around the dimly lit room. Jake was dead to the world sprawled out on a pull out bed that did not look comfortable at all. He didn't seem to mind it though. His left arm was across his chest and his right arm and leg were hanging off the end of the bed. I chuckled at the sight of my sexy husband, who, I was sure, was about to fall off the bed any moment. I made a quick trip to the bathroom, got some water and fruit, put them on the table next to my bed where I could reach them, then crawled back into bed and rearranged the pillows to make myself comfortable in a sitting position. I took a large gulp of water and ate some fruit. Finally, I reached over and carefully brought the cooing baby Jenna into my arms to nurse. Jenna wasn't good at nursing yet, but with my guidance she was learning fast. This time she latched on better and quickly began to nurse, acting like she had not nursed in days. Her only complaint was when I took the time to switch her to the other breast.

I have finished my water and fruit by the time Jenna finished nursing. After a quick, very quiet burp and diaper change, and another trip to the bathroom for me, we were both tucked warmly back into our beds. I am incredibly tired. I started to doze off before my head hit the pillow. I quickly drift into a deep, well needed sleep. Jake woke up abruptly when he landed hard on the floor. It took him a few seconds to remember where he was. He was still groggy but looked over to Jesse and saw she was still sleeping. Good, he did not wake her up. He did not hear any disgruntled noise from the baby, which was a good thing since it was so early and he hadn't had coffee yet. Jake scrubbed his hands over his face, got to his feet and stretched. He visited the bathroom and then the nurse's station to get a cup of coffee. The staff knew who he was. They were pleasant and assisted him immediately.

On the way back to Jesse's bedside he saw the water and fruit on the table. She must have got up to feed the baby. He sat his coffee on the table and carefully picked up the rocking chair and positioned it near Jesse's bed and the baby. He sat down in the rocking chair with his coffee and took a deep breath. A year ago he would have never believed he'd be here, now, with not only a wife, but a daughter too. It's funny how things work out, he thought to himself. He will never be alone again. He smiled at the thought.

Well after Jake finished his coffee and the sun began to rise, he heard the baby moving around and making cute baby noises. He had always loved babies. He especially loved all the cute baby noises they made. He could not help himself. He had to pick her up and hold her close. He was careful to support her head as he gently lifted her into his arms. He sat down in the rocking chair, looking at his daughter for what seemed like an eternity. He wrapped her up better in the blanket and then kissed her tiny cheek. "Good morning beautiful" he told her with a huge grin. "Remember me? I am your daddy. I promise to take really good care of you. You are a special little princess for a lot of different reasons, but you will always be special to me because you are *my* little princess." She stared up at Jake with a content look, and was safe and warm in his arms. Jake couldn't stop grinning at his little princess. "You have a very special mommy. Did you know that? Well, I think it's very important you know that. And you want to know a secret?" Jake pretended she said yes. In a low whisper next to her ear he said, "I love your mommy. She is the bravest and the best mommy in the whole world! And I think she's the prettiest too."

When Jake looked up he was surprised to see me awake and watching them. "I'm glad you think so" I said, smiling at them. Immediately I wanted them next to me. I scoot over and patted my hand down on the bed. "Come here family" I said to them. Jake sat on the bed and placed Jenna on top of my chest. He leaned over and kissed me gently. In a husky, quiet voice he said "Morning baby, you feeling okay?" I smiled at him and stole one more kiss before saying "I feel great. Thank you for staying with us last night." He wrapped an arm around me and I snuggled into him as he pulled us close. "There's no place else I could imagine being. I have to be with my girls. I belong with my girls." He kissed my forehead, "I can't wait to take you home today. I can't wait for us to start living the rest of our lives with Jenna. You think I should buy her a white pony? You think she will be a tomboy? I have a great idea for a tree house, in our tree, by the swing. I think I will build her a huge playhouse out by the back patio. She can play with her dolls there. We can have tea parties with her on the patio." He is so excited and is talking so fast that all I can do is laugh and hold my hand up, "Whoa, slow down dad. Let's just enjoy this part first. She will grow so fast. I want to savor each and every step of the way with her too, but it will be a while before she is ready for ponies, playhouses and tree houses."

He frowned but then shrugged his shoulders and smiled, "Sorry, guess I am getting a little ahead of myself. It's just that I have so many things I want to do with her, with both of you. I just don't want to waste one second. Not one second with either one of you." I understand what he means. It has taken me so long to meet Jake and to finally have the love that I so desperately wanted. Love that I hoped to find with Brian but instead, found nothing but pain and heart ache. Brian turned my life upside down. He never allowed me to be myself and he was never himself. It's like we were both acting. I never have to act with Jake. I am just me and he loves me for it. I am in awe of him. I love him so much and again, can't believe how lucky I am. I can't believe my life has turned out this way, but I am so thankful it has. I don't want to waste a second either.

"I don't want to waste any time either" I whisper, and then brush my lips across his. "I want to be home with you, and with Jenna. Let's start living the life we were meant to live." Carefully holding Jenna to my chest with my left hand, I reach up and run my fingers through his hair with my right hand, "I love you so much." He smiles his shy smile and my heart melts all over again. It gets me every time. He whispers back, "I love you more than you'll ever know...Damn Jess, come here." He kisses me and I feel all his emotion and passion all at once. It shoots a warm tingling sensation through me and I want to be naked, snuggled close to him. I know I can't do *that* right now so instead I slap him on the leg and say, "Okay then, let's get to it. I'll nurse her and you get the okay for me to check out of this five star luxury hotel." He didn't move. He just smiled at me. "What?" I asked curiously. "No way, if you are nursing I am watching. It's the most natural, most beautiful thing...I'm staying." I shake my head and laugh, "You are such a guy! You just want to see a naked breast!"

"Well, that's always good too" he says grinning ear to ear. "Okay, you are right. I guess I need to get the okay so we can get out of here." With that he gets up and leaves the room. I have just switched Jenna to the other breast when he walks back in. He starts packing up our things, trying hard not to look at us. "We have the okay, so as soon as you are ready we can go." I smile at him, "Come here and sit with us." He looks at me with an unsure look, "Jess, are you sure?" I laugh at my gorgeous, accomplished husband who is so nervous, "Yes, of course I'm sure. Come here, sit with me while she finishes, it wont be long, she is almost done." He carefully sits next to me and wraps his arm around me, never taking his eyes off his daughter, "Oh God Jess, she's so beautiful, I can't believe she is finally here!" I smile, "I know, she's amazing isn't she."

He kisses my forehead sweetly, "Yes, she is, and so are you. Thank you." Confused I ask, "For what?" He holds my hand and gently rubs little circles around my palm. "Thank you for just being you, and for giving me the best gift. Thank you for my daughter." Tears roll down my cheeks and he brushes them away. "Your welcome, I love you Jake." He kisses my hand, "I love you, baby." We sit happily in silence snuggled close together, fulfilled beyond belief, happier than we have ever been. Neither of us has ever experienced such intense, pure joy. We look at each other and smile, both knowing we are where we are meant to be.